DOUBLE-CROSSED

I came off the porch, one hand going for my gun while I pressed the push-to-talk with the other. "Wildfire, wildfire," I sent, as my Springfield cleared holster and shirt. My off hand met the grip on the way up and out, and the tritium sights settled on the squatting man pulling an AKS out of the straw. My finger was already taking up the slack on the trigger as the gun came to full extension, and I fired, the .45's bark deafeningly loud in the evening quiet. The first round took him high in the chest, the second in the throat, and he crumpled back against the fence, his hand held uselessly to his throat to try to stem the spray of arterial blood.

His buddy was going for the Kalashnikov, but I lined him up as I went for the far side of the yard, and fired twice more. He collapsed on top of his buddy, half of the top of his skull blasted away.

TASK FORCE DESPERATE

PETER NEALEN

Also By Peter Nealen

The Brannigan's Blackhearts Universe
Kill Yuan

The Colonel Has A Plan (Online Short)
Fury in the Gulf
Burmese Crossfire
Enemy Unidentified
Frozen Conflict
High Desert Vengeance

The American Praetorians Series
Drawing the Line: An American Praetorians Story (Novella)
Task Force Desperate
Hunting in the Shadows
Alone and Unafraid
The Devil You Don't Know
Lex Talionis

The Jed Horn Supernatural Thriller Series
Nightmares
A Silver Cross and a Winchester
The Walker on the Hills
The Canyon of the Lost (Novelette)
Older and Fouler Things

CHAPTER 1

Just like so many other times, the suck started with Bob Fagin waking my ass up.

I wasn't happy to be getting rousted out. Not that my narrow, cramped, and fairly hard shipboard bunk was particularly comfortable. Far from it. After eight hours sitting on the fantail of the *SS Lynch*, however, baking in the sun with a rifle and a spotting scope on pirate watch, I just wanted to sleep.

"It can't be time for my next watch yet," I grumbled.

"It's not," Bob said, and even though my eyes were still closed, I could hear the malicious grin in his voice. "Something's come up. Alek wants everybody up in the conference room." The conference room was another one of the accommodation compartments Captain Van Husten let us use, one deck up from our sleeping quarters.

I swung my feet out of the rack and onto the cool metal deck with a groan, digging at my eyes with the heels of my palms. "Fuck." I reached for my boots, looking at my watch in the process. "Two fucking hours. This had better be good." I glared up at him. "If this is for an announcement that you've just been declared a teen idol, I'm kicking your ass." That wiped the smirk off his face.

Bob could only be described as pretty. Pointed chin, high cheekbones, curly blond hair. He looked like he belonged in a designer clothing ad. That, along with the fact that he was the newbie in Praetorian Security's founding team, meant he caught all kinds of shit, constantly. He had shaved his head after the first few cracks, but that didn't stop them, especially when it was discovered that he couldn't grow even a goatee to save his life.

I finished speed-lacing my boots, slung my pistol belt around my hips, and grabbed my rifle. It wasn't immediately recognizable as an M1A, thanks to the Troy chassis I'd put it into. Pop-up iron sights were now backup for a tac scope. One of the things we had determined when the company started was that as long as it used one of the standard calibers, you could use any weapon you were comfortable with. We had established 7.62

1

NATO for rifles, 12 gauge for shotguns, .45 ACP for pistols, and .338 Lapua Magnum for sniper rifles. It seemed to work pretty well.

I followed Bob through the narrow space between bunks that were stacked clear to the low overhead, and through the hatch, which I had to simultaneously duck and high-step to get through. I'd hated those things on ship when I was in the Marine Corps, and I hated them just as much now.

We trotted up the equally narrow, and steep, ladderwell to the next deck, did the little duck/high-step thing again, and turned sharp left. Just like on Navy ships, the passageways were narrow, with pipes and valves presenting hazards to your head as you went by, not to mention people popping out of hatches randomly. Damn, I hate being on ship. Pay's good, though.

Our hatch was about ten yards down, and we ducked through it. The compartment wasn't big, and the table in the middle took up most of the deck space. The bulkheads were plastered with maps and charts, mostly of the Somali coastline, with red pins for pirate attacks and known or suspected pirate bases. In between the maps were photos of known or suspected pirate vessels, including two former bulk carriers that had been converted into "motherships," from which the smaller attack boats were sent out. Alek, Jim, Larry, and Rodrigo were already gathered around the laptop on the table. The usual collection of Mk 17s, Alek's OBR, two SA58s, and another M1A, this one with a Sage stock, were in evidence. We never went anywhere unarmed. I edged around to stand next to Larry, and craned my neck to see that the satellite video was up, and the Colonel was on the line.

His name was Thomas Heinrich, Colonel, US Army (ret). He looked grim, which, considering the man always looked like a cold-eyed, cadaverous motherfucker, doesn't say much, but today he looked grimmer than usual. Seeing the tight-lipped expressions on Alek's and Jim's faces, I started to get a hollow feeling in the pit of my stomach. This didn't bode well.

"All right, Tom," Alek said as Bob and I got to where we could see. "Go ahead."

The Colonel acknowledged both of us. "Fagin. Stone. I wish I could say that I was glad you could join us, but there isn't much to be glad about." He paused, his mouth set in a thin line. "Just watch. I'll fill in details as this goes." He disappeared, to be replaced with what looked like GBOS footage of a large, agitated crowd at what appeared to be a security checkpoint.

"This is the entrance control point to Camp Lemonier," the Colonel explained. Camp Lemonier, at Djibouti City Airport, was the center of any and all US operations on the Horn of Africa. "There have been crowds there for most of the last week, mainly Somali refugees trying to get food, water, medicine, what-have-you." The crowd looked less like a breadline and more like a riot to me, but I kept my mouth shut. "Some sources have been warning that various terrorist groups have been agitating these crowds, even using them for cover. A few have even mentioned this Al Masri who popped up in Somalia a few months ago."

The sea of people around the checkpoint was obviously poor; most were visibly emaciated, even in the grainy footage we had. I leaned forward, something catching my eye.

"Who's that fucker?" I asked, pointing to someone on the edge of the crowd near the camera, who was moving through the press, toward the gate. He didn't look like he was shouting, but did have his hands in front of him, and his back angled toward the camera. I couldn't be one hundred percent certain, of course, but I've seen somebody trying to hide a weapon with their body before, and that's what this looked like.

"Good eye, Stone," the Colonel's disembodied voice said. "Keep watching; it looks like those sources were right."

A few moments later there was an explosion in the middle of the crowd, about fifty meters back from the gate. The camera shook, and probably thirty people just disappeared in the blossom of smoke and dust. Larry swore. "Motherfuckers couldn't even get to the gate."

"Not their intention," the Colonel pointed out. "Watch."

As the smoke cleared, the mangled bodies became visible, not to mention the panic of the rest of the crowd. It was apparent that most of them hadn't been warned of the suicide bomber. There were wounded on the edges of the blast, some trying to crawl away, others being trampled by people trying to escape, no matter where to.

There wasn't much of any move to help anyone hit by the blast; there was just general panic, but the crowd didn't look like it was going anywhere, either. I was soon picking out small groups of armed men herding, for lack of a better term, the people into the kill zone. What the fuck?

It started coming together when the gates to Camp Lemonier began to open, and three white-painted HMMWVs rolled out. They weren't UN trucks, the UN didn't even have a presence at Lemonier, but it had become a popular paint scheme for "non-tactical tactical vehicles." Aid trucks, in other words. As you might expect, they were unarmed, which was largely why I wasn't surprised by what happened next.

Even after all these years, the RPG-7 is still plenty popular with the irregular-warfare set. It does a number on a Hummer, too. Two of them hit the rearmost truck as it was still inside the gate. The rear simply disappeared in two overlapping clouds of black and orange, and it looked like the truck almost flipped over from the force of the twin blasts. When it settled, burning, to the ground, the gate was blocked, and still open.

The camera angle didn't let us see much of what the guard force was doing, but whatever it was, it couldn't have been too effective. More RPG gunners appeared, firing through the open gate, even as the two surviving trucks were swarmed, their doors wrenched open, and the occupants pulled out to disappear under a human tide. The camera was picking up small arms flashes now, and people, mostly armed, were shoving through the gate, past the burning Humvee.

"We don't have any footage of what happened inside the camp," the Colonel said, as his face replaced the scene of fire and destruction on the screen. "What we do know is that most of it fell relatively quickly. The majority of the US personnel in Djibouti were support types, many of whom never went armed, even if they had a weapon issued in-country. I'm told that the 'special' compound took a while, but it appears to have gone silent. We have found this on YouTube, however…" The screen changed again, this time showing a crowd beating at what could only be a mutilated corpse. "The poster is saying that it is one of the 'American imperialists' who was killed at Lemonier."

The Colonel returned to the screen. "Short version, gentlemen, is that the only major US base in East Africa just got overrun, in the course of about three hours. We don't know yet if there are still live hostages, but at the moment we are assuming there are, possibly as many as two hundred."

Jim spoke up. "We just sailed past a MEU two days ago. They doing anything?"

The Colonel grimaced. "Hardly. They're still holding station, awaiting further developments. Word I'm getting from my sources is, National Command Authority doesn't want to commit troops unless there is solid proof of survivors on the ground. I have been assured that State is talking to the Djibouti authorities." The acid in his tone spoke to what he thought of that. He had retired as a colonel precisely because of his inability to get along with politicians, diplomats, and bureaucrats. "The truth is a little worse than what they're telling us. That MEU is in position, but hasn't moved in three weeks due to lack of fuel. JSOC is sitting on its hands because the money, even for them, is pretty much insufficient to mount an operation. The dollar's collapse last year pretty much grounded most of the US Armed Forces."

Alek broke in. Alek is six-foot-four, and, being Samoan, close to two hundred seventy-five pounds. When he breaks in, everybody shuts up. "I take it you're telling us this because you got us a contract in Djibouti, Tom?"

An icy smile crossed the Colonel's face. "You could say that. I've got a contact with Special Activities." That raised a couple of eyebrows. Don't get me wrong, the Colonel could be a ruthless, cold-blooded, outside-the-box motherfucker when he wanted to, but he came from the regular Army, not the Recon or SOF community, like most of Praetorian Security's operators. It was slightly surprising that he knew people in SA. "He hasn't got the assets in-country to conduct the mission, so he's calling on us. Rest assured; the pay is commensurate."

Alek held up a plate-sized hand. "Calling on us for what?"

"To find the hostages."

There was a long silence after that. We had one ten-man team on the *Lynch*. That was almost equivalent to a Special Forces A-team, yes. Sufficient to liberate something in the neighborhood of two hundred hostages? Unlikely. "You want to run that by me again, Tom?" Jim rumbled.

The Colonel held up his hands. "Don't worry, nobody is expecting just your team to go in as-is. Though I know something of the amount of gear you guys took for a simple maritime security mission," he added wryly. There was a slightly sheepish exchange of glances at that. Truth was, we had been, how shall I say, *hopeful* when we packed our gear, knowing the part of the world the *Lynch* would be steaming through. "In any case, I have already gotten Caleb's and Mike's teams mobilized and on the plane. They'll meet you there."

"Not to throw too much water on the fire, Tom," Alek said, "but even twenty guys aren't enough to bust out upwards of two hundred hostages. Not only that, but how are we going to get them out? We've only got the one plane."

The Colonel held up his hands. "I'm afraid you might have gotten the wrong impression, gentlemen. The job we're being hired for is not the actual extraction. DevGru or some such will be handling that. You are just the recon element."

Jim snorted. "In other words, they let their assets slip, and now have to hire out for their intel."

"Fair enough assessment, James," the Colonel replied grimly.

"What about the other teams' weapons?" Larry asked. Getting weapons in and out of sovereign countries could still be sticky, even in this day and age.

"Taken care of," the Colonel said, and we let it drop. The company did have certain under-the-table ways of doing things, especially in Third-World countries, so we just accepted that, come hell or high water, the other two teams would show up with all their gear, along with enough ammo to sink the *Lynch*. We had more immediate things to think about, and we could trust the Colonel--if he said we were good, we were good. It did leave one other important question still hanging, however.

"What about the *Lynch*?" I asked. Everybody turned to look at me. "Well, hell, we can't just leave Van Husten in the lurch, can we? We took the man's money."

After a moment's consideration, Alek looked back at the Colonel. "Which team is taking support duties?"

Heinrich shrugged. "Up to you. You're the ground commander."

Alek nodded. "Caleb's team gets the duty. Fifty percent on the ground, the other five helo out here to the ship. Life's gonna suck for them, but Jeff's right; we can't leave this contract hanging, especially not this close to Somalia." After the *Syndi Hampton*, and the pointed lack of reaction to that particular massacre, piracy was now considered Al-Shabaab's primary source of funding. "What all is on the way?"

"Some heavy weapons. I couldn't get enough room for any ground transpo, but Caleb's got the cash to get you vehicles on the ground. I can't guarantee that they'll be *good* vehicles, especially since I expect you'll want to buy rather than rent." Heinrich looked out of the screen with a cocked eyebrow, and Alek nodded. This was pretty standard, as we were probably going to end up beating the shit out of them. The Colonel gave one curt nod, and then continued to tick off the list. "More ammo and batteries. A couple of fuel and water bladders; empty, for weight's sake. You'll have to fill them on the ground. Some spare parts, mostly for the boats. That's about it. Caleb's going to have plenty of cash for you to purchase supplies on the ground; your best bet will be north, near the docks. That's the richer part of the city."

Everybody already had small notebooks out, and was jotting down notes, thoughts, and to-do lists. "Find the hostages" might sound like a simple enough mission statement, but it was rather dangerously general. This was going to be a bitch of a job.

The conversation with the Colonel went on for about another hour, as we got into the nitty-gritty, asking all and sundry questions that came to mind. The attack was picked apart, minute by minute. We studied their methods, their weapons, and tried to get pictures gleaned from the video of the shooters themselves. Odds were that most of the crowd wasn't in on the real plan, so we concentrated on the trigger-men. Find the trigger-men, find the hostages, was the logic. It had worked the couple of times we'd dealt with similar problems, though not of this scale, in Arizona and Northern Mexico.

From there, we moved into other details. What was the coastline like? Tides? Hazards we'd have to deal with if we did anything waterborne? What did the weather look like in the immediate future? Where were the concentrations of population in the hinterland? Roads? Terrain? We covered just about every point of orientation and intel we could. Finally, the Colonel signed off, and we got down to work.

***

Alek and I went to see Captain Van Husten. This required Alek squeezing his bulk through about five more hatches and three tiny ladderwells. I still don't know how he managed on ship when he was with Force.

I knocked on the Captain's hatch, and after a moment was answered

6

with a muffled, "Come in." I turned the latch and swung the hatch open. Alek followed me in.

Bryan Van Husten's cabin was barely larger than any of his crew's berths. In deference to his rank, there was only one bunk, but other than that, and the personal mementos on the wall and desk, there really wasn't any other sign that this was the home of the absolute dictator of this little floating country.

Of course, for an absolute dictator, Captain Van Husten was a very down-to-earth, friendly, and hardworking man, whom all of us liked, except maybe for Bob, but that was because Bob had a chip on his shoulder half the size of the ship. Bryan was a good old boy from Louisiana, who had joined the shipping company right out of his four years in the Navy, and worked his way up to skipper of his own ship. He was going bald, and a little fat, but his grin was infectious, though it slipped a little when he saw the looks on our faces.

"Mornin' boys," he drawled, standing up to shake our hands, as he always did. "What can I do for you?"

"Bryan," Alek began, while I leaned against the bulkhead, "we've had something come up. Now, we have no intention of leaving you with your ass in the breeze, but my team has to go ashore, and soon."

Van Husten frowned, as he sat back down, and motioned Alek to take a seat on his bunk. "This have something to do with that dustup in Djibouti earlier?"

"What do you know about it?" I asked.

"Just that there was some shooting and explosions by the airport," he replied. "The skipper of the *Varant* heard some of it, and saw the smoke from the docks."

"In answer to your question," Alek continued, "yes. There was an attack on the US base at Camp Lemonier. Hostages were taken, and we've been hired to help find them."

The Captain's face was grave. "How many?"

"However many survived," Alek said starkly.

Van Husten sighed heavily, and looked at his hands. "What are you planning?"

"When we make contact with Caleb's team, we'll shuttle them out here on the helo," Alek explained. "There won't be as many, but I need my team with me, and Caleb's got support for this job anyway. Then the rest of us will go ashore, using the boats we brought with us. After that, you go on your way."

"We'll move in closer to the shore," Van Husten said, his eyes on the bulkhead, thinking. "That'll save you some time getting in." He flipped open his calendar. "I think if I explain matters to Corporate, we can loiter for about five more days offshore, in case you guys need a support platform, or even someplace to lift the hostages to. Longer, if we develop 'engine trouble.'"

Alek shook his head. "You're more than enough of a target out here as it is, Bryan. Once we're ashore, move out and finish your run."

Van Husten looked at us levelly. "They're Americans, aren't they? The hostages, I mean."

I nodded. "Some of them, yes."

"I may be a fat old freighter skipper," he said, "but I'm still an American, and a vet. I may not have done some of the high-speed stuff you guys did when you were in, but I took the oath, same as you. Maybe that doesn't mean much to some, but it still means something to me. We'll be here."

For a moment, Alek and I looked at him, and then traded glances. I shrugged. I couldn't fault the man for his stance. In fact, I liked him even better than before. It was risky, and he was potentially putting himself and his crew in a lot of hot water, especially if they did get hit by pirates while running racetracks off the African coastline, but he had a determined set to his mouth that told both of us he wasn't backing down. Fair enough. It might even work out to have a sea borne platform to bring the hostages to, after getting them away from the terrorists.

"I'd try harder to talk you out of it," Alek said, "but I can see I'd be wasting my breath, and we've got a lot of prep work to do. So, I'll settle for telling you you're a damn fool, but you're my kind of damn fool. Thanks."

"Least I can do," Van Husten replied, as they stood up, and shook hands again. "Good hunting."

CHAPTER 2

I could hear the low, purring roar of our Bell 407 before I could see it. Even with my Night Vision Goggles, or NVGs, I only picked it up out of the equally dark sky and sea by the static discharge off the rotor blades and the heat off the engines. We couldn't afford the fancy new PSQ-20 Enhanced Night Vision Goggles, so we'd gone with older PVS-14s with thermal attachments. Sam was flying dark, and low, which meant he had been doing a little hunting on the way out. Or at least scouting. Too bad the pirates usually headed inshore after dark.

I flashed my Surefire at the bird three times, and got the forward running light twice in reply. I flashed one more, as he buzzed past the port side of the ship, before swinging around to line up with the stern.

As the bird came in, flaring gently, I clambered up on to the forward edge of the pad, and held up the Surefire to guide him in. Sam brought the helo to a hover, as I waved him slightly to port, then brought him down, only having to make minor adjustments as he came in. It was a calm night, with little wind. Even the swell was minimal.

Once the skids were on the deck, Sam cut the engines and the rotors slowly whirred to a stop. Colton and Bob came up onto the pad with me, to help lash down the bird, while the doors opened, and the most morose motherfuckers you ever saw got out.

Matt, Fig, Jorge, Salomon, and Drew were our replacements on the *Lynch*. It was entirely possible, if the Captain had his way, that the rest of Caleb's team would also come out to the ship to run support, but for now, these were the guys stuck with maritime security, while the rest of us got to go terrorist hunting. Sucked to be them.

Matt was short and skinny, tough as nails, and just radiating a combination of depressed and pissed as he got off the helo. He was pulling his heavy kitbag off the bird as I came up to him and clapped him on his shoulder. "How was the flight?"

He glared at me halfheartedly. "I've been on one bird or another for the last forty-eight hours. I don't want to even think about flying for at least another twenty-four." He gave the bag another yank, and it finally cleared the lip of the hatch, and dropped to the pad with a thud. The engines had finally spun down, so it was relatively quiet, except for the *thrum* of the ship's engines.

I helped him haul the kitbag, which was about big enough to haul a dead body (okay, a small one), to the edge of the pad, then he went back to the bird to retrieve his rifle. The other three, along with Colton and Bob, followed along, lugging their gear behind them.

"Alek wants to get you guys settled in berthing, then let you get some sleep before changing over," I explained. "But it's not going to be a long nap, because we've got to get ready to insert tonight. Had Caleb gotten very far on getting transpo for us before you guys lifted?"

Matt shook his head. "He had a couple of possibilities he was going to run down, mostly Land Rovers or HiLuxes, but he's not going to be able to do much until morning. He wanted me to assure you guys that he'll be at link-up on time." He shrugged. "As for down-time, we got a lot of sleep on the bird out here. We'll stash our kit, then do changeover. Maybe if there's less security noticeable after you guys go ashore, the pirates might try something." He sounded hopeful. I chuckled, and led the way.

The helipad was an after-market addition to the *Lynch*, and had been built onto the bow. That meant we had the entire length of the ship to carry their gear, mostly between cargo containers. That was fun. Several times we had to stop and put the bags down, sweating our asses off in the wet tropical heat. Finally, we got them to the superstructure, then had to squeeze, pull, and push them through the hatches, and up one ladder well, then through more hatches, until we got to berthing. Our berthing was semi-controlled chaos, as most of us were prepping gear to go ashore for an indeterminate period, so everybody's bunk was a gear bomb.

There was a chorus of mock rejoicing and insincere commiserating, mostly of the "sucks to be you guys" variety. Jim and Hank came over and helped us cram the bulging kitbags into a corner, where they'd be out of the way for the time being, then Alek came in, apparently having heard the commotion.

"Excellent, the sacrificial lambs are here," he boomed. "I know you guys are probably tired, but we're on a tight schedule. We need you to change over with the guys on duty, so we can finish prepping and get ashore before the sun comes up." There were muted groans from Fig and Salomon, but Jorge just punched Fig on the arm, hefted his short-barrel SA58, and started toward the hatch.

"Where do you want us, Alek?" Matt asked.

"Two forward, two aft, right now," Alek replied. "Rodrigo, Larry, Nick, and Tim are up on watch right now. You guys are going to have to work out how you're going to rotate; sorry to say it, but it's gonna suck any way you look at it."

Matt shrugged. "Two up, three down. Gonna be more lookouts than sentries, for a while, anyway. If Caleb and the rest of the boys come out here, it'll ease up. Hey, suckage is part of the job, right? If we wanted easy, we'd have gone to work at civilian jobs."

"What civilian jobs?" Jim growled. "Ain't much of that action going around these days." Jim was the oldest member of Praetorian Security, except for maybe the Colonel. Like the Colonel, he was retired, having left Special Forces after twenty-one years. He and Alek knew each other from crossing paths a couple of times in Afghanistan and Libya. When he had found himself unable to support his wife and daughter in the civilian world, and on a meager military pension, he had come to Alek, and joined our little mercenary start-up.

"And on that little point of light and happiness, I'm going to go hope for a few pirates to shoot in the face," Matt said, as he left the compartment.

I was already finished packing, so I slung my ruck over my shoulders, grabbed my kit and rifle, and followed Alek down to the deck. We worked our way around to the stern, where we had somewhat disrupted the regulated safety features of the ship.

The *Lynch* was a bulk carrier, and subject to the laundry list of safety regulations (that seemed to get longer every year) for such ships under the US flag. Many of these regulations concerned the stowage, readiness, and deployment of the lifeboats. Most of them carried hefty fines for violating them, i.e., doing anything with the lifeboats aside from getting in them and launching them (by the federally-approved launching checklist, of course).

That being said, there weren't any federal inspectors out here in the Gulf of Aden. We had in fact taken the lifeboats out of their cradles, and stacked them on the fantail. The cradles were now taken up with some of our special cargo.

The military calls the Zodiac F470 the Combat Rubber Raiding Craft. We always just called it the Zodiac, or Zode. We had two of them, with compact outboards, now loaded on the lifeboat cradles. I looked at them skeptically. The cradles were designed to effectively drop the boats straight off the fantail and into the water. I did not want to make that ride, especially not with weapon and ruck, and I said as much.

"We'll drop the boats first, then follow by ladder," Alek explained, as he snap-linked his ruck to the lines on the inside of the boat. "Believe me, I have no more interest than you in dropping twenty feet in a Zode."

Together, we continued to prep the boats, checking broaching lines, deck plates, sked tubes, and inflation valves. We made sure the fuel bladders were secured, the fuel lines unhindered, and the safety lines on the engines themselves were secured. Then we added extra safeties for the engines. None of us wanted to get dropped twenty, twenty-five nautical miles out at sea, just to have to paddle in. Add to that the fact that a lost engine was

11

going to come out of the responsible boat team's pay, and there was plenty of incentive to make damned good and sure that the outboards stayed attached when the boats hit the water.

The rest of the team gathered on the fantail with their gear as we worked, staging their stuff and setting to work to help out. Soon enough all the rucks were loaded and secured, the engines had been checked, and we were getting our on-person gear set and checked. Cammies, flotation, weapons, ammo, comm, fins, and survival kits all had to be double-checked.

Everyone was quiet. It wasn't nervousness, not really. We had all been through some scary shit, lived to tell about it, and buried more than a few who hadn't. We were past nervousness, at least mostly. No, this was simply a time of mental preparation for whatever shitstorm we were about to wade into. Some called it "getting your game-face on." I never called it much of anything. I just went through it, and went to work.

Alek brought everybody together after final checks; we had a time hack, and got set. We swung the lifeboat cradles out over the water, and dropped the boats, Larry and Rodrigo going in right after them. In a lot of ways, it was pretty much the same as a helocast, just jumping off a ship's deck that was twenty feet above the water, rather than a helicopter's ramp.

The rest of the team followed, two-by-two. I was in the third pair, and stepped to the edge, holding on to the muzzle of my rifle with one hand, and my fins with the other. Taking a long step, I plummeted off the deck and into the darkness.

I hit the water feet-first and reasonably vertical. I arrowed down into the warm brine, slowed, and kicked to the surface. I didn't waste any time getting my fins on and kicking out for the boat. Sure, the water was nice and warm, but the Gulf of Aden is home to quite a population of sharks. I'd seen plenty from the ship while on watch, and now I couldn't see anything underwater, which did make me a little anxious to get out. Yeah, I know, not nervous about going into enemy territory, but nervous about sharks. Go figure.

It was an easy thirty-meter swim to the boat, where Larry already had the engine in the water, and was yanking on the pull cord. It caught and rumbled to life as I caught hold of the handholds on the side of the gunwale, and pulled myself aboard. Jim was already on the starboard gunwale, pulling his fins off and clipping them to his UDT vest. Once I got a leg slung over, I pulled myself the rest of the way in and followed suit.

If any of this is sounding familiar to you current and former amphibious types, that's because, well, it should. We deliberately got the same model Zodiac as the CRRC, and used all the same procedures, for one reason: it was easy. Most of us had already trained on the Zodes while we were in, so it made it simpler to just use as close to the same equipment and procedures. Why fix what ain't broke?

It took only a few minutes for the rest of the team to board the boats, and get situated. I moved up to the bow, along with Jim. I don't know if Jim was bothered by having to be a one-man, but I was. I didn't bother to bitch about it, but I settled in for an uncomfortable ride, as Nick settled himself behind me, half on my back.

I adjusted my NVGs, pushing them a little higher so that I could look up past the rim of my FAST helmet, and see. There wasn't much to see, granted. The coast was still over the horizon, and there wasn't much shipping around here, a sign of how far things had fallen. Before what the pundits were calling the Greater Depression had started, there would have been a steady stream of ships coming and going through the Gulf of Aden, going to and from the Suez Canal. Now there was only a trickle.

We skimmed the swells, while Jim and I bounced off the gunwale with every jolt. That's why being the one-man in a Zode sucks. Unless the water is glass-calm, you just get hammered. Stomach, ribs, nuts, everything. When it's an over-the-horizon run, you can count on plenty of pain for a long time.

***

After what felt like an eternity, though, I started to be able to see the coast. It took me a second to clear my head of the fuzz brought on by over three hours of darkness and thumping, and I took a better look. We were closer than I'd thought, maybe two thousand meters. There wasn't a lot of high ground on the Djibouti coast, apparently. There were some lights to the east; that would be Loyada, the town built around the border crossing between Djibouti and Somaliland, if town you could call it. The imagery looked pretty sparse. We could see the glow over the horizon to the west from Djibouti City itself, but we weren't going there just yet.

Larry throttled back, and we slowed further, the bow of the boat sinking down to water-level. Just off the port side, Rodrigo's boat did the same. We started re-situating ourselves on the gunwales, as Jim and I sat up and started putting our fins back on.

As much as I did not relish getting back in the dark water full of tiger and bull sharks, I was one of if not the best swimmer on the team. Jim was also up there, which some found surprising, since he'd been a Green Beanie rather than Recon or SEAL. He's also built like a brick shithouse, and at first glance everybody figures he'd sink like a rock. All that notwithstanding, he beats me on timed fins half the time.

Once we were set, we both gave Larry the OK, and rolled backward into the water. Larry had put the engine into reverse, so that we weren't in danger of getting run over while we got our shit together in the water.

Jim and I swam to within an arm's length of each other, then lined up with the shore and started kicking out. We weren't as stealthy as we might like; we were kicking up quite a bit of bioluminescence. I tried not to think

13

about being a glow-in-the-dark shark lure for pretty much the whole seven-hundred-meter swim to the shore.

There was no surf zone; the beach was just there. Jim and I drifted in until we could crouch on the bottom, with our heads just above the surface, and scan the beach. I pulled the waterproof bag from around my neck and pulled out my NVGs.

We were just to the southeast of an inlet, or maybe the mouth of an intermittent river. The beach itself appeared sandy and empty. The hinterland looked to be peppered with acacia trees and leafy scrub bushes. And there was something else. As I scanned, I saw several vehicles under one particularly tall and wide acacia, glowing with heat but showing no lights. It looked like three SUVs and what I thought was probably a 3-ton cargo truck. I tapped Jim, and pointed, barely pulling my hand above the surface of the water. Even as I did, a light glimmered from the bed of the cargo truck.

It was IR; I couldn't see it with my unaided eye. It flashed three times. That would be Caleb. I reached up and triggered the illuminator on the NVGs twice, and got a single flash in reply. The support team was on site, and had the beach secure. The two of us came up out of the water and moved toward the trucks. Jim slid his Mk 17 out of a waterproof sleeve as he cleared the water, while I just drained the water from the barrel of my M1A. I had treated my rifle to hold off rust for a long, long time.

We walked in a low crouch, weapons at the low ready, staying close together, as we moved up the beach to the trucks. The recognition signal had been correct, but none of us were alive from a lack of paranoia. I relaxed a little when I saw Caleb's unmistakable huge head next to the 3-ton.

"How's the water?" he whispered, as we came up and took a knee next to the front driver's side tire.

"Nice and warm," I replied. "We good here?"

"Yeah. There's really nobody but locals around, and the Foreign Legion guys are concentrating on the area around the airport right now. We need to get moving, though." He checked his watch, sheltering the Indiglo between his body and the truck. "Sun's up in about two hours, and we've got to get those boats hidden."

If you're wondering why we were being so sneaky going in, well, when you're effectively invading a foreign country, it helps to not walk in the front door, at least not with your entire armory of high-powered rifles and explosives. We weren't interested in dealing with the red tape. We didn't have time. I turned on my radio and called out to the boats. "Coconut, this is Hillbilly. We have linked up with Monkey. All clear, come ahead."

"*Roger. Oscar Mike.*" It took a few minutes, but soon we could just hear the drone of the outboards. The boats themselves showed up quite well, with eight guys and two outboard motors providing plenty of heat. Jim and I

14

helped guide the cargo truck down to the beach, while the rest of Caleb's reduced team held security. Larry and Rodrigo brought their boats in to smooth landings on the beach, the rest of the guys jumping out as the water got about knee deep. The engines came up, and the lot of us set to getting the boats off the beach and into the back of the truck.

This was a bit complicated in the dark; we had to dismount the engines and the fuel bladders, and stack them in the front of the truck bed, then pick up the boats and load them in one at a time. It was backbreaking work, but it beat digging holes to cache the boats in on the beach, where somebody might accidentally find them anyway. I'd done that while I was still in the Marine Corps, and was plenty happy not to do it again. Once everything was on the truck and secured, we threw a tarp over it and tied it down, to hopefully conceal the fact that it was carrying two military-grade raiding craft.

We walked over to the line of three SUVs, facing the road, where Caleb had a kitbag full of dry clothes for us, and we quickly shucked out of our still soaked cammies, and changed into dry khakis and short-sleeved shirts. It looked like Caleb had gotten some pretty good wheels; two Range Rovers and a '90s Defender. The gear would have to be dried out, but for now was bagged and put in the back of the SUVs, along with our rifles, now cased. Pistols came out of rucks and were strapped on and covered. Comms were shut off before being put away. Finally, everything was loaded, and we got ready to move.

Caleb walked up to Alek and me, with a map in his hand, and set it on the hood of the Defender. He pulled out a tiny button light and a GPS. "We rented a warehouse, for lack of a better term, here, near the port." He pointed to a spot on the map, not far from the ocean, and across from what looked like a school. "The cover is an international aid organization on a fact-finding tour for the moment, so that's going to be part of our support role; going around being obnoxious and patronizing as we ask poor people how poor they are. So far we've had surprisingly little trouble with the cops looking for kickbacks--nothing we can't handle. But there are checkpoints, especially after what just went down, so pick your routes carefully. I'll be leaving in one of the Range Rovers, with the 3-ton following me." He looked at Alek, in the dim green glow of the light. "I'd suggest spacing at least ten minutes apart, and taking different routes. The warehouse is here…" He read a map grid off, and we copied it carefully. "Be advised, there are some Foreign Legion troops in the city, cooperating with the army, what's left of it. Aside from the obvious terrorist activity, there's been some new unrest among the Afar, especially with all the Issas coming from Somalia. It's a little touchy around here right now."

Alek nodded. "We don't want to tangle with the Legionnaires; that entire brigade will likely come down around our ears if we do. Plus, they're

15

not the enemy."

"At the moment," Caleb answered. "The French government is kind of shaky on the whole jihadi thing these days."

"The Legion's ultimate loyalty is to the Legion," Jim pointed out. "Best to steer clear of them in any case."

Caleb checked his watch again. "It'll be sunup soon. We've got to get the boats into the warehouse, so we'll be leaving here in about two minutes. You guys got good SA on where you're going?"

"Affirm," Alek said. "Get going." Caleb nodded, then walked to the far Range Rover and got in the passenger seat. A moment later, the engine rumbled to life, and they pulled out, heading for the nearest road, the tires kicking up dust and sand. Thirty seconds later, the 3-ton followed.

We kept the boat teams in each of the SUVs; I got in the old Defender, Alek and his team got in the Range Rover. We were going to go first--no particular reason, just a metaphorical coin-toss. We were going to go the short way, up the coast, while Alek and his boat team went around to the west, going through most of the city proper. It would be well past daylight by the time they got to the warehouse, but a convoy of big, hard-nosed Americans would probably raise some eyebrows. We didn't want any eyebrow-raising at this point. Not until we knew a little more, at any rate.

I let Caleb get about a fifteen minute head start, then put the truck in gear, and rolled out, throwing up a little gravel as we went. It was a short way to the road, which was just a dusty, unimproved dirt track, going northwest to southeast. There weren't any other vehicles on it at the moment, and I turned on and headed north.

We passed a few camels wandering on the side of the road, probably from the farm that we went by on the right almost immediately. The sky was starting to turn pale over the ocean, but I didn't rush, at least not by the standards of the local drivers. While I hadn't been in Djibouti itself before, I'd been in enough East African and Middle Eastern countries to know that while they might be lackadaisical about a lot of things, driving is not one of them. Most people in the Third World drive like fucking maniacs, and if you don't, you stand out.

The road wound through several miles of sandy savannah, dotted with scrub and acacias in the slowly growing dawn light. I took a right at a Y intersection, and we rolled due north, up the coast, toward the airport.

Camp Lemonier had been a part of Djibouti airport, but not the entirety of it. I saw a plane, looked like a Lear or something like it, take off as I drove, so the hit hadn't put the airport completely out of commission. I almost kicked myself even as I thought it. *Of course the airport wasn't out of commission, dumbass*, I thought. *How would Caleb and his boys have gotten here, otherwise?*

As we neared the runway, the fence became visible, and I saw that there was a checkpoint at the gate, manned by two men dressed in old chocolate-chip desert cammies and red berets. One was sitting behind what looked like a PKM, while the other slouched at his post, a FN-FAL slung at his side. I saw that the road split, veering away from the gate to travel along the fence, and took the outside route. I had no desire to deal with anybody from the Djibouti National Army. If what Caleb said was true, the authorities had plenty to worry about, and were likely to try to scoop up a heavily-armed band of American mercs as soon as they knew we were here. That would not end well for anyone involved, and would endanger the mission, so it was best avoided.

We bounced along the shitty track that ran along the outside of the fence, rounding the end of the runway, barely a hundred meters from the shore. "Never be able to get this close to the flight line back home," Nick said. "We'd have had fifty security vehicles on us a mile ago." I grunted agreement.

The road swung back to the northwest, still skirting the boundary of the airport, and led through close-growing acacias toward the city itself. The sun was full up by now, revealing the trash scattered along the sides of the road in all its glory.

I saw the first buildings of the city proper through the acacias, as some traffic was starting to pick up, mostly small European cars and pedestrians. Finally we bounced off the dirt road and up onto the hardball, moving north into the city.

At first glance, it didn't look much different from any other post-colonial Third World city. It was a blend of Western and Arab architecture, but gone shabby. Peeling stucco, dirt, and trash was the general motif that we saw everywhere. Junk and rubble was piled on the sides of the road, ignored by all and sundry, essentially part of the landscape.

We rumbled up the road and turned right near a large soccer field. As we came around the corner, I had to swerve wildly to avoid a truck that was tearing down the middle of the street. We got honked at, and several of the bystanders yelled, whether at us or the truck, I don't know. I got us going straight again, and we cruised toward our warehouse.

It was actually three buildings in a sort of walled complex. The wall was about four feet high, dirty white concrete, with a metal grate along the top. The metal had been painted blue at one time, but it was flaking and rusted. I had to drive around it to the north to try to find a way in, and found that away from the street, the compound was quite open. What I had taken at first to be a large, single-story building was in fact three buildings linked together in a U-shape. It was white with a metal roof, and with the windows I suspected that was going to be where we slept. The warehouse itself was almost two stories tall and built of corrugated metal, and was inside the wall. The 3-ton could be seen already backed up to the large doors in the back, so I

17

pulled the Defender over to it, and shut off the engine.

I opened the door and stepped out into the early morning heat. I hadn't really noticed it earlier, having been soaking wet at the time, but it was hot as two rats fucking in a wool sock, and the sun had just come up. I was not looking forward to the middle of the day. Even after all the time that I've spent in the tropics and various desert hellholes, I still don't particularly like sweating my life away.

The rest of the guys got out of the Defender, and we walked over to help Caleb and his boys unload the boats. As we did so, I was looking around at the setup. I hadn't seen them at first, but I picked out Jon and Billy on security, inside, watching out the windows. It wasn't bad, really, except for the part where we were right next to a major thoroughfare. That was a little uncomfortable-making.

I ducked into the warehouse along the side of the truck, which filled most of the door, to find Caleb on the port gunwale of the second boat, dragging it out of the bed. They already had the first off and stacked to the side. I stepped in to help, and we pulled it off somewhat more easily, doing the same stack, bow against the wall, tits on the ground, to let the boat drain.

"We got a hose?" I asked. We really needed to rinse the salt water off the boats and engines, but Caleb shook his head.

"No running water at the moment." He jerked a thumb toward the house. "We've got two fifty-five gallon bladders full of fresh water, and Dave's working on getting some barrels of non-potable for this sort of thing. Nothing we can do about it right now." I nodded, shrugged, and climbed up on the truck to start moving the engines. Caleb and Bob followed.

We had just gotten the first one down to the asphalt floor when we heard the crunch of gravel announcing that Alek and the rest of our team had arrived. Caleb looked at me and said, "We've got this, man. Imad's inside, waiting for you guys. He's got your team room set up, and some more information. He needs to get moving, so let's not keep him waiting."

"Right." I looked over at Jim, who nodded, and yelled at Nick and Bob that we had to get in the house. I jumped down from the truck, dusted off my hands, checked that my 1911 was still secure in its holster, and joined Larry and Jim as we walked into the house.

There was only a screen on the door going in, and it squeaked. Mike was sitting in a rickety chair just inside, and looked up as we walked in. Mike looked just as long-faced and hangdog as he always did, and he just jerked his head to the right. "Howdy, boys," he drawled. "I'd shoot the shit a little, but Imad's getting antsy in there."

"All right, we're going, we're going," Larry said. "Good to see ya, Mike."

Mike waved, and we went down the hall and into the room at the far end.

It looked like the entire north arm of the U had been stripped out and turned into a big operations center/team room. There was a map table in the center, more maps and photos on the walls, Billy's comm setup in the corner, and ten bunks against the walls on the far end. Alek, Tim, Colton, Hank, and Rodrigo were already gathered around the map table, facing Imad.

Imad David Jama was almost as tall as Alek, but skinny as a rail, and black as midnight. He had recognizably East African features, and spoke most of the major dialects fluently. He had, in fact, immigrated to the US with his parents from Eritrea back in the '90s. Most of his knowledge and considerable skill had come from sixteen years in the Special Forces. He'd been a Master Sergeant when he got out in disgust, after an op he still didn't talk about. Now he was Praetorian Security's East Africa expert, along with being a chameleon who could disappear just about anywhere on the Horn. He was dressed to do just that right now, in a loose, short-sleeved white shirt, shorts, and sandals. If you didn't know what you were looking for, you wouldn't have spotted the Glock strapped to his lower abdomen, either.

"Good to see you guys," he said as we joined the rest of the team around the table. "We've got to make this quick, because the longer I'm here flapping my gums at you, the less time I'm out on the streets trying to find these poor bastards." He pointed to the map. "The fact is, this particular base of operations is less than ideal, but that's necessary. We're quite a ways from the European quarter, where most of the Westerners hang out. That's up here, on the northwest side of town.

"This placement helps us to conceal our bigger gear, but you guys are going to be a little out of place. You're going to have to be careful coming and going. Westerners are running scared after what's been going on lately. Most of them are holed up in their hotels. After Lemonier getting wiped out, I can't say I really blame them." He looked down at the tabletop for a minute, and I took the opportunity to ask a question.

"If this is the wrong place, how come Caleb said y'all were posing as aid workers?" I inquired.

Imad chuckled. "It actually does work for aid workers, at least serious ones. It's closer to the slums. And Dave has actually set up a clinic in the shed out back. That SF training comes in handy for all sorts of things." He shook his head. "No, aid workers works for maybe one team. Trying to explain another ten knuckle-draggers coming and going at all hours is a little more difficult." He laughed. "We should have brought along a couple women and at least one fat guy. That'd make it more believable."

There was a general chuckle. We did still look rather overtly military, even with the face fur and civvies. It could get dicey, especially after what had just happened. Which was why we were armed to the teeth.

"What about local authorities?" Alek asked.

"Mostly on the north end of town," Imad replied, "protecting the president and the parliament. It sounds like a lot of what got the bad guys their crowd to hit Lemonier was a lot of grumbling going around about Guellah's fourth term, and that he's being backed by foreigners. There are a lot of very poor people here, more and more of them Issas getting out of Somalia. It's been a very fertile recruiting ground for AQ and the Brotherhood." He nodded, as though remembering something. "The Legion seems to have largely gone to ground in the north as well. Not many of them on the streets these days. The National Army is out, and there are some Legion advisors, but for the most part the troops are staying inside the wire."

He pointed to the center of the city on the map. "Most of the slums are here, spreading out to the south. More than likely, the hostages are in there somewhere, so we're going to have to go in at some point. For now, leave that to me. You guys will stand out too much. There are some wealthier parts of town where the Arabs hang out, however, on the edge of the European quarter, that you might have some luck with. I don't have to tell you the drill."

He didn't. We had done some similar things in Mexico. It was always dicey, trying to get somebody to talk to you about fanatical murderers who might be a few tables over, for all you know. Sometimes it was the only way, though.

"Any more questions?" Imad asked. When there were none, he simply said, "Good hunting," and walked out the door, already adjusting his gait to match the locals.

Alek looked around at the team. "We are short on time, but we're going to take a couple of hours to catch some rack time before we go out. We'll be in pairs, so everybody needs to be on their toes. Hit the sack."

I picked my rack, hauled my gear in, took off my boots, and dropped onto the cot as the call to prayer started to wail outside the window.

CHAPTER 3

The souk was as crowded, dirty, and noisy as any I'd been in. Imad hadn't been kidding; even a bare two miles from the European quarter, Larry and I stood out. Of course, Larry being six-foot-six, two hundred fifty pounds, white, goateed, and balding, he'd stand out just about anywhere. I am much more medium-sized, but white, black-haired, and blue-eyed still stood out here.

It didn't seem to be bothering most of the locals much. I suppose the khat helped. We got shouted at in French or English about every ten yards, rarely anything of any sort of importance or even meaning. A man in a soccer jersey walked up to us and said, "I am a policeman. Show me your passport."

Larry tried to just ignore him. As big and crazy as the bald galoot is, he's really kind of a nice guy. I am not. "Fuck off," I snarled. I took a step toward him, bunching my fists. I was about to cave his head in, and it showed. A bit of overkill, actually, I could probably have broken him in half by bumping into him, but jackasses trying to be authoritative set me off. His eyes got wide, and he scrambled away.

"Way to win the hearts and minds, there, buddy," Larry said, as I glared after the little fuck.

I tried to shake off the burst of anger. The heat was getting to me, I told myself. Well, that and the fact that he was the third fucker today to try that. Add in the stress of walking around with just Larry, in a city that had slaughtered a couple of thousand US and allied servicemen and women barely a week before, and I was on a bit of a hair trigger. Larry must have sensed what I was thinking, because his huge hand descended on my shoulder.

"Hey, take a deep breath, man. Game face," he said quietly. I tried to comply, and almost gagged. There were a lot of smells floating around the market, and not all of them particularly savory. Larry tried to hide his smile as I coughed, and clapped me on the back.

Our destination was not, in fact, the market itself, but a small café on Avenue 13. It was cooler, though not cool, shadowy, and smelled of hookah smoke. It catered to Arabs, locals, and Westerners with a taste for Arab food and atmosphere. I had a taste for neither, but we hoped to pick up or overhear some intel here.

Larry and I picked a small table where we could sit with our backs to the wall, in a dark corner where we could see most of the street. I wasn't very hungry, due to the heat, and when the server came and asked for our order, I asked for water.

"Fifty-two dollars, sir," he said.

"What?" Even with inflation being what it is, that's straight robbery. I think more than a little of that assessment came out in my tone. He got a little stiff.

"Fifty-two dollars for bottle of water," he repeated. I had to shuffle through my wallet. We didn't get paid in dollars much, these days, ever since the bottom dropped out of it, but we still kept some on hand, mostly high-denomination bills, since those were the only ones that were any good, except for getting exact change. I peeled the money off and shoved it at him with little grace. He bobbed his head and left.

As we were waiting, we watched and listened, saying little. The traffic on the street was steady. Nobody seemed to be in much of a hurry, and in this heat, why would they be? It took almost twenty minutes for my bottle of water to get to the table, unsurprisingly. I twisted off the cap and took a gulp. It was warm, but I was bathed in my own sweat, and thirsty.

I had noticed another Caucasian on the far end of the café, sipping on a bottle of something and just lounging. I kept watching him, and saw that he was doing much the same thing we were; he was carefully observing the people going past, as well as in and out of the café. He was watching us, too. I was starting to suspect he'd made us when he made eye contact, and lifted his bottle in salute. Fuck.

I nudged Larry, as the other man finished his drink, got up, and started to weave his way across the café toward us. Larry nodded fractionally. He had already spotted the guy.

My attention was suddenly drawn to a rising human noise outside. The man approaching us turned his head to look toward the unmistakable sound of an increasingly restive crowd, but didn't seem overly concerned. I tried to continue to watch both, as he came closer.

He stopped at our table, and in faintly accented English, asked, "May I join you?"

"Sure," Larry said easily. He was relaxed in that particular way that said his hand was within inches of the grip of his STI Tactical under the table, if not on it. The man inclined his head, pulled up a chair, and sat down.

He was around six feet tall, brown-haired, and gray-eyed. He was dressed in a green short-sleeved shirt and khaki shorts, with good hiking boots. And, unless I missed my guess, he was armed.

"Fine day, isn't it?" he said, casually, looking out on the street. He noticed my attention to the crowd noises coming from up the street, and smiled. "Don't worry about that, my friend. Just the daily protests. It's nothing to worry about, yet. When you start hearing screams or gunshots, then it's time to worry."

"Have to say, I haven't seen many other Westerners out and about today," I observed.

"Indeed not," he replied. "A lot of that--" he gestured toward the noise "--is aimed at foreigners, particularly Westerners. The opposition has long believed that it's foreign money propping up the President, and with his landslide election to a fourth consecutive six-year term, they are getting a little upset with the West these days."

"Have you been here long?" Larry asked. "You seem pretty well versed."

"I have been stationed here for four years now. It is home, of a sort." He smiled.

"Legion?" I asked. He nodded.

"*Sergent Chef* Arno Kohl, at your service," he said. I raised my eyebrows. I didn't think anybody used "at your service" anymore. "And yourselves?"

"Lou," I replied. I jerked a thumb at Larry. "This is Bud."

He laughed. "Hardly the most inventive cover names, but as I was not born Arno Kohl, I suppose I have no room to argue." He looked us over. "What brings you to delightful Djibouti?"

"We're with a refugee aid organization," I replied, pulling out one of the phony business cards that Sam had cooked up. They looked professional, and in fact they were, having been made through an online company that specialized in them. The fact that no such organization as Team Refuge existed was beside the point.

He studied it as though it were genuine, though, nodded, and handed it back. "Veterans, yes? I have met a few such, turned to relief work."

"It's an exclusively veteran organization," I replied. I was talking out of my ass, since we didn't really have all that thick a back story for Team Refuge. I had to be careful that I didn't go too overboard. Not only did that present problems for the rest of the teams, keeping up with my lies, but it could awaken some suspicion in our new friend. I didn't trust this Legionnaire, especially since we were in the country without the knowledge of the US Embassy or the local authorities.

He was a pleasant enough conversationalist, though. He spoke at length about the city, and a few of his experiences with the Legion.

"So, Arno," Larry said congenially, "I haven't seen much Legion presence out on the streets today. And you're not in uniform. Last time I was around the Legion, you guys wore your uniforms everywhere. What's

23

going on?"

Kohl grimaced. "The French government has issued strict 'hands off' orders for the demi-brigade," he answered. "We have an arrangement with the President, but apparently that doesn't extend to dealing with this rabble."

"I understand the opposition is just pissed that the President stays in power no matter what the people want," I said. "Pro-democracy demonstrations and suchlike."

"That's what they say," he said derisively. "And a lot of them certainly are just that--they want a functioning democratic republic. But a lot of these people are Somalis, driven out of that *scheissloch* of a country as the wars worsen." He took a gulp of his drink. "There are plenty of infiltrators among the Somalis--Shabaab and Al Qaeda, and plenty of Sudanese who are happy to help." He leaned forward. "They are appealing to the poor Muslims to unite and drive out the infidel-influenced President. Then they can set up an Islamic state here, on the only major port on the Horn."

"Why would the French want to sit back and allow that?" I asked, genuinely curious.

"Because they don't want to piss off all the jihadis in their own country," Larry snorted.

"Exactly," Kohl said. "*Verdammt* cowards are overrun with Arabs and Algerians now. Entire tracts of Paris are off-limits to infidels. The Republic is hanging on by a thread, and they are terrified of doing anything to further inflame the Islamic population. If they do, the rioting might overthrow the whole country." He spat.

"You don't seem to like the French much," Larry commented amusedly.

"Of course I don't, I'm German," Kohl said. "The Legion gave me a chance when I had to get out of Germany. I am loyal to the Legion, not the fucking French."

"*Legio patria nostra*," I said quietly. He nodded emphatically, and smote his hand on the table.

"So, what, the entire demi-brigade is just staying inside the wire?" Larry asked.

"Essentially," Kohl said. "As soon as the attack went down, the *Colonel* recalled all of our units, except for the higher-profile advisors, to the operations base. We are to stay static, inside the wire, until we receive orders otherwise."

"But liberty's fine? Even with the attack, and the unrest you were talking about?" I was starting to suspect something about our German friend. It was confirmed when he froze, then smiled.

"You are most astute, *meine freunde*," he said, leaning back in his chair. "As it turns out, *mon Colonel* is no fool. He has a few of us out on the

24

streets, to keep an eye on things."

"So he's getting ready to act, even if his higher headquarters isn't?" Larry was leaning forward, his forearms on the table, paying close attention.

Kohl had gone slightly colder, and was eyeing us both carefully. "I wouldn't know," he said. "He does not reveal his plans of action to me. I am only a *sergent-chef*."

"Of course," I said apologetically, even as my ears pricked up. The noise down the street had changed. It was getting louder, and taking on a distinctly nasty edge. I was starting to feel my hackles rise. "I'm sorry, I was just curious." I nudged Larry, who looked over at me, and saw how I was listening. He cocked his head, and his face changed. Trouble.

Kohl heard it too, and also saw how we reacted. I was hoping that he'd write it off to our being veterans, like we'd told him, but he didn't say anything about it. He just put a handful of francs on the table and stood. "I think we had best get elsewhere, my friends," he said, cool professionalism in his tone. "It sounds like things might get a bit ugly today after all."

"I agree," I said, standing up as well, and starting to move for the street. As I did so, Kohl stepped close to me, and spoke in a low undertone.

"I will see what my contacts can find about what you're looking for, my friend. I will be 'in touch,' as you Americans say." I looked at him in surprise, and he smiled, then hurried out of the café.

I looked at Larry, shrugged, and we followed him out.

The street, which had been bustling with hucksters, merchants, and shoppers, was now deserted, left to the trash and standing, brackish water. The noise of the crowd was coming from the west, in the direction of the traffic circle at the end of Avenue 13. We promptly turned and headed the other way.

We were already several blocks down the street by the time the crowd cleared the corner. Crowds don't usually move all that fast, and I was extremely thankful for that. From the scraps of Arabic chanting I could pick out, we would be targets if anyone in the crowd spotted us.

Looking up, I spotted a balcony that we could climb up to, and pointed it out to Larry. I wanted to get a better picture of what was going on, and watching the crowd for a little bit might be informative.

"And if the house is occupied, we get compromised that much faster," Larry objected. "And if we get compromised, odds are we get torn apart by the crowd. I'm not in favor of that."

I hesitated for a moment. I really wanted some more information to go back with, but Larry had a good point. Finally, as the crowd got closer, I shrugged. "You're right. Bad idea. Let's get moving."

The trouble was, as much as we wanted to get out of sight, I didn't want to cut through the slums. We'd have to go in there eventually, but going in blind and in broad daylight was not a course of action I was comfortable with. But the crowd was getting closer, spreading out along Avenue 13, even as it seemed to be generally pushing north. We had to either go to ground or find a different route.

"Fuck it," I finally decided, and ducked into an alley leading to the slums, Larry close on my heels.

***

We wove through the filthy back alleys, piled with trash, and often with raw sewage running down what passed for streets, which were mostly bare dirt or crumbling asphalt. Increasingly run-down brick and stucco buildings started giving way to ramshackle hovels built out of cardboard, plywood, corrugated metal, canvas; anything their desperately poor occupants could get their hands on. The filth was staggering, the emaciated faces watching us suspiciously a testament to the nightmare of living in such squalor.

Some of the people were friendly, calling out greetings in French or Arabic. A lot of the kids were excited at the strange faces, and ran alongside us, laughing. There were groups of young men, however, whom the others seemed to avoid. These guys were hostile, mean-mugging us as we went past. I was glad of the weight of my 1911 strapped to the small of my back, covered by the fall of my shirt, but hoped I wouldn't have to use it. That would only draw attention, something we really, really didn't need at the moment. I was still nervous about how much that Legionnaire, Kohl, had guessed.

Several of the hostile young men were moving as we passed, and I started to notice a pattern. "We're getting encircled," I muttered to Larry, as we crossed another cramped intersection.

"Who are these guys?" Larry asked.

"Best guess?" I replied, stepping over a running stream of sewage. "Some of the young radicals that Kohl was talking about. I think we're in trouble."

Ahead of us, one of the groups of young men was blocking the alley. The ones in the front were all chewing. Great. Khat. Which meant, that aside from all the Islamist claptrap and hatred of Westerners that the jihadis had been putting in their heads, they were high as a kite. We were indeed in trouble. A lot of trouble.

I tried to turn the corner to get away from them, but another group was blocking that way. I started cussing under my breath. This was not going to end well, for anyone involved. They didn't appear to have guns, but they didn't need them to be dangerous. I started to reach for my pistol. Larry was moving laterally, getting a better angle on the ones we'd just turned away from, no doubt getting ready to throw down himself. I found myself kind of wishing I had that STI of his; fifteen rounds of .45 versus the eight I had in my Springfield sounded really good right about now.

My hand was under my shirt, my fingers touching the butt of my 1911, when there was a torrent of loud Somali from behind us.

The old man was so skinny I half expected him to collapse just from walking. His bones stuck out from his flesh, and his shirt hung off him like a clothes hanger. He was spry enough, though, and had some considerable lung power, as he yelled at the young men confronting us, and waved angrily at them. One of them said something, only to be cut off with another torrent of angry words. Finally, the young men turned away, shooting glares of pure hate at us, and drifted off into the rest of the slums.

"Forgive," the old man said, in broken English. "Boys. No enough discipline."

"Thank you, grandfather," I said. I spoke in English, as I didn't know any Somali. "God be with you." Not exactly the local blessing, but I hoped it would suffice. The scrawny old coot with rheumy eyes had probably just saved quite a few lives by intervening. I wondered if he knew it. I suspect he did.

"*A salaam aleikum*," He replied. "*Nabakey.*"

I put my hand over my heart. That much Somali I had learned. "*Nabakey.*" The old man nodded, waved his skeletal hand at us, and walked back into the maze of alleys.

"Huh," Larry said. "Good of him."

"Sure was," I replied. "Let's get out of here before we need him to come back."

Looking up at the sun, I got re-oriented, and this time busted a hard left, moving east to try to get out of the slum, and back over to the Boulevard De General De Gaulle. That would get us close enough to the industrial areas along the shoreline, and hopefully allow us to avoid any more such unpleasant encounters.

CHAPTER 4

We got back to our little urban base camp as the sun was going down over the city. Most of the rest of the team was back, and we gathered in the op-center to go over what we'd found out.

It was mostly atmospherics, and some background info we hadn't had going in, which was about what we'd expected. We didn't exactly blend in here, and that was a liability when it came to getting intel. I was pretty sure we'd have to start working sources, something of which I knew next to nothing. Hey, I know my strengths and weaknesses. Shooting and blowing stuff up, I'm good at. Recruiting sources in an entirely foreign culture; not so much.

There was a picture forming, however. Larry and I had gotten a little of it from Arno Kohl, but other pieces were starting to come together.

The President had just changed the rules for the second time, allowing himself to run for a fourth six-year term. There had been plenty of outrage the last time, when he had done the same thing, and been elected by a suspicious 80-something percent. He apparently didn't even try to mask the election fraud this time, with something closer to one hundred percent. This alone wouldn't be much of a surprise. Kleptocrats were a dime-a-dozen in this part of the world.

The trouble was, the president was the single richest man in East Africa. Meanwhile, some sixty-percent of the men in Djibouti were unemployed, and living in the crushing poverty we had gotten such a good look at that afternoon. Envy is a powerful tool in the wrong hands.

Much of his wealth came from the port, i.e., from foreigners. The Islamists, from Eritrea, Sudan, Egypt, and Somalia, were capitalizing on that, especially in the slums. Anger at the rich, fraudulent president had started to build.

There were demonstrations. They started out peacefully, but the president's security forces had heard some of the grumbling, and overreacted. Over a hundred people died in the resulting massacre, and the demonstrations turned into riots. The president hadn't been seen outside the presidential mansion since.

There had been more riots, some aimed at the security forces, but most at the Westerners or even the equally poor Afar. There were militias forming in the slums, and even in some of the more affluent parts of the city. The military was being held close to the presidential palace, and after an entire squad was killed and mutilated in the slums, they didn't venture too far from the main drags.

Lemonier had been a target because of the growing outrage against Westerners. Nobody seemed to know why they'd gone after a guarded US military base, but were still leaving the European quarter pretty much alone, but that wasn't really our concern. It was obvious to me, as more of the story came out, that the opposition had been entirely co-opted by Shabaab and Al-Qaeda types, probably with several other random jihadi organizations thrown into the mix. The Muslim Brotherhood wasn't making any secret of its presence in most of the mosques, either.

The bigger picture was, if anything, even more ominous than upwards of two hundred hostages in the hands of psyched-up Islamist terrorists, in the middle of a city that was about to set itself on fire. Djibouti was the only major port on the Horn. That made it very, very important, strategically. If the Islamists were able to install a strict-sharia state here, they could put some serious economic hurt on the West. As if the piracy coming out of Somalia and the worldwide depression weren't bad enough.

As we were discussing the worsening intel picture, Imad came back. He looked grimmer than usual, as he joined us at the map table.

"Most of the people who might talk are scared shitless," he explained, as he leaned on the map. "Can't say I blame them. There are some seriously scary motherfuckers in town." He started ticking off names. "Mohammed Khasam and Ismail Farah I know for certain are here. Farah made his name with Al-Shabaab a few years ago, for his enthusiasm with a tapanga when dealing with captured AMISOM soldiers. Khasam was almost as bad, although he tended to prefer to drench his victims in gasoline and set them on fire.

"I also heard somebody mention Omar Sadiq Hasan, a particularly nasty Sudanese bad boy, who cut his teeth massacring fellow Muslims in Darfur. He's got at least five hundred deaths to his name, and he claims as many as seven hundred. I can't confirm yet whether he's here, has been here, or is on his way."

He looked around the table. "The Colonel was right, Al Masri is here; at least that's what I was getting from the whispers. Most of the people here aren't as afraid of him as they are of the Shabaab types, since he tends to go for bombings and paramilitary attacks more than the kind of up-close tribal violence that the others are known for."

"Do we have any idea who this 'Al Masri' is?" Bob asked. "'The Egyptian' doesn't tell us very much."

Colton, who acted as the team's intel specialist, shook his head.

30

"Nobody knows his real name, and in all his videos, he's wearing a shemaugh over his face. There was a theory floating around that he's actually several people, but somebody did a voice analysis of several of his messages, and it's definitely all the same man."

"I don't suppose anybody you talked to said they knew where these assholes are," Alek ventured.

Imad snorted. "If I even thought it real loud, they got skittish. Nobody wants to have anything to do with possibly crossing those fuckers."

Alek wasn't happy. "What about locating the hostages? Any luck?"

"Well," Imad said slowly, "maybe." He obviously wasn't comfortable with what he had. "There's someone who offered information. He didn't say what, but he made it clear that he expects to be well paid for it, and for the risk he's taking even talking to me." He rubbed his hand over his jaw. "I'll be honest; I'm more than half-expecting it to be a setup."

"More than likely it is," Jim said. "Is it worth following up on?"

"Right now, it's the only lead we've got, really," Imad replied.

"Then we'll take the chance," Alek said. "Where are you meeting him?"

"Outside the city, at a farm in the south." Imad pointed out the location on the map. "He gave me a pretty good description. He wants to meet tomorrow, at sundown, and we'd best have a good amount of cash for him, or he won't talk."

"Did he specify that you had to be alone?" Nick asked.

No, but if there are too many of us, he'll get spooked," was the answer.

We started studying the farm in question, and pulled up some imagery from Google Earth. It was on the south side of the major canal that ran along the southern edge of the city, and there was a fair amount of vegetation on the imagery. It appeared to be walled, and there was also a large conglomeration of what looked like small shacks less than two hundred meters to either side. I didn't like it, and I wasn't the only one. It might be quiet and remote compared to the middle of Ahriba slum, but if there was shooting, there was going to be a lot of attention, real quick.

"I'll go in with Imad, as backup," I said. "Probably can't be packing too much heat--" Imad nodded at my glance, and I turned back to the map "-- so pistols only, soft armor, and comms." I traced the treeline on the imagery. "It looks like two or three guys, with rifles, should be able to get over the wall here, at the northeast corner. Situation's going to dictate, but it looks like there should be a fair amount of shade and junk to hide in back there."

"Assuming they don't have somebody back there already," Jim pointed out. Jim liked occasionally usurping my place as the team's resident Voice of Doom.

Larry was looking down at the map and imagery, and stroking his

31

goatee with a frown. "I don't like it." He pointed to the only visible entrance to the walled compound. "We can't see if there are any good alternate approaches, or if this is the only way in or out. You could easily get in there, and have them slam the door shut behind you. And where are we going to stash vehicles if a fast exfil is necessary?"

"Here." Jim was pointing to the open ground by the canal. It was less than two hundred yards from the farm. "If everything goes to hell, go over the back wall, and sprint for the trucks. It's a short distance, and we can even support from the trucks."

We studied the problem for a while longer, then I finally straightened up. "You know what? I think we need to do a drive by in the morning. Get a look at the ground beforehand. One more truck roving around isn't going to attract too much attention, as long as we don't loiter too long. Imagery's great, but there's a lot we can't see. Not to mention--" I checked the time stamp "--this is five years old. Things well could have changed."

There were noises of general agreement. We figured out a scheme of maneuver for the leader's recon, and then retired for a few hours shut-eye, while we could.

***

Imad and I pulled the Range Rover back into our compound a little after noon. The recon had gone as smoothly as could have been expected; we got a good look at the farm and the surrounding ground, and didn't think we'd been noticed, at least not insofar as we were casing the place.

The fact was, we had to be very careful as to our movements. The exodus of Westerners from the city, with the majority of those who stayed staying holed up in the European quarter, was severely limiting our camouflage. It's hard to blend in in an African country when you're one of the few Caucasians walking around.

Imad parked the truck next to the warehouse, and we got out, grabbing our rifles off the floor. We were harmless tourists as far as anyone looking in the windows could see, but we were still loaded for bear out of sight.

It was hot as hell. Even with the Range Rover's still-functioning air conditioning on, it had been sweltering. When I got out and stepped into the direct sun, I wanted to wilt. I hadn't been this hot since Libya. My shirt was sopping with sweat.

There were three reciprocating industrial fans going in the op-center, but they didn't seem to do much besides circulate the hot air. At least none of Rodrigo's electronics were overheating yet. I pulled out the camera that we'd been "sightseeing" with and started downloading the pictures onto one of the laptops.

We had already discovered one hitch in the plan that we couldn't see from the imagery. What looked like a wall around the farmhouse was in fact a fence, made of corrugated sheet metal. That presented a problem--while it was possible to quietly scale a mud or concrete wall, a man in load bearing gear with a rifle wasn't going to get over a sheet-metal fence without making a hell of a racket. The more I thought about it, the worse our options were getting. Somebody was going to have to walk into that fence, and there weren't a lot of vantage points to cover the inside, if any. On top of that, getting overwatch into position before dark was going to be a bitch. There wasn't a lot of cover or concealment between the road and the house.

While I was pondering this, and cleaning up the photos, Hank turned away from the comm laptop he was covering, and called out, "Hey, get everybody up. The Colonel's on the line. Says it's important."

There was a fair amount of rustling and grumbling from the far end of the room, as Imad started rousting the rest of the team out. Most had racked out, or tried to. It could turn out to be a long night, so Alek had invoked the oldest bylaw of soldiering: get what sleep you can, when you can. It was too hot to get much, but any rest is useful.

The team shuffled over to the bank of comm equipment, most wearing little more than shorts, but with weapons still close at hand, along with at least a couple of spare mags. Nobody was under any illusions about our security situation. Mike's team was handling most of it, to their chagrin, but none of us could afford to let down our guard too far, even if we were technically in a secured location.

Hank swiveled the laptop so that everybody could see it, and touched the key to activate the speaker/mic combination. "Everybody's here, Colonel."

Heinrich's pixelated portrait came on the screen. Even as blurry as he was, he looked haggard. I knew he was doing everything he could back in the States to get us as much intel as possible. The fact that there wasn't much available that we couldn't find on the ground here wasn't going to stop him from trying, and staying up nights to do so. One of the reasons we liked the guy.

"Gents, I got Rodrigo's rundown of what you've got so far. I know it sucks trying to get an in with these people on such a short timeframe. But I'm afraid that we've got even less time that we might think." He reached to the keyboard beneath the screen. "This got posted on YouTube about four hours ago."

The video program beeped, and a link came up under the picture. Hank reached in and clicked on it, then maximized the video that came up.

The picture was of a shemaugh-swathed man in a green fatigue jacket, sitting in front of a black flag with Arabic lettering on it. It looked like every other jihadi propaganda video that had been floating around for the last thirty years.

The man started to speak in Arabic, followed a second later by an

33

accented English voice-over. "Praise be to Allah, the most merciful, the most compassionate. Muslim brothers everywhere, *as-salaamu aleikum, wa rahmatullahi wa barakaatu, wa bad*:

"*'Fight those who believe not in Allah nor the last day, nor hold that forbidden which hath been forbidden by Allah and His Apostle, nor acknowledge the religion of truth, even if they are of the people of the Book, until they pay the* jizya *with willing submission, and feel themselves subdued.'*

"I address our Muslim brothers, subject to the oppression of the infidel West, who yet rise in the name of Allah to strike with us at the depraved Crusaders.

"All over the Ummah, they set their bases on Muslim ground. They kill our children, and rape our women. They defile our soil with their presence, and oppress the Ummah with their depravity. Their arrogance tells them that they are untouchable, that they rule land, air, and sea.

"But, my brothers in Islam, they are not invincible, they are not unconquerable. Allah has delivered them into our hands, as He once delivered them into the hands of abu Bakr, Salah ad-Din, and our dear brother, Osama, murdered in his home by the cowardly killers of the Crusader Americans. Just as Osama once struck at the Crusaders in Islamic East Africa, to show their weakness, so have we now struck at their necks, and destroyed their largest base in this ancient Muslim land.

"Yes, my brothers, the infidel base from which they sent their cowardly drones to murder our faithful brothers in Yemen, Somalia, and Oman has fallen, and we have taken many captives. We hold these hostages as a warning to the West; that if they act against the Ummah anywhere, these will feel the wrath of Allah, at our hands!" He shook his fist at the camera, and from behind him came cries of "Takbir!" and "Allahu akhbar!"

"See the loathsome infidel soldiers, humbled and broken at our hands," he said, gesturing to his right. The camera panned to show about a half-dozen young men, dressed in tattered remains of uniforms or PT gear, kneeling on a concrete floor. Their hands appeared to be tied behind their backs, and their feet were tied or taped together. The back three had sacks over their heads, but the front three were uncovered. All of them showed signs of severe beatings, and one was hardly able to stay upright. His face was crusted with dried blood from one or several cuts on his head.

As the video continued, two more masked men, dressed in shabby fatigues and with some AK variants slung on their backs, stepped to the bloody-faced man and grabbed his arms. He didn't resist as they roughly dragged him over to the black flag and forced him to his knees.

My fists were clenched, and my jaw was working with rage. I knew what was coming.

"*The punishment of those who wage war against Allah and His*

34

Apostle, and strive with might and main for mischief through the land is execution, or crucifixion, or the cutting off of hands and feet from opposite sides," the shemaugh-swathed terrorist intoned, as he lifted a tapanga from the table in front of him, and stepped over to stand over the kneeling American. To cries of "Allahu akhbar!" he put the edge to the young man's neck, and began to saw.

Blood sprayed, and the young man screamed, a horrible gurgling that died in a few seconds as his trachea was cut through. His murderer kept at it, sawing away at flesh, bone and gristle as blood drenched the remains of the man's Air Force utilities, and the hands of the butcher that was killing him. With a few hacks and a couple of jerks, the severed head came free, and the terrorist held it up, to the now near-hysterical shouts of "Allahu akhbar! Allahu akhbar!"

"This will be the fate of all infidels!" he shouted. "Let the faithful take heart, and let the Crusader West tremble in fear! Allahu akhbar!" The video ended.

For a long minute, there was only silence. Deadly silence. Heinrich didn't interrupt it right away.

"That poor bastard," he finally said, "was Senior Airman Kyle Phillips. He was a data technician at Lemonier. Near as we can tell, the motherfucker who sawed his head off is Al Masri.

"Unfortunately, we can't gather much from the video. Concrete floor, white walls; could be anywhere over there. One thing we can get is that they may not be keeping all the hostages in one place. We only saw six, and from what we've been able to ascertain, including the statements on several jihadi websites, they have a lot more than that."

He sighed, and his shoulders slumped a little. "Look, I'm sorry I had to show that to you guys. But we're trying to get you any information that we can, and if the CIA has anything, they aren't telling us." He shook his head angrily. "We're getting precisely dick in the way of support."

"Do they want the hostages back or not?" Nick demanded. "They had a fucking JSOC compound in that base; they've got to have some information to help us out."

"They don't want any governmental fingerprints on it," the Colonel replied. "At least not until they have a slam-dunk. If this goes south, the only involvement that they have is thirty deniable contractors."

"They're going to have a lot worse than that!" Alek exploded. "That poor kid is just the first. If they don't get their shit together, they're going to have a lot of dead hostages on their hands, not just thirty dead contractors they'd rather didn't exist."

"It's the Iran hostage situation all over again. They're dithering, and the administration doesn't want to risk an op going bad. Like I said, you guys are deniable. Hell, you're more than deniable, you're potential

35

scapegoats. The mainstream media still hasn't let go of the Blackwater meme." The Colonel didn't bother to hide his disgust.

"So what the fuck are we still doing here?" Bob snarled. "Let's pull chocks and get the fuck out."

"We're still here because we're getting paid to be here," Alek said, a thoughtful expression on his face. "Not only that, but those poor bastards might have a fighting chance because of us." He looked around. "Nothing changes. We find the hostages, and we call in the cavalry."

"And if there's no cavalry?" Jim asked quietly. "If they decide it's too dangerous?"

"Then we kill, steal, and hijack our way to where they can't say it's too dangerous, and call them to pick the lot of us up." There was a set to Alek's jaw. I knew the feeling. None of us was comfortable with the situation, but we were even less comfortable with the suits back in the States playing politics with American lives. Just like Captain Van Husten had said, we had all taken the oath, and nobody ever released us from it. "Believe me, I'm not letting those fuckers off the hook."

There was a moment of silence, as everyone absorbed the new reality. As bad as it sucked, there was no whining, no, "We're screwed, man!" Just quiet, angry acceptance that the job was going to be harder, and likely, not all of us would be going home after it.

"If we're going to go ahead and push on," Larry said, "we'd probably better finish getting ready for this meet tonight."

And with that, we got back to work.

CHAPTER 5

Imad and I were sitting in the Defender, which we had idling on the dirt track about a hundred fifty yards from the entrance of the fence, watching the meeting place as the sun crept toward the hills to the west. Our loose shirts hid soft armor vests, pistols, and multiple spare mags. Tiny Bluetooth headsets were hidden in our ears.

"Not a lot of activity," I observed. I'd expected more overt guards.

"He's being cautious," Imad said. "He seemed like the cagey type when I talked to him." He stopped suddenly. "There. Just inside the fence." I saw what he was talking about. There was a man standing there, in the increasing shade of the fence and a wide-topped acacia.

"Can you tell if it's our boy, or one of his pals?" I asked.

Imad squinted. "Too dark, can't tell. I think he's a little too short to be our boy, though."

I looked at my watch, checked against the position of the sun. "Almost sundown."

"Yeah." He pulled out his Kimber and brass-checked it for the third time. Satisfied, he holstered it and pulled his shirt back down over it. "Game time." His voice was already slipping into his East African accent.

We got out and shut the doors. I walked around the front of the truck to join him, and he led off toward the farm. I kept about five meters distance, to the right and slightly behind him.

The farmhouse was surrounded by a five-foot sheet-metal fence, along which grew a row of acacias. The house walls were built from what looked like cinderblock, with a dusty metal roof. There was a lot of junk piled against the inside of the fence.

We walked slowly through the gate, if that's what you wanted to call it. It was really just a gap in the fence. There were four young men standing or squatting around in the dusty yard, watching us intently. One of them pointed toward the house, but none of them spoke. Imad nodded to them, and we walked up onto the rickety porch. There were two windows and a badly-fitting screen door. I stationed myself next to the door while Imad went inside. I leaned my back against the cinderblock wall, and watched the four young bucks watching me.

The screen door slammed, and a man spoke in Somali, greeting Imad. Maybe it was me, but he sounded nervous. I folded my arms loosely, trying to look non-threatening, while still being in a position to get to my gun fast.

The conversation continued in the house. I knew it could take a while. Members of tribal societies rarely get straight to business. There has to be a certain amount of small-talk and "getting to know one another" beforehand. I couldn't understand more than a few words, but it seemed to be going amicably enough.

Outside was uncomfortable. Not only were the bugs coming out, including swarms of mosquitoes, which made me glad of the mefloquine that Colton insisted we take every week, but there was something else, a certain tension. The four guys in the yard kept watching me, without speaking. The two squatting near the west fence would occasionally talk to each other quietly, but I couldn't pick anything out. There was none of the friendly welcome that could be heard inside.

The sun was below the horizon, and the sky was quickly going from orange to purple and black. The shadows were getting deeper, though one of the squatters was smoking, so I could see the two of them well enough. The heat was starting to recede. It was probably down to a hundred already, and felt comfortably cool. The air smelled of dust, shit, and smoke.

Voices from inside started to get more animated. Imad was getting insistent about something. It sounded like he was pressing his questions, and they weren't being answered. The other man was making placating noises. My paranoia was starting to make itself felt, especially as one of the loitering young men in the yard walked around back of the house. Soon enough, the one who had been standing by the gate followed him. The other two stayed squatting by the fence, next to a pile of straw.

Imad was getting loud. Whatever the other man was saying, Imad didn't like it. I carefully flexed the fingers of my gun hand. I could feel the situation going to hell already.

There was a crash from inside, and Imad let out a particularly vile curse in Arabic. It wasn't just indignation; that was our gone-to-shit signal.

I came off the porch, one hand going for my gun while I pressed the push-to-talk with the other. "Wildfire, wildfire," I sent, as my Springfield cleared holster and shirt. My off hand met the grip on the way up and out, and the tritium sights settled on the squatting man pulling an AKS out of the straw. My finger was already taking up the slack on the trigger as the gun came to full extension, and I fired, the .45's bark deafeningly loud in the evening quiet. The first round took him high in the chest, the second in the throat, and he crumpled back against the fence, his hand held uselessly to his throat to try to stem the spray of arterial blood.

His buddy was going for the Kalashnikov, but I lined him up as I

38

went for the far side of the yard, and fired twice more. He collapsed on top of his buddy, half of the top of his skull blasted away. I needed to calm down. I was shooting high.

The other two came running around the side they'd disappeared around before, even as gunfire erupted inside the house. I cranked off the last five rounds in the gun at them, and they ducked back behind the cinderblock, as I jumped behind a pile of trash and rubble, dropping the mag out and grabbing a fresh one from my belt. The pile wouldn't provide much cover, but I didn't intend to stay there that long.

Even as I bunched my muscles to move again, one of them stuck the barrel of an AK-47 around the corner and opened fire, spraying the corner of the yard on full auto. The rounds cracked overhead and smacked into and through fence and trees, as I dropped to my belly, and tried to get a shot. In the background I could hear an engine roaring, and hunkered back away from the gate.

There was more gunfire from the far side of the house. It sounded like a .45, and was answered by a scream. The gomer shooting at me ran out of ammunition, and I took the opportunity to fire a couple of covering shots, then scrambled to my feet and ran for the back corner of the house. If I could circle around behind him while he reloaded...

The engine roar got louder, along with the sound of flying gravel, and then the Range Rover was smashing through the gate, and skidding to a stop. The windows were open, and two battle rifles were stuck out and began to spit flame. Heavy 7.62 rounds started pulverizing the corner where the shooter had been.

"Hillbilly, going around the southeast corner," I sent. "Watch your fire."

"Affirm," Larry's voice came back.

I heard footsteps pounding on the porch in front as I went around back, gliding along in a slight crouch, my pistol at the low ready. There was the familiar rattle of the gomer's AK as he tried to blindly return fire, but as I peeked around the corner, he was too far back from the corner to have a hope in hell of hitting my teammates. I leaned out, put the front sight post on his center-mass, and shot him. He crumpled, and everything went quiet.

"Hillbilly, coming out." I did *not* want to be mistaken for a gomer. Unlikely, given my size and build, but it always pays to be careful. I reloaded with my third and last mag as I came back around to the front.

Imad was already in the truck, and Larry and Jim were on a knee to either side, rifles up. Alek was behind the wheel. "Get in," he said. "We've got to get moving." I complied quickly enough, grabbing my rifle off the floor in the back. We hadn't wanted to leave anything in the Defender when we'd left it, so we'd stashed our heavy stuff with the backup vehicle. As soon as I was in, Jim got in the passenger seat, and Larry squeezed into the back.

As Alek threw the Range Rover into reverse, and roared out of the farmyard, Larry started patting me over. "I'm fine," I told him. He finished his blood sweep anyway, and then leaned across me to Imad. I pushed his arm back. "I'll check him." It was standard procedure for us to check each other after a firefight. Sometimes you can get hit, and the adrenaline is just going so strong you don't even notice. I ran my hands over Imad's arms, legs, and back, checking for blood. Nothing.

"What the hell happened?" Alek asked, over the noise of the engine and the gravel under the tires.

"It was a simple robbery," Imad said. "They didn't have any info; they just knew we had money." We stopped at the Defender, and, instead of continuing the debrief, Imad and I jumped out and ran to our vehicle. Imad slid behind the wheel, while I got in the passenger side, reloaded my .45, and pulled my rifle up onto my lap. The rest of what had happened could wait until we got back to the compound.

We split off from the Range Rover. We'd take different routes back to the compound, to keep our footprint small. This wasn't like Afghanistan or Libya, where there had been an established presence, and convoys were common.

As we pulled away, headlights off, we could see people starting to converge on the farm, as well as a couple of HiLuxes, each with several armed men in the back. I took a closer look with the NVGs, and they looked like militia, not official security forces. In fact, I couldn't hear any sirens, or see any flashing lights. It looked like things had gotten so bad the local authorities really weren't venturing anywhere outside their strongholds in the city.

This was probably going to create a stir. I doubted that the guys we'd shot were the only ones who knew there were going to be Westerners at that farm tonight, and the shootout was probably going to tip somebody off that there were more than just scared tourists and idealistic humanitarian organizations in town. I cussed under my breath. Between the lack of support from the States, and now this, the job was looking more and more impossible by the hour.

If they thought the US had sent JSOC after them, the bad guys were likely to just kill the rest of the hostages, or, almost as bad, move them. Not that we had any sort of reliable intel on even their general location.

We wound through the streets, taking a complicated and serpentine route back to the compound. There wasn't a lot of traffic. The streetlights were on, and there were people out walking around, but there was a furtive undertone to their movements. People were scared.

When we got to the compound, we found quite a crowd there. The lights were on, and Billy was walking along a line of locals, most of them

40

showing injuries, directing some to one room or the other. I got out and walked over as Imad parked the truck, careful to leave my rifle in the cab, and my pistol concealed. These people didn't need to see what we really were.

"What's going on, Billy?" I asked, as I walked up.

He didn't look up from the woman he was examining. She was bleeding from a wound on her head. There was quite a bit of blood, but head injuries are like that. I didn't see any flowing, just a slow ooze. "There was a riot in the southern slums a couple hours ago," Billy said. "Nobody seems to know what started it, but it turned into Afar versus Issa really quick. Sounds like a few people died, and we've gotten a few dozen wounded and injured here. Dave and Colton are inside, treating the worst of them." He pointed one gloved hand toward the side of the building that Dave had turned into an aid station. "You want to help me triage?"

"Let me make sure tonight's trip is put to bed; then I'll be back out," I said. I pushed past the line of wounded Djiboutians, and into the main building. The line continued in the hall, leading to the southeast wing of the building, while the door to the northwest wing, our team room, was tightly shut, with a sheet tacked over it. I slipped under the sheet and opened the door.

Alek, Jim, and Larry were coming in from the other side, with Imad. Imad had my rifle in his hand and held it up for me before putting it on my rack. I nodded my thanks, and waited at the map table as the others secured their gear.

"I told Billy I'd go out and help him triage the local wounded after this," I announced, as the night's team gathered at the map table. Alek nodded his acknowledgement.

"So," he began, "How does this affect our situation?"

"We can't know entirely," Jim said matter-of-factly. "It's going to depend on how many people knew about what was going down tonight, and how closely they connected Imad with us here. Worst-case, the bad guys know there are some heavy hitters in town, know it's us, and act on it." He rubbed his jaw. "Not to put too fine a point on it, but it sure as hell didn't help us, any way you look at it."

There was a moment's pause, as we all thought over the implications. Then I had an idea. "Wait, we know that Khasam and Farah are in town. We don't know what Al Masri looks like, but we've got photos of those two. Anybody want to bet they're taking a big part in the demonstrations that keep turning into riots around here?" That got everybody's attention. "Maybe, if we start watching the demonstrations, we can get eyes on one of these fuckers and tail them. They might lead us to the hostages, or at least to somebody else who can."

Everybody mulled it over for a moment. "We'd still need to be able to trail him inconspicuously," Alek pointed out. "As we've discovered before, that can be difficult here."

"Overwatch team," Imad put in. "I'd be on the ground. Two teams in vehicles on the outskirts, positioned to move in and take up the trail when he leaves the crowd."

"It could work," Jim said.

"All right," Alek said. "We've got some planning to do. But first, for the sake of OPSEC, let's go help get these locals treated, and out of here."

Leaving our weapons with Rodrigo in the team room, we crossed over to the aid station to lend a hand. There were probably upward of twenty people in the room, men, women, and children. Most of the injuries were blunt trauma, from beatings or thrown rocks, but some sported lacerations, likely from knives or tapangas. Colton was stitching a young woman's arm, where half her bicep had been cut off, and had been dangling down to her forearm. The kid next to her looked to have been hit with a rock; he was bleeding from a nasty abrasion on his shoulder. I pulled on a pair of latex gloves and squatted down in front of him, to start to clean the wound.

"Fuckin' nuts, man," Colton declared as he tied off another suture. "Nobody can tell me why it started. None of these people ever did anything to anybody, and it's not like it's their fault their president's a fucking klepto."

The dirt and grit out of the gouge in the kid's shoulder, I reached for gauze and started to gently bandage it. The kid was just watching me, his chin tucked in, not making a sound. "The bad guys are trying to create chaos, so they can take over. Chaos leads to more chaos," I said. "When you break down a society, everything breaks down, even the decency of a lot of the people, and shit like this is what happens."

We continued to work well into the night, patching, stitching, and splinting. Fortunately, there weren't really any critical cases that we had to either keep around or try to take to the hospital, in the north of town. A little after midnight, we were able to send them all home.

***

It was three in the morning when I woke up. I couldn't remember the dream, just the sick, disquieted feeling it left me with. For a few minutes I lay there, sweating, staring at the ceiling, trying to will myself back to sleep. I had only managed to drift off an hour before.

It wasn't working. There was a faint red light splashed on the ceiling, and I looked over to see Larry sitting on his cot, reading by the red glow of his headlamp. Guess he couldn't sleep, either.

I sat up with a muffled groan. I didn't want to be awake, but I knew from past experience that I wasn't going to get to sleep for a while when I felt like this. Larry looked up, putting a finger in his place in the book as I swung my feet to the floor.

"One of those nights, huh?" Larry asked.

"Yeah." I put my head in my hands and rubbed my eyes. "What're you doing up?"

"Same reason," he said. "Couldn't sleep." He held up the book, one of the monster hunter books he'd gotten me hooked on. "Thought I'd catch up on a little reading."

Larry and I went back a ways. We'd been on the same team in the Philippines, just before we'd gotten out and hooked up with Alek and Jim to start Praetorian Security. We'd been in half a dozen hellholes together since.

"You never made it to Libya, did you?" I asked.

"Nah, just the PI," he said, setting the book down on the rack next to him. "Twice before our team, then the deployment we did."

Suddenly struck by a memory, I grinned. "You remember that one night on Mindanao, something like a week before everything went to shit? We were about two miles outside of that tiny-ass village that nobody knew the name of."

Larry chuckled. "When Lucky woke up with a banana spider two inches above his face?"

"And sat up right into it." I shook my head. "I'm still amazed he didn't start shooting. He sure freaked out far enough."

"Lucky was always a little high-strung," Larry said. "What happened to him, anyway?"

"Don't know," I admitted. "He got out right after we got back from that deployment, and I kind of lost track of him." Larry just nodded. That happened in this business. A guy you had spent every waking moment with for a year or more got out, went home, and just kind of dropped off the map.

After a long pause, Larry asked quietly, "Why'd you ask about Libya?"

"Ah," I searched for an answer that would make sense. I wasn't entirely sure, myself. "This just kind of reminds me of the situation over there. What with the complete chaos, what starved, beaten version of a civil society they had there breaking down. It wasn't pretty. It ain't going to be here, either."

Larry murmured thoughtfully. "Can't save every situation, brother."

I snorted. "Can't save any of 'em, is how it's starting to look."

Larry leaned back and swung his feet back up on his cot. It creaked dangerously under his weight. "You know, I remember you saying once, 'The world is fucked. Any student of history should be able to see that clearly enough. The only thing any of us should worry about is doing the right thing. Probably won't change anything, but that doesn't stop it being the right thing.' Sound familiar?"

I shrugged. "Yeah, sounds like something I'd say."

"It's a sage bit of wisdom," he said, putting his hands behind his head. "You should probably think about it."

I flipped him the bird and lay back down on my cot. Morning would come soon enough.

CHAPTER 6

Damn, but I was getting tired of the Djibouti heat.

Larry and I were in the Defender, slowly cruising in random circles in the back streets, about a half mile from where there was another demonstration going on. We could actually hear the rising and falling roar, even over the sound of the engine. Whatever was being said, it was getting them good and riled up.

"I've got eyes on Khasam," Bob whispered over the radio from the overwatch position, which was actually the other Range Rover, where he was crouched over a laptop, controlling the tiny Aeroseeker UAV that was hovering over the crowd. "He's standing on top of a Nissan van, with a bullhorn. Can't make out what he's saying, but it's loud, it's angry, and it's aimed to the north."

"Who else is around him?" I asked.

"Looks like a bunch of his goons," was the reply after a moment. "Nobody who wants to look important."

"Probably too much to hope for that we might be able to bag more than one of the assholes," Larry said. He was lounging in the passenger seat, one massive arm resting on the open window. His other hand was down on the butt of his STI, which was holstered on the side of the seat.

I took another turn, this one leading away from the traffic circle where the day's crowd was gathered. The flaw in our roving tracker plan was becoming obvious now that we were on the ground. The fact was not all that many people in Djibouti City drove that much, and only a few of the streets were fit for cars. Our orbits were severely limited, and we were running the risk of being too far out of position to pick Khasam up when he decided to leave.

I was looking for a place to park, within a distance where we could close fast on foot, when I got a call from Imad.

"Hillbilly, Spearchucker." He sounded worried.

I tapped the push-to-talk. "Send it, Spearchucker."

"Just a heads-up. This guy is pushing. It's the same bullshit as always, but he's trying to get the crowd really riled up, and I think he's succeeding." There was a lot of background noise; Imad was sub-vocalizing

45

into his bone mic. "A lot of the usual crap about Western exploitation, the president is a thief and a puppet, blah, blah, blah. But he's calling for a lot of blood and violence." Another roar of sound drowned him out. "He just called for the president's severed head to be paraded through the streets." It was getting really hard to hear him through the crowd's yelling. "This is going to turn into a riot any minute now," Imad said.

"Shiny has eyes-on," Alek called. "Get clear." None of us wanted to lose Imad, and if he got caught in a riot, we very well could.

"Moving." He signed off.

I found our spot, and pulled off the main street into the market on the Rue de Bender. We could still watch down the street, where the crowd was milling. What we could see from here was not pretty. The market was almost deserted, and the people we could see out on the street were heading indoors, fast. You could almost feel the rage in the air.

As I shut down the engine, I caught movement out of the corner of my eye, and followed it, to see what looked like a platoon of Djiboutian army soldiers, in uniform, and armed, coming into the market area, and starting south down the Rue de Bender.

They weren't moving fast, kind of a slow, hesitant walk. The looks on their faces as they sort-of marched past our Land Rover was a mix of put-on courage at best, and sheer terror at worst. They were dressed in a mix of chocolate-chip and desert tri-color cammies, with Vietnam-era steel pots and Y-harnesses. Their weapons were even more of a haphazard mix. I saw M16s, FN-FALs, AKMs, a FAMAS or two, a Galil, and several G-3s. The guy with the huge officer shoulder-boards was in back, chivvying the rest on.

"Fuck me," Larry said, as they trudged past us. He keyed his comm. "Spearchucker, Monster. I hope you're clear, buddy, because there's about a platoon of National Army troops headed for that crowd, and they look shaky enough to start shooting pretty quick."

"That's just one section," Bob announced, from overwatch. "It looks like at least a company is coming south, and they've got armored vehicles behind them. Looks like a mix of a couple Ratels and about a half dozen AMLs. None of the infantry have riot gear, either. Just weapons."

"Keep eyes on Khasam," Alek called. "Spearchucker, are you clear yet?"

There was another burst of noise, the roar of several thousand human throats sounding their anger, and then Imad could be heard, barely. "I am...st edge of...tight...can't..."

"Spearchucker, I don't care if you have to shoot your way out, get the fuck off that street," Alek said. Even over the radio, his voice sounded tight, stressed. I found myself gripping the steering wheel of the Defender until my knuckles turned white. I forced myself to relax. Imad was good; he knew what he was doing.

46

"Coconut, Spearchucker." There was less background noise this time, and I started to breathe a little easier. I could see Larry relax just a bit, too. "I'm out, di-di-ing east on a back alley. I'll link up back at the compound."

"Roger." Alek sounded about as relieved as I felt. Larry and I looked at each other, and I raised my eyebrows. He blew out a sigh of relief.

The troops were getting closer to the crowd, which had noticed them for the first time. The northern edge of the mob, and it was a mob now, was starting to turn to face them. There was just a lot of shouting and fist-waving, but the first rock was only a matter of time. And the way those boys were keyed up, it would turn into a blood bath as soon as it happened.

I really didn't want to stick around for that. Aside from the likelihood of stray rounds coming our way, I can't say I particularly care for watching massacres.

"Shiny, where's our boy?" I called. Khasam was our whole reason for being out here. We couldn't let the impending disaster on the streets keep us from focusing on the mission.

"He's still on top of the van," Bob reported. "Only now he's got an AK, and he's waving it at the government troops."

"Fuckfuckfuckfuck," Larry started muttering, thumping his meaty fist against the door. "Motherfucker's going to get himself martyred, and we're back to square one."

"No, wait," Bob said. "Hold on a second..." There was a sudden flurry of supersonic *crack*s overhead, followed a fraction of a second later by the rattle of an AK-47. "Fuck. He just shot at the troops, then jumped down off the van."

We could see the chaos as the troops down the street tried to scramble to get out of the line of fire. The crowd saw their reaction and roared, smelling their fear. The mob surged forward, and rocks started to fly.

An AML armored car was rolling past us. The vehicle commander was up out of the turret, his hands on the spade grips of an M2 .50 cal. He racked the gun as the car came closer, but didn't fire, yet.

"He's moving," Bob called. "Looks like he's heading northeast, into the tight alleys. Monster, Hillbilly, he's yours. Move fast, I could lose him any minute in there."

"I'm on it. Give me some directions," I said, as I bailed out of the Defender.

"Go to the southeast corner of the market, and keep pushing up that road. If you turn south after about a block, I should be able to talk you onto him."

I did as he said, even as I heard all hell break loose around me. The chatter of small arms fire was quickly joined by the heavy pounding of at least one heavy machine gun. "Hillbilly, Monster," Larry called. "I'm moving. The National Army just opened up on the crowd, and somebody is shooting back from the buildings. It's a full-on firefight out here." There was a sudden loud bang. "Oh shit, that AML just got hit with an RPG."

Great, I thought, as I wove through the abandoned market stalls at a run, trying not to slip on the trash and puddles on the ground. As if it hadn't been bad enough here already, Khasam had just managed to provoke a massacre. Nobody was pulling this country back from the brink now.

The alleys were deserted, except for a handful of people who peered around corners or out of windows. They knew what was happening out there on the street, and they were scared shitless. Smart of them.

Bob was keeping me pretty well abreast of Khasam's movements, but he kept losing him for brief periods as he went under overhanging roofs or rounded corners quickly. The good news was the guy was making a pretty much straight line, as much as he could. "It looks like he might be heading for Block 215," Bob guessed. "If you head there, you should be able to catch him. Just be advised, he's still got a couple of his goons with him, and they've got AKs."

"Roger." I ran harder, hoping to get ahead of him, to where I could hunker down and watch. I had no illusions about going into his bolt-hole alone. I just wanted to see where his bolt-hole was. And hoped that I didn't run into any tribal checkpoints along the way.

Just as I thought that, I turned a corner and saw a barricade across the alley, with a couple of locals squatting in front of it. They were chewing khat, and one had an ancient-looking, rusty FAL across his knees. The other had what looked like a Browning HiPower shoved in his shorts, in front of his shirt.

I changed directions fast, ducking down another side alley. I was going away from the path I wanted, but better to detour than get caught. I went about a half a block, then turned back the way I had been going before the checkpoint and kept jogging through the dusty, debris-littered alleyways. At least they didn't twist and turn much, which made it easy.

"He's almost to that big building on Block 213," Bob reported. We had numbered all the blocks in the city, for ease of reference.

If I had my bearings right, I was almost a block ahead of him. I dashed another three blocks, and slowed down to loiter where I could hopefully see him pass, two blocks to my south.

"All right, I got him." Khasam was a skinny, chicken-necked motherfucker, dressed in the loose shirt and baggy pants that seemed to be the national dress in Djibouti. There were two more with him, just as scrawny, and considerably less than intimidating, except for the AKMs they were carrying. Of course, an AKM carried over the shoulder by the barrel, like one of them was doing, is a little less than immediately useful, but I was glad to see they didn't seem all that well-trained.

None of them were really looking around; they must have figured they were home free. Fair enough. I wasn't going to touch them now, anyway. I watched them continue down the alley they were on, and trotted ahead to catch them at the next intersection. I got to where I could see Block 215, and peered around the corner.

Okay. *There* were the professionals. There were guards on the low wall around the three warehouse-sized buildings. They looked alert, armed, and they didn't look local. There were a few black Africans, Somali Issas unless I missed my guess, but the majority of them were unmistakably Middle Eastern. They were still dressed locally, but their weapons looked reasonably well-maintained, at least as far as I could see from two blocks away, and they weren't holding them like Daddy's shotgun.

"Monster, this is Hillbilly," I called, very quietly. I probably needn't have bothered, since the cacophony of the fighting in the streets to the west would have drowned me out. It actually sounded like it was getting closer. "I think I have eyes-on Khasam's bolt-hole. He's not being subtle about it, either." I counted. "I have six armed males on the north side of the compound; appear to be locals and Arabs. Small arms, but no heavies in sight."

"Roger," Larry replied. "Coconut, you copy?"

"Affirm," Alek replied. "Shiny, you have eyes on?"

"I do," Bob said. "Taking pictures now. Be advised, I'm running out of loiter time."

"Hillbilly, Coconut," Alek said. "Stay in the area for now, but try not to get noticed. Let's make sure he's sticking. Once we know he's going to be there for the night, we can set up the hit."

"Roger," I whispered, listening even more intently to the street battle. This could get interesting.

***

As it turned out, I didn't end up having to dodge a running street fight. About a half hour after it started, the shooting started to peter out. There were still sporadic bursts of gunfire, and a pall of black smoke hung over the main streets to the west, mostly from burning automobiles and armored cars. But somebody had apparently come out on top. I just couldn't tell who from where I was.

I did a couple of orbits of the target compound, trying my best to look like a reporter or a tourist. I couldn't say how well it worked, as it looked like I was the only white guy on the street. Most of the real reporters were holed up in the European quarter, and the tourists were gone. That had to be a hit to the local economy, too.

People were starting to venture back out, with the fighting apparently over for the time being, and I had to start fending off the usual weirdness, like jackasses in shorts and no shirt claiming to be customs officials, not to

49

mention the pickpockets. I guess as hard as I was trying to be inconspicuous, I still stood out too much. I was very glad that Larry was cruising back and forth on the Boulevard du General de Gaulle, only a couple of blocks away, and in constant radio contact. If the bad guys in the compound figured out that I was casing them, it could get a little hairy. I made a point of never looking directly at the compound when I might be in sight.

The sun was going red behind the smoke. I squeezed the push-to-talk. "It's getting dark, and he hasn't come out yet. He's sticking."

"Good to go," Alek replied. "Come on in. Monster, Hillbilly's inbound."

"Gotcha, Hillbilly," Larry said. "De Gaulle and 13."

"Roger," I answered. "En route."

I couldn't make it look like I was dashing for extract, any more than I could afford to relax, just because I was getting away from Khasam and his jihadi buddies. I did risk a single glance back at the compound. *See you soon, motherfuckers.*

CHAPTER 7

The Range Rover slowed without ever quite stopping, and Jim and I bailed out, dashing into the shadows of the alley.

It was just past one in the morning. Fortunately the moon was down already; we would have had to push regardless, but the lack of illum was handy. Add to that the fact that the power was out in large swathes of the city, and we had plenty of deep shadows to hide in, occasionally lit only by the sputtering glow of the fires that were burning near the market.

The violence had continued sporadically throughout the evening. The short confrontation in the streets that I had mostly only heard had just been the beginning. The crowd had had its blood up, and attacked the National Army troops ferociously, especially after the front few ranks were gunned down by the scared soldiers. The loss of two of their armored cars to RPGs fired from roofs nearby had broken the government troops, and their attempt at riot control had turned into a bloody rout.

Since then, bands of rebels had pushed into the government-controlled segments of the city, looting, burning, and killing. As near as we could tell, there wasn't a lot of rhyme or reason to the killings; anyone who got in the way, who could be conveniently tagged as Western or a Western puppet was a target, which largely meant anyone who wasn't part of the gangs.

All of this was happening a couple of miles away from our target, which was fine with us.

We weren't going to be mistaken for locals tonight, if we were seen. Both of us were in full kit--assault vests, FAST helmets, and ATACS desert camouflage, with suppressed rifles, and pistols in drop holsters. NVGs revealed everything through the shadows, in an eerie green tint.

Jim split off, cat-footing around to the north side of the ramshackle building where Mike had dropped us off. I went the other way, circling around toward the east side. I moved very carefully, watching where I put each step. All the trash made for a noise minefield in any Third World alley, and this one was no exception.

I continued down the alley, making for the southeast corner of the target compound. As I got close, I heard a *crack*, immediately followed by what might have been the faint sound of a body falling.

I carefully sidestepped around the corner, keeping behind my rifle. I had the scope off, and was running with the old PEQ-15 laser mounted on the forearm. NVGs make it difficult if not impossible to sight a rifle normally, so we mounted infrared lasers to give us an aiming point. It wasn't as accurate as properly aimed fire, but at close quarters it more than did the job.

There was the corner of the wall, and the crumbled gap in it that was Jim's and my breach point. I saw a tiny blip of light green luminescence at the base of the gap, but no other thermal hits. I crept forward, half-crouched, my rifle at the low-ready. Jim was already at the corner, covering the breach point with his suppressed Mk 17. He turned his head as I came up, saw me, and went back to the gap. He took his hand off the foregrip to hold up one finger, and then gave a thumbs-down.

I keyed my radio. "Coconut, Hillbilly. Kemosabe and I are in position. One tango down at the breach point."

"Roger," came Alek's muted voice. "There's some activity at the front; looks like they heard something, but they're not sure what." There was a pause. "Shiny, Monster, you in position? We've got to kick this pig soon."

"This is Monster. Thirty seconds."

"We've got company," Jim hissed. I started moving toward the breach point, even as I heard voices raised in Arabic. They'd spotted the body. "Coconut, Kemosabe. We're made; we've got to go loud, now."

"Do it." There was no hesitation in Alek's reply, and I immediately heard the muted cracks of suppressed fire toward the front. I went in the breach point fast but smooth, coming around the crumbling edge of the wall with my rifle already coming level with the bright thermal silhouette of one of the tangos, who was walking warily toward his buddy's corpse, his AK already half-lifted. The bright IR dot settled, and I squeezed the trigger twice. With two hushed *cracks* blending almost into one, the tango crumpled.

Jim was right on my heels, and slammed two rounds into another tango coming around the corner of the building, just as I shot two more behind the first, tapping one in the chest twice, then shifting to the second as fast as my brain registered that the first was down.

Colton and Nick were coming through behind us, to take inner cordon duties; making sure that not only did no squirters get out through our breach point, but that when we went in the house, nobody came in behind us and shot us in the back. They took a knee at the corner of the first house, positioned to cover the west and south sides. Jim and I dashed for the door.

It wasn't much, just hollow wood, so I didn't even have to reach for the sledgehammer strapped to my back; I just kicked the door in, planting my boot about an inch below the handle. The latch broke away from the door and splintered the jamb, then I was in, Jim on my heels, my rifle up and ready to end anything that looked like it was going to put up a fight.

The hallway went the full length of the building, with doors on either side, most all of them closed. I simply flowed to the first one, kicked it open, and went in, immediately clearing the corner in front of me, then sweeping across the room. Jim was on my ass through the door, button-hooking around to cover the other corner. Nothing. Mark the room, move on.

We came back out into the hallway, and into a shitstorm.

Apparently, one or more of the rooms down the hall were sleeping quarters for tangos. They were spilling out into the hall, in various levels of undress, with weapons. One of them saw me come out of the door and yelled, raising his pistol.

I was already halfway out into the hallway. I just kept going, charging toward the opposite door, even as I smashed the shouter to the floor with a pair of suppressed shots. I slammed my shoulder against the door and it splintered and gave, spilling me into the opposite room. There was another gomer lying on a mat on the floor, reaching for his Kalashnikov, and I shot him, even as Jim opened up from the last room.

A quick glance showed me that this room was clear; somebody was looking out for me. One-man clears are very, very inadvisable. I moved to the door, leaned out into the hall, and added my fire to the devastation that Jim was already causing. I tracked my muzzle back and forth across the tangled mass of bodies in the hallway, pumping rounds into heat signatures. My mag went dry, the bolt locking back, and I ducked back into the room, ripped the empty out, and rocked in a fresh one before sending the bolt home and getting back into the fight.

I leaned out just in time to see Jim put a single round into the head of the last tango moving, who was trying to crawl away. With no more movement in the hallway, I crouched to retrieve the empty mag, and slipped it into my drop pouch before marking the room I was in. I looked across at Jim, who nodded, still covering down the hallway. I came out of my room and headed for the next.

The rest of the sweep was quick and uneventful. Apparently, the gomers had all piled out into the hallway at once, making things much easier for us. Three rooms were obviously sleeping quarters, with the floors practically carpeted in sleeping mats. Another looked like it had been a kitchen.

"Coconut, Hillbilly. Building Three is clear," I called. "No hostages, approximately twenty tangos, no unknowns, two shooters up."

"Building One, clear," Alek replied. "No hostages, two tangos, no unknowns, four shooters up. Moving to Building Four."

"Roger. Moving to Building Four." I tapped Jim on the shoulder, where he was covering the front door. He came smoothly to his feet and followed as I headed back to the door we'd breached on the way in.

"Hidalgo, Key-Lock, this is Hillbilly. Two coming out."

"Roger, come ahead," Nick called. I wouldn't have exited the building until I got the go-ahead from the inner cordon. Doing otherwise is a good way to get shot by your own team.

I led the way, rounding the corner and heading for the north end of building two, keeping low to avoid any fire from the windows. There were no lights on, and it was dark enough inside the compound that I didn't figure they could see us, but it never paid to take chances. In less than a minute we joined Alek, Rodrigo, Bob, and Larry at the front door. Alek was in the front of the stack, where he preferred, and he kicked in the door and went in as we fell in at the rear.

There was no hallway; the entire building was one large room, with scattered mats on the floor, and several stacks and crates of weapons and comm gear. There were only three gomers. One of them lifted a FN 5-7 and was smashed to the floor by at least three pairs of shots. A second ran toward us, shouting, "Allahu akhbar!" and met the same fate. The third stood there, waiting for us.

We didn't have our lights on, the NVGs were enough. There was a lantern in the room, illuminating the jihadi flags on the walls, including the black and white al-Shabaab war flag. There was a table covered in pictures, two laptops, and several weapons, Kalashnikovs and Makarovs.

It was also enough light to see the mocking smile on the third terrorist's face, as he watched us, his hands at his sides. Bob and Larry started to glide along the wall toward him, as the rest of us kept our rifles trained on him. He just stood there, that small smile on his face.

Just before Bob got within arm's length of him, he said something in Somali, smiling broadly, then raised his hands and shouted "Allahu akhbar!" I saw his hand curled around something, and yelled, "Trigger!"

Six suppressed shots still made a pretty impressive noise as Mohammed Khasam's head was splashed into a red mist of blood, brain, and bone, and he dropped to the floor like a puppet with its strings cut. Ordinarily, bullet impacts will not cause explosives to detonate by themselves, but none of us wanted to take that chance, or that a suicide vest would stop the rounds and give him time to hit the trigger. When he collapsed and did not explode, we all breathed a tiny sigh of relief. Larry moved up and carefully removed the trigger from his hand. He held it up; it was a garage door opener.

"Figure he's still live," Alek said quietly. "We've got five minutes. Tear this place apart. Kemosabe, let's arrange a tragic bomb maker's accident."

Rodrigo and I took security on the door, while the rest of the team went to work. Jim checked the corpses for explosives first. The runner had had a grenade, which he hadn't pulled the pin from. Khasam had nothing on him, but Larry called Jim over a moment later.

The IED was under a tarp next to several crates of PETN. It would have been a hell of a boom, and none of us would have left much to get sent home. Maybe some teeth, if they could be found. It made Jim's job easier, though.

"Don't even fuck with it," he said, picking up the trigger from where Larry had set it on the table. "We'll get a decent distance away, and use this on the way out."

Alek and Bob were going over the materials on the table, shoving pictures and documents into drop pouches. How much of it would be useful, we didn't know. It didn't matter. The longer we were on the target site, the more chance Murphy had to rear his ugly head.

We had been on-site for about four and a half minutes when Alek keyed his radio. "Cleghorn, Coconut. Ready for exfil, meet us at the gate." He let off, then keyed again. "All stations, collapse on the gate."

There was a chorus of acknowledgments, then Alek was behind me, thumping me on the shoulder. I went out the door we had come in, rifle still up and ready. Nothing. An IR light flashed from the far corner, and I returned the flash. A moment later, Tim and Hank came around the end of the east building, where they had been holding inner cordon duties. I heard footsteps behind me, where Rodrigo was covering, as Nick and Colton closed up with the rest of the team.

A moment later, we heard the rumble of a diesel engine, and then the 3-ton was out front, with Jon and Chad in the back, manning two of our M60E4s, which they had laid over the top of the slats around the bed. It wasn't fancy, and accuracy was going to suffer, but it would work for a hasty technical.

The guys who had been on inner cordon set up hastily on a knee around the truck, while the rest of us piled on the back. The bed was positively bristling with weapons by the time the last two got on. Alek beat on the roof of the cab, and Cyrus hit the accelerator, speeding us out of there.

CHAPTER 8

The team room was quiet. Colton and Nick were going through the pictures and laptops we had taken from the target site. Most of the rest of us were sitting on our cots, sweating and cleaning our rifles.

Something was bugging me. I tried to just focus on weapons maintenance, but finally gave up. The M1A didn't get all that dirty anyway. I finished putting my rifle back together, stood up, and walked over to Alek's cot.

"We need to talk," I said.

He looked up from his OBR. "Uh-oh. Have I been leaving the toilet seat up again?"

"Oh, fuck off," I replied, as he laughed. "We've got some serious shit to discuss."

"All right, all right," he said, still chuckling. "Let me finish putting this back together, and then we'll have a sit-down." I went back to my bunk, shaking my head.

It didn't take long. Alek put the rifle back together with a speed and ease born of long practice, then came over and sat on Bob's cot, across from me. "All right, Jeff, what's on your mind?"

I leaned forward, my elbows on my knees. "What would we have done if we hadn't schwacked everybody on that target site last night? What if one or more of them had surrendered?"

"We'd have grabbed them," he replied.

"And done what?" I asked. "We could lock 'em up in a room in that garage out back, but then what? None of us are trained interrogators. For fuck's sake, we've got twenty-five guys on the ground, hanging in the wind, fuckin' blind. We can't afford to take detainees, at least not for any length of time. We've got to keep 'em fed and watered, at least, and we don't have the time or the facilities to interrogate them effectively. And I'm not sure I'm comfortable with the options I could come up with."

For a long moment, Alek sat there and thought, looking at his hands. "You're right," he said quietly. He stood up and started toward the comm end of the room. "Come on. We've got a call to make."

It was the middle of the night back in the States, but when the

Colonel came on the satellite link, he didn't look like a man who had just been awakened. I suspected that he had been up already. "What's up, Alek?" he asked.

"Problems," Alek replied. "We hit Khasam's hideout last night, killed everybody and we're sifting through what the site exploitation brought out. Fortunately, none of them surrendered, so we didn't have detainees to deal with.

"Jeff brought it up just now, and I agree with him," he continued. "If the Agency wants us to do the dirty work on the ground, they need to provide some more support. We're undermanned for this, and we have zero room for error. We also don't have the training, facilities, or gear we need for the intel side of this operation. If they want us to find these guys, we need intel, we need backup, and, if it comes to it, we need somewhere to take detainees for processing. We can't do it. We don't have the time or the logistics."

Heinrich shook his head. "I've been trying, Alek. So far I've been stonewalled on most of it. They're telling me that there are no assets available in that part of the world."

"Bullshit," I put in. "There was a JSOC compound at that base, and they expect us to believe that they don't have any assets at all?" I folded my arms. "Bullshit."

"Look, gents," the Colonel said, "there's a lot of politics going on behind all this. I don't know all of it, but it's putting a real monkey-wrench in trying to get you guys more support. The military has been warned to keep out of Djibouti's territorial waters and airspace. I've been told it's because of worries about casualties, but the fact is, I just don't know." He gusted a sigh. "Look, get me a list of what you need, and I'll make a few more calls. Maybe I can get somewhere this time."

"We need real-time sat and electronic intel," Alek said, ticking points off on his fingers. "We need everything they've got on recent terrorist movements in-country. I know that everything those boys in Lemonier saw got sent back to the States and backed up. We need all of it, if we're going to come anywhere near finding those hostages. You know, I know, and they know that we're dealing with a finite time schedule here." He tapped another finger. "We need somewhere to process and deliver detainees. I don't care if it's offshore, over the border, or in the middle of Bumfuck, Egypt, we need somebody here who is trained on this sort of thing. We're trigger-pullers, not interrogators."

He took a deep breath. "And, on top of all that, we need to know what the plan is to get these guys out when and if we find them. They're talking something close to 200, most of whom will be in need of medical attention and transport. Who's coming for them? Where? Where's extract for this operation? We *have* to have that information, and we need it yesterday."

The Colonel just nodded. "I've been harping on half of that list for the last week, Alek. But I'll try again, and see if I can get something more substantial than the bureaucratic runaround I've been getting. I'll call you guys back when I've got something." The link went dead.

**

Things were getting worse out in the city. The Islamist militias were now openly attacking government forces wherever they could be found, which was fewer and fewer places as they went to ground and hunkered down behind walls and barbed wire. The president was running scared, especially with few of his European backers even bothering to return his calls. Given what we had heard of the chaos in Europe after the collapse of the euro and the subsequent disintegration of the EU, that should have come as a surprise to no one.

It had turned out that the Sudanese butcher, Omar Sadiq Hasan, had insinuated himself into the opposition to such a point that he was being put forward as the next leader of an Islamic Djibouti. This was bad news, especially as we suspected, from what Imad had heard, that he had had some part in the attack on Lemonier. The question was, did we risk taking him out? We needed more information.

Meanwhile, refugees were fleeing the city, and militia checkpoints were going up. The government only owned the port area now, and the Legion's 13th Demi-Brigade was still staying put.

Imad had slipped back out into the city. He could pass for Afar or Issa if he liked, and was gregarious enough that he could easily slip into just about any group of people and be accepted. I hoped that he wasn't trying to infiltrate any of the militias, but gathering information was his primary task right now, and he'd do what he thought was necessary to accomplish that.

The rest of us stayed in the compound. The streets were even more dangerous for Westerners now, and all but the hardiest aid workers and journalists had run. Almost overnight, the tourist industry in Djibouti had been extinguished. We could handle ourselves, but Alek had decided that it was going to be more productive to hold tight, and wait for word from Imad or the Colonel, whichever came first.

Of course, given our cover, we qualified as one of those particularly hardy groups of aid workers. There was almost constantly a line outside of Dave's aid station these days.

As it turned out, the Colonel beat Imad to the punch.

**

We rolled through the darkened streets in the brown Range Rover, lights out to avoid attracting attention. There weren't many people out on the streets after dark lately, aside from militias, but there were checkpoints, and we wanted to avoid those at all costs.

Colton was driving, weaving a serpentine route through the streets and back alleys of the city, heading southeast toward the coast. He had his FAST helmet on, his NVGs clipped to them, and his rifle jammed between the seat and the gearshift next to him. Hank was sitting in the passenger seat, similarly kitted up, with his Galil ACE 53 across his lap. Alek and I were in the back seat, fully geared up with vests, helmets, and rifles.

Nobody talked. We didn't have much to talk about, anyway, and everyone was a little on edge. The reason why became abundantly obvious when we rounded a corner, and abruptly slowed. Colton muttered, "Oh, fuck."

Alek and I leaned forward to see past Colton and Hank, and saw the checkpoint in the middle of the street. It didn't look like much, just a pile of junk and old tires across the road, with two gomers lounging next to it. Neither looked to be all that alert; in fact, one looked like he was asleep.

"Plan B," Alek hissed. He and I immediately bailed out, leaving our rifles. We hoped to get past this without any shooting.

I went left, while Alek went right. I soft-footed it down the side alley, trying to avoid kicking any of the cans or other detritus, and looking for the next break in the haphazard shacks. I found it in seconds, and started working my way around toward the checkpoint.

A dog started barking to my left, and I froze, looking around, but I couldn't see it, even with the thermal imagery turned on. Whether it had smelled me, or was just barking, I couldn't tell. Oh well, nothing to do about it. I kept going.

After a moment, I heard the crunch of gravel and trash as Colton started rolling again. I was getting closer; I could hear the two gomers at the checkpoint chatting quietly in Afar. Just as well we were trying to go nonlethal here; from what we'd seen, most of the Afar were miserably poor, and just caught in the middle of the crapstorm that was enveloping the city. These guys were probably just neighborhood militia trying to defend their families.

I turkey-peeked around the corner, and could see the checkpoint. I was about four long strides from them, and they hadn't heard shit. Plus they were smoking, so there went their night vision. It went away even further as Colton flipped on the headlights.

They both started, and threw up their hands against the glare, squinting and yelling in Afar. I came around the corner and started moving.

I got to my target a second before Alek. I came in low and fast, just behind him as he started walking toward the Defender, loosely cradling an ancient, battered Mosin-Nagant. I wasn't subtle. I came up and hammer-fisted him at the base of the skull. Lights out. I caught him as he crumpled, and dragged him over to the side of the street. Alek was down on the ground, choking out his gomer. The Afar twitched and struggled a little bit more, then went limp. Alek gently moved him out of the line of traffic, as

Colton turned the headlights off again. We got back in, hastily closing the doors, while trying not to make too much noise. Colton was rolling before the latches clicked.

We got the rest of the way out of the city without incident and headed for the open desert.

After about another fifteen minutes, Colton brought the vehicle to a stop and shut off the engine. We sat there for a few more minutes, watching and listening. A hyena trotted by a few hundred yards away, followed by what looked like a jackal a minute later. There was no sound but the wind and the pinging of the engine as it cooled.

Once we were satisfied that we were alone, Alek and I got out, pulling our rucks out of the back, and each pocketing several IR chemlights. We staged the rucks next to the vehicle before starting to set up the LZ, marking a T with the chemlights.

Soon we could hear, faintly, the sound of the Bell 407, coming in from the ocean. Alek was on the radio with Sam, murmuring quiet instructions, as the two of us waited on a knee, next to our rucks. I held my rifle at the alert. We were pretty sure we were alone out here, but you never really knew.

The low roar of the helo increased, and I spotted it, low and fast over the horizon. We hadn't heard of any SAMs being used out here, and the rebels didn't seem to be organized enough to have coast watchers to keep anybody out, but complacency gets you dead, especially when you're working on the shoestring that we were on.

Sam brought the bird in hard and fast, flaring at the last second and kicking up a shitstorm of dust, sand, and gravel. I ducked my head to avoid the worst of it, but it got in my eyes and teeth, and down the back of my shirt, anyway. Par for the course. He could have brought it in gentle as a lamb, and the rotor wash still would have sandblasted us.

Alek and I grabbed our rucks and ran, hunched over, for the helo. The side door was already open, and Fig was leaning out, rifle leveled, watching the surrounding territory for threats. I beat Alek to the bird, tossed my ruck onto a seat, and clambered in after it. Alek was only a few feet behind me. No sooner were we both on the bird, than Fig was pulling the door shut, and Sam was pulling pitch.

We banked hard, still less than one hundred feet above the ground, and then we were moving, the nose pitched hard forward, screaming out toward the Gulf of Aden at barely 150 feet.

He kept it low and fast, dipping even lower as we got out over the water. The rotor wash kicked up a wake, which glowed faintly with bioluminescence as it churned beneath us. The sky was clear, the moon nearing its zenith, and reflecting off the mild waves.

Sam didn't take a straight course, but followed more of a long Jhook, coming around and approaching the *Lynch* from the north. It had been over a week, but Van Husten was still steaming racetracks in the Gulf. I hadn't heard what excuses he was making to his employers, but we rather appreciated it.

Somebody was on the edge of the helipad, guiding Sam in with a handheld light, just as I had done earlier. He drifted in from the port, sidling in to land directly on the H. Sam was nothing if not a perfectionist when it came to his flying.

The skids settled and the rotors started winding down. Fig led the way off the bird, and started lashing it down as Alek and I collected our rucks and headed for the superstructure.

Matt was waiting in the team room, along with a slender man with salt-and-pepper hair, who grinned as he saw us. Matt took his leave as soon as we walked in, muttering something about having to get some sleep before he took over watch again.

"Well holy shit," Alek said. "Good to see you, Danny. Didn't know you were going to be the one they sent out here."

The graying man's grin turned slightly sheepish. "Well, as it happens, I'm the sacrificial lamb who's been made responsible for this goat rope."

Alek got serious at that. We dropped our rucks at the hatch and went to sit down at the table in the middle of the compartment. "Tom didn't mention that you were the guy who called."

"The Colonel doesn't really know me," the man called Danny replied. "At least not by sight. And I'll admit, I didn't really go to any great lengths to fill him in on our past association." I thought I remembered who Danny was, now. He had been one of Alek's platoon commanders, one of the better ones, who had gotten out and disappeared into Special Activities. "It wasn't really relevant to the job."

"The job, I should tell you," Alek said bluntly, "is a clusterfuck." His ham-sized fist hit the table. "What the fuck, Danny? No info, no support, just, 'Here's what happened, oh by the way there are maybe as many as two hundred hostages in the middle of this shitstorm, go find 'em.'"

Danny didn't flinch at either the blow to the table, or Alek's outburst. "I know, Alek, I know. You think I didn't try to push for more? You think I liked throwing you guys to the wolves? Hell, I'm not even supposed to be here, right now, and I'm sure as hell not supposed to get on that helo and go ashore with you." He took a deep breath.

"Look, here's the deal." He leaned forward, elbows on the table. "The administration is in panic mode right now. Ordinarily, something like this would be responded to with drone strikes. It's how they like to do business. It's something pretty risk-free that they can point to in press releases to show they're tough on terrorism. Doesn't really do much, but

62

they're politicians, they don't give a fuck about results, they just want the *appearance* of results.

"Trouble is, Lemonier was *the* drone base in the region. Most of the rest that were started up got shut back down for one reason or another. Sure, there's a small one up north, near the Eritrean border, but they only have a couple of Reapers.

"Not only that, there are hostages. They can't just start throwing Hellfires around without risking dead hostages as a consequence. Their main action item has been effectively taken off the table."

"So what?" I asked. "There's still the rest of the military."

Danny looked over at me. "I wish that was the case, brother," he said. "But the budget cuts, the collapse of the dollar, and all of these bullshit interventions in the last five years have spread things way too thin." He pointed in the general direction of the Indian Ocean. "That MEU out there? I guaran-damn-tee that half its helos won't fly, mainly from lack of parts. They're pretty short on fuel, too. They have to gas up at each port, just enough to get them to the next one." He shook his head. "The greatest armed force in the world is a hollow shell of itself. It's worse than the Clinton years. Training is lacking, too. Oh, there are some outstanding NCOs who are still hanging in there, in spite of what's looked like a concerted effort to force out the experienced ones, and they're doing their damnedest to get their boys trained up, with or without equipment, fuel, or ammunition. But there are fewer of them every year.

"Let's face it, guys; you are the best equipped and trained force for the job, as few of you as there are."

For a long moment, Alek just looked down at the table, at a loss for words. When he looked up, his voice was quiet. "It's really that bad?"

Danny nodded sadly. "It is. We're as bad off as the Russian Army in the '90s. You'd weep to see how many of our guys are either on welfare, or missing training to moonlight for enough money to feed their families.

"There's more. They've realized that they can't let people know that they've essentially left us defenseless, while assuring everyone that they were just 'trimming the fat,' and that what would be left would be a leaner, 'smarter' force. It's dawned on them that if they try to intervene in Djibouti, and get stomped by a Third World force because their troops are now under trained and equipped with poorly maintained crap, the cat is out of the bag. They're panicking about it."

"So you're saying that we're not getting any support because there really isn't any support to be had?" I asked. The true horror of what was going on was starting to set in, and I was starting to feel a little sick.

"Mostly." Danny's face was grim. "I've managed to persuade the powers that be to let me go in-country, along with some electronic eavesdropping gear, and a few small surveillance UAVs that you guys can't get on the open market. I also brought about two million, in Australian Dollars and the new Reichmarks." I knew that those two represented pretty much the strongest Western currencies at the moment. "And, I'll be your interrogator if you do take detainees."

"Danny," Alek said slowly, "what about the hostages? If the military is in as bad shape as you said, how the fuck are we going to get them out when or if we find them?"

He shook his head. "They're still scrambling to get enough assets together. To be honest, it may well be the Aussies that have to come get them. They've at least still got a decent force, if not the power projection we used to have. The new Bundeswehr is getting stronger, but the administration has managed to thoroughly piss the Germans off, not to mention that they've got their own problems."

There was a long, slightly stunned silence. It had really come to this. The United States had covertly hired a small private military company to do the job it had rendered itself unable to do. Holy shit.

* * *

The conversation continued for a while, as Alek and I picked Danny's brain about every sordid little detail of the situation. Before we knew it, it was almost dawn. We wanted to get back, but trying to insert into that mess in daylight was less than advisable. We bedded down on the ship to get some fitful sleep, while we waited for dusk.

CHAPTER 9

We didn't get much sleep, as it turned out. It had only been a couple of hours when Matt rousted us out.

"We're being followed," he said. We grabbed kit and rifles, and headed topside.

The sky was clear and brassy, the sun beating down on the water. We got up on top of the superstructure, where Salomon was sitting post, behind his VEPR .308. He looked over at us as we came out of the ladderwell, and then pointed. I took the proffered binoculars, letting my rifle hang from its sling in front of me.

There were three boats on the water, about half a nautical mile behind us. It looked like two dingy skiffs and a brightly-painted blue dhow. The dhow was pretty big, probably about a hundred feet long. Even from this distance, with the binos I could make out the KPV 14.5mm heavy machine gun mounted in the dhow's bow. Pirates.

I handed Alek the binos. "This job just keeps getting better and better, doesn't it?" I said dryly. He peered through the binos and grimaced.

"We'd better be ready to take out that 14.5 gunner fast," he said. "He could ruin our whole day." He studied the view a little longer. "I think I see a couple of RPGs in the smaller skiff. This could be fun."

He lowered the binos, and handed them back to Salomon. "How do you want to play it?" I asked.

His jaw set. Anger sparked in his eyes. "We lie low until they get close, then fuck 'em up. I've had it with this shit. I want those fuckers dead."

I knew how he felt. After the metric ton of shit we'd had dropped on us already, this was the last fucking straw. I grinned humorlessly, and headed below for the weapons locker. I wanted something a little bit more substantial for this, at least to kick things off.

The weapons locker was really little more than a cargo container, fitted with multiple racks for various weapons that we carried with us as a matter of course on these sorts of high-risk jobs. I cranked open the doors, and headed for the back.

It took a little bit of shuffling, but I was able to come out with a bandolier, and a long drag-bag, which I slung over my shoulder and headed back topside, securing the doors behind me as I went. I trotted up the ladder wells, breathing hard, and came back out at the lookout on top of the superstructure. Alek and Salomon were already bent over their rifles, peering through optics at the oncoming pirate vessels. I went over next to Alek, and unzipped the drag-bag.

One of my MOS's in the Marine Corps had been 0317, Scout/Sniper. My first job in the high-risk contractor world had been as a "Defensive Designated Marksman" which is a fancy way of saying "sniper" that doesn't get the plant-eaters' hearts all aflutter. I had kept current, and was one of the top shots in Praetorian Security, if you don't mind my saying so.

The rifle I pulled out was my baby; a Sako TRG-42, chambered in .338 Lapua Magnum, with a Surefire muzzle brake and HorusVision scope. I could reach out and touch someone out to over a mile with that baby, and I loved it. I hadn't taken it ashore before, but was already planning to when we headed back. I quickly scrambled up on top of the flat superstructure, to the side of the lookout post, and laid out the drag bag for the bipod legs. The five-round box mag slid into the weapon, and I worked the bolt, locking the first round into the chamber, and settled behind the gun.

The wind was fairly calm, but there was still enough swell for it to be a tricky shot. I would have to time it just right, taking into consideration the flight time of the bullet. The boats were getting closer, and I'd let them get closer still. I wanted that KPV gunner, and I wanted him before he could get anything like an accurate burst off.

Of course, pirates being what they are, they'd probably start ripping bursts off high, to try to frighten the poor, defenseless merchies into surrendering, to be ransomed to their company. Suckers.

Danny had appeared back on top of the superstructure, carrying a Mk 17, and settled in the prone a few feet from me. I glanced over briefly as he climbed up, and then went back to my scope.

The dhow was rising and falling on the swells, but I thought I was getting a pattern established. A couple hundred more yards, and he was mine.

Of course, no sooner had I thought that than he opened fire. I saw the ten-foot muzzle flash of the heavy machine gun a split second before the rounds cracked by overhead. A couple seconds later, the *thud thud thud* of the gun rolled across the water.

I dare anybody not to flinch at least a little bit when something that big is being shot at you. Those rounds are the size of my thumb, and packing half again as much punch as a .50 BMG round, and the tracers look like someone had set baseballs on fire and started throwing them at your head. It is not a happy experience to be on the receiving end.

Even as I picked my head up off the deck and put it back to the scope, I could hear the helo spooling up behind me. Alek was serious about taking the fight to these assholes. Good.

It was hard to see the gunner past the enormous flash of the weapon, but I breathed slow and easy, and settled my hold on him, using the Horus grid. I had to adjust slightly for the extra heat coming off the barrel; it would raise the impact of the bullet, however slightly. The .338 laughs at turbulence that would throw a .308 round high and right.

One more breath, and my finger slowly tightened on the trigger.

The gunner stopped firing, and turned to shout something to his buddy on the port side, laughing. The trigger broke.

Even with the muzzle brake, the .338 had a hell of a kick. It slammed back into my shoulder, with a hammering *boom* that echoed out across the water. I lost sight picture for a split second, through the flash and concussion of the shot. When I settled back in, the KPV was unmanned.

"Good hit," Danny called out. "Went into his upper left chest. Tango down."

I worked the bolt and moved to the next target. One of the pirates, wearing a loose, flowered shirt and carrying an AKS, was looking toward the heavy gun in shock. I took in the slack on the trigger again. Another bone-rattling *boom*. Another pirate gone when I got back on the scope.

By now they had figured out that something wasn't right, that this placid bulk carrier had teeth. The dhow slowed, and started to turn to port. The skiffs scattered to either side. Behind me, the 407 came to full roar, and I felt the wind as it started to lift off.

Despite the sudden realization that they were in a bad situation, the pirate vessels were now close enough for Alek, Salomon, and Danny to start firing. Two more pirates toppled into the bottom of one of the skiffs, as I blasted a third off his feet and over the gunwale of the dhow.

There was a lot of yelling going on down there now, and I saw one of the pirates on the larger skiff start waving his AK in the air and shouting. He smacked his coxswain with the back of his hand, and gestured threateningly at the others in the boat, then pointed his AK at us and ripped off a burst. Apparently, he was either very brave or coked out of his mind, and was determined to take the ship. Whichever it was didn't matter to me. I swung my muzzle around to line him up.

That's where things got problematic. The skiff was coming on fast, as the coxswain laid on the throttle. The bow came up out of the water, and rooster tails sprayed up behind the boat. I had a split second to line him up for a shot before he was going to be too close, and under my horizon.

I didn't make it. Cursing, I abandoned the sniper rifle, grabbed my M1A, and rolled off the roof of the superstructure and back down into the lookout, barely missing Salomon. Alek was already coming off the lip, and heading for the hatch, while Salomon and Danny continued engaging the farther skiff. One of Salomon's casings hit me in the cheek as I went past, and I brushed the hot brass off with another curse. I don't think he even heard me.

Alek and I rattled down the ladder well as fast as we could, kitted up and carrying rifles. The narrow, steep steps were a pain in the ass when speed was an issue.

We got to the main deck, and ran through the cramped passageway toward the port side. Alek slammed through the hatch, reeling a little at the impact with the heavy metal. I was right behind him.

The pirates already had a boarding ladder hooked onto the lip of the gunwale, and sporadic fire was snapping up toward the top of the superstructure. I hadn't heard of pirates being this aggressive with a defended ship before, but like I said, maybe this guy was just doped out of his mind.

Alek and I got to the gunwale, just as three more bullets smacked into it. The helo roared by overhead, and I heard Alek speak into his radio, saying, "No, they're too close to the ship. Go handle the others further out." That was when I realized I hadn't turned my comm on. I did so hastily. Alek looked over at me, and I nodded. With that, we popped over the lip of the gunwale, following our rifles over.

There was already one pirate on the ladder, starting to climb up. Alek and I shot him simultaneously, and he folded in on himself and dropped back into the skiff, landing on one of his compatriots. The aggressive jackass with the AK was yelling incoherent hate up the ladder, when I shot him in the throat. I had been aiming high chest, but high angle shooting can get interesting. He dropped to the bottom of the skiff, clutching his spurting neck, his gurgles lost in the cacophony of our fire. Alek shot the coxswain and two more pirates at the stern with a series of hammer pairs, so fast it all blended together into a roar of sound. I finished off the pirate who was lying under the fallen climber, as he tried to crawl out.

The roar of the Bell 407 was joined by the stutter of automatic weapons fire, and I looked to the stern to see Sam bring the helo in a long, slow turn over the second skiff, while one of our guys leaned out the door with an M60E4, and raked the boat. There was some sporadic return fire for a second or two, but it didn't last long. Fragments of wood and fiberglass flew up as the stream of 7.62 rounds hammered the boat. The gunner ceased fire, and I could see, even from this distance, that the skiff was lying a bit lower in the water, and starting to list to one side.

The helo made one more slow turn around the skiff, then pitched forward and went for the dhow.

There was some more serious opposition coming from the pirate mothership, as they had gotten a gunner back on the KPV. Fortunately, they weren't very good shots, especially as Sam was keeping the helo weaving through the air, until he suddenly came nearly to a halt, flaring up and presenting the gunner's side to the ship. The KPV tracked away from the helo, and the M60 opened up, hammering the KPV gunner to the deck.

Sam made three passes, each time low and slow, letting the gunner work the ship over from bow to stern. When he pulled pitch for the *Lynch*, the dhow was sitting dead in the water, with some smoke starting to rise from its stern. As we stood and watched, the smoke thickened, getting black, and flames started to lick up from the cabin in the back. I don't know what he'd hit, but there wasn't going to be much left of the dhow in an hour or so.

Alek took hold of the boarding ladder and heaved it off the gunwale, where it clattered against the skiff before flipping into the ocean. Then, as the skiff started to drift away, he shouldered his rifle, and put a mag into the hull, keeping his group as tight as he could. Water started to pour into the skiff, stained red as it lapped around the bodies.

For a moment, he and I just stood there, watching the skiff sink. The bloodletting hadn't changed the ultimate suckiness of our situation. Nor had it really assuaged the anger at the hard place we found ourselves in. I just stared at the bloodied bodies as they were taken by the ocean, and felt nothing.

Alek clapped me on the shoulder as the helo flared overhead, coming in to land on the helipad, and I followed him back into the superstructure.

Behind us, the sharks gathered for their feast.

CHAPTER 10

Danny had set up next to the comm station, at the far end of the team room. He was poring over imagery while keeping a pair of earbuds in, plugged into the SIGINT scanner he'd brought along.

I came in from another fruitless night reconnaissance. We didn't dare go out in the daytime anymore. While Alek, Danny, and I had been out on the *Lynch*, an Issa militia had attacked a group from *Medicins Sans Frontieres*, and killed two of them with tapangas, while screaming about foreign infidels. The third, a French national, had been rescued by a squad from the Legion, which had been dispatched only because the team had been from France. Overall, the Legion was still holding to a strict "hands-off" policy as far as the civil unrest went.

Danny looked up as I dropped my gear on my cot. "You guys are back early."

I slumped onto the cot, my rifle across my knees. "It was come back early, or get in a firefight," I replied. "Too many militia out there tonight. We don't want to draw any more attention to ourselves, at least not until we've got a target site for the hostages." I grabbed a water bottle and pounded about half of it in one pull. "You getting anywhere?"

Danny sat back in his chair and rubbed his hands over his face. "I'm starting to think that they're not here."

"What?" That got my attention.

He shook his head in frustration and gestured to the imagery on his laptop. "There should be some sign. Logistical movements, extra guards, something." He glanced over at me. "How much of the initial imagery did you guys see?"

I shrugged. "Just the video of the initial assault, and a couple of gomers dragging mutilated bodies through the streets. That's it. I didn't know there was any more."

"Fuck," he muttered. "I told those assholes to give you guys everything." He sat up and searched on his laptop, before another photo came up, then leaned back and said, "Take a look."

I got up and walked over, leaning over his shoulder to look at the screen. It showed the main gate at Lemonier, from an angle that suggested it

71

had been taken from just over the horizon. There were triumphant gomers standing on the walls and on top of the mangled gate, waving rifles and RPGs in the air. And below was a line of people, unarmed, their hands on their heads. Most of them looked to be wearing uniforms. It was a long line, too.

"Is that what I think it is?" I asked. It looked like the fucking Bataan Death March.

"If you think it's our people getting herded out of Lemonier after the attack, then yeah, it is." He switched back to the images he'd been looking at. "The satellite that took that picture went below the horizon and lost contact only a moment after that. The one that was supposed to take its place got shot down by a Chinese A-sat last year, and hasn't been replaced."

He pinched the bridge of his nose between thumb and forefinger. "From that image right there, we know that there were at least two hundred in enemy hands after the assault. That should leave a pretty big footprint, wherever they are; they might not feed them much, but starving hostages to death is counter-productive, and even at minimal rations, enough to keep two hundred people fed is going to be noticed. But I haven't seen dick that points to that kind of logistical effort anywhere around here."

"You think they've killed them all already?" I asked, a sudden icy ball settling in my gut. Maybe we were here for nothing...

"No, a mass grave would show signs, too," he said. "I've seen them before, and I know what to look for. They're either not here at all, or they're being kept in multiple different places."

"That way nobody can really mount a successful rescue op," I said, realization dawning. "If we find one group, they might execute the rest when we go after them." These fuckers were getting clever. This spoke of a level of sophistication that I hadn't heard of Islamists using before.

"They've got some damned good COMSEC too," Danny said. "Not encryption, these assclowns wouldn't even know what it means. But if there are hostages here, nobody's talking about it.

"It's this Al Masri dogfucker," he said after a moment, staring at the screen. "We knew he was smart, but usually even the smart ones have let their ideology get in the way of strategy. For some reason he hasn't. He's not trusting Allah to fill in the blanks."

"Has he done something like this before?" I asked. I didn't actually know a lot about Al Masri. I knew he was reportedly connected to several Salafist terrorist organizations, and was considered a member in good standing of the Muslim Brotherhood. But specifics were hard to come by in open-source materials.

"Not at this level," was the reply. "He was the power behind the attacks in Bahrain a couple years ago, that ended with the Emir dead, parliament suspended, and the island in Iranian hands. We don't know if that was his desired endstate, but he showed some real strategic brilliance there. Then, once the Iranians moved in, he dropped off the map, only to show up in Somalia last year, where he orchestrated the retaking of Mogadishu from AMISOM, mainly by assassinating leaders and luring platoons of AMISOM troops into fire sacks where they couldn't fight back without killing a lot of civilians. A lot of civilians did wind up getting slaughtered, and the population turned against the AMISOM mission. Once they had Mogadishu back, they started hitting the Kenyans, even managed to drive them out of Kismayo, and back into the hinterlands. In a matter of months, Al-Shabaab owned southern Somalia again."

"And we still have no idea who this asshole is?" I asked. Maybe the CIA had information that we didn't.

Danny just shook his head. "Nope. His nickname suggests he's from Egypt, but that could just be a ploy to throw his enemies off the scent. For all we know, he could be a fucking German who speaks Arabic really well. Adam Gadahn was a fat-assed American with a high-pitched voice, and he was on the 'most wanted' list of Al-Qaeda maggots for a long time."

I sat there and looked at the imagery on Danny's laptop for a moment, while Danny squinted at the ceiling, his hands behind his head. How the fuck were we supposed to find a ghost? Or, for that matter, find where the ghost kept hostages?

"So what are we looking at?" I asked, finally, an unpleasant sensation gnawing at my guts. "How the fuck are we going to find the hostages and get them out?"

"We keep going up the chain," Alek said from the doorway, his rifle tucked under his arm and his vest in his hand. "Like we did with Khasam. We're going to have to be careful, and try to make it look random, so we don't tip them off that that's what's happening. They'll definitely kill the hostages then."

"And what if they're not even in the country anymore?" Danny asked. "We can't take on the entire revolution here in Djibouti, even if the hostages' lives weren't hanging in the balance. For one thing, while we're doing that, the trail's going to get colder."

"Do we have a trail right now?" Alek asked bluntly.

Danny frowned. "Not really."

"Then we keep going as we are until we pick one up," Alek said, walking over and depositing his gear on his rack. "No other course of action that I can see, unless we suddenly get an intel windfall tomorrow." Danny said nothing. There wasn't much to say.

"Is anybody still coming to Dave's clinic?" he asked suddenly, a thoughtful look on his face.

"Yes, and no, we're not going to start grilling the locals as to whether or not they've seen any hostages," Alek said flatly. "If we're not compromised now, we sure will be as soon as that happens. For all these people know, we're just a meaner-looking version of Doctors Without Borders, and I'd like to keep it that way." All the same, I had found myself wondering how long that was going to last. After the French docs had gotten hit, how long before some angry gomers got it in their heads to hit the other clinic full of Westerners, conveniently too close to the Afar part of town?

"I'm not talking about openly asking pointed questions, Alek," Danny said, annoyance creeping into his voice. "I'm not stupid, and I'll remind you that I've been at this particular game longer than you have. There are ways to get information without the source even knowing they've given it to you. I'm just thinking that we do need to start engaging the locals who come to the clinic more. Something useful might come up in conversation."

Alek nodded thoughtfully. He had a point. "Unfortunately, none of us speak Somali very well, aside from Imad."

"I do," Danny said. "And although I'm a little rusty, my field med skills haven't completely atrophied."

"And if you're in the clinic, who's going to keep looking over all the rest of this stuff?" Alek asked, motioning to the laptop and the imagery pinned to the wall.

"This crap isn't getting us anywhere," Danny admitted. "I think it's time to rely on some good, old-fashioned HUMINT." He stood up and stretched. "And, coincidentally, I happen to have the training for that, too."

As he stepped to the door, heading for the clinic on the far side of the building, he turned back for a moment, a serious expression on his face. "Oh, yeah, I almost forgot. We might have a bit more of a time limit on this op than we thought. With the threat of the rebels taking over, the Ethiopians are starting to mobilize. No word on actual movements yet, just the initial mobilization orders, and an increase of radio chatter on the border."

That feeling of being between a rock and a hard place just wasn't going to go away. "Only a matter of time, I suppose," I said heavily. "They can't afford to let the only port they have access to taken over by Islamist hardliners. They'd be strangled."

"That's not all," Danny said. "I'm starting to get mutterings that the Eritreans have noticed the mobilization, as well."

Alek sighed. "Which means they'll be coming, if for no other reason than to fight the Ethiopians. Great." His shoulders slumped. "We've got to find what we're looking for. Fast."

***

For three more days, we waited and listened, playing aid worker, and keeping our weapons close at hand, albeit out of sight of the people we helped. The entire time, we waited for the gunfire or explosion that would announce that we were the next target.

While the city seemed locked in a never-ending riot, somebody was putting some backbone in the government troops, who were holding the port and the presidential palace. The latter wasn't actually that hard, as it was situated on a man-made peninsula, and really only had two points of access. Still, they hadn't yielded any ground in several days. I suspected the Legion had something to do with it, until a tall, fit man walked into our clinic, looking around with a hawkish stare that missed nothing.

He was actually lighter-skinned than Imad, and had a thin beard and mustache. He was in mufti, but carried himself with the unmistakable bearing of a career soldier, and not one from around here. I'd seen enough of the Djiboutian National Army to peg this guy as an outsider. If I had to guess, I would have said Ethiopian. Which opened up a whole other can of worms.

I caught Dave's eye, as I continued bandaging the shrapnel wounds on the little boy in front of me. He'd been too close when some jackass launched an RPG at random, and had caught about three dozen splinters of metal and pulverized concrete. Fortunately, none had hit his eyes; he'd heal fine. If he lived so long.

Dave jerked his head at me, then at the tall man standing in the door. I saw he had his hands full, up to his elbows in an unconscious woman's blood as he tried to save her. I washed my hands in the corner and met the newcomer's eyes. "What do you want?" I asked. Maybe not the usual question one was supposed to get from an aid worker, but I wasn't really an aid worker, so what the hell.

"I have heard that there are Americans here," he said, in accented, but flawless, English. "I was understandably curious; most Westerners have fled or are staying locked down in the European quarter. I wished to see these extraordinary Americans."

"Well, you've seen us," I said brusquely. This guy was fishing, and I more and more suspected he was Ethiopian, probably an advisor to the National Army. The Ethiopians had been pretty close to the US for a while, getting a fair amount of support from Task Force Horn of Africa, the survivors of which we were now searching for. But in the last few years, rumor had it that they were turning more and more to the Chinese. In other words, I had no idea what this guy might be planning if he suspected we might be here for some other reason than aid work.

"I am surprised," he admitted, as he walked further into the clinic. "I would not expect aid workers to be so doggedly staying on, especially not after a major American military base was recently overrun. Or hadn't you heard about that?"

"Oh, we've heard about it," Dave replied without looking up. "Jeff, can you give me a hand? I need a clamp." I hurried over to where he was kneeling over the woman. Her upper leg had been severely wounded, but someone had had the presence of mind to throw a tourniquet on. Dave was now trying to find the artery. I grabbed a clamp off the table next to him and reached in.

The tall man stepped over to loom over us as we worked. "Can I be of assistance?" he asked.

Dave actually looked up, nonplused. "Sure, I guess." He pointed with an elbow at the table. "Put on some gloves, first." As dirty as the place had been when we'd found it, Dave had personally scrubbed and sterilized it, and he'd be damned if somebody put their dirty hands on one of his patients without precautions. Dave had been an 18D, Special Forces Medic, and had collected very nearly enough medical knowledge to become an MD. He just would rather work this way. He said it paid more these days, and he was probably right. He also just didn't want to work in an office, for some stuck-up hospital administrator.

The tall man dutifully pulled on a pair of sterile rubber gloves, and leaned in. Dave pointed to a Surefire next to the table. "Hold that so I can see." The man picked it up without a word, and shined the light into the wound.

The wound was a ragged one, and had slashed across the thigh. As near as I could tell, it had only nicked the artery, but that was enough. Dave had his suture kit nearby, but he was trying to find the artery first, which was difficult. Pinched off by the tourniquet, it had shrunk. Fortunately, it hadn't been severed, so it couldn't retract into the leg.

I used the clamp to pull open the wound, allowing Dave to get better access to the artery. I heard him grunt as he got enough room to work, and he reached for the sutures, which the tall man quickly handed to him. I glanced at the woman, noticing her features for the first time. She was really quite attractive, if a little on the scrawny side. Good thing she was out, too. This would hurt like hell if she was awake.

Dave worked as deftly as he could in the small space of the wound, while the tall man moved carefully to keep the light on his hands. I still didn't know who the guy was, and I was still gun-shy about his being here, but he'd had some training, and appeared to know his way around some trauma medicine.

Finally, Dave leaned back and took a deep breath. "Thanks, guys," he said, consciously or unconsciously including our visitor. "Just have to sew up the wound now." He waved us away, and I walked over to the trash bag tied to a cot in the corner, and peeled off my gloves. The nameless visitor followed.

As we got out of earshot, I turned to face him. "All right, who are you, and why are you here?" I asked.

He smiled, showing even, white teeth. "I am…a friend. I spent some time in the United States, and had some dealings with a number of the personnel who were stationed here a few years ago. It is possible that some of them were still here when the attack took place.

"I simply wished to meet these other Americans I'd heard about, and ask if they had heard from their friends in west Balbala?"

The hackles went up on the back of my neck. He smiled again, shook my hand, and left.

Dave finished tying off the sutures in the woman's leg, and stood up as I started out of the room. "What the hell just happened?" he asked, seeing the look on my face.

"We just got a tip from Ethiopian intelligence," I said over my shoulder as I went out the door. "I've got to find Alek."

CHAPTER 11

"There. I think that's it."

Danny was pointing at the tablet sitting on his lap, as we cruised back and forth on the roads outside Balbala.

Balbala wasn't really a town in and of itself; it was a slum that had started as a squatter community, outside the barbed wire fence erected by the French around Djibouti City itself, during their administration of the country. Almost thirty percent of the country's population lived in the shanties of Balbala, and most of them were unemployed and dirt poor.

And, if what our nameless Ethiopian friend had told us was correct, there were American hostages somewhere in there, as well.

Danny, Jim, and I were running recon. Jim drove the Defender, it being the oldest and most beat-up looking vehicle we had. We really didn't want to stick out any more than necessary out here. If the whispers that Danny told us had come to JSOC before the attack were anything to go by, there had been a lot of Shabaab and al-Qaeda activity in Balbala for a lot of years now.

Danny was running two of his miniature drones from the pad on his lap, while I kept my rifle at my feet, and my pistol in my lap, holding security. None of us were all that visible from the outside, through the dirty windows, but we did our best to avoid getting too close to anybody.

I half-turned to where Danny was sitting in the back seat. "I can't see it from here, dude."

He handed the pad forward to me, while shifting his own HK45C to his lap in its place, and looking out the window. I didn't know exactly what all Danny's military experience was, but Alek had implied pretty strongly that he knew his shit, so I didn't question him. He held security while I looked at the pad.

He had both drones circling, one with a thermal camera, the other with regular photo imagery. Both were presently focused on a cluster of what looked like planned housing, although gone as dingy as the rest of the slum.

"The housing complex?" I asked, looking back at him. "This bunch of one-to-two-story apartments on the south edge?"

He didn't look at it, but kept his gaze outward, scanning for threats, or signs that we'd been compromised. "Yep."

I looked back at the pad. The complex was big, and looked like it could be made up of as many as thirty separate buildings, all kind of walled together. It looked like a fucking nightmare, from a raids perspective.

"What makes you think that?" I asked, not sure if I wanted to know the answer.

"Sentries. There are armed men on the roof, and a lot of spotters around on the ground."

I looked more closely, zooming in with the photo imagery. There were about a half-dozen men scattered on the roofs of the buildings, mostly in places where they wouldn't be immediately visible over the short parapets that were standard in Arab architecture. I looked as close as I could, and it did seem as though they had weapons, though the angle and distance made it hard to make out what they were. There seemed to be several groups hanging around near the corners of the complex, as well. No sign of weapons on the ground.

"This is the Hodan district," I pointed out. "A lot of rich assholes from Dubai live in these complexes. We could just be looking at their security setup."

"It's possible," he admitted. "However, there isn't anyplace else in Balbala with that level of security. Unless our mysterious Ethiopian friend sent us on a wild goose chase, I'm saying that this is the most likely spot that they might be keeping hostages."

"Even if it is," I replied, trying not to think about what would happen if the Ethiopian had put us on the wrong track, "This is going to be a nightmare to clear. At least one three-story, shooters on the roof, multiple buildings with connecting walls...we'd need damned near a company to do this right, and we've got ten shooters."

Danny was silent. I kept staring at the compound as the drones circled overhead, and Jim swung us around another turn. How the fuck were we supposed to do this?

"We need more and better intel," Danny finally said. "I've got some ideas. Let's head back."

***

We got back to our compound to find four HiLuxes parked out front, each with about five hard-nosed looking individuals sitting in them, watching us impassively as we drove into the garage. They were a mix of Westerners, North Africans, and black Africans. I smelled Legion as soon as I saw them.

"What the hell are these guys doing here?" Danny murmured, as we got out, carefully keeping our weapons out of sight. He was answered when we walked into our team room to find Arno Kohl standing there with Alek and Imad.

"Ah, my friend Lou!" Kohl exclaimed. "Or is it Jefferson?"

I looked at Larry, who nodded reassuringly. "It's Jeff, actually," I replied warily, looking at Alek. "What's going on?"

"It seems we're getting some unofficial help," he said.

"*Mon colonel* has been made aware of your presence, and has agreed to let several of us quietly...what is the American term? *Moonlight*, yes?" Kohl grinned.

"So, what? You want to play aid worker too?" I asked, lifting my eyebrows. Kohl just laughed.

"For an aid worker, you make a good professional soldier, *meine Freund*," he replied. "I did not wish to call you out where others might hear, but I recognized what you were the moment I saw you in that café. Come now, two obvious professionals, concealing semiautomatic pistols and body armor, in-country a mere week after a major terrorist attack on an American military base? You might fool a lot of the locals, but I have been around too long."

"You mentioned you had sources," Larry pointed out. "Have they happened to mention that our cover is blown?"

"Hardly. They still think that the explosion that killed Khasam and so many of his friends was an accident. Very good work covering your tracks, by the way," he said approvingly. Alek grinned.

"So, what have your 'sources' told you?" I asked, as I walked over to my cot to deposit my duffel full of weapons, ammo, and optics. "Anything we can use?"

"I'm still pursuing the two who might have some more information," he admitted. "They tend to be a bit...close-mouthed when it comes to the possibility of getting their heads cut off if they talk to me. Well, one is," he amended. "The other is something of a jihadi himself, but I have enough blackmail on him to get him to talk, if I can find him. So now he is avoiding me." He frowned.

"However, some whispers have come to my attention. Especially after you gentlemen took care of Khasam. By the way, did you get anything useful out of him?"

Alek shook his head. "Motherfucker had an IED trigger in his hand. Had to kill him first."

"Pity," Kohl opined. He pointed to the map on the table, which was increasingly more of an enlarged photo mosaic of the city and its environs. "Still, it seems Khasam was small-time. He was an engine of chaos, a bomber, torturer and murderer brought in to further the unrest. He tagged along on the attack on the base, but had little if anything to do with its planning." His finger came to rest on the Hodan district, where we had just come from. "One of my sources, who almost entirely lives on the money I give him to keep his eyes open, has seen several of the major jihadists coming and going from this complex, here. It seems they have some friends in Dubai."

Danny had come in a couple of minutes before and was standing next to the door, leaning against the jamb. "Makes sense," he put in. "We've suspected a lot of terror money goes through Dubai for a long time."

"Unfortunately, he has not seen any hostages," Kohl continued. "However, he assures me that if they are in the area, they are in Balbala, and they are probably there."

"We need a damned sight more than 'probably,'" Larry said, folding his arms.

"No kidding," I said. I turned to Alek. "We got a look at this complex today, and Danny thinks that it's probably the place, too. Problem is it's fucking huge, at least for our level of force. A hard hit is out of the question, without solid info on the hostages' location."

"Can I ask a question?" Rodrigo asked suddenly, from his cot.

"What's up, Rod?" Alek asked.

"I thought we were just the recon force," he said flatly. "Some high-speed SOF motherfuckers were going to come swooping in to rescue the hostages as soon as we found them. So, if we've found them, where are our assaulters?"

All eyes turned to Danny.

His shoulders slumped. "I don't have an answer for you, gents. I've called in, and no one's available. All I'm getting is to stand by, and keep the intel coming."

"Somebody should have been on standby as soon as we hit the shore," Hank said. "But from what Danny's told us, we shouldn't be surprised that they weren't." Hank looked like a biker, with tattoo sleeves, a shaved head, and blond goatee, but he was usually soft-spoken, when he talked at all. As always, his tone was low and reasonable. "So I'd say that what we have to figure out now is this; what are we going to do with the situation as it is?"

Alek looked around at all of us. "Gentlemen?" One word, but it carried a dozen questions. All of which could be answered with little more than a nod. We weren't leaving those poor bastards in enemy hands if we could help it. It was a hell of a risk, as we were effectively declaring war on the terrorists who had kidnapped our countrymen. We were putting ourselves, as well as the remaining hostages, at a lot of risk. But, if we just sat on our hands and waited for the military to do something, odds were they'd either all be dead, or buried where we'd never find them.

It was a Rubicon moment. Once we decided that we were it, there wasn't going to be any going back or slowing down, until every last imprisoned American was accounted for, or we were all dead. Nobody hesitated, shrank back, or protested. Satisfied, Alek turned to Kohl and asked, "Just how far are you and your fellow Legionnaires ready to go as far as moonlighting?"

"Far enough," was Kohl's response. The humor was gone from his voice. He was dead serious. I admit, I found it a little surprising to hear that kind of commitment to rescuing Americans coming from a Legionnaire, especially a German Legionnaire.

"All right, we've got some planning to do," Alek said.

***

"Five minutes."

I eased my head around the corner of the three-story building across the street from the target complex. I could see one guy on the roof, ostensibly holding security, but he did not have a weapon in his hands, and he was smoking. There wasn't anyone on the street anymore, and the lights were out. A little creative tinkering with the fuel line to the generator that was the sole remaining source of electrical power in this little enclave of Dubai in the middle of shanty central had seen to that.

It was quiet, and can't-see-your-hand-in-front-of-your-face dark. Perfect. We were just waiting for the signal to go.

I was trying not to think about what a long shot this was, and just focus on what we had to do.

The signal was a series of *snaps* overhead. The silhouette of the sentry I was watching, who was sitting on the roof of the nearest building in the complex, suddenly jerked, a dark mist exploding out of his back, and he slumped down to the roof, dead. There was a slight slope to that roof, but not enough for him to slide off. Across the complex, the other sentries died, as Hank and Jim hit them from distance, with suppressed RND 2000 and Noreen Bad News rifles.

As soon as the first shot went by overhead, not silent, but quiet enough not to wake anyone who was still alive on the target site, Bob and I were moving.

We got to the base of the wall at the north end of the complex in seconds. Neither of us was heavily kitted; we carried suppressed pistols, ammo, smoke grenades, radios, NVGs, and soft armor. The rest of the weapons were in the duffel that we carried between us. We needed to be quick and quiet.

I turned and put my back against the wall, cupping my hands in front of me. Bob put his boot in my cupped hands, and I hoisted him up onto the wall. He caught the top and levered himself up into a prone position on top of the wall, and then reached down for me. I grabbed his hand, and hauled myself up to where I could grab the top, then he let go and dropped down on the other side. I hefted up the duffel bag, then followed as quickly as I was able, dangling my right hand and leg down like a spider, then swinging down to the ground as quietly as possible, using my knees to cushion the impact.

83

We were in a small courtyard. There was some withered, patchy grass on the ground, but it was mostly dirt. I was facing a one-story building to my front, and what looked a lot like a gymnasium to the left. The doors to the gym were closed, but there was a single door and window into the one story. Bob was already at the door, and I padded over to the window, depositing the duffel next to the door.

Slowly and carefully, I eased my NVGs into the corner of the window, and peered through them, with most of my head and body crouched out of sight. The light intensifier didn't do much, as it needed ambient light to see, but the thermal showed nothing, either. The house was empty. In fact, as near as I could tell, it looked stripped down to the walls.

I signaled Bob, giving him the thumbs-down to indicate a dry hole, and pointed to the gym. He nodded, and moved toward the little gatehouse style building that led to it.

As we moved, I carefully keyed my radio, which was set as quiet as I could get it, and sub-vocalized into my throat mic, "One, clear."

Bob and I got to opposite sides of the door leading into the foyer, or whatever it was. Bob reached for the door handle, and I drew my pistol. I leveled it at the crack in the door, and nodded to Bob, who eased the door open with a barely audible *click*.

Nothing. The foyer was empty. I moved in, buttonhooking through the doorway to make sure. Dust and a couple of folding chairs. Nothing else. On to the next door.

There was a gomer just inside the gymnasium. He was sitting in a chair, the front legs off the floor, tipped back against the wall. His AK was leaning against the wall beside him. He was fast asleep. A moment later he was dead, unaware that he would never wake up. A suppressed .45 makes little more noise than the action cycling, especially with a good suppressor, which I had.

I continued clearing the big room, moving to the right, while Bob took the left. There was a lantern at the far end, but it was too dim to reach us. The crowd in the middle of the room showed up fine on thermal, though.

There were about twenty people in the middle of the room, sitting in an attitude that suggested they were bound. Probably why there was only one other guard there, whom Bob dispatched with a quick pair of shots.

There were low sounds from the prisoners, but no questions, or even loud reactions. I could see several of them flinch at the sounds, though. Neither Bob nor I had said a word, and the second guard had been as alert as the first. The prisoners knew something was happening, but not what. I suspected that by this time they had been brutalized into making as little sound as possible. That could come in handy, or it could be a liability. We'd have to see.

I switched on the IR flashlight under my pistol. I don't usually like

84

having extraneous crap hooked to my weapon, but right at the moment, I was glad I'd brought it along, especially as Bob crept over to the lantern and doused it.

These were our hostages, all right, or at least some of them. They were sitting back to back, with sacks over their heads and their hands and feet tied. They were dressed in their shorts and T-shirts, with no socks or boots. Fuck. That could be a problem getting them out.

I padded over to one who seemed to be sitting up straighter than the others, and put my hand on his shoulder. To his credit, he didn't flinch. "Listen to me very carefully," I whispered. "We are Americans, and we're here to get you out. Do you understand?"

He nodded, slowly. He probably suspected it was some kind of trick. Being in captivity can fuck with your sense of reality after a while. "Good," I whispered. "Do you know where the rest of the hostages are?"

He shook his head, and from his posture, looked like he was about to say something. I squeezed his shoulder. "Never mind. I'm going to take your hood off. You're still not going to see shit; there aren't any lights on in here. When I cut you loose, I need you to start helping me get the rest untied and up. Can you do that?"

"Yes," he whispered hoarsely. "What about the guards?"

"Taken care of for the moment," I told him. "But we need to keep quiet. We don't want to wake up the whole neighborhood." He nodded, as I pulled his hood off.

He was young, maybe mid-twenties. His haircut suggested regular Army or Marine Corps, though it had gone a little shaggy, along with a couple weeks' worth of beard. He looked like he'd been beaten, though not so badly that he couldn't function.

He had been tied with baling wire, and it was a simple matter to get it unwound from his hands and feet. He rubbed his hands when he brought them in front of him, then went to work on the hostage next to him, whispering that the Americans were here.

Unfortunately, it was too much to ask that all of them would be as level-headed about their situation as the young man I had initially freed. As I turned to covering the door we had come in, some damned POG burst out crying when told that the Americans were here to rescue them.

"Shut that motherfucker up!" Bob and I hissed almost simultaneously.

There was a scuffle as several of the newly freed hostages, who were a little more aware of their situation, piled on the guy to keep him quiet. I listened carefully at the door. Nothing. Everything was still quiet. I keyed the comm. "Coconut, Hillbilly," I murmured. "Found some twenty hostages in Building Two. Getting them sorted out now."

"Roger," came the faint reply. "Nothing else so far. I'll get Schultz moving." We had taken to nicknaming Kohl "Sgt. Schultz." He had needed it explained to him, and wasn't terribly amused when he got it. This only ensured that we'd use it more.

The last of the hostages was getting cut loose. The weeper had been gagged by his fellows, using the sack that had been over his head. I approved. We did *not* want anyone knowing we were here until the sun came up and we were long gone.

The sudden sound of shouting in Arabic and the rattle of AK fire dashed those hopes.

Alek's voice crackled over the radio. "Go loud, we're made. Push to Building Two and strongpoint until the trucks arrive."

I looked at the guy I'd freed first. "Can you shoot?" I asked, grabbing him by the shoulder. I hoped he could, but I knew a lot of training requirements in the military had gone to shit lately; some, especially in the Air Force or Navy, never even touched a weapon after basic.

"Yes," he replied. "Where do you want me?"

I steered him toward the door. "Cover right here, and check your targets before you shoot at anything," I said, as I picked up the AK that the gomer wasn't going to need anymore, and handed it to him. "There are friendlies on their way here."

"Roger," he replied, taking a barricade stance on the door, the rifle held in a firm alert carry. Good, he did know what he was doing.

"Bob," I called, as quietly as I could, "Give somebody with their head screwed on straight that other gomer's rifle. I think we're going to need it." I opened the duffel, which I'd left just inside the foyer, and shucked out my rifle, rocking a mag into the well and racking it as quietly as I could. The suppressor was already on the barrel. I handed the three spare AK magazines the dead gomer had in a chest harness to the kid I'd armed, and he tucked them into the elastic of his shorts.

"What's your name, kid?" I asked, over the growing sound of shouting and sporadic shooting outside. I didn't know what they were shooting at, as all of our shooters should have been inside, but odds were, they didn't know, either.

"Sack," he replied. "Sgt John Sack, USMC." He must have been part of the advisor group with TF Horn of Africa. "Who are you guys?"

"I'm Jeff," I replied. "As for who the lot of us are, let's just say we're some pissed-off old gunfighters who got hired to find you, and deal with the rest of the pleasantries when we're somewhere more secure than here." I finished speaking as a gomer came slamming through the gateway into the courtyard in front of us. I shouldered my rifle, and drilled him in the chest with a tight pair of shots.

There was a flurry of shots from further down the complex. It sounded like people were coming awake, and Alek, Larry, Colton, and Tim were having to fight their way through as they cleared. My little reverie was cut short as four more yelling gomers tried to come through the gate, and Sack and I cut them down.

There was another fusillade from the left, and then an IR light flashed from Building One. "Hillbilly, Coconut. We're in Building One."

"Roger," I replied. "I have eyes-on. How far out is Schultz?"

"Five mikes," was the reply, as all hell broke loose.

There was a roar of engines, and more shooting. Fires were starting to flare up, and in the flickering light, I could see movement outside the gate. The shouting was turning into a cacophony now, and there was more small arms fire aimed toward the buildings, and up in the air. We'd stirred up a hornet's nest.

I tapped Sack on the shoulder, and indicated that I was moving to the gate. I wanted a better view of what was going on, as well as a better shot at anybody coming.

"Hillbilly, Coconut, this is Kemosabe," Jim called. "I don't know what just happened, but the whole goddamned neighborhood is awake, and coming out of the woodwork. There are burning tires in the intersection, and at least three technicals on the street. I'm counting at least a hundred fighters, and that's just on the streets. Watch how much you expose yourselves; I'm seeing shooters in the upper stories of the buildings to the north."

"Roger," Alek replied. I hunkered down a little lower at the gate, while glancing over my shoulder at the three-story buildings across the street. I was covered, barely, by the wall, and I was in the shadows, so unless they had night vision scopes, they'd have a hard time seeing me. I still felt as exposed as hell, though.

I could just see down the street toward the south. It was a narrow sight window, but it actually gave me a pretty decent field of fire, at least insofar as the buildings allowed. And I immediately saw four militiamen running toward us, AK-47s held at waist level. I opened fire, the suppressor keeping any muzzle flash to a minimum. It would have blinded me otherwise. The two lead fighters dropped in the street, while the other two scrambled out of my line of fire.

I shrank back as my hiding place was suddenly hammered with a barrage of 7.62 fire. More small flames stabbed from the open door of Building One, as one of the other guys opened up in reply, but was soon silenced, as the volume of fire increased. Rounds smacked against the wall next to me, and snapped through the gateway, hammering against the building. I heard a sharp yell of pain, cut off as quickly as it came, from the doorway.

"Everybody all right?" I yelled, as I ripped the mag out of my M1A and rocked in a fresh one.

"Caught a bullet fragment," Colton called back from the doorway. "I'll be fine, just stings like hell."

I picked up the nearly empty mag where it had dropped, and stuffed it into a cargo pocket. "Where is Schultz? We're going to get overrun here if we stay much longer!" I yelled.

"He's circling the area," Alek yelled from the window, over the roar of shooting and shouting. "He's in unarmored trucks; they can't get close without getting shot to ribbons."

Fuck, fuck, fuck, fuck. "Can we get out to the south?"

Another burst of firing from the other side of Building One answered that question. "Negative, they're coming in that way, too."

The fire from the street had slackened somewhat, so I risked reaching out into the gateway to snag one of the dropped rifles, but quickly ducked back, as a fresh storm of shots blasted dust and chips of concrete in my face. I racked my brain to remember the layout of the exits from the recon. There had to be a way out of here, preferably out into the desert to the south, where there were fewer hiding places for gomers to pop out of.

The fire slackened some more as they lost me as a target, so I ducked back out and ripped a handful of shots off. I was rewarded with one high-pitched wail of pain as I took cover again. The return fire was, if anything, fiercer than before. But I'd gotten another AK. I tossed it back toward the door, where Sack caught it and passed it to another hostage who could fight.

Another group of gomers tried rushing the gatehouse, and were met with gunfire from the house. One got past, and actually made it inside the wall, before I blew his head off from two feet away. Blood and brains splashed messily, and he crumpled to the ground.

"Jeff!" Sack yelled from the door. "What's going on?"

"We're fucking surrounded, is what's going on!" I bellowed. "Now either shut up, or get out here and fight!"

I should have known better. The crazy bastard, barefoot and in his skivvies, dashed out to join me at the wall, his AK held in a tactical carry. There was a *crack*, and a bullet smacked into the wall of Building One as he passed, probably aimed at him.

"Crazy fucker," I snarled at him, shoving him back against the wall. "Can the rest of them move?"

"Some are going to need help," he replied, "but yeah, I think so."

"Go get 'em ready," I said, shoving him back toward the gym. "And keep your damned head down!" I laid another suppressive burst down the street, and then ducked back into cover. "Alek!" I yelled.

"I hear you, brother," came the shouted reply. "Plan B, let's do it!"

"Shiny, get 'em moving," I called over the radio, slinging my rifle across my chest. I dipped into the duffel at my feet.

Colton yelled, "Coming out!" and ducked through the door to take up security on the gate, facing north, as I came up with two of the concussion charges we'd put together. They consisted of two one-pound blocks of TNT taped together, with a tubular nylon handle about two feet long and a ten-second time fuse. I had about a dozen HC smoke grenades in the bag, as well.

Colton was shooting, engaging any shooters he could see on the street. The rest of the team came out of the house, while Tim still held security on the window, in case anyone tried to come at us through the house. Tim was also, I noticed, keeping a prisoner; the guy was on his face on the ground, with Tim's knee in his back. Alek came to me, and grabbed one of the concussion charges. I had placed one next to me, and immediately grabbed a smoke, pulling the pin and lofting it over the wall to the north. Let those fuckers in the buildings across the street see us through that.

"Bob!" Alek yelled through the open door of the gym. "Let's go, get 'em moving!"

No sooner had he finished speaking, over the storm of gunfire outside, and the snapping reports of Larry and Colton shooting back through the gate, than Sack yelled, "Coming out!" and led a line of hostages out of the gym's foyer.

"Coconut, Kemosabe," Jim called over the radio. "Goldwings and I are keeping them off the crew-serves, but you need to get out of there. It looks like half of Balbala is headed in your direction." His statement was punctuated by another *crack*, as either he or Hank shot another gomer trying to get on a machine gun mounted on one of the technicals out on the street.

I looked over my shoulder, and the ragged band of hostages looked to be all out in the courtyard, some coughing as the thick white smoke from the grenade started rolling over the top of the wall. I nodded at Alek, and we both grabbed concussion charges. Lighting the time fuses, we both started to whirl the charges on the end of the nylon, getting them some good momentum before we lobbed them over the wall. No sooner had mine left my hand than I was diving for more smokes.

The charges went off thunderously in the street, blowing smoke and dust up over the wall, and shattering glass all over the block. We immediately followed with about six smokes, as fast as Alek and I could pull pins, throw, and grab the next ones. As we were lobbing smoke grenades, Larry and Colton pushed out onto the street, firing as they moved.

Sweeping my rifle back up from where it dangled in front of my chest, I hefted the duffel and tossed it to the fittest-looking hostage I could see who didn't have a weapon. "Hold on to that!" I yelled. "Now move!" Then I charged out the gate, and took a knee near, but not on, the wall, facing north.

The intersection to the north of the complex was like a scene out of hell. The gomers had rolled tires out into the middle of the intersection and set them on fire when they started attacking us. One of the concussion charges had landed on one, and scattered burning rubber all across the street. Flames flickered on the ground, through the roiling clouds of smoke, while muzzle flashes strobed above, bullets snapping by overhead, seeking our lives. The fire had slackened, and several bodies lay in heaps on the streets, from both our fire and the explosions. Some of the gomers were still staggering around, firing wildly in our direction. They were blinded by the smoke. The thermal elements of our NVGs removed any such handicap from us.

We gunned them down in the street with their fellows.

Larry, Colton, and I formed a line of shooters across the street, trusting to our fire to keep us alive, as Alek, Tim, and Bob chivvied the hostages down the street, toward the open desert, where we hoped that Kohl and his buddies could pick us up. Tim still had his prisoner, holding him by the collar with one hand, pushing him down the street. I could hear more shooting behind me, as they fought their way through another group of gomers trying to come around to the south. I couldn't focus on them. My fight was to the north.

Time seemed to slow down, and everything took on a certain clarity that only comes to me when things have well and truly gone south. Larry was shooting so fast it sounded like his DSA FAL was on automatic, but I could hear every single shot. Colton was actually firing bursts. I was simply shooting pairs, every time my IR laser settled on a target.

Gomer. Two shots. Next target. AK in hand. Two shots. Gun goes dry, yank a fresh mag from its pouch, use it to hit the mag release, and sweep the empty mag out of the well. Rock the fresh mag in, and send the bolt home. Shotgun. Two shots. Next target.

We were holding the line, but the hostile fire was getting more intense, not less. Jim hadn't been kidding; gomers were flooding out of the alleys and back streets of Balbala. We had well and truly kicked the hornet's nest. Dimly, through the noise, I heard Alek yelling over the radio. "Hillbilly! Bound back!"

I was close enough to Larry to hit him on the shoulder, and he immediately ceased fire, came to his feet, pivoted, and dashed to the south. A few seconds later, he opened up again, his shots snapping past to my left, and I followed suit, bounding past him about ten meters. I pivoted on my right foot, dropping to my knee and bringing my rifle up, and started firing again as soon as I stopped moving. Colton turned, coming to his feet.

The bullet caught him at the base of his jaw.

He spun halfway around and dropped to the pavement like a sack of rocks. I was moving before I could even yell at Larry to hold, running forward to grab him. Larry was right next to me, laying down fire to cover my rush to Colton.

90

He was still alive, gurgling through the ruin of the lower half of his face. There wasn't time to do anything for him; can't put a tourniquet on a face wound. I grabbed his arm, and hoisted him into a fireman's carry. Fortunately, he was a skinny guy, and I hefted him easily, while Larry kept shooting, cursing a blue streak.

I tried to settle Colton across my shoulders as I ran. Larry keyed his radio as he dashed back behind me. "Seabiscuit's down, Hillbilly has him, coming to you!"

"Roger," came Alek's reply. He was breathing hard, his voice rasping over the comm. The firing behind us picked up, as we dashed past Tim and Bob, who opened back up as they saw we were clear.

My lungs were burning, and every muscle was protesting under Colton's weight, as he bounced painfully against my shoulders. My left shoulder and arm were wet with his blood. I panted with exertion, but didn't dare slow down.

We cleared the south end of the complex, and sprinted across the road, heading for the mounds of dirt and tailings that had been left from the construction of the complex and similar projects nearby, hoping to find some cover. I was trying to gasp some encouragement to Colton, trying to keep him fighting to live, but all I managed were hoarse pants.

I staggered around the edge of a berm where Alek had gathered the liberated hostages, and slumped to the ground, trying to ease Colton off my shoulders. Two of the hostages were there as well, and helped me lower him to the ground. I made sure to put him on his side; on his back, he'd likely choke to death on his own blood.

I ripped out the med bag at his waist, and went to work, daring to use a small red lens flashlight. They knew where we were, anyway, as Rodrigo and Nick were on top of the berm with M60s, laying down covering fire as soon as Tim and Bob got out of the way.

I needn't have bothered. Colton was dead. Either the bullet or the fragments of his jaw must have severed his carotid artery. I was covered in his blood, and he wasn't moving or breathing. His eyes stared sightlessly at the night sky.

I threw the med bag in the dust in fury and grief. "Where the fuck is Kohl?!" I bellowed at Alek.

Alek just pointed, where two old 5-ton trucks were rolling up the road, flame stabbing from the FN MAG machine guns mounted on the cabs. The lead truck skidded to a halt between us and the gomers in a cloud of dust and gravel. Kohl leaped out of the passenger door, FAMAS cradled in hand, and ran around to the rear, where he sent a couple of desultory bursts downrange before unhooking the tailgate and letting it fall. Then he waved us toward the truck, while taking a knee and starting to suppress the enemy.

I was starting to lift Colton's body when a hand clasped me by the shoulder. It was Sack. "We'll get him. I think we need you to shoot right now." I almost decked him and went back to carrying my brother-in-arms, but his common sense penetrated the emotional shock, and I remembered that the more guns we had in the fight, the more likelihood we had of getting the rest of us out of this alive. It was too late for Colton. Maybe it wasn't too late for the rest of us.

Bending low, I dashed forward, coming to a knee next to Kohl, and opening fire. A group of gomers was trying to rush us from the small cluster of huts on the other side of the north-south running road. They didn't make it far. Kohl, Alek, and I gunned them down, even as three machine guns swept across them, peppering the shacks at the same time.

Kohl was a good shot, I'll give him that. He kept his rifle on semi, putting controlled pairs into any target that presented itself. And there were plenty. The militia was enraged that we'd invaded their turf and taken their hostages, and they were out for blood. Another group of about twenty came boiling out of the alley between building complexes, and into Rodrigo's fire. He laid windrows of them down in the dusty street.

We were taking fire, but it was mostly high, as the enemy was suppressed by the withering barrage of machinegun fire. I kept killing anything that presented itself, listening for the shout that everybody was on the trucks.

Finally it came. "Let's go!" Bob yelled from the back of the lead truck, even as he leaned out the back and kept shooting. Looking back, I saw that Kohl, Alek, and I were the last ones on the ground. I punched Kohl's shoulder, and he got to his feet and ran for the truck. A moment later, Alek tapped me, and we got up and ran.

Helping hands reached down to pull us into the back of the truck. They didn't have a lot of strength left in them, but those hostages who still had some spark of defiance in them were determined to help. Sack was on his belly on the truck bed, leaning out below Bob, shooting the AK I'd handed him. As soon as I was on, I reached down and grabbed the tailgate, hauling it up and cutting off Sack's fire, as Alek pounded on the back of the cab. With a lurch, the truck was moving, the Legionnaire on the gun up top still laying down the hate.

We rolled toward the open desert, leaving the hell of smoke, fire, and blood behind.

CHAPTER 12

It had been a long, bumpy ride. Kohl's driver, Leon, had taken a winding mess of barely rutted tracks, wadis, and occasionally just cutting cross-country, into the desert south of Djibouti City. We wanted to get as far away from Balbala as possible, before we even thought about heading back to our HQ. Odds were good that we'd have to relocate that pretty soon, anyway.

For the moment, we were stopped, the engines shut off, in a small wadi, surrounded by acacias that loomed like black umbrellas against the lighter background of the desert at night. Nick and Rodrigo were in the backs of the trucks, looking over the hostages. Some were rather the worse for wear, and a few really hadn't handled their captivity well. Two were almost catatonic, and had needed to be lifted by main force into the trucks.

The rest of us, Alek, Bob, Tim, Larry, and I, stood a little way away, in the bottom of the wadi. Colton's body lay at our feet.

His face had been covered by a bloody shemaugh, and his gear had been stripped. Looking down at him, he looked…shrunken. He'd always been skinny. We'd blamed his unnatural speed on the fact that he wasn't much more than skin and bones; he didn't have as much weight to drag around as the rest of us. That, plus his first name, had led to his callsign.

But now, skinny-ass Colton looked frail, like the flesh had all melted off his bones. The clinical part of my brain explained that this was due to the fact all his blood had run out. The rest of me could only stare, numbly, at my friend's corpse.

Colton wasn't the first brother I'd lost, and wouldn't be the last. It's a dangerous profession we'd chosen. It didn't make it hurt any less when another one of us went down.

"We've got to bury him," Alek said quietly. "No way are we going to be able to take him back with us."

There was a general murmur of assent. Getting out of here, especially with hostages, was going to be hard enough. Plus, we had no way of preserving his body. He'd rot before we got within a thousand miles of the States.

For another long moment, no one said or did anything. I could see

Bob shaking, silently weeping. He and Colton had been pretty tight, as the soft-spoken runner had been the most welcoming to the new guy on the team. After a moment, he turned, his shoulders still shuddering, and walked to one of the trucks. He returned with a shovel, and began digging in the dry, hard-packed dirt.

As the grave got deeper, the sound of an approaching vehicle could be heard. Alek turned away, listening, and then keyed his radio. "Roger, that's us...Affirm, I have eyes on you. Come on in."

A blacked out HiLux soon trundled into the wadi and coasted to a stop next to one of the 5-tons. The engine went quiet, and a man got out and walked toward us. As he got closer, I saw it was Danny. He didn't say a word at first, just walked up to Alek, grasped him by the hand, and pulled him in close. "I'm sorry, brother," he said quietly. Alek just nodded; then Danny faced the rest of us. He walked over to Colton's body, and bowed his head.

Bob had stopped digging, and was staring at Danny. "What the fuck are you doing here?" he asked.

"That's enough, Bob," Alek growled, but Bob wasn't going to be put off. He was digging his best friend's grave, after all.

"No, this motherfucker stayed back, while we went into that fucking hornet's nest, and now Colton's fucking dead. And he's got the balls to come here and say he's fucking sorry?!" Bob's voice was starting to rise in volume.

"I said shut your fucking mouth, Bob!" Alek snapped. "I made the call as to who went, and who stayed back. I was the one who decided Danny had to stay back and work support. This motherfucker has been through worse shit than you can imagine, so shut the fuck up."

Bob shut up. It was hard to see his face in the dark, but he still didn't look happy about it. Danny, if anything, seemed even less so. If he had worked with Alek before I knew him, that meant he had been in on some hairy shit. I wondered how many other friends and comrades he'd had to bury. I decided I probably didn't want to know.

After a few minutes, Larry stepped down into the grave. He put his hand on Bob's shoulder, and gently took the shovel from him, then started digging, while Bob stepped up out of the grave. While Larry dug, Danny motioned to Alek and me to come with him.

We walked around behind the HiLux, where Danny blew a deep breath up past his nose, folded his arms, and leaned back against the tailgate. "You said you picked up one of the gomers?" he asked, all business.

"Yeah," Alek said. "An Arab. Young kid, too, maybe twenty. He's in the truck with two of the Legionnaires watching him."

"Not sure I like having them too involved," Danny said.

"I don't either, but we all needed to be down here," Alek said, indicating Colton's shrouded body.

"I understand. Let's just get him somewhere where I can talk to him soon, okay?" Danny replied. "And I mean *soon*. I got word from Langley just before I came out here. The Ethiopians crossed the border an hour ago."

"Well this just keeps getting better and better, doesn't it?" I said. "Fuck. How long does that give us?"

"Depending on how fast they move, they could be at the city by sunup," Danny replied.

"Motherfuck," Alek swore. "We've got to get these guys out of the country now, then."

"And try to find out where the rest are," Danny agreed. "Twenty is something, but it's supposed to be only about a tenth of the number they grabbed. Which means that the rest are in even worse danger now." He rubbed his chin. "I think we do need to move our operation out of the city, though."

"I agree," I said. "No way we're going to be able to work much inside the city with the Ethiopians steamrolling it." That gave me pause. "How are they justifying this? Peacekeeping? The official government's still intact, if a little pinned down at the moment."

"I don't know, I haven't heard," Danny replied. "We have to assume that they're moving to secure the port, though, which means they'll have the city locked down in a matter of hours."

Danny looked over at the 5-ton, where our unwilling guest was sitting in the bed, with a black Legionnaire watching him, FAMAS pointed loosely in his direction. "I'm afraid our guy here might be the key to getting to the rest of the hostages in time. As soon as we're settled, I'm going to need some time with him."

"Agreed," Alek said, starting toward the grave. "I'll speed this up. We need to move."

***

In the end, there wasn't any ceremony. Those of us who prayed, prayed silently, as we gently lowered Colton's body into the hole, and covered it over. Bob marked the grid on his GPS, in case we ever managed to come back. It wasn't likely, but there had to be hope.

Then we loaded on the trucks and got back in the war.

***

We roared up the road, following much the same route to the compound that we had on the first day. We were still ahead of the Ethiopian incursion, but Danny was getting semi-regular updates from a satellite as it passed over. There was almost an entire mechanized division heading for Djibouti City. They weren't stopping or securing anything else as they went, not that there was much between the Ethiopian border and the port. They were coming, and coming hard.

Our little three-vehicle convoy rolled up to the compound just as the sun was coming up and the call to prayer was starting to echo across the city. Hank came out and pushed open the gate. Pulling all three trucks inside, we started getting the hostages out and under cover. Dave would have his hands full for most of the day.

Hank helped Rodrigo manhandle our unwilling guest out of the back of the 5-ton, and into the shed against the seaward wall of the compound. He'd stay there for a while, until Danny went to have a chat with him. The Legionnaires then loaded back up, while Kohl shook our hands and thanked us for the excitement. They left after that, going back to where they were supposed to be.

Then most of us went inside, and promptly collapsed into an exhausted sleep, some of us outwardly trembling from the adrenaline dump. Unfortunately, grief and the memories of the night before precluded it being a restful sleep.

***

When I cracked my eye to see that it was Bob shaking my ankle, I groaned. "Not you again. What's gone to hell now?"

"Something's going on up north," Bob said, looking slightly confused. I guess my crack about him being the permanent bearer of bad news went over his head.

I swung my feet out of bed, still in my boots. None of us undressed much to sleep anymore. My drop holster clipped onto my belt, and I scooped up my rifle before lurching over to our little op-center while I tried to rub the ache out of my eyes.

Larry and Rodrigo were still getting up as well, but the rest of the team was gathered around the feed from one of Danny's UAVs. At first I couldn't tell what it was showing, exactly, just a cloud of dust and smoke. Then, as I looked closer, I swallowed, hard.

"Is that the Presidential Palace?" I asked carefully.

"Yeah, it is," Jim said heavily.

The southern half of the crenellated palace was a smoking crater. It looked like whatever had gone off, had exploded right at the base of the palace. I was betting truck bomb, but a rocket was also conceivable. Even as we watched, through the pall of smoke and still-settling dust, what was left of the southwest tower crumbled, slumping into the crater with another billowing cloud of dust.

"How'd they get that close?" I asked.

"Suicide bombers," was the reply. The camera panned back, showing the trail of devastation along the west road. It looked like they'd had enough car bombs to take out any checkpoints, then blast through the outer wall, before letting the final strike in to the palace itself. The entire western harbor was overlaid with a pall of black smoke.

"Any word on the president?" Rodrigo asked.

"Right now, the rebels are saying he's dead," Tim answered. "The government radio station is insisting he's alive, and safe." He shook his head. "Looking at that, I'm a little inclined to take the rebels' word for it."

"What are the Ethiopians doing?" Jim asked. Tim tapped a key, and the scene shifted to outside the city.

There was a FOB growing in the desert, straddling the N5 highway. I was reasonably sure there was another one on the N2. There were already berms going up, and as the tiny UAV whirred silently overhead, it showed columns of trucks, troop transports, and tanks. There were also several Hip and Hind helicopters, both on the ground, and orbiting above. I was frankly surprised our UAV hadn't been detected and shot down, yet.

"There's a lot of chatter, but no movement, yet," Tim said.

"Only a matter of time, regardless," Larry said. He stroked his goatee. "Even if the president's alive, they'll probably move in to shore him up."

For a while we watched the beehive of activity outside the city, as a relatively modern FOB, that didn't look too much different from one of ours before the big draw down, took shape. Finally, Alek spoke.

"Start getting the gear ready to move. We've got to be ready to head for the beach tonight."

"We calling it, then?" Nick asked, hooking his thumbs in his pistol belt. "I thought we were doing pretty well, running around with all this going on."

"We're at least getting out of the city," Alek replied. "Whether we're canc'ing the whole thing or not probably depends mostly on what Danny finds out from our guest in the shed. But movement in the city is going to be severely hampered if the Ethiopians take over. Most of their COIN doctrine and tactics come from us. I don't know about you, but I'd rather not have to deal with that, especially if it turns out that the hostages are somewhere else, and we wind up playing hide-and-seek with the Ethiopians instead of the fuckasses we're supposed to be hunting."

"And what about the targets here?" I asked quietly. "Are we just going to let them go? Figure they're out of our reach?"

"You're talking about the bastards who led the attack in the first place," Alek said. It wasn't a question, but I nodded anyway. He sighed. "I don't like it any more than you do, but we were hired to find the hostages, not get the bad guys who took them. If we can do both, so much the better, but the hostages are our objective. We simply don't have the manpower to do both."

"Don't need a lot of manpower to take people out," Hank remarked. "Rescuing people seems to take a lot more."

"It does," Jim said, siding with Alek. "But that doesn't take away

97

from what we were hired to do. There are still a lot of hostages left, and their life expectancy probably just got a lot shorter, thanks to what we did last night. They can't afford side missions."

He was right, and I conceded, as much as I was hungry for blood after last night. As exhausted as I was, I had still seen Colton falling to the street every time I closed my eyes. I could still see the faint echo of that image, lurking behind my eyelids. It went together with the Senior Airman getting his head sawed off, simply for being an American in territory the Salafists claimed. Fuck them. I wanted them all dead.

Fortunately or unfortunately, rage alone cannot dictate operations. Alek and Jim were right. I didn't like it, though, and I confess I let my bitterness over Colton's death get the better of me. I stalked off to my rack and sat down, with my back to the rest. Childish, I know. I'm not proud of it. But I just had to get away a little bit, and try to restrain the roiling urge to smash, rend, and destroy that was threatening to claw its way out of my chest.

As I sat there, grinding my fist into my palm, Alek suddenly loomed over me. "Come on, brother, let's walk," he said. I didn't say anything, didn't even look at him at first, but finally heaved myself to my feet. He clapped one huge hand on my shoulder and steered me out of the room, into the hallway between the team room and the clinic.

He turned to face me as the door closed, and folded his arms. I couldn't meet his eyes at first. Alek and I had known each other a long time, and we'd had to bury several of our brothers. He knew how I reacted, and I knew that understanding, concerned look in his eyes that he got every time. And right at the moment, I didn't want to see it, because it might dampen my fury.

"I worry about you, Jeff," he said finally. It was the same way he'd started every one of these conversations for the last ten years. "I know what you're thinking. You want to go back in there, and burn the whole city to the ground. You want to make a mountain of dead bodies and blackened skulls, as retribution for Colton."

"And all the others those motherfuckers murdered," I snarled. "Including that kid who lost his head on the fucking internet."

"I know, brother." Alek kept his voice low and inexorably understanding. "You're a barbarian, a berserker. A fucking Viking. But I know you, and I know that you still understand why we can't do that. And that you wouldn't, not really, even if I gave you the chance."

I glanced sharply at him. "You don't think so?"

"I know you better than that." He nodded. "You're still a good man, the same good man who was ready to shoot another team leader when he started acting like he was going to use those Libyan farmers as target practice. However strong your rage-monster is, that conscience of yours is

98

stronger. I've seen it. And I know you know it."

I studied the dirty floor under my boots. He was right, and at that moment I hated both of us for it. It's a conflict I've had to live with my entire adult life, and it's one that's cost me a lot of sleep, and probably a few years of my life. Part of me is a throwback, a savage killer from a long-lost century. In another life, I might have been a reaver, leaping off a longship with an axe in my hand. But another part followed the old code my Dad had taught me that a real man always followed. Never cheat, steal, lie, murder, or disrespect a woman. It kept me in check. And at times like this, my bloodlust cursed that part of me, the part that wouldn't let me cut loose and sate my appetite for death and destruction.

Most of the time, I'm very glad of that cast-iron moral compass. It keeps me a man, instead of a monster. It also helps me to keep sight of what can and can't be done, regardless of my own personal desires.

But sometimes, like now, the sheer inability to follow through only made it worse. I raged, gritting my teeth together at the sheer injustice of life and the fucked-up world we live in.

Alek had seen it all before, and continued to talk, softly. "If we had time, I'd be right there with you. We'd find a way, Ethiopians or no, to make these bastards bleed for this. But we don't have the time. More importantly, the rest of those boys and girls who got dragged out of Lemonier don't have the time. As soon as we hit that place last night and found hostages, the countdown timer started. We've got to move, and hope we can come back and settle the score later."

"Won't happen," I muttered, bitterly. "They'll just get away with it again, even if we take all their human shields away. None of the bleeding hearts back home will pay us to go after 'em, especially if one of them becomes the 'legitimate leader' of a 'sovereign country.'" I took a deep breath, trying to dissipate the poisonous rage. "You're right, though, damn it. But don't expect me to thank you for it, not yet."

He grinned, and clapped me on the shoulder again. "Wouldn't dream of it. Now let's go see how Danny's doing."

CHAPTER 13

We met Danny coming out of the shed. He shook his head before we could even ask anything, and pointed toward the main house as he walked past. Alek and I looked at each other. Alek shrugged, and we turned around and followed him inside. The door slammed shut behind me and Danny turned to lean against the wall.

"He's cracking," he said confidently. "Little fucker hasn't had any real training." He rubbed a hand over his two-day stubble. "I already have one particularly interesting little bit of information about him." He grinned tiredly and humorlessly. "That's Ali Mustapha, the Emir of Dubai's nephew, in there."

That presented a whole new wrinkle to this already nasty little jumblefuck. There was a lot of money in Dubai, and there were a lot of other connections throughout the Arab world. Whatever information we got from junior, he could turn into a serious problem, especially if his uncle got word that he'd been snatched. "Any idea if he's here on business, or is he just joyriding along for a little jihad over the summer?" Alek asked.

"Don't know yet," Danny admitted. "Could be either, but he sure seems to have expected it to be a walk in the park. Kid's scared shitless."

"Prestigious," Alek said, contempt dripping from every syllable. "Little punk wanted a taste; well he got it, didn't he? And now he's regretting it."

I had, if anything, even less sympathy for the kid than Alek did. If he wanted to play at "kill the infidels," he got to deal with the backlash. It still didn't take away from a problem that was starting to niggle at the back of my mind, now that I was getting over my initial reaction, and accepting that we'd have to move to hunt down the rest of the hostages. "One problem," I said. "Assuming that you can wring out everything he knows, Danny, what the fuck are we going to do with him? I'm all for shooting him and leaving him in a ditch, but that could cause even more problems. Can we disappear him to Gitmo or someplace? And if so, how?"

Danny nodded. "That's the next thing I have to do, is make a few calls to arrange for processing of this guy once I'm done with him. Right now I'm just concentrating on mission-essential information; how many hostages, where, how long, etc. He's likely to be plenty valuable on other levels as well, but we've got to get him to the people who specialize in these sorts of things. However much he knows, it's going to take a long time to squeeze him dry."

He knuckled his eyes. The guy looked exhausted. Most of us had at least managed to get a couple hours of sleep, but I realized that Danny had gone right to work on Mustapha as soon as we got back, which put him at a minimum of thirty-six hours on his feet. "How are the guys we got back doing?"

"I haven't checked on them yet," Alek admitted. "We've been a little preoccupied with the president of this little flyspeck country apparently getting assassinated."

"What?" Danny looked up abruptly. "When did this happen?"

"About an hour ago," Alek said. "I'm sorry, brother; I didn't realize you hadn't heard. Suicide truck bomb to the south side of the palace. The government's saying he's still alive, the rebels are saying he's dead, and the Ethiopians are talking a lot but not moving. Yet."

"Fuck," Danny cursed tiredly. "We already looking at a way out?"

"Out of the city, at least," Alek replied. "Depends on how, and how fast, we can get the liberated hostages out of the country and back into US hands."

"I might have some help inbound on that," Danny said. "A bulk carrier just passed through the Suez Canal about two days ago. It has a South African registry, but is owned by a front company; it's an Agency asset, one that is technically 'off the books.'" He grinned lopsidedly. "Keeps the budget-cutters from snagging it. It actually does some legitimate business, but is primarily intended to be in the vicinity of littoral operations, so that officers have some sort of seagoing transport to call on."

"Great," I responded. "And we've got two Zodiacs and an old transport plane. Not going to help us much getting twenty-odd bodies out to a ship."

Danny chuckled. "Which is why it always has an AP.1-88 hovercraft in its hold."

I stared at him blankly. I had no idea what he was talking about.

"It's a cargo/passenger air cushion vehicle," he explained. "Can carry up to 80 passengers. They should be offshore by tonight or early tomorrow. Under cover of darkness, the hovercraft will come in, pick up the hostages, and get them out to the ship, where they'll be cared for until they can be returned to the States."

"That is of course assuming that the hovercraft doesn't get shot to shit coming in," Alek pointed out. "How long is the ship going to loiter?"

"Not long," was the frustrated reply. "Langley has determined that it needs to mimic the movements of a genuine freighter as closely as possible.

102

It can be in the area, but it can't stay, like Bryan Van Husten is doing with the *Lynch*. Speaking of which, how much longer is *he* going to be able to stay put?"

Alek grimaced. "Not long. His partners are already making unhappy noises about the risk he's running, not to mention the fees that he's incurring, not getting his cargo to its destination in time."

I hadn't heard that part yet. It was sounding like what little support we had was starting to evaporate, and we were still stuck out here in the cold, figuratively speaking, with a mission that nobody else was willing to stick their necks out for.

Danny gusted a sigh. "Let's go check in with my ship, make sure they're on schedule."

I jerked a thumb at the shed. "What about Junior?"

"Heh. Let him stew for a bit."

***

The ship, the MV *Baxley*, was on schedule, and in fact the ACV would be making landfall that night. We set to getting the hostages ready to move. Danny disappeared back into the shed, to work on his "guest" a little bit more, hoping to wring the information we needed out before we had to turn him over to handlers on the *Baxley*.

I was prepping to go out with Nick, scouting for another hidey-hole. Frankly, this one was starting to put my teeth on edge; we'd been in one place too long. I wasn't the only one, either; with the common Recon/SOF background most of us shared, staying in a hide for very long got uncomfortable. Where else we were going to set up was looking a little problematic, but we were primarily looking at setting up in what was left of Lemonier. There were a few squatters who had settled in there, but for the most part, it was abandoned. We'd be leaving at nightfall.

We never got out. I had just finished double-checking my kit and weapons, and lay down on my cot, sweat-soaked as it was, when something stopped me. At first I couldn't place it; it was faint, far-off. But after a moment I nailed it, and my blood ran cold.

It was a distant rumble, made up of the roar of engines, the squeal of treads, the tramp of feet, and the thump of rotor blades. The Ethiopians were moving, coming up the main roads, aiming to secure the city. And we were still in it.

I swung my legs back off the cot and thumped my feet to the floor, accompanied by another five pairs as everybody else who was trying-- generally without success--to sleep in the stifling heat got up, grabbing for weapons and gear. Bob and Rodrigo made a beeline for Dave's clinic, to get the hostages ready to move.

"Get the fuck up!" Alek boomed unnecessarily as he came in the door. "We've got company; we've got to be ready to move, now."

Tim was already starting to break down the bare-bones comm suite he'd left up, and Hank, Larry, and I ran outside to get the vehicles prepped, dragging our kit with us. Fortunately, old habits die hard, especially in what was, for all intents and purposes, enemy territory. We'd been packed for a breakout the entire time we'd been in place. Nick and Jim were tearing maps and photos off the walls as the rest of us pounded out into the courtyard.

We were too late. As I came out into the courtyard, two BTR-60s and a Humvee, all flying Ethiopian colors from their antennas, rolled up to the compound and stopped, troops pouring out of the backs of the BTRs and deploying on the street. It was a good perimeter, but it should be, considering how much training the Ethiopians had gotten from the United States in the last ten years.

We stopped and waited, fanned out across the courtyard, facing the gate, as a Humvee rolled up to it. It was an older job, without the up-armor kit or the protected turret. Thin sheet-steel sides, and an open turret with a DShK heavy machine gun mounted on it. The gunner was turned to face us, though he kept the muzzle of the gun pointed at the sky. Four more Ethiopian soldiers came in on the flanks of the vehicle, covering the gate, though their AKM and G3 rifles remained pointed at the dirt.

The three of us faced them quietly, letting our own weapons hang from their slings, or, in Hank's case, carefully placing them on the ground. I kept my hands out to my sides. Damned if I was going to reach for the sky like a hostage.

The passenger door of the Humvee opened, and a man with a thin mustache and the shoulder boards of a senior lieutenant stepped out. A moment later the back door opened, and our bearded visitor from the clinic, who had tipped us off about Balbala, got out. He was now in uniform, his shoulder boards bearing the four stars of a captain. Together, the two men walked toward us, unarmed. That was a good sign, or at least I hoped it was.

The captain strolled up to us as though it was just another day, we weren't armed to the teeth, and there weren't soldiers with enough firepower to go through our vehicles long-ways behind him. "Good afternoon, my friends," he said, and reached his hand out to me. Slightly nonplused, I shook it. His grip was firm and strong. "How is the woman we helped your friend to heal?" he asked me. "Is she recovering well?"

"Last I heard, yes," I replied carefully. "The people we help don't always come back to tell us how they're doing after we send them home."

"That is good to hear," he said, doubtless referring to my assessment of the woman's health. "And your countrymen in Balbala? Were you able to contact them?"

"As a matter of fact we were," I replied. I was tempted to relax, if ever so slightly. The man seemed to genuinely be on our side, but if there's one thing I've learned in my time overseas, is that one is only ever on his own side. If the interests of his country matched ours at the moment, so be it. If not, then he would turn on us. He might do it regretfully, and I liked to think that this man would regret such an action, but he'd do it anyway, and in a heartbeat.

"And are they well?" he asked. His tone never changed, it remained polite and conciliatory. Yet I sensed there was an unyielding hardness in the man if crossed. I wasn't sure why he was playing this polite double-talk game, but as long as his men weren't leveling weapons, I was willing to play along. Through the corner of my eye, I could see Alek and Jim watching from the doorway. No weapons were in sight, but I knew they were there, ready to go into action in a heartbeat.

"The few that we found are, generally speaking, yes," I answered. "Some are better than others, but they will be going elsewhere soon." I could feel Hank's eyes on the back of my neck, and I could almost hear Larry thinking about how he might be able to get around on the flank before this went pear-shaped. I started praying that nobody did anything stupid. I didn't want to get gunned down in a courtyard by Ethiopians.

"I am glad to hear that," he replied, stepping closer. I resisted the urge to back up. He lowered his voice. "I am sorry, my friend, but we are here to make sure that you leave. My superiors know of your presence, thanks to me, but cannot allow you to continue your operations in the city once we have secured it."

I grunted. "You sound pretty optimistic about 'securing' the city," I said. "The locals haven't had a lot of luck in that department."

He smiled coldly. "The Djiboutian National Army is not the Ethiopian Defense Force, my friend. We will secure the city, and end the violence that is threatening the stability of all of East Africa. But you will not be here." He gestured to the BTRs outside. "These will stay here to make sure you do not get into trouble. As soon as you are ready to leave, they will escort you to your point of departure."

"And what if there are more Americans in the city?" I asked.

"Then we will find them, and make sure they are safely returned to your country," he answered. Then he stepped back, and looked around at us. "You have twenty-four hours to prepare to leave. Good day, my friends." He turned on his heel and walked back to the Humvee, the senior lieutenant following at his heels. The Humvee roared off, but the soldiers remained at the gate. Two now watched the outside, but two were still faced in, toward us.

I jerked my head at Larry and Hank, and led the way back inside. This called for some renewed planning.

***

It was not a happy conversation.

We were stuck, truth be told. None of us wanted to fight the

Ethiopians, even if we could. It was a losing proposition from the get-go, and it wasn't our mission here. We were in Djibouti to find American hostages, and if we killed a few terrorists in the process, so much the better. That was it.

As we were discussing the matter, Danny came in. "Somebody mind explaining to me why there are Ethiopian troops at our gate?" he demanded.

"Sorry, Danny," Alek apologized. "We didn't want to interrupt you, and figured you'd find out soon enough, anyway." He filled Danny in on the situation and the Ethiopian captain's ultimatum. Danny frowned, and rubbed his stubble.

"I suppose it's just as well," he said, jerking a thumb in the general direction of the shed. "Our boy cracked." He sat down heavily. The lines were getting deeper on his face, and there were dark circles under his eyes. As tired as we all were, Danny had been working at least as hard as we had been, if not more so. He took a deep breath. "They were smart. The hostages aren't in one place, or even two. They're scattered all over in groups of twenty or so. I've got the locations of two more of these groups. He also let slip the name and general location of a guy who will know where the rest are. Some gomer called Abu Sadiq."

"Who the fuck is Abu Sadiq?" Bob asked.

Danny shrugged. "No idea. Never heard of him. Could be he's a new player, could be one of the same old bad guys with a new alias. Don't know."

Jim had a thoughtful frown on his face, as he leaned on the table. "So where are the next two groups?"

Danny smiled, thinly and humorlessly. "Not here. One is in Berbera, across the border in Somaliland. The other is in Qardho, which, if you've never heard of it," he said in response to the blank looks from all of us, "is a small town in the middle of Puntland." He scratched his beard. "Abu Sadiq is a little farther away; his main bolt-hole is apparently in Kismayo." There was a chorus of curses at that. Kismayo was eight hundred miles away, as the crow flies, on the southern tip of the Islamic Emirate of Somalia. As the crow walked, it was more like fifteen hundred miles, through pirates, terrorists, and at least two shooting wars; the continuing civil war between *al-Shabaab* and the New Federal Parliament of Somalia, backed up by the African Union, and the continuing Kenyan occupation of western Somalia, against the *al-Shabaab/Hizb-ut-Islam* insurgency.

And that was assuming we were able to get out of Djibouti without the Ethiopians escorting us the wrong direction. I wouldn't put it past them to do their damnedest to keep us "out of trouble."

"Do we dare go after the hostages first, or Abu Sadiq?" Larry asked. "I'd think it would be better to get the intel first."

Alek grimaced and looked at the table. "I wish I knew the answer."

He looked around at all of us. "Opinions, gentlemen? I'm not sure there's a right way to jump, here. The bad guys probably already know we busted out the first twenty. There's bound to be a backlash, and soon. Trouble is, if we go after these two groups, we could be condemning the rest to death, while we try to find Abu Sadiq. So here's the dilemma: do we take what we can now, or try to map out the whole package, and see if we can't get some SOF support to grab as many of them at once as we can?"

One by one, each weighed in, and it was pretty unanimous. While we hated to leave those guys in enemy hands longer than absolutely necessary, it just made more sense to try to put the hits as close together as possible.

Of course, the enemy always gets a vote, too.

CHAPTER 14

True to his word, the captain showed up again the next morning, after a night of sporadic gunfire and explosions. From where we were, it didn't sound like the Ethiopians were steamrolling the city the way he'd assured us they would, but when I pointed this out, he shook his head emphatically, and insisted that it was just "mopping up." I wondered where he'd heard that particular euphemism, and if he understood what it usually turned out to mean.

The Ethiopian soldiers didn't interfere with us, but made their presence felt anyway. They had been kind enough to supply an ancient Ural 375 truck to help transport the hostages to the shore, where Danny had told them the hovercraft was landing. We had been informed that we would be getting on it, as well, so he had called ahead to have it configured to take our vehicles.

There was something close to a squad of well-armed troops lining the courtyard as we climbed onto our trucks. Two more Humvees flanked the gate, with DShKs pointed at the sky. The captain smiled and waved as we started out the gate. He had helped us with the Balbala raid, but was more than happy to see us gone.

His smile faltered when the first salvo of rockets went over, heading south.

I knew the sound of 107s. And coming in that kind of a swarm, they had to be from an actual Chinese Type 63, somewhat similar to a WWII German Nebelwerfer. It seemed like the rebels were ratcheting things up a notch.

A second and third salvo *buzzed* overhead, coming from different parts of the city, even as we heard the rolling thunder of the rockets hitting downrange. I could guess where they were aimed, and from the wide-eyed look on the captain's face, I suspect he could, too.

I was in the passenger seat of the Defender, with the window rolled down, and could just hear the captain's radio go nuts. It was in English, but I couldn't make out what was being said. I didn't need to.

"Everyone inside!" he shouted, waving at his men, and us. "Everyone get to cover!" Even as he said that, there was a fusillade of automatic weapons fire from the north. It sounded close, and several of the shots snapped by overhead.

None of us needed a lot of urging. Even as the Humvee gunners swiveled their DShKs to the north, we were bailing out of the trucks and looking for some kind of overhead cover. Unfortunately, the building didn't really qualify as such; sheet metal doesn't stop rockets all that well.

But most of us had been under indirect fire before. While the Ethiopians cringed, and a lot of them dove for the dirt, we headed for the north wall. Not much overhead cover, no, but if the rockets were at a low enough angle, the wall would cover us decently. I noticed that I wasn't the only one with rifle in hand; everybody was armed, which the Ethiopians hadn't been comfortable with, but when the metal starts meeting the meat, fuck their comfort level.

There was a pause, likely as they reloaded their tubes, and Larry, Jim, Alek, and I started pushing toward the gate, and the sound of weapons fire. We didn't say anything about it, didn't even look at each other. We just went.

However, the Ethiopian captain saw us and yelled. "No, my friends, I cannot let you go out there!"

"Fuck off," Alek growled. "You think we're just going to cower here, while the rebels overrun us?"

The captain was on his feet now, from where he had thrown himself in the dust, and was brushing off his uniform, as he kicked one of his soldiers up out of the dirt. "I am sorry, but I have very specific orders. This is not your mission any more. I cannot let you loose in the city, interfering."

He had no sooner finished speaking than there was a *bang* from the north, near the old railroad tracks, almost drowned out by the *whoosh* of a PG-7V warhead. Half a second later, the PG slammed into the side of one of the Humvees at the gate. The concussion thumped through the gate, hammering our lungs and ears, as smoke and grit blasted into the air. When the smoke cleared, the DShK was down, the gunner slumped in a bloody ruin in the turret. One of the Ethiopian soldiers was crawling out of the back door, furthest from the blast.

The shockwave had knocked the captain off his feet. I reached down, grabbed him by the shirt front, and hauled him up, sticking my face close to his. "That is what we're trying to 'interfere' with, motherfucker!" I snarled at him. "Those are your troops dead in that truck, not ours. Now you can worry about your orders, or political fallout, or whatever has your fucking panties in a twist, while more of your people get killed, or you can let us out to kill some of these assholes, and hopefully save some of your men's lives." I let him go, and he fell back down on his ass, looking up at me with that slightly bewildered look of somebody who had just gotten caught in an explosion, then had somebody yell at him while still trying to regain his equilibrium. "Your call."

He didn't have much to say, especially as AK fire started coming through the gate and smacking holes in the side of the building behind us. I left him sitting in the dust and pushed out with the others.

As we cleared the destroyed Humvee, which was starting to burn, I saw that the situation was a lot worse than I'd expected. There were at least a hundred people in the streets, and most all of them were armed. I saw AKs, FALs, and even a few G3s. There were more climbing up on the rooftops, with rifles, PKM and RPK machine guns, and RPG-7s. The ones in the front of the crowd were firing sporadically, and inaccurately, mostly from the hip or with the rifle held out at arm's length in front of them.

One ran forward, stopping in a half crouch, stuck out his rifle, and sprayed about a ten-round burst at us. I dropped to a knee, as the rest scrambled for cover, leveled my rifle, and dropped him with a pair to the chest. He collapsed in the street, his AK flying from his hands. Then all hell broke loose.

The Ethiopians were mostly huddled in the shelter of the other Humvee, or the two BTRs, and for some reason the heavy guns on the BTRs were silent. One went silent permanently as two PG rounds hit the turret. The explosions tore into the vehicle, and the remains of the turret were half knocked off the mounting ring. The volume of fire was increasing, especially as the Ethiopians kept to cover, only popping out to fire two or three rounds at a time. We spread out, got down, and started dropping gomers.

I had found my position was a little too exposed, so I moved to the corner of the non-burning Humvee, got down on one knee, and opened fire again. I shot a yelling gomer with a FAL, and, incongruously, water-wings on. The round went low, and he spun to the street, clutching his shredded guts, screaming.

"Up!" Alek yelled, over the increasing roar of small-arms fire. "Take the machine gunners and the RPGs!"

I tracked up to the roof, where an RPG gunner had just popped up, aiming at the truck I was kneeling behind. The PG-7 round looked fucking huge, even from this distance. My shot took him in high center chest, and he staggered, a dark red stain spreading across his torso, before slumping and falling off the roof. His slack body dropped onto the head of another fighter, who was half-crouched behind the corner of the building, holding his AK out and sideways as he fired at us. I don't know exactly what happened on impact, but neither man moved again.

It was one of the most intense firefights I'd ever been in. Half the time I was only barely lining up the target before firing. Gunfire rolled along our small line in a constant roar, as we gunned down rebel fighters as fast as we could squeeze the trigger, recover from the recoil, and move on to the next target. Meanwhile, the volume of return fire just kept growing. I shot another fighter, in a white shirt, shorts, and sandals, as he ran forward. His legs went out from under him as red blossomed on his shirt, and he tumbled head over heels to the street.

Then I ducked back down behind the Humvee, as a stream of RPK fire started pinging into the metal and the street right in front of me.

"Alek!" I yelled. "I'm starting to think this might not have been the best idea!"

He was hunkered down behind a stack of cinderblocks outside the long warehouse to the east. "I'm starting to agree!" he shouted back. "Fall back by twos! We're going to go firm. Jeff! See if that captain can make himself useful, and get us some supporting fires, air if he can get it! The rest of us will get the Ethiopians inside the compound!"

I nodded curtly, and dashed back through the gate, to where the captain was starting to shake off the shock and concussion and was getting his men organized on the walls.

I grabbed him by the arm, and yelled in his ear, over the noise of Jon and Chad opening fire from the gateway with our two M60E4s. "We need supporting fires, helos if you can get them!"

He shook his head. "There are no helicopters! The only ones that might have been available were hit by rockets while they were on the ground."

"Fuck!" I bellowed. "Get your people inside, and get that other BTR shooting. We're going to be overrun if we don't get some heavier fire on those assholes out there."

"Yes, yes," he shouted, and started out onto the street, where he started signaling and yelling to his troops. The still-operational BTR started moving, as the Ethiopians ran toward the gate, covered by Alek, Jim, and Larry, bolstered by Jon and Chad alternating long bursts over the top of the wall. I saw a group of at least five bad guys go down in a heap as Chad played his fire across the street. The machine guns were doing an increasingly effective job of sweeping the street clear, but that just meant they'd find another avenue of approach to come at us.

As the last of the Ethiopians scrambled through the gate, and the captain started directing them to other defensive positions around the compound, Alek punched Larry in the shoulder. Larry and Jim immediately came to their feet and dashed back inside, passing where I was leaning out into the gateway, opposite Alek. I took up firing, and yelled at him, "Alek! Turn and go!"

He was up and moving, his legs pumping, as 7.62 rounds kicked up dust around his feet. A rock rolled under his foot and he stumbled, going down to a knee. I started to dash out to help him, but he scrambled back to his feet and barely beat the hostile fire inside, as the BTR rolled in front of the gate, closing it off. The turret turned, and the 14.5mm KPVT in the turret opened up with a series of painfully loud, chunking *bangs*.

The BTR's gunner let off after about fifty rounds. The sudden drop-off of shooting seemed eerily quiet, even though we could still hear the rockets going over, and what sounded like fierce fighting elsewhere in the city. The group attacking here had apparently decided to back off for the moment. We had a breather, for a little while.

Mike's team was back on its security positions at 100 percent, now bolstered with Ethiopian soldiers. The initial shock of the attack seemed to be wearing off, and their officers and NCOs were getting a handle on things. The rest of us met with the captain in the corner of the U-shaped building. He was talking with his higher headquarters on what looked like a Russian manpack radio.

He finished, shoving the single headphone back into the canvas carrier. "The rebels waited until we were well into the town, then attacked out of the slums," he explained. "It was well-coordinated, and they are far better armed and organized than we'd expected."

"Does this sound like a homegrown Djiboutian rebellion to you?" Caleb asked.

The captain shook his head. "No, it does not. These people are horribly poor and uneducated. They couldn't have afforded all the arms and munitions without outside help, not to mention the tactics and strategy are too complex." He looked around at us. "I suspect the Eritreans are behind this."

"Maybe," Danny replied. He hadn't made his status known to the Ethiopians, and none of us were going to let them know, either. As far as the captain knew, he was just another team member. "Maybe not." He wasn't any more forthcoming. I suspected he recognized what was going on, but wasn't interested in necessarily enlightening the captain about it. Couldn't say I blamed him.

"Can we get some support?" Alek put in, changing the subject. "We do need to get these hostages out of here, and we can't do that while they're shooting us to ribbons. I'd prefer helos, but if you can get a couple more armored vehicles here, that might help."

The captain shook his head. "They did a great deal of damage with the rocket attacks. Our main Forward Operating Bases are in disarray, much damage, many fires. We have small units cut off and isolated throughout the city. Higher is trying to put together a rescue column, with tanks and BMPs, but they will probably not be ready to move until tonight, or tomorrow morning." He shrugged apologetically. "And this will likely be the last place they come to. They will be starting on the other side of the city."

Alek blew a sigh. "Fuck. All right, then, let's get a rotation set for security, and get all the ammo broken back out. I have a feeling we're going

113

to need it." He looked over at Caleb and Danny. "We've got a couple of calls to make, ourselves."

***

Alek, Larry, Jim, and I watched as Danny paced along the wall, his satellite phone held to his ear. He was not happy.

He spoke quietly and calmly, though, even while his jaw clenched angrily. We couldn't tell what was being said, but he was talking to Langley and looked pissed, so that couldn't be a good sign.

After a few more minutes of low, heated conversation, he took the phone away from his ear and killed the connection, then walked over to us.

"Washington wants to go after the two groups of hostages that we know about," he began. "They are convinced that the longer they wait, the greater the risk of losing them."

"They might not be all that wrong," Larry pointed out. "Especially after Balbala."

"Maybe, maybe not," Danny replied. "Point is, if we're going to go after Abu Sadiq, we're going to have to move fast."

I glanced back at the Ethiopians. "That may be easier said than done," I muttered.

"I wouldn't worry about them," Danny said. "They want us out of the way, the sooner the better. I'm actually more worried that Langley is now going to decide to stick their oar in, and fuck everything up a month into the op."

"Why now?" Jim asked, his face impassive. I think he suspected the answer, but wanted Danny's take.

Danny laughed humorlessly. "Because it just dawned on them how far out in the wind we are, with no ass. My report on the Balbala raid sent up some red flags, so now they're scrambling to try to catch up, while simultaneously trying to make it look to the seventh floor that they didn't completely screw the pooch from the get-go. We can expect some more support, but it might not be what we want or need."

"Who is the lead on this op, Danny?" Alek asked quietly. "You or me? Or some Fobbit paper-pusher at Langley?"

"Technically, I am," Danny replied. "Operationally, you are. I'm here to support, and to try to keep Langley from fucking too much up."

"And does Langley accept that?"

Danny grimaced. "With very poor grace, but yes. For the moment."

"Then they'll stay out of the way if I say so?"

Danny paused, as if reluctant to answer. "Well?" Alek asked, watching him closely.

Danny took a deep breath. "They'll stay clear if I tell them. I am reasonably certain of that." He rubbed his beard. "They do want us to make contact with a guy down south, in Kenyan-occupied territory. They're insisting he can be a valuable asset."

"You don't sound convinced," I pointed out.

He shook his head. "I know the guy from a few years back. He's…well, I don't think he's screwed together all that tightly, if you know what I mean. I think he's a loon, but he's got people at Langley who think he's one of the best Africa hands they've got. Not sure if that's saying something about their judgment, or the state of the Africa desk, but there you go."

Jim and I cussed, but Alek just smiled tightly as he glanced down at the ground. "And how far from Kismayo is this guy?"

"He's in Baardheere. About two hundred miles north."

"So technically, he's on the way there?"

"Technically, yes." Danny didn't look too happy at the admission.

"Fine," Alek said, his hands on his hips. "We'll try to make contact with him. But our priority is this Abu Sadiq, and finding the rest of the hostages."

"Actually," I pointed out, as some more sporadic gunfire went by overhead, "I'd say right now our priority is getting out of this compound, with all our gear, in one piece. I doubt the gomers are going to let us waltz out of here." I looked at Danny. "Do you think we can get that ACV to come in closer? Like at the shoreline about a hundred yards from here?"

"It's possible, provided I can get the pilot to come that close to the shooting," Danny replied wryly. "These guys aren't planning on being combatants; they aren't like Van Husten."

"Well, what are they getting paid for? Support, right?" Larry demanded.

"They're getting paid to transport Company cargo quietly and discreetly," Danny said. "That doesn't necessarily include coming in to a hot landing site, in their book."

The snap of bullets passing by overhead started to increase. "Well, call them up and tell them," Alek said. "I think we have the second wave to deal with." Danny nodded, and we headed for the west side of the compound, where most of the shooting seemed to be coming from.

I ducked into our clinic/team room building, and moved to a window that was high enough to see over the outer wall. The wall itself was only a couple of feet from the building on the west side, so it would be pretty easy to shoot over. I kept back from the window to keep from silhouetting myself, and peeked out.

There wasn't much to see; the gomers were generally staying out of sight, popping out to fire a few shots wildly in our direction, then ducking back down below the low wall around the school across the street. I couldn't see how many of them there were, but it wasn't enough, or they weren't coordinated enough, to put out much in the way of overwhelming fire.

As I peered out, movement on the other side of the window caught the corner of my eye, and I glanced over to see Imad doing the same, his Mk 17 cradled easily in his hands. He squinted against the glare from outside, and asked, "Do you see what I see? Right, just on the near corner of the soccer field?"

I looked, and my blood ran cold, as I saw what he was talking about immediately. "That looks like a mortar team setting up to me," I said. "That what it looks like to you?"

"Yep," he replied, bringing his rifle to his shoulder. I followed suit, and settled my crosshairs on the gomer holding the tube. Imad's rifle *boomed* a fraction of a second before mine did. My target dropped like a puppet with its strings cut, red splashing from his chest. I didn't see which one Imad had shot at, but I didn't worry about it. The guy had been a competitor at the International Sniper Competition at Fort Benning a year before he joined us. You didn't worry about Imad hitting what he aimed at.

I caught another gomer running for the dropped tube, bent over to try to get below our fire, and shot him. The shot was a little wide, and took him in the neck instead of the torso. He fell, anyway, and I went to looking for more targets.

"We need to make sure they can't get that mortar back up," Imad said, just after his rifle hammered the air in the room again.

I cracked off a snap shot at a running gomer who started toward the tube, then changed his mind. His sudden change of direction saved his life, and he dropped to the dust and out of sight as my bullet went past his head, close enough he had to feel the shockwave of its passage. "We're going to have to get the Ethiopians to push out, instead of turtling," I replied.

Imad reached for his PTT; we all had radios on now. "Coconut, Spearchucker. The gomers are setting up a mortar tube on the soccer field across the street. Hillbilly and I have them pretty well suppressed for the moment, but I'd like to get some shooters across there and take out the tube itself, before they can get to it and reposition it where we can't shoot them while they set it up."

"I'll see what we can do, but our new friends aren't too keen," Alek replied. I almost lost the last word as I snapped another shot at a head that popped over the roof, and missed by a hair.

Bullets were smacking into the wall in front of us, and a few ripped through the walls of the building itself, fortunately mostly overhead. I didn't know what the building was made of, but apparently, it wasn't all that solid. They hadn't quite figured out where the fire that was keeping their mortar out of action was coming from, but they were increasing their volume of fire to make up for it. I ducked back as a bullet smashed into the window frame, blasting dust and plaster into my face.

"What I wouldn't give for an RPG right about now," I remarked to

Imad, as he pumped three quick shots out in response.

"Hey, that's a good idea," he said. "You think any of the Ethiopians might have one?"

"Why the hell didn't I think of that?" I snarled. I wanted to smack myself in the head. I keyed my radio. "Coconut, Hillbilly."

"Hillbilly, Coconut," Alek came back. "No go on advancing, their captain doesn't want to risk it. He insists that armor is coming, and will clear the streets."

"Roger," I replied. No big surprise there. "Option Two: do any of the Ethiopians have RPGs? We can talk them on from here; hopefully they can do enough damage to put that tube out of action permanently."

"I'll check," Alek said.

A moment later, Larry came over the net. "Hillbilly, Monster. I've got an RPG gunner, and we're heading for the outer wall at the south end of the CP building. I'll let you know when we're in position and ready to fire."

"Roger, Monster," I answered. "Make sure you've got a shot at the soccer field."

"Affirm," he replied. He was breathing a little hard. Larry is a very large man. He doesn't like running around much. "Give us a minute, we might have to relocate."

A storm of AK fire hammered against our position, and Imad and I were forced to drop to the floor, getting below the top of the outer wall. The air was filled with dust and chips of concrete and plaster. "Might have to hurry that up, buddy," I called to Larry. "It's getting a mite hot here." I was able to pop up and rip off a couple shots as the fire slackened, doubtless as most of them went dry at once and had to reload. But I was answered with another ferocious fusillade that chewed away more of the window frame, and had to duck back under cover.

There was an explosive *whoosh* from off to our left, outside, and a PG round slammed into the wall across the street. It barely had time to arm, and while there was a lot of dust and splash, I wasn't sure it did much on the other side. My hunch was borne out when, a few moments later, the firing resumed, although it was a little less enthusiastic. As the dust settled, I could see the huge dark splash mark on the wall, with a hole the size of my head in the middle of it. Anybody on the other side of that wasn't happy, to say the least.

Larry's new buddy fired again, the backblast rattling the windows again. This one went over the wall, and caromed into a tree. The trunk shattered in a cloud of dust, smoke, and splinters, and the tree fell with a crash. I couldn't tell if it had taken out any of the bad guys. I hoped it had.

The gomers were getting a lot less interested in sticking their heads up, however inaccurate our friend with the RPG was, and Imad and I were able to get back to work. "Monster, Hillbilly. Can he get any closer to that tube?"

"He seems to be aiming as best he can, Hillbilly," came the reply. "I'm not sure we're going to get sniper accuracy out of this guy."

"We don't need to," I retorted. "The RPG isn't a sniper rifle, and it's two hundred yards away."

"I don't think this guy's been shot at before," Larry said. "He's not all that steady, and I'm not going to try to take the launcher away from him, either."

Yeah, that probably wouldn't be a good idea, especially surrounded by his buddies, who all were armed, and had a BTR at the gate.

With the slackening of enemy fire, Imad and I were able to start playing catch-up. Bracing rifles against the pitted, shattered window frame, we started carefully picking off anyone who stuck their head up to shoot. It actually didn't take all that long before the combination of our shooting and Larry's buddy's random RPG fire broke them. The remainder fled, only sporadically visible between the buildings and bushes of the school, leaving the mortar tube lying abandoned on the soccer field.

Of course, it was only then that the BTR's gunner decided to open up on the school, blasting huge holes in concrete and plaster with the 14.5mm slugs. I still doubt he actually hit anyone.

***

The rest of the day saw only sporadic attacks and potshots. Apparently, the rebels had decided that they didn't really want to fuck around with us. I guess we played too rough for them.

Finally, as the sun started to go down, the captain confirmed that the makeshift armored column was on its way. We started getting ready to move again.

CHAPTER 15

The column approached slowly, heralded by the growl of engines and the squeal and rattle of tank tracks. They were coming from the west, along the Avenue Gamal Abdel Nasser. More sporadic gunfire was answered by heavy machine guns. The Ethiopians got on their trucks and the one BTR still in action, having stripped the hulk of the other one once the shooting died down. Most of us mounted back up in our own trucks, but Imad, Alek, and I stayed out on the ground to talk to the captain.

"We can get the craft to come in on the beach here," Alek was explaining, pointing to a map spread on the hood of the captain's Humvee. "At least then we can get the hostages out of harm's way faster."

The captain was nodding. "Yes, yes. We will escort you there, easily. Can the craft take your vehicles?"

Imad and I traded a look. "We won't be going on the hovercraft," Alek said. "We'll be staying here with the vehicles."

The captain frowned. "I have told you, we cannot allow you to remain in Djibouti."

Alek put up a gigantic hand placatingly. "And we won't. We'll be leaving just as soon as we are assured that the hostages are safely out to sea. We are just going somewhere else."

The captain shook his head again, raising his voice over the increasing noise of the tank tracks now just outside the walls. "I am sorry, but my instructions are clear. You are to leave the country as soon as possible. Getting on the hovercraft is as soon as possible. If it will not carry your vehicles, then you will have to leave them behind."

I folded my arms in front of me and glowered. "Are you going to reimburse us for them, then? We're not in a position to put aside the loss of these kinds of assets lightly." Of course, Caleb hadn't paid all that much for any of them, relatively speaking, but the less of a paper trail we left, the better.

"Again, I am sorry, but I do not have instructions to that effect," he said stubbornly. "My instructions are to escort you out of the country, and I will do that." He jerked his head to indicate the T-62 that was heaving into view through the gate. "And you do not have the wherewithal to resist, so I

119

suggest you do not try."

Unfortunately, he had a point. We weren't in a position to argue with tanks and APCs. Which just pissed me off even more, and from the expressions on Imad's and Alek's faces, I wasn't alone. But Alek finally shrugged, and walked away, back to his truck. I guess we were going out to the ship.

With the column holding security, the first truck of Ethiopian soldiers started moving, and we were waved at to follow it. As we rolled through the gate, I was able to get a look at the armored column that had come for us.

They looked like hell. There were two T-62s, a T-72, and three BTR-60s, along with three Ural trucks. The armored vehicles looked scarred and battered, with signs of several glancing hits from explosives on their hulls. One of the BTRs was actually smoking pretty bad, choking black fumes wafting from its exhaust. Most of the soldiers watching us from the beds of the trucks were wounded, with hasty bandages peeking through torn cammies. A lot of them looked pretty shell-shocked, too, and just stared around with wide, vacant eyes.

Fortunately, the drive was short; around the corner, head south a hundred yards, turn again, and drive three hundred yards to the ocean. Danny was in Jim's truck, already on his sat phone, and I could already see the plume of spray in the dying light as the hovercraft came in toward the beach.

The tanks took the main points of the perimeter. One of the T-62s rumbled past us toward the south, its squeaking treads throwing up small rooster-tails of sand as it went by. The commander was up out of the hatch, without a helmet, his hands on the spade grips of the DShK mounted on the cupola. We stopped our trucks high on the beach, and started unloading gear from the 3-ton. Getting the boats onto the hovercraft was going to be a bitch. I just hoped there was room.

The AP.1-88 hove into view, spray jetting out from underneath its black skirts. The hull was painted a standard white and red, and from a distance, it might be mistaken for a US Coast Guard craft. It drove up onto the beach easily, the saltwater spray being briefly replaced by sand before it grounded, the fans turning just enough to keep the skirt inflated without bringing the vehicle off the ground.

By the time it stopped moving, we already had most of the gear staged within a few yards. We first escorted, or in some cases carried, the hostages on board. Danny frog-marched Ali Mustapha up the ramp and aft. Mustapha was flex-cuffed, blindfolded, and gagged. We got a few looks from the Ethiopians about that, but I didn't care, and I was pretty sure Danny didn't, either. The kid had been hobnobbing with assholes who murdered Americans and took hostages. Fuck him. Once most of the hostages and our "guest" were aboard, we started hoisting the gear aboard. Several of the hostages came back down to the beach to help. When we tried to wave them off, they insisted, so we finally let them carry some of the lighter stuff.

The boats, as expected, were the hardest part. The AP.1-88 is a passenger craft, and wasn't designed to carry a lot of cargo. It's primarily a ferry. There wasn't a hold or well deck to secure the boats and engines, so we wound up having to hoist them up onto the roof, and lash them down.

By the time we finished, it was full dark, and the Ethiopians were getting very nervous. I saw a couple pairs of ancient AN/PVS 7B night vision goggles, and the tanks had night sights, but for the most part, they had no night vision capability. They would have to rely on the tanks' searchlights, and those were vulnerable to small arms fire. They were at a disadvantage at night, and they knew it. I thought about pointing out to the captain that he could let his men know that the rebels didn't have any NVGs, either, but given how they'd just fucked our plans up, I wasn't inclined to throw them a bone. Apparently, neither was anyone else.

Of course, I realized I was assuming the rebels didn't have night vision. Certainly we hadn't seen any sign of any, but we hadn't seen any sign of the number of Type 63s they had, either.

Alek was the last man on. He stared at the Ethiopian captain, who was standing at the front of his Humvee, illuminated by the headlights, for a moment, then turned and stalked up the ramp. Two of the crew dragged the ramp back up and secured it. Then the deck started to vibrate harder, and the fans increased their turns until there was a howling scream coming from below us. I felt the whole craft wobble slightly, as the air pressure pushed the skirts up above the sand. Wind started to whip around us as the propellers mounted on the back went into reverse, pulling the vehicle off the beach.

I turned and ducked into the passenger compartment, to get out of the wind and spray. The place had been pretty well split, with the hostages forward, and the Praetorian operators aft with their gear. Most of the hostages looked quite a bit better, as the coast of Djibouti receded behind us. They were still in shorts and T-shirts; we hadn't had extra clothing for them. Fortunately, it was hot enough not to matter all that much.

It was a quiet trip. Most of us either slept, tried to, or just sat on our gear, staring out the windows at the Gulf of Aden. It was too noisy to talk much, even if we'd been inclined to. I know I wasn't.

I kept thinking of that Ethiopian captain, and wanting to punch him in the face. Sure, he'd tipped us off about Balbala, but then he'd turned right around and screwed us. Taking our trucks was going to put a serious damper on the operation, especially if we had to go inland to Baardheere. He had to know that, but didn't care. He just wanted us out of his hair. Which begged the question in my mind, why had he even helped us in the first place?

I never did find out the answer to that question.

Turning from my reverie, I looked out the port, and saw the running lights of the *Baxley* getting closer. The sea state wasn't bad; it usually was relatively calm on the Gulf, especially as compared to the nearby Indian Ocean. The *Baxley* actually looked like an island, hardly moving with the swell at all.

The hovercraft slowed as we came alongside the ship. I wondered exactly how we were going to get on; bulk carriers aren't exactly like amphibious assault ships, they don't have loading ramps or well decks like alligator navy ships do. My answer came a few moments later, as two of the ship's onboard cranes swung out over the side, extending out until the cargo hooks were directly over the hovercraft. As one, they started lowering the hooks, while crewmen scrambled up onto the roof of the hovercraft, to where what looked like attachment points had been bolted or welded, I couldn't tell which.

I watched, fascinated. There wasn't any sign that they were going to disembark us or the hostages before hooking up. Were they just going to lift the hovercraft, cargo, passengers, and all, into the hold?

A moment later my question was answered as the crew secured the hooks to their attachment points, then climbed down off the spray-slick roof. One of them lifted a small radio to his mouth, and the cables started to pull taut. Below me, I felt, and heard, the fans slow and stop. Then we were rising up, out of the water, swaying slightly with the now-noticeable motion of the ship.

The cranes lifted us more or less straight up, until we were above the level of the gunwale, then started to retract their arms, pulling the hovercraft in, over the deck. The more I watched, the more obvious it became that the cranes weren't going to be able to get us into one of the holds; they weren't built with the range of motion to get two cranes lowering cargo into a single hold. But instead, they just retracted until the craft was all the way over the edge, and then let it, and us, down gently to the deck, next to the second cargo hatch back from the bow.

We stopped moving, and one of the crew came back from the pilothouse, and announced, "We're going to unload now, gentlemen. Once we've got everybody off, we can readjust and stow the hovercraft in the hold." There was a general bustle, as we started grabbing our gear and manhandling it toward the ramp, which was now being extended to the cargo hatch next to us.

There was still some hurried organizing to do, but none of us were planning on staying aboard all that long, so we found a corner of the hold, piled our gear, sat down against it, and went to sleep.

***

I woke up with a stiff back, a serious crick in my neck, and a sore buttock from lying on the steel deck. I levered myself up to a sitting position with a groan, and several *pops* from protesting muscles and joints. I'd put my body through a lot, between eight years in Recon and Special Operations, followed by this job. You'd think I'd get enough, eventually, but for some of us, it just doesn't work that way.

I hauled my protesting carcass to my feet, looking around the dimly lit hold. The cargo hatch was closed, and dim green lights provided the only illumination. The hold was only about half full, and most of that cargo was in crates. Usually bulk carriers hauled grain, or some similar bulk cargo, that was poured into the holds and needed a bulldozer to load and unload.

Our corner was a jumble of gear, kitbags, weapons, and sleeping men. Imad was lying flat on the deck, his head barely pillowed by a jacket. Bob was on his side, his legs tucked up under him, his head on his kit, and Jim was semi-sprawled in almost a sitting position against the mound of his gear, his head lolling back, his mouth open and snoring.

My stomach growled, and I stretched before looking for the way out of the hold. I found it around the back of a shipping container, marked with a big green glowing "EXIT" sign. The hatch opened onto a ladder well, which led up to, conveniently enough, the galley.

I didn't know exactly what time it was, but the galley was pretty empty. A couple of crewmen, or guys I assumed were crewmen, were sitting at a table in the far corner, but aside from Danny sitting at a closer table hunched over his laptop, there wasn't anyone else there.

Danny looked up as I came in, and tiredly waved me over. I grabbed a couple of pastries from the open counter next to the hatch and complied.

"Dude," I said, as I sat down, taking a bite out of what I thought was supposed to be a bear claw. "Don't you ever sleep?"

He shook his head wearily. "Only when I can afford to." I started to see why the guy was going gray. He squinted at me, his eyes bloodshot. "Is Alek up?"

I shook my head. "Snoring like a sawmill."

A half-hearted hand wave. "Let him sleep. This'll keep for another couple hours. He's not going to like it any more than I do, though."

I got that sinking feeling in my gut. "Oh, hell. What now?"

He looked up at me without raising his head. "Well, when I said that we'd be getting more support from Langley, I wasn't lying. Unfortunately, that support hasn't come in the form I'd hoped." He swiveled the laptop around so I could see it.

The photo on the screen was of a jovial, bearded African, wearing a woodland camouflage jacket over a white t-shirt. He was smiling broadly at the camera, and had an AK-47 in one hand. "This is Mohamed Al-Jabarti," Danny explained.

I frowned. I'd heard that name before, though I didn't recognize the guy in the photo. Then it clicked. I snapped my fingers. "The pirate?"

He nodded, and swung the laptop back around to face him. "The same. He's become something of a 'godfather' for piracy operations out of Harardhere and Hobyo. With the upswing that Al-Shabaab has enjoyed in the last couple years, thanks to Al Masri and his ilk, a lot of the 'authorities' in the area have taken to worrying more about Islamists overrunning their fiefdoms than pirates. Gives the likes of Al-Jabarti pretty much free reign."

"So what's he got to do with us?" I asked. "They want us to nab him too, in addition to meeting your contact in Baardheere?"

"Nope." Danny leaned back in his chair and ran his hands through his hair. "They've paid him a rather sizeable sum, and we're supposed to link up with him. He's going to get us into the country, equipped with vehicles, and pointed in the right direction."

"What?!" I almost came out of my chair. "We're supposed to do business with fucking Somali pirates now? Have they forgotten just why our company was out here, within range to do their dirty work, in the first place? We came out here to fend off, and if possible, kill these bastards, and now they want us to work with them, trust them? What inbred, soft-headed fucking retard is running things at Langley?"

Danny shrugged, and put up his hands to placate me. "Not my call, brother, and believe me, I've already given them an earful about it. They won't listen, and they won't budge. They insist this guy is mercenary enough that he'll help us out for three million."

"Three million what? Dollars?" He shrugged again. "Oh, fuck me," I swore. "They really think this guy is stupid enough to think three million dollars is much money anymore? We'll get sold to Al-Shabaab as soon as we set foot on the ground."

"What's this about getting sold to Al-Shabaab?" Alek demanded from the hatchway.

Danny explained. Alek's response was loud, long, and profane. The crewmen across the galley stopped talking for a moment and looked over at us. Danny waved Alek to a seat. "It's not quite as bad as all that, gents. Don't get me wrong, it's still pretty fucked up, but we're pretty sure that Al-Jabarti isn't doing business with Shabaab. Hell, there was a major shootout between his outfit and Shabaab types in Harardhere just a month ago. Word is that he hates Shabaab with a passion."

"Maybe he hates Shabaab," Alek pointed out, "but that doesn't say he necessarily hates Al Masri and his people. Did anyone think to point out that we're still figuring out just who we're dealing with here to the big brains on the seventh floor?"

Danny leaned forward again, putting his elbows on the table. "Look, Alek, I've brought it all up. Problem is, we don't have another way to get into Somalia right now. We might be able to get ashore up here in Puntland,

124

but we frankly don't have shit in the way of assets there. Even Saracen International got kicked out down there, when the UK government went after them a year ago. We'd have to get transport, intel, everything on the fly, and probably have to throw around a lot more cash than the three mil that Al-Jabarti is supposed to be settling for."

He ducked his head as he gusted a sigh. "Look, I'm not saying we trust the fucker. That's why you guys are so heavily armed and paranoid. He's using this to gain some advantage, I know it and you know it. We just have to use him, and try not to get killed in the process."

For a minute Alek and I just looked at him. Finally Alek broke the silence, his voice a low rumble. "So this is what we've come to," he said heavily. "Trying to hire pirates to help find our people."

"Hey, we work with what we've got," Danny said. "No offense to you guys, but if I had any choice, I'd be doing this with Delta, not you. It is their job, after all. But they're 'otherwise engaged' at the moment, or so I was told." He laughed, a short, sharp bark. "Hell, it's kind of old school, when you think about it. We've used criminals of all stripes in the course of intelligence gathering over the decades."

I didn't like it. From the look on Alek's face, he didn't like it, and I knew Danny didn't like it. But it was all we had. I looked over at Alek, and caught his eye. I wondered if he was thinking the same thing I was--was it time to back out of this job? I hated to leave hostages in enemy hands, but this was increasingly looking like a suicide mission that was just going to get them killed faster.

But we weren't going to do that. For all we get characterized as soulless mercenaries, getting our kicks and hefty paychecks off of human misery, we really were still the same guys we'd been when we were in uniform. We couldn't walk away from this. It wasn't about the pay anymore. We'd find a way.

We'd find a way.

***

The dhow that floated alongside the *Baxley* was actually in pretty good shape, for what I'd seen of ships and boats in that part of the world. The paint was reasonably fresh, and the engine didn't smoke all that much. There were Somalis lining the sides, dressed in weird combinations of camouflage uniforms, web gear, and brightly colored, loose clothing, and carrying a smorgasbord of weapons, ranging from ancient bolt-action Mausers and Enfields to AKMs and FALs.

A rickety plank had been set up between the dhow and the bulk carrier that we were supposed to walk down, with our weapons and gear. The fact that we were told it was okay to carry our weapons openly was supposed to be a sign of good faith by Al-Jabarti and his people. I didn't buy it, and from the gimlet-eyed looks most of my teammates were giving the

125

pirates, I wasn't the only one.

The plank bowed significantly under each of us, and we went down one at a time, always making sure that the last guy was off before we stepped on. Even so, I wasn't convinced it was going to last through the whole team. It creaked dangerously, as if the swaying up and down from the swells wasn't enough.

I was next. I shouldered my kitbag, kept one hand on the grip of my rifle, and started down. Imad was waiting at the foot of the plank to grab my kitbag or me, depending on which was about to overbalance first. But I made it down, half tightrope walking, half running, and stumbled down onto the deck of the dhow.

I swung my kitbag off my shoulder at the last moment, and it took most of the impact. Imad grabbed me by the elbow to help steady me, and I nodded thanks, before hefting the kitbag again, and heading for our little corner of the deck.

There wasn't a place for us below deck. We had a corner of the deck aft, behind the pilothouse. I supposed it was good enough from a security point of view; they could only come at us from two directions if they wanted to. On the other hand, there was nowhere to go. We were pretty much boxed in if this went south.

I was second to last. Jim was the last guy on, and as he came around the pilothouse, I saw the plank lowered to the deck. I say lowered, but it was really more like dropped. It clattered and bounced on the deck, before being lifted by two laughing Somalis and stowed against the gunwale.

Beneath us, we felt the diesel engines rumble as they spooled up to start moving. Black smoke chugged out of the stern of the dhow, and we started to pull away from the *Baxley*.

The dhow was considerably lighter than the bulk carrier, and as we motored out into the Gulf of Aden, we soon started to feel the relatively light swell a lot more. Good thing I didn't get seasick. I knew a lot who did…and Rodrigo was looking positively green at the moment… After a few minutes, he got up, went to the stern, leaned over, and emptied his stomach into the dhow's wake. Several of us chuckled, and he flipped us the bird behind his back, still leaning out over the water.

There wasn't a lot of chatter as we bobbed across the Gulf. Most of it was because we were all paranoid as hell sitting on a pirate ship off the Somali coast. We mostly sat and watched the water, or our hosts, and kept our weapons close. Except for Rodrigo, of course, as he kept getting up to puke every hour or so.

I didn't keep my compass out, but I've got a pretty good sense of direction. We were heading pretty much due east, toward the Horn. We were on our way.

CHAPTER 16

The trip took three days. Every evening, the dhow would pull in at a beach along the Puntland coast and the pirates would get off to cook dinner. The Somalis had brought a coop of chickens and two goats on the dhow, and regularly slaughtered one or two for fresh meat in the evenings. They kept the leftovers for lunch the next day. We mostly kept to ourselves, though the pirates were friendly enough, and offered to share their food and tea at every meal. We had plenty of backpacker's meals that we were able to heat up, but usually accepted a little bit of the pirates' food, to be polite. One thing many of us had learned a long time ago was when you are in a tribal culture, accept hospitality when it's offered. It's important to them, and if you reject it, you could be insulting your host, who just might feel the need to avenge the insult with gunfire or explosives.

Mostly it wasn't bad. It tended to be spicy, and thoroughly cooked. I've got to hand it to them, they did know how to cook. Didn't make them any less a bunch of bandits whom I'd happily shoot in the head if they gave me a reason, but the food was good.

Now where we started getting a little perturbed was when we didn't turn south when we motored past the Horn. We kept going east, toward Socotra Island.

The island was technically a part of Yemen. It also was not where we wanted to go. But when Alek and Imad remonstrated with the crew, they got smiling reassurances that everything was all right, and that Mr. Al-Jabarti wanted to talk to us, face to face. Since he was on Socotra, that was where we were going.

The island loomed, mountainous and rocky, out of the Arabian Sea. Clouds had gathered on the peaks of the central mountains, and inland was obscured by hazy sheets of rain. The dhow made its way along the northern coast, giving us views of white sand beaches, looming red sandstone outcroppings, palm trees, and other, weirder plants. Imad explained that Socotra had been isolated for so long that a lot of the plant life there wasn't found anywhere else in the world.

Rodrigo expressed his lack of interest by barfing up his breakfast, while dolphins leapt alongside the dhow and chattered at him.

About five hundred meters offshore, the dhow slowed, the engine noise diminishing to a dull putter. I had been half-sitting, half-lying against my gear, and when I heard the engines slow, I looked up, to see two skiffs roaring across the waves to meet us. Up on the shore lay a town that looked almost medieval, except of course for the power lines and various trucks, cars, and SUVs. Blocky buildings ranged from white plaster to dark limestone blocks. I saw two relatively short minarets. "Anybody know what town that is?" I asked.

"Hadibu," Imad replied, from where he was sitting on his own kitbag. "I asked. It's the largest town on the island, with about nine thousand people. Apparently, our host likes to stay at a hotel just outside of town."

"Joy," I replied, levering myself to my feet. "So I suppose that this is the welcoming committee? Or should we be locking and loading right now?"

"I'm already at Condition One," Bob said. "Aren't you?"

I glared at him. "Figure of speech, dumbass." That got a petulant glare from Bob, and chuckles from Jim and Larry. Alek wasn't paying attention to any of us, instead watching over the side at the approaching small boats.

"So what are the rules for carrying weapons on Yemeni territory?" Bob asked.

Larry snorted. Jim looked over at Bob and raised his eyebrows. "We're going to visit a pirate," Larry said. "What do you think?"

"It's not like we gave a damn for Djiboutian gun laws, now is it?" Tim said.

"But this is going to be broad daylight, in a place that isn't imploding," Bob protested. "How do we know we won't get picked up by the authorities if we're packing rifles?"

"We won't take rifles," Alek said, still watching the skiffs. "They'll search us for weapons before we go in to see him, anyway. Pistols only."

"Won't they take those, if they search us?" Bob asked.

"Of course they will," Jim replied. "But I don't feel like being unarmed around a bunch of pirates any longer than necessary. Do you?"

"Not all of us are going ashore, anyway," Alek said. "The guys staying back will keep watch on the weapons and gear, while Danny, Larry, Jeff, and I talk to Al-Jabarti."

Rodrigo groaned. I'd guess he wasn't too thrilled about having to stay on the pitching dhow and be seasick some more. Still, nobody questioned the cautious approach. Nobody needed to.

***

The two skiffs pulled alongside the dhow, and our hosts threw over a couple of rope ladders, probably the same ones they used to board ships they were aiming at hijacking. No, I didn't have much in the way of charitable thoughts for these clowns, no matter how friendly they were. Three million dollars were making them friendly, not any natural inclination to be neighborly. I knew what scum suckers like these had done, both at sea and in ports in Kenya.

Alek led the way, unwilling even now to not be the first one into harm's way. It didn't matter that we were already in harm's way, even on the dhow. We were all dressed pretty much the same, in various iterations of khaki trousers and short-sleeved tan shirts. We carried our pistols openly, mostly in drop holsters, and our backups less openly. Several of these backups would doubtless be confiscated before we got near Al-Jabarti, but we were sneaky bastards, and had a few other tricks up our sleeves that they shouldn't know about.

I followed Alek, while Danny and Larry stayed topside, watching both the pirates down in the skiffs as well as the ones on the dhow. We weren't being particularly friendly, and a few acted hurt, but fuck 'em. The ladder wasn't terribly well kept up. The nylon rope rails were fraying and salt encrusted, jabbing my hands with splinters of stiff, fibrous nylon. The rungs were almost worse. I thought they were aluminum, but they were so crusted with salt and corrosion it was hard to tell. My boots wanted to slide off each rung as I put my weight on it, so I had to go down very carefully.

Alek had moved to the bow of the skiff, which was tinier than I'd imagined. We had spoken up on deck about trying to get all four of us on one, but with the three pirates on the lead skiff and the four on the other, that didn't look likely. Just one more thing to make us uncomfortable and paranoid; we were being split two-by-two, and outnumbered on all fronts. Damn, I hated this situation.

I joined Alek in the bow, sitting on a plastic jug, and trying to get as low as possible. The skiff wasn't the best quality, either, and on the waves it felt like it would be awfully easy to get tossed overboard. Alek was actually sitting on the bottom of the boat, wedged against one of the narrow board seats, still managing to have his hand near his pistol, even in that awkward position. I tried to get stable as the skiff pulled away from the dhow, and Danny and Larry climbed carefully down to the second boat. Danny clambered down more quickly and nimbly than I did, while Larry descended slowly and stiffly, reminding me of nothing so much as a bear trying to climb a ladder.

Just as soon as both Danny and Larry were in the boat, the coxswain gunned the outboard, and we started racing over the waves toward the shore. It was a bumpy ride; if the outboard had had a little bit more muscle to it, it might have been really miserable. As it was, it was just uncomfortable.

The surf was minimal, tiny one-to-two foot waves, but the boat had just enough speed on it that spray was soaking me in the bow as the coxswain drove us as hard as his sputtering outboard could go toward the beach. The beach itself was a mix of sand and rocks, with the town looming up just beyond it.

Both boats ran aground just shy of the beach itself. Apparently the slope was very shallow, going out a fair distance, which would explain why the dhow stayed out at sea, while the skiffs came to get us. Alek and I clambered overboard, splashing into ankle-deep water, and started going ashore, where two HiLuxes waited for us, surrounded by armed Arabs and Somalis. I was momentarily thankful that I had a titanium dive knife strapped to my ankle above my boot, instead of one of my better steel ones, as we waded up onto the beach. Strange, the things that go through your head sometimes.

One man, standing next to the cab of the front truck, walked forward to meet us. He was tall and thin, and while he was darker than most Arabs, he wasn't obviously Somali, either. He was dressed in what I was starting to think was a uniform in this part of the world; loose tan slacks, sandals, and a loose, untucked beige shirt. Unlike his fellows at the rear truck, he wasn't carrying a rifle, but there was an old Browning HiPower shoved in the front of his pants, with the shirt pulled up under the grip. He might have thought it was intimidating, but I just imagined him going for his gun and blowing his nuts off. Why do gang-bangers and pirates always think the same stupid shit makes them look tough?

The man walked forward to greet us, with the same polite smile on his face, holding out his hand. Alek shook it, and then he went around to the rest of us. "Welcome to Socotra," he said, in only slightly accented English. "Mr. Al-Jabarti is looking forward to meeting you, and sent me to escort you to him. My name is Ibrahim. Come with me." He waved us along, and started back toward the trucks.

We followed without comment, but kept our spacing, hands near our guns, and eyes always moving. Granted, it seemed like a pretty elaborate scheme for a trap; if they'd wanted to kill us, they could easily have done it as soon as we were on their dhow. But, as we had all been reminded so many times on deployment with the military, through spray-painted warnings on concrete Texas barriers, complacency kills.

We ignored the passenger of the second truck, who was waving for a couple of us to get in the back, and all piled into the bed of the first HiLux. The guy in the second was getting frustrated, and leaned out of the window to harangue us in Somali. I turned the glare on him, and after a moment he shut up and pulled himself back inside the cab. Alek nodded to me silently. I've been told that while I'm by no means the biggest guy on the team, that's a close race between Alek and Larry, I can be the scariest. I take that to be a compliment.

The driver of our truck slammed it into gear, and we took off from the beach, bumping and caroming off of bits of coral and rock the size of softballs. The driver was trying to take off like a bat out of hell, but it wasn't working all that well, with coral, sand, and rock spraying out from under the tires. They finally bit, and we were on our way.

It was a short drive, up a shallow, rocky incline, across the main paved road, and turning onto a dirt road that led to a limestone building with a hand-painted tin sign out front that read "Taj Socotra Hotel" in English and Arabic, with a royal crown in the background. The courtyard was walled, with an arched gate overshadowed by the stepped, blocky main buildings. It looked like effort had been made to make it look like classic Arabic architecture, with arched windows on the second floor.

Our escort pulled up beside the outer wall, and we piled out. The half-Arab looking guy, Ibrahim, waved at us to follow him again, and led the way through the gate and into the courtyard. Danny waved away an inquisitive goat that trotted up to us as we went in.

There was actual grass on the ground inside the courtyard, and it looked like the staff actually worked to keep it growing. The yard wasn't very large, with a sizeable amount of it taken up by the steps leading up to the front door. We ventured into the dark, cool shade of the lobby.

Once we were inside, it really wasn't that dark. The walls were plastered and whitewashed, the floor was tiled in shades of orange and beige, and the windows had white and blue curtains over them. It actually was rather pleasant, considering that a Somali pirate godfather was staying here. But then, I suppose even bad guys would choose pleasant places over shitholes if they could.

Our guide waved at the single receptionist, who had a stockless AK variant sitting next to his chair, and led the way up the stairs to the second floor, and stopped at the first room. There were two men outside the door, with pistols stuck in their waistbands much like his, and one of them was chewing what could only be khat. Which meant he was likely to turn aggressive and dangerous at the drop of a hat. Ibrahim turned to us and said, almost apologetically, "Please hand over all weapons, and hold your arms out at your sides." We complied, at least with our overt pistols, and at least one knife. I waited to see if they'd find my backup. The frisking was short and sloppy. They didn't find the titanium knife at my ankle, and I didn't feel like letting them know, either. A quick glance at Alek and Larry confirmed that both of them still had at least one weapon still stashed away. Knowing Larry, he probably had a .357 somewhere.

With the search complete, and all of us nominally disarmed, Ibrahim knocked on the door, and a Somali answered, with another AK slung across his chest. They spoke quietly in fast Somali for a moment, then the doorman opened the door fully, and let us in.

The room reminded me of the lobby, with the brightly painted walls

131

and light-colored drapes on the windows, which were topped by colorful half-moon designs in stained glass. There was a single bed, and several cushions on the floor, which was covered by a dark green and black patterned rug. A bookshelf against the wall held a small TV, which was presently tuned in to what I took to be Al-Jazeera. An air conditioner, set into a plywood frame, hummed on the wall above the bed.

The man sitting on the bed reminded me of a description I'd read of a Somali warlord in the south in the '90s. "A black Stonewall Jackson," had been the term, and this guy seemed to fit it. He had a high forehead, his otherwise full head of salt-and-pepper hair receding slightly at the temples. His beard was long, bushy, and full. His eyes held an easy good humor, but behind it, I could see the signs of a sharp and ruthless intellect that missed little. Which only made sense. Pirates on the Horn of Africa tended to be a pretty anarchic bunch. It would take a hard-nosed, canny son of a bitch to become a "godfather" out here.

Al-Jabarti smiled a shark smile of even white teeth, and spread his arms in greeting, though he did not get up. "Ah, our American friends are here," he said. "Welcome to my little vacation home." He motioned to the cushions on the floor. "Please, sit down. Ibrahim, can you have some tea sent up?" His English was flawless; hell, the guy spoke it better than I do. Ibrahim nodded and left, and the doorman stepped out into the hall. He kept the door open, though.

We crowded into the relatively small hotel room, and took seats on the cushions. While we waited for the tea, there was some inconsequential small talk, as is usual in Africa and South Asia. It is considered rude to get straight down to business, and even pirate godfathers are concerned with the niceties, apparently.

Ibrahim came back with a battered silver tray, five small glasses, and a silver teapot. He set the tray on the floor in the center of the room, and poured the tea, then stepped out. Al-Jabarti motioned for us to go ahead, so we each took a glass. He waited for us, then took his own and sipped it. I noticed that none of us touched any of the tea until he had drunk it, and a flicker in his eyes told me he'd noticed, as well. A quick grin momentarily dispelled any fears of an angry reaction to our lack of trust.

For a few more minutes, we sipped tea, and Al-Jabarti talked about the weather, the fishing, and how the tourism had died down in the last couple of years. It was a shame, really. It had brought plenty of money to the people of this isolated island. The fact that his activities probably had had something to do with it he blithely ignored.

Finally, Danny set his tea glass down. "Mr. Al-Jabarti," he said, "I am curious as to why you brought us here. I was assured that your fee was paid in full."

Al-Jabarti smiled as he leaned back and spread his hands

expansively. "This is not about money, my friend," he said jovially. "I wished to meet the men I am doing business with."

"Except we're not doing business," Danny said flatly. "The CIA is paying you to get us into Somalia, and equipped with ground transportation. That's it."

"That is still business, my friend," Al-Jabarti pointed out, smiling. I was getting the impression that he was enjoying the hell out of the CIA doing business with pirates. "Besides, I did not want it to be said that I let my clients go into the situation in Somalia without all the facts."

That rang some warning bells. Danny was watching Al-Jabarti very closely, and, while I'm pretty sure it wasn't abundantly obvious to the pirate, the rest of us tensed, just a little.

"What facts?" Danny asked levelly.

Al-Jabarti motioned toward the TV. "It seems that your escapades in Djibouti have not gone unnoticed."

I looked at the TV, which had been muted, and which I had been ignoring since entering the room. But now I saw that a man with his face masked by a shemaugh, who was gesturing as he spoke into the camera. I didn't read much Arabic, but I could make out "Masri" in the subtitle at the bottom of the screen. My blood went cold. I looked over at Alek, who had gone pale, or at least as pale as a Samoan could.

"What happened?" Alek asked, quietly and calmly. I doubted Al-Jabarti understood just how dangerous Alek was when he got that quiet and calm. Larry flexed his gun hand, and I already had mine resting on the knife hilt above my boot. Yes, we were being paranoid; there was no real reason to assume that whatever had happened would necessarily lead to our being attacked on Al-Jabarti's own turf, but what had been going on for the last couple of weeks was not calculated toward making us the trusting sort. If this was a double-cross, Al-Jabarti would die, it was that simple.

Al-Jabarti grew more somber, but there was still a glint of what looked like humor in his eyes as he announced, "Al Masri has executed twenty-five of his prisoners in response to your raid on his friends in Balbala."

He paused for dramatic effect, doubtless wanting to see our reaction. Larry obliged him.

"I'm going to take him apart," the big man said, grinding his teeth as he stared at the screen. "I'll kill him one piece at a time."

Al-Jabarti raised his eyebrows in some surprise, and actually smiled, then called out something to Ibrahim outside the open door in rapid-fire Arabic.

"What is it?" I demanded. Danny was staring at the TV stony-faced, and Alek was giving Al-Jabarti the gimlet-eye.

"I was telling my friend Ibrahim what your man said," he replied. "It seems that Americans understand revenge, after all. After many of your operations in our part of the world, I had begun to think that you did not."

"Never mind differing philosophies of revenge," Danny said. "How does this change our contract?"

"You have much less time than you may have thought," Al-Jabarti said. "This of course increases the risk for my people, and drives up our price. If you want to get into Somalia, with the vehicles you have asked for, we will need five million dollars, in the next twenty-four hours."

I almost got up and stabbed him in the throat right then and there. How the fuck were we supposed to get another two mil in cash in a day, out here in the middle of Bumfuck, Nowhere?

But Danny didn't move, or bat an eye. He stared down Al-Jabarti and simply said, "Let me see what I can do."

Al-Jabarti gave another of his expansive gestures, and said, "Of course, of course. Ibrahim can show you to a room where you can stay for now. I will be here for another three days, but, as I said, you need the money in one if we are to do business." He smiled again, as if this was all just friendly haggling.

Danny nodded again, and thanked him politely, then got up and ushered us out to Ibrahim. None of us spoke as the pirate's right-hand-man escorted us down the hall two more rooms and let us in to another that was functionally identical to Al-Jabarti's but with two narrow beds instead of one. Alek, Larry, and I sat down on the beds, while Danny pulled out his sat-phone from its waterproof case and started dialing a number.

"Damn it," Alek muttered. "That motherfucker." Larry sat back against the wall, the bed groaning under his weight, and stared stonily at nothing. I just watched the door and thought of horrifying and bloody ways to end Al Masri's life.

CHAPTER 17

We didn't see Danny much for the next few hours. We had our weapons back, and kept them close at hand, just in case, but none of the pirates made any threatening moves, or even tried to talk to us.

For the most part, we stayed in the rooms they had showed us to, but as night fell, and the temperature dropped, Larry, Alek, and I moved out into the courtyard. The clouds that had draped the mountains inland were spreading over the town, and a cool breeze was coming in off the ocean.

The conversation, while quiet, was not nearly as cool as the weather. We had spent most of the last couple of hours brainstorming what amounted to increasingly unlikely and violent ways of getting off the island and into Somalia. Trouble was, none of them looked like they were going to work, short of trying to hijack Al-Jabarti's entire organization. Yeah, I know. Not exactly feasible, especially given that our assets were pretty much limited at the moment to four men with about eight pistols and probably around sixteen knives.

The worst part, the part that had us all paranoid as hell and watching every doorway, corner, and window, was that if this was a complete double-cross, we were pretty well fucked. Alone, on an island that, if it wasn't completely run by the bad guys, was at least generally friendly to them, we wouldn't have a chance if they turned on us. Oh, we'd take down plenty of them in the process, but we'd go down, even so.

It was in the midst of this murmured conversation, sitting in plastic chairs around a dusty folding table, lit by a couple of naked light bulbs overhead as night descended, that Danny came back to join us. The conversation cut off, and three pairs of eyes turned to look at him.

Danny pulled up one of the blue plastic lawn chairs and sat down without a word. He propped his elbows on the table and looked around at us. "So," he began. "What did I miss?"

"Contingencies," was Alek's laconic reply. Larry and I didn't see fit to add anything more.

Danny took a deep breath. "Mind filling me in a little more? If this is going to go sideways, I'd like a little warning."

"How about you fill us in on the situation first," Alek replied.

"That's going to kind of color which contingencies we end up going with."

"I'm working on getting the money to pay Al-Jabarti," Danny replied. "It's not easy to get my hands on five million dollars on short notice, even black funds. Hell, especially black funds. The money just isn't there anymore."

"That's just fucking awesome," I put in. "Let's try to do business with a pirate, who, just for the sake of argument might be a little greedy, since he's, oh hey, a fucking *pirate*, without having either enough cash to pay him off, enough force to intimidate him, or enough dirt to blackmail him. That sounds like a *great* idea."

Danny looked around at us again, and got hard, angry stares in response. He held up his hands. "Look, guys, I'll get us into Somalia. I just need a little more time."

"We're running out of time, Danny," Larry said quietly. "And so are the guys we're trying to find."

Danny put his head in his hands. "I know, I know." He jerked back up and looked around at us, something close to despair in his eyes. "What do you guys want me to do? I haven't got a bottomless supply of cash. I haven't got the backup you guys want. I can't just wave my hand and make this all better. I'm stuck in the same shit-sandwich with the rest of you."

There was a long silence after that. We had mostly come to like Danny in the last couple of weeks, but the problems with the people he answered to were starting to spill over into our working relationship. For several minutes nobody said anything, mostly staring at the table or the bugs swarming around the light bulbs hanging precariously on the sides of the hotel.

Then Alek raised his head and looked around, catching our attention. He just said, "The Nogales job."

I traded glances with Larry. None of us had ever said much about the Nogales job. Suffice it to say that in the course of securing a client's property against a particularly vicious smuggling arm of one of the cartels, we had come into possession of a considerable sum of drug money, destined to be used for who knows what north of the border. We hadn't turned it over. For one thing, there wasn't anybody down there to turn it over to. Half of Arizona had been effectively turned over to the Cartels. Aside from Phoenix, which was an ever-shrinking island of American control, there really weren't any effective authorities south of Sedona. We hadn't even been supposed to be there; Americans were told that if they went south of the demarcation line, which of course the Cartels ignored, they were on their own. So we'd kept the money, stashed it against when we might need a large amount of liquid capital.

From the look in Alek's eye, he was figuring that that time was now.

Larry shook his head. "We'd never get it here in time."

There is still such a thing as a wire transfer," Alek pointed out. "Things are going to hell, but not that far."

"Out here?" Larry asked. "Not going to happen."

"Actually," Danny said, frowning, "there's a Yemeni bank that does still do that here. It's called the CAC Bank. Now what the hell are you guys talking about?"

Alek looked down at the table for a moment. He spoke without looking up. "There is an emergency fund that we might be able to tap. This will pretty much clean it out, but it might be possible, if we can manage to transfer the funds to this bank, and not lose most of them to bureaucratic top-skimmers along the way." He met Danny's eyes. "Don't ask where it came from, or even how it exists. Technically, it doesn't."

Danny held his gaze for a moment, then nodded. "I'm pretty good at keeping secrets," he said. "Nobody needs to know where it came from. If anyone asks, it came from one of the other black funds that they don't know about."

Alek nodded silently, got up, and went inside to call the Colonel. The rest of us followed shortly thereafter, to get ready to leave.

***

Things went surprisingly smoothly. The online fund transfer went through with only a few thousand dollars going to various fees and, let's face it, bribes, to get it past the bureaucrats and bean counters. That was a lot of money to move, and doubtless raised some eyebrows in certain governmental circles. The Colonel would be dealing with the IRS in short order, and they were getting meaner by the day. I almost pitied them.

The IRS weren't our concern at the moment. We carried over one hundred pounds of paper money into Al-Jabarti's rooms, and let him leaf through the bills. He smiled expansively, and spoke rhapsodically about how he knew we were good people he could do business with, and apologized for the necessities that led to the higher price, but assuredly we understood the costs of doing business in this part of the world, especially if he was risking making an enemy of Al Masri to do it. My ears pricked up at that part. If I heard that right, it sounded like Al Masri was not only well known in these parts, he was considered a very major player. Which still begged the question of just who the hell he was, and how did we get to him.

But, first things first. We were invited to share a meal with Al-Jabarti, and while none of us were particularly thrilled at that idea, Danny pointed out that we had to. It really was a throwback to the SOF days in Libya, cozying up to bastard warlords to get the help to try to bring down the military-Islamist regime in Tripoli, which had killed Qaddafi only to turn out to be as bad or worse. They'd been assholes, too, but we'd had to work with them, even though they turned out just making things worse in the long run.

Still, we swallowed our rancor and sat around the short table with the bearded, jolly pirate, ate his spicy food, and pretended to be friendly. They had brought the rest of the team ashore for the night, along with all the gear, so we were well prepared if they tried anything, but no treachery was forthcoming. We ate and made small talk, if rather stiff, uncomfortable small talk. Al-Jabarti apparently was fascinated by several Hollywood stars, a couple of whom I'd never even heard of, and a couple more I was surprised he'd even heard about, as I was under the impression they weren't working anymore. I was frankly bored to tears, aside from the tense professional paranoia that kept me watching both the pirate kingpin and his lackeys for any false moves.

After a couple of hours spent talking about the apparently scandalous life of some brunette actress whose name I can't remember, we finally called it a night, and thanked Al-Jabarti for his hospitality. He smiled expansively and shook all our hands before we retired to what had turned into a suite of rooms on the bottom floor, where we set security and settled down to grab a few hours' sleep before setting out again the next morning.

***

The next morning dawned cool and clear, with a slight breeze coming off the ocean. Most of us were up long before the locals, packing up what little gear we had broken out during the two days we'd been on Socotra. Of course, we had to wait three more hours for the pirates to rouse themselves to even start getting breakfast, before getting on the boats and heading out to the dhow that would take us to Hobyo.

The sun was high in the sky, the clouds were starting to gather over the inland mountains, and we'd been sitting on the beach with our backs against our gear and rifles across our knees for a while when two Toyotas finally started toward us from the hotel. Jim grumbled something about "lazy-ass gomers won't even walk that far," as we started to get up. I shoved my ball cap back on my head, as I'd had it pulled down to shield my face from the burning sun for a while.

The two SUVs came to a stop about fifty yards from the shore, and pirates started piling out, most carrying AK's, but few carrying any extra ammunition for them. Most of them ignored us and started piling onto the boats that were pulled up on the sand. We started hefting our gear to load it back up.

To my mild surprise, Ibrahim got out of the passenger seat of the white Toyota Land Cruiser that had led the way from the hotel, and walked over to us, with a small satchel over one shoulder and a wide, if phony, smile on his face. "*A salaamu aleikum*, my friends," he said cheerfully. "Are we ready to go?"

"Been ready for a couple of hours," Larry said bluntly, and Ibrahim's smile slipped just a little. Not the way in that part of the world, but we were increasingly uninterested in making friends with this pack of thugs, no matter

138

how much the CIA might want us to. Danny gave Larry a sharp glance, then looked at Alek, who made a point of not noticing the faux pas. *Fuck their niceties,* was the message, and though nobody said as much, it was equally obvious that the message had been received, loud and clear. We loaded our gear onto the skiffs and helped push them off the beach, jumping in with the lower legs of our trousers soaked with salt water.

It was a quiet trip out to the dhow. The pirates chattered amongst themselves in a weird patois of Arabic and Somali, and we kept to ourselves. Ibrahim tried to be friendly, and make small talk, especially showing interest in our kit and our guns. We weren't very forthcoming, and Danny's features were getting clouded with a combination of worry and irritation at our intransigence. I had no doubt we were going to be treated to a lecture on hearts and minds as soon as he could get us out of earshot of the pirates, but none of us cared. We'd all been there before.

As it turned out, he wouldn't get much of an opportunity to admonish us in private. Ibrahim didn't leave us alone much, in spite of the "fuck off" signals we were all putting off pretty strongly. As the dhow chugged along the north coast of Socotra and toward the open ocean between the island and the Horn, he was always there, leaning against the rail, chattering away. Couldn't tell you most of what he talked about; it seemed like the guy knew far more about American pop culture than any of us were even remotely interested in. After an hour I wanted to dump him over the side just to get him to shut up.

***

It was a long trip, and this time the pirates seemed to be on a little bit tighter schedule. There wasn't any stopping on the coast every night; we just kept sailing. This was, of course, absolute misery for Rodrigo, as he didn't even get any relief for his seasickness when the sun went down. I spoke quietly to Alek about it. We needed to make sure Rodrigo was out of the way for a little while when we did make landfall, as he'd need to recover some strength and nutrients in his body before he was much use in a fight. Right now he was just a liability.

We rounded the western tip of Socotra in the midafternoon, and were passing the rocky shores of Abdul Kori Island by the time the sun started to sink toward the western horizon. Seabirds shrieked overhead as we passed a few hundred yards from the sheer cliffs at the eastern tip of the island.

Night descended like a leaden blanket on the ocean, and before long the only light was from the lamps in the dhow's cabin and the stars overhead. The pirates had quieted, their conversations little more than murmurs as most of them bedded down below decks, and the only other sounds were the chugging of the engines, and the slap of waves against the hull. We stayed in the bow, leaning back against our gear, our kit on and weapons close at hand, at least two guys up at all times. If Ibrahim noticed our paranoia, he gave no sign, but curled up against the starboard gunwale and went to sleep.

I stood second watch, until Larry relieved me, then I lay back against my ruck and closed my eyes. It was surprisingly peaceful, even out here, surrounded by pirates, on one of the most dangerous stretches of ocean in the world. The gentle rocking of the swells and sound of the waves lulled me off to dark, dreamless sleep.

***

I woke to considerably less gentle swells, and a leaden, threatening sky. The wind was whipping in from the east and battering the dhow, as it rode the increasingly unruly waves. I felt the first stinging drops of rain, and reached for the weather cover stuffed in the top flap of my ruck. I'd been in a couple of storms at sea before, and wasn't looking forward to one on a rickety dhow. I glanced around, and saw that even Ibrahim had retired to the cabin, or below decks, while Jim, Nick, and Bob labored to strap down several weatherproof tarps over our perch in the bow. I levered myself to my feet, swaying a little to get my balance against the swells, and went to help.

The wind was picking up, hard, and snapping the corners of the tarps, threatening to yank them out of our grasp. With a fair amount of struggling, stumbling, and swearing, though, and increasingly soaked to the bone by stinging, wind-driven rain, we got them tied down over our gear at least. Most of us couldn't fit underneath, at least not with enough room to breathe, but we took what shelter we could in the lee of the cabin and hunkered down. Rodrigo looked positively corpse-pale, which was a good trick for a brown guy.

We huddled against the stinging rain and wind, braced against the increasingly violent swells, for a good four hours. At least that was what my watch said. It felt like a whole hell of a lot longer than that. Through the soaked, freezing misery of it all, I couldn't help but still think that we were behind schedule, and likely failing the poor bastards in enemy hands, the longer we stayed out at sea.

Of course, once we got ashore, that was only the beginning, but I had no idea at the time just how pear-shaped things could get.

***

Five days. Five fucking days of wet, cold, rocking misery, covering a distance that should have only taken two. That storm was only the first. Two more came rolling in on its heels, slamming into us from the Indian Ocean and tossing the dhow around like a wood chip on a pond in a thunderstorm. Part of the reason it took us so long to get where we were going was that the crew stayed out of the weather as much as they could, and got us swept off course by almost one hundred nautical miles.

We were so soaked to the skin that most of us had pretty much given up on ever being dry again. After the first squall passed, we'd pretty much taken to just leaving our rifles and M60s in waterproof weapons bags, and our pistols were so slathered with silicone to keep the water off that if it weren't for the downright aggressive checkering set into the grips, we'd never have been able to keep hold of them.

The skies had pretty much cleared as we hove into sight of Hobyo, which slowly rose above the dusty horizon to the southwest, a low-lying collection of concrete buildings, swathed in low trees, crowned by a square, white tower. There were still clouds scudding across the sky from the east, and as I craned my neck to look past the cabin, I could see what looked like another squall line starting to form out to sea.

Rodrigo was in bad shape. He'd been so seasick that he could barely take any food or water, and he was weak, dehydrated, and borderline hyponatremic. He was dry heaving more than puking at that point, for lack of anything to bring up, and when he did bring something up, it was more often than not dark green bile. We'd have to carry him ashore, and he wouldn't be good for much until we could get some food and fluids in him. Figure a couple of days, at least. Which was bad, as those days were going to be spent in bad-guy country.

Nobody said much as the skiffs started to come out to us from the white sand beach, rocking as they crested the gentle breakers and motored out toward the dhow. Ibrahim was back with us, smiling and trying to make small talk, but he was generally rebuffed with monosyllables or inanities like, "Yeah, sure, great." His smile slipped again, and he looked put out, saying something about bad manners. I couldn't make it out, as I was trying to help Rodrigo up, along with Nick, who was on his other side.

None of us had time for Ibrahim, especially as we were levering our gear over the side and into the skiffs below, hopefully without dropping them in the drink. Imad and Bob were down in the skiff, catching kitbags and rucks with their rifles slung across their backs. Jim and Larry had already crossed over to the second, and were helping spread-load the gear.

It took a relatively short time to get down into the skiffs, even with having to essentially lower Rodrigo down. He tried, hard, to get down by himself, but he was so weak from being that sick for five days that he was unsteady, and his grip on the rope ladder wasn't strong enough to trust. Over his protests, I tied a sling rope around his chest and helped lower him to the skiff.

Danny and I were the last ones off the dhow. The crew was gathered near the rail, watching us, but not saying much. I didn't like the looks we were getting. They made my back itch. Or maybe that was just the five days of being wet.

I clambered down the salt-encrusted rope ladder, my rifle swinging slightly across my back, and squeezed into a spot on the crowded, low-in-the-water skiff, between Bob, Imad, and a pile of rucksacks. The Somali at the tiller wasn't talking, and wasn't even looking at us much. Imad leaned over to me, and over the noise of the outboard and the swish of the water against the hull, he stage-whispered, "I've got a bad feeling about this, man."

"Me, too," I replied, glancing at the coxswain. "Danny can repeat what the Agency says all he wants. I don't think it was a very good idea to trust these assholes. Especially now that they've got our money."

Imad nodded. "Head on a swivel?"

"Hand on a gun," I replied, and tried to lean back against one of the rucks.

It was a short run to shore. The coxswains took the skiffs all the way in, beaching them in water ankle deep. There were a ragged assortment of Bongo trucks, Toyota Land Cruisers, and HiLuxes arrayed on the beach, along with what looked like entirely too many young men wearing loose clothing and shemaughs and carrying weapons. AK-47s, FALs, PKMs, RPGs, and even a couple of FN MAGs could be seen. There was a lot of firepower on that beach. I flexed my hand around the pistol grip of my rifle, and saw the rest of the team start doing similar things, checking mags were seated, quick, surreptitious brass checks. This didn't look like a welcoming committee so much as it did an ambush.

Granted, I am a bit paranoid. I came by that paranoia honestly, though, and so did the rest of us. We got off the skiffs and started pulling our gear out, as the pack of Somalis started down the beach toward us.

I glanced around at my compatriots. Everyone was calm. Nobody was obviously ready for a fight. At first glance, the untrained eye would only have seen eleven men unloading piles of gear from two boats and carrying it onshore. Innocuous, unremarkable, and non-threatening.

But there was a tension, a coiled-spring alertness, to everyone's movements. No one picked up more gear than they could drop easily to get at a gun. Eyes, while never settling for long, never really left the Somalis.

Ibrahim walked up to meet the heavily armed group of Somalis, and started jabbering quickly to the man in the lead, a tall, rangy type with a round face and aviator glasses on. The man handed him an FN HiPower.

One thing this particular band of skinnies wasn't very good at was concealing their intentions. They started telegraphing their envelopment before they'd even started moving, and that was a bad idea.

A split second after the first gun had started to come up, we were all up, facing outboard, guns up and covering them. The look of shock that they all, to a man, had on their faces was fucking priceless.

Imad barked at them in Somali. At first they balked, though none of them was stupid enough to try to bring his gun up while being covered by eleven battle rifles. I was keeping my muzzle pointed at one of the MAG gunners. Those machine guns could do a lot of damage if they didn't go down first, and there really wasn't any cover here. If any of them so much as twitched, I was drilling them first. I could see by the look in the guy's eyes that he understood that, and didn't want to die.

The tall guy in the lead was pissed. He snapped something at Imad, who replied shortly. I kept watching my chosen machinegunner, who was getting more scared by the second. I was suddenly tempted to grin at him, just to see what his reaction would be. Funny, the thoughts that go through your head in such situations. One wrong twitch and this beach could turn into a bloodbath, and I was getting tempted to mess with one of the bad guys' heads.

Imad took a step forward, menacingly raising his weapon for emphasis. It looked kind of like skinny posturing, but I knew Imad well enough to know that he had just shifted his point of aim from the tall guy's chest to his head. A glance at the tall guy confirmed that, mirrored shades or no, he had seen that as well. He spat something angrily in Somali, and, holding out his hands, bent to put his AKS-74U in the sand.

One by one, the others followed suit. Alek stepped up beside Imad. "On the ground," he snarled. Imad translated, jerking his weapon for emphasis. Slowly, glowering at us, the tall guy waved at his compatriots, and took a step back, away from his weapon. The rest did the same, with varying levels of alacrity. Then, one or two at a time, they got down on their stomachs in the sand. Ibrahim and the tall guy were the last to comply.

Alek jerked his head, and Tim, Larry, and Hank moved forward, digging in their gear to come out with zip ties to use as hasty handcuffs. They weren't gentle. Hands were jerked behind the pirates' backs and hastily though thoroughly cuffed with single zip ties. Some of them winced, and a couple of them actually cried out as Hank yanked the ties tight, but the tall guy stayed impassive, staring at Imad with what I expected was supposed to be a wordless promise of bloody retribution to come.

Bob, Nick, and Jim hurried to the trucks behind our captives, and began checking them out, while Alek and I covered the pirates and Rodrigo and Danny started collecting the weapons that were now strewn on the beach.

There was a scuffle by the trucks, and I glanced up to see Nick choke-slam a pirate against the hood of a HiLux. The kid's weapon clattered to the ground, and Nick tossed him in the sand on the other side of the truck, then stepped over to put a boot in his back. Another quick zip-tie, and the last pirate was trussed and out of trouble. For the moment, at least.

Danny and Rodrigo were now festooned with slung weapons, and were trudging over to the trucks to deposit them in the backs, assisted by Tim, Larry, and Hank, who were now free to help. Imad, Alek and I advanced on the bound pirates, and Alek dug his boot toe under Ibrahim's chin.

"Don't think we'll forget this," he said, glowering down at Ibrahim, who was squinting up at him, his neck bent at what had to be a painful angle. "If I had more time, I'd make you and your boss pay now. But I haven't got the time, and I'm not in the habit of shooting people with their hands tied behind their backs. So just make sure it sinks into that thick skull of yours, and tell all your buddies, too--" He crouched down to get closer to the pirate, and grabbed him by the beard, twisting his head up further to make solid eye contact. "--We'll see that this kind of backstab doesn't go unpunished. Rest assured. But before that, make sure nobody follows us, because if we see dust behind us, we're likely to make life very short for anybody making it. I don't give a fuck if they're just watching. We'll kill them anyway. And when we're done with our business down south, we will come back here and kill every single living thing in this town. Clear?" Using the man's beard as a lever, he forced Ibrahim to nod his understanding, then dropped his head in the sand and stepped over him.

Keeping an eye on the pirates, we moved to the vehicles. Nick had grabbed a HiLux with a PKM mounted in the bed, while Bob and Jim had each snagged a Land Cruiser. The Bongo wouldn't have done all that well cross-country, so I was glad nobody had decided to try to take one of those. Alek waved everyone in next to Nick's HiLux.

"All right, change of plans," he said, as half of us listened while facing outboard, particularly facing the town. There was an increasing amount of movement over there, and I could make out more than a few faces turned our way, watching curiously. We were still over four hundred meters away, and there had not been any shots, so they probably couldn't tell what was going on over here on the beach, but it was only a matter of time before some of the pirates' buddies figured out something wasn't right and came to investigate. Knowing Hobyo's reputation as a pirate town, I had no doubt that if that happened, about half the population of the town would be coming at us. Maybe not quite as bad as Black Hawk Down, but pretty fucking close, and we were out here in the open with no cover. It was not a comfortable-making situation.

"Nick, how much fuel have we got?" Alek asked, pausing in his rundown of the change of plans.

"The trucks are all around three-quarters, and we've got about four five-gallon jerry cans in the back of the Land Cruisers," was the reply. "It'll get us a ways away from here."

Alek grimaced. "Not far enough, but we'll have to chance it." He looked over at Danny. "Where can we find fuel around here?"

The spook scratched his beard. "There aren't exactly Shell stations on what passes for roadways here. We'd have to find somebody with a fuel truck, or a working gas station, and those are pretty few, from the briefings I've gotten. Especially in the last couple of years. Harardhere will almost certainly have fuel, but it's crawling with pirates, and Al-Jabarti will probably have agents there, if not a cell of his own. The guy's got his fingers everywhere in the area."

144

"Can we make it to Harardhere on the gas we've got?" Alek asked Nick.

The Texan was studying the map. "Should be able to. Looks like about seventy-five, eighty miles. Some rough country along the way, but no reason we can't make it, unless one of the trucks catches a bullet in the gas tank."

"Uh, Alek?" Larry said. "We might want to get moving, and finish this planning session on the move." He nodded toward the town. "We're getting a bit more attention than I like." He wasn't kidding. There was a crowd gathering on the south end of town.

Alek looked up, squinting slightly. "Right. Everybody mount up, and have your comms live. We'll finish this Oscar Mike."

We scrambled into the vehicles, and Nick gunned the HiLux's engine even as Bob grabbed on to the grips of the PKM to keep from getting thrown out of the bed. Sand blew up from three sets of tires in rooster tails as we fishtailed into motion.

Behind us, Hobyo exploded into activity as the pirates figured out what was happening.

CHAPTER 18

Our three vehicles bumped and rattled onto the hard-packed track that passed for a road out of Hobyo, heading southwest along the coast. Nick led the way in the white-and-rust-colored HiLux, while the two brown Land Cruisers followed in trace. This might not have been the best decision tactically, as the HiLux was the only truck with a mounted machine gun, but in our Land Cruiser in the rear, Jim pulled one of the two M60E4s out of its case strapped to a kitbag, and broke out the back window. We now had a rear gunner.

And it looked like we were going to need it. In defiance of Alek's warning to Ibrahim, dust was rising in great plumes over the outskirts of the town, as a veritable mob of trucks and SUVs came roaring out after us. Already, a few of the more enthusiastic gunners were firing away, their muzzle flashes blazing in the dust, even though they didn't have a hope in hell of hitting us from that distance and on the move.

Jim, wisely, held his fire. We'd likely need every round. Wasting ammo wasn't our way, anyway.

Nick was pushing hard, and the SUVs were struggling to keep up with the HiLux. The cloud of dust we were putting up was fast getting thick enough to act as a smokescreen. Trouble was, it also pointed out where we were as effectively as a big neon arrow in the sky pointing to us. Not that there was really anywhere to hide. The Somali coast is flat and dusty, with little more than knee-high scrub. The acacia groves that had grown in Djibouti were nowhere to be seen.

Fighting the wild bouncing of the Land Cruiser, I clambered over the back seat and onto the pile of rucks in the rear, trying not to bounce into Jim too much, or hit him with my rifle. There was too much dust to see much through the scope, and we were moving too violently for anything resembling a good shot, but having another gun facing our pursuers might be a good idea.

Alek was talking over the radio, but I couldn't hear him. Turned out that my earpiece had fallen out, so I hurriedly stuffed it back in, managing to punch myself in the ear a couple times in the process, as well as bouncing off the Land Cruiser's roof and possibly bruising my tailbone on Larry's ruck frame. "...lose these guys," Alek was saying. "If we can't do it by ten klicks from Harardhere, we're going to have to turn and fight."

Struggling to hold down the 60 with one hand, Jim keyed his radio. "Boss, if we try to stop these guys cold, they'll chew us to pieces." He squinted through the dust, which was billowing into the vehicle through the broken rear window. "I can see at least ten technicals; figure about eight to ten guys in each. I say we brake-check these mothers and see if we can chew 'em up a little at a time."

"Good call," Alek came back. "Vic One, Vic Two, spread out and fall back to come on-line with Vic Three."

No sooner had the transmission ended than I could see, through the shifting clouds of brown to our flanks, the other two trucks veer off to come alongside us. I looked over just in time to see the back window of the other Land Cruiser break, and two muzzles poke out of the dark cavern of the back. Bob was braced in the back of the HiLux, crouched behind the PKM. I turned my attention to the rear, as Alek called over the radio, "Brake-check in ten seconds. Be advised, we're going to be moving again about ten seconds after that, so make it count. Five...four...three..."

I braced my back against the back of the seat in front of me, and leveled my rifle. Beside me, I could feel more than see Jim do the same. Then, suddenly, Tim mashed the brake, and we were shoved hard against the seat back, then lurched toward the open window as the vehicle came to a skidding stop in a billowing cloud of grit.

I recovered fast, bringing my eye to the scope, even as Jim opened up, the heavy, rapid *thumpthumpthump* of the M60 filling the back of the SUV with cordite and hot brass. I could see silhouettes, but little more through the dust, but that was all that I needed. I milked the trigger, slamming a 7.62 round into a gomer briefly visible as a darker shape in the brown before he dropped like a puppet with its strings cut. I tracked across the jumbled line of enemy vehicles, which were veering and skidding to a panicked halt, as the combined storm of fire from Jim's M60 and Bob's PKM shredded the lead vehicle, an old deuce-and-a-half with a DShK mounted on the cab. Targets appeared as fleeting, man-shaped shadows in the haze and confusion, and I probably missed at least as often as I hit, but I saw enough go down, hurt or dead, to be effective.

A moment later the tires were spinning, throwing up billows of sand and dust between us and our targets, and we were shoved back toward the rear door again as Tim stomped on the accelerator and started us moving again. A massive dust cloud rose behind our three vehicles, completely obscuring us from the enemy's sight, as well as hiding whatever devastation we had wreaked on our pursuers.

"ACE reports!" Alek snapped over the radio. "Everybody all right?"

I rocked the mag out of my M1A, checked it, and shoved it in my dump pouch with some difficulty, as I was half-sitting on the pouch. As I rocked in a fresh one, I called up, "Hillbilly, used eighteen rounds, up and up."

Jim had checked his M60's box. "Kemosabe, one hundred fifty rounds expended, up and up."

One by one, each member of the team checked in, giving their ammo expenditures and affirming that they were unhurt. A couple of 7.62 rounds had impacted the HiLux's bed, as Bob rather shakily reported. It sounded like one or two had come uncomfortably close to him.

As we got further away, and the initial dust cloud started to disperse, we saw that there were still pirate trucks on our tail, but they had been thinned out considerably. I found myself wishing for mines.

Once all the ACE, or Ammo, Casualty, Equipment reports were in, Alek came back on the net. "Listen up. It looks like we thinned the herd some, but we need to break contact with these mothers. Five hundred meters, we brake-check again. If that doesn't sufficiently discourage them, then we bombshell. Right seaters, get ready to copy the rally point."

I was keeping an eye out for more bad guys, but I could hear Rodrigo up front call out, "Ready to copy," which was chorused by Hank in the other Land Cruiser.

"Coordinates are--" Alek spooled off the numbers. "The rally point is south of Harardhere. I don't want to make a straight line in there, in case these punks have called ahead. Upon reaching the rally point, if none of the other trucks are there, attempt to get comm, and hold position for no more than six hours. If there is no contact after six hours, move to the secondary rally point." He rattled off another string of coordinates. "If you cannot reach the rally point, attempt to get comm, and, if necessary, move on foot to the secondary rally point."

I glanced over at Jim. If it hadn't been obvious just how far out in the cold we were on this job before, it sure was now. We were making plans that in the old days, working for Uncle Sam, would have ended in escaping and evading for friendly lines. Here, there wasn't any such thing as friendly lines. Bad-guy country was everywhere.

Just as I was thinking that, Danny broke in on the circuit. "If you can't link up with the rest of the team, find a way to make it to Gaalkacyo. It's the capital of Galmudug, and it's big enough you should be able to lose yourselves long enough to arrange a flight out. Just make sure you ditch your long guns before you go in. The security forces might get a little twitchy."

Alek agreed. "You can still get a flight to Kenya out of Gaalkacyo. If you get cut off, get the fuck out." I hoped and prayed that nobody got cut off. We couldn't really afford to lose a third of the team at this juncture.

We were coming up on five hundred meters. Easy to do, when

you're tear-assing across the desert at forty klicks an hour. Which isn't all that fast on the road, but offroad, it's pretty fast.

It was a repeat of the previous engagement. Alek counted down, the drivers stomped on the brakes, and we lit up our pursuers. This time, they were a little more ready for it, and the return fire was getting pretty thick, especially since they slowed down when we did, so as not to pile into a big jumblefuck when we suddenly stopped.

It didn't do them a lot of good, though. As a rule, Middle Eastern and East African troops don't do much aiming, apparently going by the principle that Allah will make the bullets hit. This tends to mean that they quite literally "spray and pray," most of their fire going high, and sailing off to Lord knows where, and probably killing some hapless sheepherder a mile away. We didn't work like that.

In spite of our less-than-optimal shooting positions, sitting braced between back seat and back door, on an uneven jumble of rucksacks and gear, Jim and I made the best of it. Jim held the 60 tight into his shoulder with the broom handle foregrip, and stitched tight, thumping bursts into the enemy trucks. I propped a knee up on a ruck, and rested my elbow on it, to get a little bit more stability. The 8x magnification on the scope still made things bounce a little, but it was easy enough to get on target, at least as far as it went. The dust and grit was still obscuring everything, and a lot of the finer dust was settling on my scope lenses, in spite of the shock of the rifle's firing.

Bob was laying it on, hammering at the HiLux in the lead. Even through the clouds of dust and flying sand, I could see the puffs of dust, shrapnel, and smoke coming off the truck as it was peppered with a heavy stream of 7.62 fire. Jim was alternating between that truck and an ancient Land Rover, which now had a smoking engine compartment and shattered windshield.

A couple of savage *crack*s announced a pair of hits on our vehicle. I glanced up to see the bullet furrows in the roof, and quickly got back on scope to try to find the shooter. Turned out there was a pirate with a SVD crouched in the scrub about twenty meters away from the trucks, taking potshots at us. I pumped three rounds at him, and he vanished into the shrubbery. Then we were moving again, and I couldn't see anymore.

Again, the ACE reports went up. Larry had gotten grazed this time, but it was nothing more than a burn. I was starting to worry about our ammo stores. We were in enemy territory, without the kind of support we might have gotten as a SOF asset. We had extra ammo in our kitbags, but we couldn't afford too many of the kind of pitched fights that had been all too characteristic of this job.

"Anyone see any further pursuit?" Alek called. I squinted through the brown fug behind us. My eyes were starting to grate in their sockets from the dust.

After a few moments of searching, I keyed my radio. "This is Hillbilly. I don't see any sign. Looks like they're still stopped where we hit them."

"Roger," Alek replied. "We'll go another five klicks, and then turn inland, provided there's no further sign of pursuit or observation. I don't want to be making straight lines out here." I couldn't agree more.

It was a quiet five kilometers, except for the banging of the SUVs and everything in them as we bounced across the barren landscape. The dust was filling everything, and I coughed as it coated my throat. I kept squinting against the sandpapery feeling in my eyes, trying to see if our little friends were still up to their mischief. But the hazy horizon stayed clear.

Finally, we slowed and started to turn west. The East African savannah stretched flat, dry, and featureless in front of us. This was going to be navigation by time, azimuth, and speed; there weren't any landmarks to follow.

There also wasn't any place to hide for a long, long way. Which worked against us as much as it did for us.

We hadn't been on our new course for very long before Jim prodded my elbow. When I looked over at him, he pointed. I peered along his pointing finger and saw the distant plume of dust to our southeast. I lifted my M1A to look through the scope, but we were moving too much, and I couldn't focus on the dust cloud. I called up to Alek anyway.

"We've got a dust cloud, looks like vehicles moving north/northeast from the vicinity of Harardhere. Might be our little pals' buddies."

"Any sign they've made us?" Alek asked.

"Not yet…" I stopped. The dust cloud had changed, as if it was aimed in our direction now. "Could be. Looks like they've turned inland."

There was a pause, doubtless filled with Alek's cussing up a storm in the cab of the HiLux. "Push it harder, gents," he finally radioed. "Let's try to open up the gap, and keep it open."

"Gonna be tough, trying to keep the gap wide enough until nightfall," Jim radioed from beside me. "We'll be out of gas long before then."

There was another pause, and then Alek came back over the net, his voice firm. "Plan B, then. Bombshell in five. We'll see you guys at the RV point."

"Bombshelling" is an old anti-tracking technique, where if the quarry is a group, they scatter in all directions. The idea is, the tracker can't follow all of them, and will more likely lose the spoor when it is from one individual, and not going in a particular direction. How well it would work with vehicles on the open savannah, we couldn't tell, but it was a better chance than just trying to outrun whoever was back there on severely limited fuel.

"Coconut, Hillbilly," I called. "I'd suggest we hold off until we've got some cover. They see us split at a distance, and they're probably going to just split up to go after us. Let's find a wadi or something where we can get out of line of sight, then split."

"I hear you, Hillbilly," Alek came back, "but there isn't jack out here. At least not enough to disguise our dust."

"If we can't get something between us and them," I argued, "we should stick together. More guns means more chances of staying intact. I don't feel like getting run down and slaughtered piecemeal."

"I'm going to throw in with Hillbilly, boss." It was Hank's gravelly voice. "If we had a break in contact, then fine, but I don't think it'll work this way."

There was a pause as we continued to bounce brutally across the plain, the dust of our pursuers rising into the brassy morning sky behind us. I imagined that Alek was poring over the maps and imagery he would have had spread across his lap, trying to find a solution.

The fact was, we needed fuel. I didn't know where there was gas to be had out here, but from what little I knew about central Somalia, there probably wasn't much outside of certain population centers, and most of those, at least close to the coast, were dominated by pirates. Of the others, we couldn't be certain which ones were "friendly," by which I mean wouldn't shoot us on sight, and which ones were in the hands of Al-Shabaab or one of the other Islamist militias. We had a long way to go, and going on foot wasn't in the cards. We didn't have the time.

I kept squinting into the rising sun to try to see our tails a little better. After a moment, in spite of the jouncing, I made out a crucial detail. "Coconut, Hillbilly. Be advised, it looks like our pursuer is just an outrider. I say again, the main body appears to still be heading toward Hobyo."

"How many outriders, Hillbilly?" Alek came back quickly.

I squinted some more. The dust was coating my Oakleys, making it even harder to see through the haze and glare, but after a moment I called back, "Looks like two trucks, Coconut."

"Are they continuing to pursue?"

I was about to say yes, when I noticed the dust seem to dwindle, then change direction. "Negative, negative," I called back, breathing a sigh of relief. "They are turning back and rejoining the rest of their convoy."

"Bet their homies told them that the bad guys who hit them were way more than just three trucks worth," Tim cracked. "I mean, they couldn't admit that they got shot to shit by only eleven guys."

"Good point," Alek conceded, "but not one I'm willing to bet the farm on. Keep an eye on 'em, and let's start figuring out where the hell we're going to get some gas. I think Harardhere is probably out. More than likely, the bad guys called ahead, and they'll be waiting for us."

"Nearest town is Balli Gubat," Imad announced. "Don't know much about it, but there was something in the briefings we got from Danny that the Galmudug military had an outpost in or near it these days, to threaten the pirates."

"What do we know about the Galmudug military?" Larry asked.

"Their leadership is mostly what's left of Aidid's boys from the '90s and early '00s," Danny replied. "They've got a reputation for being ruthless, hard as woodpecker lips, and some of the most efficient, experienced, and well-trained soldiers in Somalia. The only thing that's really kept them from overrunning the operations in Hobyo and Harardhere is their logistical and money shortfalls."

"Aidid?" Imad asked. "Is it really a good idea to risk tangling with them?"

"Well…" Danny sounded a little hesitant. "I'm reasonably sure they won't shoot us on sight, which is more than can be said for the people behind us. If we can manage to convince them that we're here to put the hurt on Al-Shabaab and Al Masri's merry motherfuckers, I'm hopeful that they'll at least sell us some gas."

"'Hopeful?' I'm not all that comfortable with 'hopeful,' Danny," Jim replied.

"Everybody pipe down for a minute," Alek called shortly, and the net went quiet.

For rather more than a minute, we bounced across the desert in relative silence. I watched the dust cloud to our east, but it didn't come any closer, as the sun climbed in the sky. Finally, Alek made his decision. "We get close to Balli Gubat, and lay low until sundown. Then we'll send Imad in, with four of us close by as backup. If we have to, we steal the gas and get out. If we can, we'll see what supplies we can buy from the Galmudug troops, and hopefully some kind of safe passage, at least through the region itself."

It wasn't perfect, but it was a plan.

CHAPTER 19

Larry, Hank, Bob, and I scrambled forward through the scrub, bent half over, our NVGs lowered in front of our FAST helmets, before spreading out and going to ground, crouching in the low, prickly brush deep enough that we would be lost in it to an observer from the town, without obscuring our own view.

In my head, I was cussing. It had been a pretty hellish five-klick movement from the shallow wadi where we had done what we could to conceal the vehicles. The oppressive heat hadn't lifted much once the sun went down, so we were all sweating profusely under our kit, which had included about three liters of water per man. The ground had been soft and sandy most of the way, which makes it twice as hard to walk as over firm ground. Add to that the vicious, thorny tangle of the brush out in the desert, and we were all about as miserable as we could get. I was reasonably sure I was bleeding in several places under my trousers, but with all the sweat, it was hard to tell.

Focus. On task. I swept my gaze across what I could see of the tiny town of Balli Gubat, the darkness turned to shades of green. Directly ahead I could see a large enclosure made of shrubs just like many of the livestock enclosures that we had been seeing all over the place out here, only this one was considerably taller and thicker. From the imagery, there were a handful of these thicker, taller enclosures in the town, all apparently around wells. For obvious reasons, water was the primary concern of the people who lived here.

Imad was already at the enclosure, and starting past it. I could see down the track that served as a main road through Balli Gubat, which also ran past the same large enclosure, heading straight to the town square/well area. It was there that the Galmudug soldiers had set up, and I could see a couple of them gathered around a fire barrel. I couldn't see a lot of detail with the NVGs, since it showed mostly their heat signature, but it looked like they were wearing cammies and some sort of chest rigs. One had an AK variant slung, while the other looked to be unarmed, until I caught sight of the PKM leaning against another barrel.

I flicked on the IR laser on the PEQ-15 affixed to my rifle, laid it on the AK-carrier, and waited for Imad's move.

Imad was going old-school, without night vision. While he was still dressed in our pseudo-field uniform of baggy cargo trousers, T-shirt, and hiking boots, as opposed to much of any local attire, he wasn't fully tac-ed out, and only had his Kimber holstered high on his hip, under the trailing edge of his shirt. He'd look pretty non-threatening at first glance.

He paused just inside the shadow of the enclosure, back where the two paramilitaries couldn't see him in the glow of the fires, and called out in Somali. It apparently was a hell of a shock to hear a voice calling out from the darkness, especially as it looked, from a cursory sweep of the surrounding buildings and enclosures, like they had the town under a curfew. The one with the AK started, and got tangled in his sling trying to bring his AK around. I put my laser on his chest, my forward elbow braced against my knee, and waited. The other one was reaching for his PKM, swinging it up with the ammo belt rattling loudly in the nighttime quiet, and I saw another IR laser from my right track in on him.

The AK wielder yelled out a challenge and took a step forward. He couldn't see shit, especially since he'd been staring at the fire a moment before. Imad barked a warning to him, explaining in Somali that there were two rifles trained on him and two more on his buddy. That gave him pause, and he rattled off a suspicious-sounding query. My guess is he figured that maybe he was being bluffed.

Imad answered calmly, explaining that he had business to conduct, and that the men in the bushes with guns were only there as a precaution. He then demanded to see the soldiers' commanding officer.

The PKM gunner yammered at his fellow, who snapped at him then reached for something and lifted it to his lips. He spoke into what had to be a small tactical radio, and even from where I was I heard the crackling response. Seemed they had their radio turned all the way up, probably so they'd hear it if they fell asleep. Some professionals.

The rifleman yelled at Imad that someone would be coming, and demanded he step into the light where they could see him. Imad agreed, but not before reminding them that we were out in the dark with rifles, ready to shoot them if we thought he was in danger. From their body language, I think they hoped he was bluffing, but were afraid he wasn't. They weren't prepared for something like this; they were supposed to be guarding a tiny rural town against rag-tag pirates.

Of course, it wasn't hard to guess that part of their job, since they were in the middle of the town instead of outside, was to enforce the curfew on the locals, who might or might not be entirely in favor of having the former USC/SNA troops in their town. But that wasn't our business, and we couldn't afford to care.

After about ten minutes, an ancient UAZ jeep came growling down

156

the main drag from the north. There was a driver, passenger, and one soldier standing in the back at a machine gun mounted to the roll bar. I couldn't tell what kind it was through the NVGs, but that it was the size of any number of medium MGs was enough. I shifted my laser to the gunner. If this blew up on us, I'd need to take him out of the picture first.

The UAZ came to a stop a few yards from the guards and the passenger got out. I couldn't see a lot of detail with the thermals, but he was dressed in fatigue trousers, a T-shirt, and beret. From his swagger, I somehow got the impression that if it had been light out, he'd have been wearing mirrored aviator sunglasses. I did make out that there was a pistol on his hip, but no rifle. With the MG watching over him, he didn't really need one.

He didn't approach or speak to Imad at first. Instead he strode up to the guard with the AK, who was already starting to cringe. He stopped in front of the man, stared at him for a moment, and then punched him in the face.

It wasn't much of a punch--most of us could have taken it standing up and kept coming without even blinking. But the guard fell on the ground, where Beret Boy kicked him and started screaming in Somali.

Now, I've already established that my Somali sucked. But even I could tell what was being said to the poor bastard on the ground, as his commander started stomping on him, while he tried to cover his head with his arms. He'd been on watch, and, regardless of how outclassed he was, we'd gotten the drop on him. Beret Boy was *pissed*.

Imad didn't interrupt. He just stood there with his back to the enclosure behind him, a bare two paces from the shadows, his arms folded.

Finally, Beret Boy finished beating and berating his subordinate, and with one last perfunctory kick, he turned to Imad and swaggered up to look him over. Imad just stood there, coolly returning his arrogant gaze. After a moment's posturing, which Imad refused to answer, the guy demanded to know who he was, and why he was there.

Imad calmly replied that we had been attacked by pirates, that we were mercenaries here to fight pirates and Al-Shabaab, and we were looking for fuel. He didn't mention payment at first. It never paid to let these kinds of thug soldiers know you had money.

He didn't have to, of course. Any mercenary outfit or NGO out here would have money of some sort. Beret Boy was doubtless aware of that, and starting to calculate how much of it he could get and for what risk.

But his first question seemed to throw Imad for a bit of a loop. I couldn't make it out, even if I'd been able to understand the language, but Imad asked a question in return, that sounded like he was trying to clarify what he'd just heard.

For a while, there was just the two of them talking, overwatched by

157

the gunner on the truck and the driver, who was now sitting half out of the driver's seat, an AK across his lap. The PKM gunner who'd been on post there in the square was now helping his battered comrade toward one of the enclosures off to the side of the square.

As Imad and Beret Boy talked, I saw Imad reach into his pocket and draw something out. Beret Boy flicked a lighter to take a closer look, and I knew it was one of the gold Krugerrands that we'd brought for just this purpose. As quickly as he'd shown it, Imad slipped it back into his pocket and started to take a step back.

Beret Boy started getting agitated, and his voice rose until I could hear it pretty clearly in the bushes. My earpiece clicked.

"Hillbilly, Spearchucker," Imad called quietly. "Can one of you switch to your vis laser for a second? I need to make a point."

I didn't say anything back, but just reached up and flicked the switch on my PEQ. The beam in my PVS-14s didn't appear to change as I moved it off the UAZ gunner, but Imad pointed at Beret Boy's chest, and the man started, as he looked down and saw the red glowing dot hovering over his heart and lungs. I kept it there for just long enough to get the point across, then switched back to IR. No reason to give them a possible line back to my position, which they would pick out sooner or later.

Imad continued to slowly move back toward the shadows, and called out something in Somali as he went. Then he was back in the darkness and moving toward us pretty quickly.

I blinked a tiny green LED light on my vest, down in the weeds where they shouldn't be able to see it from the square, but Imad picked it up, and vectored in toward me. Behind him, I could hear Beret Boy yelling, and saw him gesturing wildly at his subordinates. I didn't lower my weapon, but kept the UAZ gunner covered while Imad moved. If this had gone south, I wanted to put the hurt on these mothers as fast as I could.

Imad rustled through the brush and took a knee beside me, his knee touching my foot. "What was that all about?" I whispered.

"Let's get some distance first," he replied. "Not sure I trust him to hold tight until morning."

"Is that the deal?" I still hadn't stirred from my position.

"Yeah, the commander will be here in the morning, and he'll make the decision as to whether or not to sell us supplies, take us prisoner to ransom back to the US, or just kill us and take our money and weapons," he said dryly.

"Great." I circled my PEQ laser on the side of the UAZ, using that as the signal to fall back to our consolidation point. The others blinked once, then vanished. "Okay, let's move."

I rose from my crouch, my knees protesting, and did my best to glide through the grasping bushes. The rasp of the thorns and branches against my trousers and the crunch of sand and gravel under my boots sounded impossibly loud, even over the yelling and commotion back in the town. I didn't like the tone in Imad's voice, and was increasingly expecting to get swarmed by pissed-off Galmudug soldiers any moment.

But we reached the consolidation point without incident, and the link up with Larry, Hank, and Bob went off without a hitch. Crouched in the tiny depression, Imad filled us all in, just in case things went pear-shaped on the way back to the trucks.

"Well, the guy with the beret is apparently the equivalent of Sergeant of the Guard, though he identified himself as a Captain. He said that their Colonel, named Qasi, wasn't there, though I'm not entirely sure if he wasn't there, or was just asleep or passed out. He doesn't know if the Colonel will agree to help us, even for gold, but we should come back in the morning. He said that it might be possible, especially if we are going to cause trouble for the Egyptians." That turned heads, even as we lay in a three-sixty, facing outward for security.

"Yeah," he said, seeing our reaction. "That's what I thought, too. Seems there's a substantial Arab presence down south now, mostly from Egypt, Sudan, and the Arabian Peninsula. I'm guessing he's talking about Al Masri and his bunch, though how he's drawn this many foreign fighters, I don't know. He didn't seem to know, or care, either."

"What about the pirates?" Bob asked in a loud stage whisper. Damn, I knew he could be quiet, but he'd get excited sometimes.

"I don't think we really need to worry about them this far west," I said, notably more quietly. "They're not going to tangle with a Galmudug military unit, not willingly. They've taken some setbacks from the Galmudug forces in the last couple of years, when they've pushed further inland."

I turned my head to direct my whisper back to Imad. "Anything else?"

"Not yet. Guess we've got to see what this Colonel Qasi says in the morning."

"All right, then," I said, levering myself back up to one knee, and turning my head so that I could be heard, without taking my eyes off my sector of the horizon and the town perched on it. "Let's move back to the trucks, link up, fill in the rest of the team, and start getting a plan together for the morning."

***

The morning in Balli Gubat was bright, windy, and hot. The five of us from the night before had come to see Colonel Qasi, geared up and rifles in hand. We wouldn't be mistaken for anything but Americans, but our hope was that between the threat of our firepower and their hatred of Al Masri and his goons, we'd be able to deter violence and do some business.

There wasn't much sign of the locals as we came up the dusty track to the town square. A few goats bleated in the enclosures we passed, and there were a few children's eyes watching us before being swept away by frightened parents. The locals didn't know what was going to go down this morning, and they wanted to keep their families out of the way if shooting started.

The square was empty as we walked up. I spotted several groups of Galmudug soldiers in varying degrees of uniform, mostly consisting of old tri-color or Russian camouflage trousers and t-shirts, though a few were wearing camouflage blouses as well, usually not quite matching the trousers. Most were wearing combat gear, though that didn't consist of much more than an old AK chest rig, or cartridge belt with mag pouches.

They were trying to be nonchalant, and there wasn't as huge a display of weaponry that might otherwise be expected. That didn't mean that we couldn't spot them anyway. AK-47s predominated, though there were a couple of SKS variants, and I thought I saw a G-3 or two.

Hank and Bob took the left, and Larry and I took the right, spreading out into the square. We kept our posture about as nonchalant as the Somali soldiers did. We didn't bother to watch our backs, because the trucks were down to the south, just barely visible over a slight rise in the ground, with no fewer than three sniper rifles covering us and anyone near us who might start feeling froggy.

I glanced at my watch. Morning was getting on, and there was no sign of anyone here to meet us aside from the soldiers scattered around the square. They might have managed to look less like an ambush if there had been locals in the square too, but the locals didn't appear to be interested in serving as human shields. I made eye contact with Hank across the way, and he nodded slightly, his hand flexing ever so slightly around the pistol grip of his Galil ACE. There was no other word or action, but everyone was primed.

It felt like a long time, standing there in the sun and the dust. There wasn't much noise, especially since there didn't appear to be much in the way of power in the town. A generator chugged somewhere and goats bleated out of sight. Several of the soldiers were talking quietly among themselves, but none approached us, and we returned the favor. They watched us, we watched them. Time crawled, as we baked in the rising heat.

It must have been nearly an hour before there was a rising chatter of voices, and several of the soldiers started to straighten up, and try to look a little more menacing. One of them, not much more than a kid, with an ancient SKS that I could see the rust spots on, lifted his rifle toward me and puffed up his chest. I just watched him impassively, refusing to rise to the bait. Of course, he took this to mean I was afraid of him, and got even more of a big head. Before he could cause any real trouble to where I might have to shoot him, the officers showed up.

Unsurprisingly, Beret Boy was in the back. I recognized his silhouette, anyway, from the night before. He didn't look like nearly the big man he'd acted like in the wee hours. He still tried to maintain his swagger, but the attitudes of the other men around him put the lie to it.

I picked out Colonel Qasi right away, though he wasn't anything like what I was expecting. He was short, wiry, and didn't walk with the swagger that his men did. He had short, iron-gray hair and an equally gray, neatly trimmed beard. His fatigues were plain green, totally unadorned, and his pistol belt and holster were plain green webbing. He carried a battered but clean-looking AKM slung barrel-up on his shoulder.

He walked up to Imad and offered his hand. Imad shook it calmly, betraying nothing. We watched--silent, still, hands on weapons.

"So," Qasi began, in nearly unaccented English, "Captain Ould-Ali tells me that you are asking for our help." His voice was cold, his face expressionless. "Why should we help you?"

"To begin with," Imad said calmly, "Because we have mutual enemies to the south. The Islamist militias--"

Qasi cut him off with a slash of his hand. He sneered. "You Americans. You always say that you are here to help, to fight our enemies, if only we take sides with you, surrender ourselves to your operations. You will come to our country, wave your high-technology weapons and the bad people will all go away. Then we will all live in peace and harmony, according to your American ideas. You know nothing of our country, and you never have." He waved his hand toward the south. "I was in Mogadishu the first time your soldiers came; I have more in common with Al-Shabaab, Allah curse their names, than I do with you."

"We're not here to try to remake your country," Imad insisted. "But if you help us, maybe we can help you, by killing a few of your enemies, while we carry out our mission."

Qasi snorted. "You weren't going to remake Iraq, Afghanistan, or Libya, either, were you? Where are those people you 'helped' now?" He gesticulated vaguely in what was supposed to be the direction of each of the stricken countries that had been the battlefields of the opening decade of the 21st century. "Iraq all but belongs to the Persians, the Taliban rule Afghanistan again with an iron fist, and the Salafi Party has overthrown the Libyan transitional government. The people you 'helped' are dead or in prison. So why would I expect your 'help' to end any differently?" He looked around at the rest of us, his lip curled.

"Besides, if you think to fight Somalis with so few, you should go home now. With all the power that you brought the last time, we sent you fleeing. These are too few," he said scornfully.

"I never claimed to be able to send all your enemies fleeing at our approach," Imad countered. I watched the Galmudug soldiers carefully, the hackles on my neck going up. Imad was getting his back up, and that could get really bad. I almost said something to him about dialing it back a little, but this was the wrong time and place for backseat driving. "You don't want our help, fine. We can pay, though. All we ask is some fuel and supplies, and we'll be on our way."

"Just like that?" The scorn had not left Qasi's voice. "Your countrymen do not have a presence in this country, American. There is no one to pressure the people to do what you want; there are no helicopters to come rescue you. Why do you keep thinking that the world will simply bow down to your will any longer?"

"That's our problem," Imad replied. "Like I said, we can pay for the petrol and we'll leave."

"Maybe I just kill you, take your guns," Qasi suggested. "Then you aren't my problem or anyone else's. Your people sent so few of you, I doubt they would even miss you."

Imad's voice had gone cold and hard as granite. "You might. I promise you that a lot of your soldiers would die before we went down, and you'd be the first. You think that these four are all I have?"

There was a long pause, as Imad and Qasi stared each other down. I was going over target engagements in my head, picking out who I'd shoot first, second, third, etc. There wasn't a lot of cover in the square. If Qasi decided to try to be a hardass, it was going to be a bloodbath.

After what felt like a small eternity, as the sun beat down, sweat dripped, and flies buzzed, Qasi regained his sneer. "Pay? What will Americans pay with? Your money is worthless."

Imad jerked his chin at Ould-Ali. "Your man knows. I showed him the gold last night."

Qasi's eyes narrowed. He didn't want to lift a finger to help us, but if we had gold, he wanted it, almost as much as he didn't want his head blown off.

Finally, after an agonizing stretch of thinking, he curled his lip again, but this time it didn't have the weight of contempt behind it. He was negotiating, but trying to make it seem otherwise, especially to his troops. I still didn't relax. As soon as you relax in these sorts of situations, that's when Murphy decides to bend you over.

"Petrol is expensive," he said. "Especially these days. Do you have enough gold to pay for it?"

Imad just stared at him stonily for a moment. When he spoke, his voice held as much contempt as Qasi's had. "You must either be stupid, or think that I am. Which is it?"

I think it was at just about that point that Qasi started to realize just what kind of people he was fucking with. And he didn't like the realization. He kept his face straight, but there was a shift in his demeanor. I don't know

162

if any of his minions picked up on it, but he knew he'd overstepped, and was on more dangerous ground than he had imagined.

Imad continued. "Gas might be expensive, but gold is even more so, and somebody in your position would have to know that. So either you're an idiot, and I should just go ahead and take what we want, over your dead body or not, or you're trying to rob me, in which case I should kill you and take what we want anyway."

Qasi was starting to sweat, and not just from the sun. He had to make a decision. His arrogance might have just fucked him, and he knew it. He also knew that how he reacted in the next few minutes would have long-standing consequences with his men. Scanning around, I could see them watching intently. More than one had a thoughtful look on his face. If Qasi jumped the wrong way, he could wind up undermining himself with his subordinates.

"We are very far from any petrol station," Qasi said. "Petrol will be more expensive here. Say, two Krugerrands for one hundred gallons?" It was robbery, pure and simple, even with petroleum prices being what they were. At its worst, two ounces of gold could have bought two hundred fifty gallons.

Imad glared. "Okay, apparently you really do think I'm stupid." He was bluffing more than anything else. We needed the gas, and ultimately would pay whatever we needed to. But we were playing a tricky game here. We couldn't afford to show Qasi that. It might be seen as weakness, which would be exploited, and might get us killed and tossed into a wadi. Not right away, of course, but we didn't want an ambush waiting for us, either.

"One Krugerrand, two hundred gallons," Imad said. Which was still considerably higher than average gas prices at the time, but not nearly as high as Qasi was trying to extort out of us.

"You are the ones in need of the fuel," Qasi said, seeming to relax a little. "Two Krugerrands, two hundred gallons."

"You might get one for one hundred fifty," Imad replied. "You want two? Three hundred gallons."

"We cannot afford to give up that much fuel," Qasi protested, apparently relaxing fully into the role of haggling merchant, more so than I expected a commander to. Made me wonder what really got this guy his rank. "One hundred twenty-five for one Krugerrand."

Imad made a great show of thinking it over, but the truth was that it was probably about as good as we were going to get, and we didn't have the time to fuck around. We needed to get moving, and the sooner we could get gassed up and get on the way, the better.

Finally, Imad nodded tightly. Qasi smiled just as mirthlessly, and turned to yell at one of his soldiers in Somali. I think he had reached the point where he was going to simply be glad to get rid of us. Were we to cross paths again, I suspected things wouldn't be so pleasant or friendly.

I keyed my radio. "Coconut, Hillbilly. Deal is done, bring the trucks up."

"Roger," Alek replied.

We didn't help the Galmudug soldiers who were bringing up the rickety trailer full of five-gallon jerry cans and two rusty steel drums. The four of us who hadn't spoken maintained our air of stone-faced hired guns, watching as Imad checked each of the containers, before grudgingly handing over the one-ounce gold coin. Qasi inspected it carefully before accepting it and pocketing it with equal ill-grace. By that time, the three vehicles had pulled up, and Jim, Alek, and Danny started loading the fuel into the backs of the trucks, while we stared down the soldiers.

There was no trouble. We just stared at each other like boys and girls at an early high-school dance, while the fuel got loaded, which, since a lot of it was in the two drums, didn't take a lot of time. Okay, granted, like boys and girls ready to shoot each other dead at the drop of a hat, but you get the idea.

With the last of the fuel loaded, we fell back to the trucks, Bob quickly clambering back on the PKM in the back of the HiLux that he had essentially claimed as his own personal property, and covered the rest of us as we loaded up. Qasi stood watching us, his arms folded across his chest, trying to look stern. To this day, I'm convinced the only reason he dealt with us was to preserve his own skin, after Imad assured him he'd be the first to die if he tried anything.

We left Balli Gubat in a cloud of dust, but we did look back. Just because you're paranoid doesn't mean they're not out to get you.

CHAPTER 20

We pushed hard, rattling and bouncing over the desert, changing direction about five times in an hour, hoping to at least make it harder for Qasi's goons to follow us if he decided to come after us. I held on for dear life and listened to the suspension protest in agony as we jounced over the arid, rocky ground. It was only a matter of time before something went bad, and we had a notable dearth of replacement parts. We had gas now, but other fluids were pretty lacking. I knew what this sort of environment could do to vehicles.

After about an hour, our headlong rush began to slow, and then stopped. We circled the vehicles in a small laager, smack dab in the middle of nowhere. Rodrigo, Tim, and Jim, who were driving, stayed in the vehicles, Hank, Bob, and Larry stayed on security, and the rest of us got out and gathered in the middle to go over our situation.

I glanced up at Bob, still standing in the back of the HiLux, and couldn't help but comment, "We're going to have to use a crowbar to get that PKM away from Bob when this is over."

There were dry chuckles. "He does like that gun," Hank agreed from the perimeter. "Can't blame him."

"Just because you never met a cheap communist gun you didn't like," Rodrigo called out the open window. Rod being an FN fan boy, he could always be counted on to rag on Hank's love of AK's and Galils, which were Israel's AK-based service rifles. It helped ease the tension a little.

"All right, settle down," Alek said. I looked around as the small team got quiet. We were all filthy, unshaven and haggard, crusted with dried sweat and dust. I couldn't tell about the others, especially as none of us would likely complain about it out loud, but I was exhausted and I hurt. My joints felt like they were full of sand and I was battered and bruised from the hell-bent-for-leather ride across the desert.

We crouched in the sand between the vehicles, and Alek spread out his map on the ground before looking around at us. "All right, thanks to Imad, we're good on fuel for a couple of days, at least. Danny and Rodrigo secured about thirty gallons of water from one of the outer wells during the night. It'll have to be purified, but we've got water for about the next two and a half days."

"We should be able to hit the Webi Shebelle by then," Danny put in. "Still going to have to filter the hell out of the water, probably with chemical purifiers as well, but it'll be water." Nobody said anything. None of us wanted to drink unpurified water from anywhere in Africa. The chemical purifiers would ensure it tasted like shit, and it would be hot as hell, but at least none of us should get the galloping shits from it.

Alek looked at me. "How are we doing on ammo?"

I had checked during the pre-dawn hours while we waited for the meeting with Qasi. "We came with enough that even after that firefight on the way out of Hobyo, we've still got about a combat load and a half per man, give or take about a hundred rounds," I said. I was counting two hundred rounds of 7.62x51 as a combat load. "We'll have to be stingy with it, and try to avoid trouble when we can." Again, there were no comments. We did our damnedest to hold to the rifleman standard as described by the late, great Jeff Cooper--disabling first-round shots out to five hundred meters. Of course, real-world that wasn't always possible, but we always strove to hold to it. The limited ammo supply and lack of imminent resupply would only reinforce that.

"Well, we're not here to try to take down the entire network, just to find our guys," Alek said. "I think I can safely say that our plan to try to get the Galmudug forces to help us based on their antipathy toward Al Qaeda and its allies here wasn't the best idea. From here on out, unless absolutely unavoidable, we are avoiding contact with any locals if at all possible." That could be a tall order, given what little I knew about the nomadic population of Somalia. When I thought about it a little more, though, I reasoned that we were traveling in local vehicles. We didn't have to look like locals close up, just from far away. Preferably very far away.

"That said, we do need to do some movement during the day," Alek continued. "We're on the clock; there's no telling when Al Masri is going to get a wild hair and decide to teach the Great Satan a lesson by executing some more of his hostages. I'd like to only move at night, but we've got over five hundred miles to go just to get to this contact in Baardheere. Best case, that puts us two days away, and I'm not expecting best case, not by a long shot." Which he almost didn't even need to say. Whoever was paying the bills for this job, Murphy was most definitely in charge.

He squatted down and pulled out his knife to point to the map. "We don't have a lot of up-to-date intel on what areas to avoid here, so we're going to have to play a lot of this by ear. Terrain looks mostly flat, but as we all know, flat is relative in the desert, especially when we're dealing with vehicles. We haven't got much in the way of parts, fluids, or even spare tires." He traced several lines with his knife point. "These are known major roads or tracks. We want to avoid them as much as possible, and see if we can't arrange to cross any of them that we have to at night." There were a number of semi-amused grunts, and he shook his head. "I know, I know. Probably not going to work out that way."

He continued to use his knife as a pointer, this time tracing a thin black line drawn with a map pen. "This looks to be the most direct path we can take to the vicinity of Baardheere, while avoiding most habitation. We can't guarantee that we'll miss the nomads, of course, but we can avoid any towns or villages." The knifepoint slid along the acetate-covered paper. "We push inland from here, and pass about thirty klicks north of Geedaley before turning south again." He circled a spot on the map. "Imagery shows what looks like some pretty rough country here; we'll avoid it if we can, but keep an eye on it as a bolt hole if we take contact. From there," the knifepoint continued its path, "we should have a fairly straight shot for about two hundred fifty kilometers before we start running into the rougher country near the Shebelle River. I'm not going to lie, that river is going to be a major obstacle. Imagery shows it lined with farms; we're going to have a tough time finding a covert way across it. We may have to cover a fair amount of ground north or south before we can find a crossing point.

"Once across, we'll continue to push west for another fifty klicks, and then turn south. Like Geedaley, I want to skirt wide around Baidoa. We'll come out on the plains to the south, and push for the Juba north of Baardheere. Once we're in place on the northern outskirts, it'll be up to Danny to get us in touch with our contact."

He looked around at us again. "We're looking at something over seven hundred kilometers, and I want to get us there in two days. If you're not driving or on lookout, try to get some rack time in the trucks while we move. There won't be a lot of halts, I hope."

He proceeded to list off a series of tentative rally points. With such a long route, there were a lot of them. We hauled out little waterproof notebooks to write them down. We went over reaction to contact and down vehicle SOPs one more time.

Alek called Hank over to go over the comm stuff, and Danny took his place on security. Hank started ticking things off on his meaty hands. "We're low on batteries. Most of the short range radio batteries I can recharge; I brought a solar charger for that, but the big-ticket stuff is getting low. Unfortunately, I don't know of any good way to procure more, especially in the disputed areas around here, so go easy on the radios. If you're not a VC or a lookout, keep your radio turned off."

There weren't all that many questions; we had all done this before. There was no fire support piece, either. We had no support; no air, no fire support, no casevac. I don't know about the others, but I tried not to think too hard about it.

Before we climbed back on the trucks, Alek went around to each of us, asking pertinent questions. It was a good way to make sure everybody had the plan set in their mind. Satisfied, he grunted, "Let's go, gents. Miles to go before we sleep."

With various creaks, groans and cracks, we got up and headed for our vehicles. I slid into the passenger seat next to Jim; I'd be taking the vehicle commander slot for the first leg. I gave Jim the brief rundown of the plan. He asked a few clarifying questions, then nodded.

"Hell of a fix we've gotten ourselves into out here, ain't it?" he said, watching ahead through the dusty windshield as we lurched into motion.

Things started to go poorly within the first hour. We had to divert farther to the north around Geedaley than we'd planned, as we ran into an impenetrable wall of sand dunes. If we'd had better vehicles, not to mention more confidence in our equipment should one get stuck, we might have gone straight through, but we didn't trust them that far. We wound up going another fifteen klicks north just to get around the dunes, and even then, there were a few iffy parts where sand started to go soft under the tires, and only skillful driving kept us from digging a truck to the axles.

We found ourselves getting into the eroded badlands that Alek had specifically talked about avoiding. The ground, while peppered with brush, was either carved into runnels and pits, or was soft riverbed-type sand where it lined the channels. We actually did get one of the SUVs stuck, and it took almost a half hour of backbreaking, sweaty work in 120-degree heat to get it moving again. More lost time.

We had to cut hard south for about fifty kilometers to make sure we got well clear. By this time, the sun was already starting to dip toward the western horizon. It would be dark before we got even half the distance we'd been hoping for.

There wasn't any griping; there wasn't a man here, except maybe for Bob, who hadn't had at least eight years' experience in the field before going to work for Praetorian. Once you leave the wire, Murphy takes over, like it or not. There's an old saying; "No battle plan survives first contact with the enemy." I'd revise it to say, "No battle plan survives the first step outside the wire."

The sun disappeared under the horizon, and we continued through the brush-strewn plains, driving without lights, our NVGs lowered in front of our eyes. We might be heard, but we wouldn't be seen, especially not by the dirt-poor nomads who lived out there in the hinterlands. It was not the most comfortable I've ever been driving at night, especially since we didn't have any IR headlights. We were driving on ambient light alone, and there was precious little of that.

Finally, as the terrain started to get bumpy again, and we almost lost the HiLux to another sand hole, Alek called a halt. We'd get moving again just before first light.

***

"Fuck."

It was the first word either Jim or I had uttered in about two hours. It also seemed entirely appropriate, given the noise we had just heard.

"Coconut, Kemosabe," Jim called over the radio. It was his turn in the passenger seat. In the back, Larry and Hank had been awakened by the loud bang from the undercarriage. "Need to call a halt. We've got a mechanical problem back here."

I heard Alek's voice, tinny and quiet, through the handset that Jim had attached to the radio. "Roger. We'll be back at your pos in a second."

I pushed open my door, which creaked and rasped from all the dust and sand in the hinges, and levered myself out into the only slightly more unbearable heat outside. The A/C in the truck worked, but only barely. I knelt down in the dirt and sand, shoving a low, prickly bush out of the way and peered into the shadows underneath.

"Yep," I called out heavily. "Axle's broke like a fucking twig. We ain't going anywhere."

We were still thirty klicks shy of the Shabelle River. Every direction was the same dun, green-spotted plain. The land was a lot flatter than I had expected from the imagery, but that didn't mean it was smooth. We'd hit a rut, and the axle had snapped, loudly and finally. I pulled myself back up tiredly. My buttocks ached from the hours spent in the vehicle.

The HiLux came back around in a wide turn, and rolled to a stop a few yards away. Alek got out tiredly, as Larry and Hank clambered out of our stricken heap. "What's up?" Alek asked.

"Broken axle," I replied. Larry and Hank were already pulling gear and supplies out of the back.

"Son of a bitch." There was almost no inflection in Alek's voice. "Guess we're spread-loading."

"Yep," Jim replied, pulling his own ruck out and starting to haul it toward the HiLux. "Clown car time."

Danny and Imad were already climbing out of the other SUV and coming over to help. We'd have to strap more of the rucks to the outside and tops of the vehicles, to have room for men inside. Not just clown car time; it was gypsy wagon time.

I reached into the back for the shitty tool bag that we'd found under the floorboards. "Might as well strip it," I said. "If one of the others breaks down, we should have some spare parts--spare tires at least."

"Good idea," Alek said. "Let's siphon the gas tank, too."

Stripping an SUV in the middle of the desert with minimal tools really is as hard as it sounds. Maybe harder. The worst part was getting the tires off. We didn't have a jack, and ended up having to work out a lever

169

arrangement with some pipes that had been in the back of the HiLux when we grabbed it, that fortunately we hadn't thrown out. Finding a place to carry all the crap we stripped off the kaput Toyota was even worse. We now had eleven men, their weapons and gear, and spare parts, tires, water, and fuel, to cram into or onto two vehicles.

"We're going to have to go more slowly," Nick said, standing next to the cab of the HiLux. "I'd say no more than ten miles an hour; five would be more like it. Especially with the extra weight, these trucks aren't going to last much longer against this abuse."

Alek started to lean against the fender of the defunct SUV, then snatched his arm away with a curse. Jim chuckled tiredly. "Metal tends to get hot in the sun, Alek," he pointed out. Alek flipped him off.

"It's already midday, and we're not even across the Shebelle yet," Danny pointed out. "Can we afford to lose the time?"

"We'll lose even more time if we lose another truck," Nick pointed out reasonably. Danny nodded, scratching his salt-and-pepper beard. He looked at Alek and shrugged.

"So much for two days," he said with a rueful chuckle.

Alek half-grinned, half-grimaced. "Par for the course. I guess I was being too optimistic."

I grunted as I heaved another tire into the bed of the HiLux. "How many times have I told you? Optimism just gets you screwed. Accept that the world is fucked, that everything is doomed, and when things work out, you're pleasantly surprised."

"Okay, Voice of Doom, we get it," Alek retorted. I laughed at him as I pointlessly dusted my hands, which were encased in tac gloves anyway.

Alek looked around. "We probably should hold here until dark, anyway," he mused. "We're less than twenty klicks from the river. If the imagery isn't lying--" he tried to glare at me before I could add any of my words of wisdom on the likelihood of that "--there should be a place to ford pretty much straight ahead."

***

The Webi Shabelle, or Shebelle River, starts in the Ahmar Mountains in Ethiopia, and meanders southeast into Somalia, before turning southwest to parallel the coast past Mogadishu, until it joins with the Juba River and flows into the sea just north of Kismayo. Along with the Juba, it is one of two primary sources of water and irrigation in Somalia. Its floodplain could be a breadbasket, but the chaos in Somalia since the fall of Barre's regime in 1991, coupled with destructive flooding and severe droughts, had taken a severe toll on Somali farming.

We were hoping that some of that destruction of farms might have opened up a place for us to cross relatively unobserved.

***

Our two remaining vehicles rolled across the Shabelle floodplain, trying to drive as close to silently as possible.

Of course, there's only so quiet you can make a vehicle, especially at night. The air cools, most of the daytime sounds die away, and any sounds that are made travel farther, and stand out more jarringly. The internal combustion engine is not a fundamentally quiet mechanism, and one that has been subjected to the rigors of operating in East Africa is even less so. Add to that the crunch of gravel and sand under the tires, the creak of the suspension, and the occasional bump of equipment or weapons against metal or plastic when a bump is hit, and it gets even worse. The slower, the better.

However, we couldn't afford to go too slowly, as the floodplain was soft and sandy, and we were constantly at risk of getting stuck. Get stuck out here, and we were made, no question about it. We probably wouldn't be able to get unstuck and across the river before daylight.

The preoccupation with stealth, while we had been tearing pretty handily across the desert until the axle snapped, was due to the fact that the Shabelle floodplain was some of the extremely limited fertile farmland in central Somalia, and so was thoroughly lined with farms. If anyone was up and about, which was still possible, they'd notice us. We didn't want any word of our whereabouts getting to the bad guys, whether by force or bribery. As for our presence, we were pretty sure that was already known; shooting the shit out of the Hobyo pirates had to have made the word-of-mouth version of the six-o'clock news, which anyone who has been in the Third World can attest, is faster than anything on the 24-hour news cycles back in the States, even before half the cable companies went under.

But nothing said we had to make it any easier for the bastards.

The HiLux seemed to slow ahead of us, and then slewed hard to the left, then the right. Nick had hit a soft spot, and had to act fast to wrench the truck clear of it before he bogged down. At the wheel of our Land Cruiser, Jim made sure to go wide around it.

I was riding shotgun at that point, having relieved Danny about an hour before. I checked the GPS and the map with my key-fob-sized red lens, under my shemaugh to cover any light from being seen outside the cab. We were just about to our near-side rally point. I keyed my radio. "Coconut, Hillbilly."

"Roger, Hillbilly, I see it," Alek called back, before I could say anything. "Another two hundred meters." Which was damn near spitting distance, and Jim took his foot off the gas. We were barely idling as it was, but we still had enough forward momentum to coast to a stop near the HiLux.

Ahead, I could barely see the darker line of the low trees that covered the banks of the river. The moon wasn't supposed to rise for another hour, so we didn't have a lot of light to work with, aside from IR floods from PEQ-15s. There was enough to see that we were a good distance away from any human habitation. The desert was flat and empty, dotted with the dark spots of the ubiquitous low bushes.

I got out as Jim killed the engine, leaving us in relative silence, aside from the noises of the cooling engine and what sounds we made moving around. I didn't dally, but slung my rifle, checked my radio, and headed over to the hood of the HiLux, where Alek and Hank were already on a knee, facing the river.

I came up and sank to one knee beside Hank. "You ready?" I whispered. He just reached out and tapped my shoulder with a fist. I tapped Alek in turn, and led out. Hank rose smoothly to follow me, and we headed down toward the riverbank.

We moved carefully and smoothly, hands on our rifles, but not up and in the red. At least, not until we heard the grunting down by the water.

Unless you've ever heard a crocodile grunt close to you in the dark, you don't really know what fear is. I'd face a twenty-to-one firefight happily long before I want to hear that sound again. When I realized what it was, I damn near shit myself. Nobody in their right mind wants to go fucking around with crocs in the daytime, much less at night, when you can't see the scaly fuckers.

I immediately turned on the thermal feature on my NVGs, only to remember that the crocs are cold-blooded, and probably wouldn't show up very well. "Fuck!" I hissed under my breath, as I sank to a knee in the sand. Hank came up next to me and took a knee at my shoulder.

"What's up?" he asked, his voice barely a whisper.

"Crocs," I replied, and I heard muffled swearing.

"We've got to get across somewhere," he said after a moment.

"I know," I whispered in reply. "And there isn't likely to be anyplace else on this fucking river that doesn't have crocs, too." I gnawed at it in my head, but couldn't see any way around it. We were going to have to ford in the face of crocodiles, and to do that, we'd have to go in and check that the river was fordable before we tried to drive vehicles into it. Damn it.

I didn't turn to look at Hank, but kept my eyes out, watching the only faintly visible long shapes down by the shore moving around. "We still have to do this, but I'm going to call the rest of the team up to cover while we do. I am *not* going into that water with all those fucking dinosaurs in there, with just the two of us." Without waiting for his reply, which turned out to be little more than a fist thumped lightly on a shoulder in agreement, I keyed my radio. "Coconut, Hillbilly. At the river. Be advised, there are crocodiles on the banks at the least. Request you bring up the rest of the team to cover while we conduct Fordrep."

"Roger, Hillbilly," Alek called back at once. I breathed a little easier. It was still going to be risky as hell, but I felt a little better about checking out the river crossing when there were other guys with thermals and guns ready to kill any ancient reptilian predators that wanted to make me or Hank into midnight snacks.

The two vehicles growled up to us, starlight glinting off the windshields, and came to a stop about fifty meters from the riverbank. The rest of the guys got out, weapons ready, and spread out, while Alek came over to where we were kneeling.

"What's the matter, gunfighter? Some lizards got you shaky?" Alek whispered. I couldn't see his grin, because I was still watching the crocs, but I could hear it.

"Fuck you, Alek," I replied. "You go down there and wrestle with those fuckers."

He clapped me on the shoulder with a plate-sized hand. "I'm just fucking with you, brother, good call. I wouldn't want to chance that shit, either, and there's no good reason to. Damn it," he continued. "We should have thought of this during planning."

"Too long out here, and no real place to go firm and get some rest," Hank pointed out. "We're going to have to watch that, or we might miss something even worse."

"Amen, brother," Alek agreed. "Hopefully we can stand down for a day or two whenever we link up with this contact, though the way the rest of this clusterfuck has been going, I'm not counting on it." He blew a huge breath out. "Now, has anybody got any ideas as to how to scare away crocs without waking every nomad, farmer, or local militia within thirty miles?"

"Anybody here from gator country?" I asked. "I knew one weird Cajun back during my time in Recon who might have had an answer, but I don't, aside from driving the trucks right up to the shore."

"Which kind of defeats the purpose of doing a ford recon, but I see your point," Alek said. "And no, we don't have any swamp runners on the team, but you knew that."

I heard the rasp of his hand rubbing his stubble. "I guess we go ahead and try to ford, one vic at a time, and if we start running into trouble, either back up, or get pulled out. We'll just have to take it slow, so that we don't get stuck. I still don't know what this riverbed is made of, and for some strange reason, there's next to no information on it in any of the intel we've got."

"Figures." I took my eyes off the crocs long enough to look back at him, even though he wasn't much more than a looming shadow at my shoulder. "Call the play, boss."

He reached back to key his radio. "All pax, back on the trucks. Due to reptile hazards, we're going to wing this one. HiLux goes first, with tow lines ready in case we've got to yank it out. We'll be fording blind, so we'll take it slow. Go ahead and hook up the tow lines first, just keep them slack until they're needed." We had managed to find some very long ropes, almost

120 lines. They were a lot longer than the tow straps that we'd used in the military, which were twenty feet long, if you were lucky. Of course, there was the question of how well they'd hold up to the vehicles' weight, but then again, they were all we had.

It took a few minutes to get the lines out and tied securely. Most of us were out around the vehicles, on a knee in the sand, on security but mostly handling croc watch. Nobody wanted to tangle with those things, which made me feel a little better about borderline freaking out about them.

Finally, the murmured command, "Mount up," came over the radio, and I piled back into the right seat of the Land Cruiser. The HiLux was already moving; we had lost enough time here already.

Jim moved the Land Cruiser close behind the other truck, and only stopped at the edge of the bank, which was steeper than I'd anticipated. It still wasn't bad, and really was nothing to these vehicles, but it wasn't as shallow as I might have expected a ford to be. The HiLux' nose dipped down to almost a forty-five degree angle, as Nick eased it toward the water. I couldn't see a lot of detail aside from the thermal signatures, but Bob looked to be holding on to the PKM in the back for dear life.

The truck nosed into the water...and kept going. Fortunately it was a HiLux with a snorkel. I'd been pleasantly surprised to see that, though I realized that it was unlikely that the pirates had known what it was for, or cared. The water was up to the hood, and was threatening to go higher, but then the truck leveled out, and continued to push across the river.

About halfway across, the left front corner suddenly dipped, almost throwing Bob out of the bed and into the water. The truck stopped almost as abruptly, and then started to ease backward, as Nick worked to get them out of the hole in the riverbed. Jim had his hand on the gearshift, ready to throw the Land Cruiser into reverse to pull them back out if Nick couldn't recover.

But the HiLux eased backward, righted itself, then turned about forty-five degrees to the right and forged on ahead, pushing around the hole. The rest of the riverbed failed to produce any similar nasty surprises, and soon the HiLux was clawing up onto higher ground. Jim threw the Land Cruiser in gear and started forward, before the tow line could go taut.

I wasn't sure how well the Toyota SUV was going to handle the river. It didn't have the fording kit that the HiLux did, and I was more than a little concerned that we'd wind up flooding the engine as well as the exhaust. Jim was similarly concerned, so he floored the engine, driving as hard as he could to get across the river before the water could do too much damage.

Water flowed in the door, the current and sheer volume of the river forcing it past the battered weatherstripping. Everybody lifted their weapons to chest level to keep them out of the muddy flood, though my pistol was getting a good bath. I'd have to strip and clean it as soon as I could; even with the Slipstream treatment, I didn't want that crap in my beloved 1911.

I let out a breath I hadn't realized I had been holding, as we surged up out of the river, fishtailing a little on the muddy bank. The water started flowing out of the cab. We were all soaked to the waist, and it was going to be chilly until the sun came up. Nothing unfamiliar, there wasn't a one of us hadn't spent the most part of the last ten years or more either wet, gritty, too cold, too hot, or some combination thereof. Didn't mean we wouldn't bitch about it. The grumbling from the back was starting already, until Jim growled, "Shut the fuck up," and the complaints subsided. For the moment.

***

The land began to rise as we came out of the Shabelle River floodplain, though it never turned into highlands. More desert went by in the dark, a little rougher perhaps than to the northeast where we'd started, but we were still able to maintain about a forty kph rate of march. By the time the sun came up, we were fifty miles south of Baidoa. We could be on the outskirts of Baardheere by noon.

CHAPTER 21

We didn't make it that far before the HiLux slowed and stopped. We were in the middle of nowhere, nothing but flat, scrub-dotted plains as far as the eye could see. We'd seen some camel-driving nomads earlier, but now, with the sun rising higher in the sky and the horizon already starting to shimmer with heat, there was no sign of life.

Alek got out of the HiLux' cab, looked back at us, and circled his hand over his head. Assemble. Something was up.

Except for the two drivers and two on security, we all piled out and huddled around Alek on the ground between the trucks, rifles carefully held muzzle-down across knees, except for Imad, who kept his muzzle-up, I think largely as a fuck-you to the "Rambo" comments that had been made the first time he did it, on one of our border jobs.

"What's up?" I asked, as I lowered myself to a knee. Like everyone else, I was still keeping one eye on the horizon.

Alek jerked a thumb at Danny. "He just got a phone call from Langley. Seems things have potentially gotten more complicated."

Danny launched in without much preamble. "The final push to force the Kenyans and the Ethiopians out of the country has apparently started. We have gotten reports from Baird that Malouf Ali Awale's Lashkar al-Barbar is advancing on Baardheere. They're moving relatively slowly; they're a lot like the Janjaweed militias up in Sudan, and are terrorizing villages on the way, particularly any that have helped the African Union or the Kenyans in the last few years, but they are on their way, and in force. Langley sent me some satellite imagery that backs all this up, as well."

Hank raised a finger. "Question; who the fuck is Lashkar al-Barbar? I've heard of Shabaab, obviously, and AQEA. Who are these fuckers?"

"Lashkar al-Barbar is a relative newcomer," Danny explained. "They grew out of the cooperation between Shabaab and AQ, and we have some indicators that Al Masri was closely involved in its founding. It is essentially the Somali version of the Taliban's old Brigade 055 or Lashkar al-Zil. It's a semi-autonomous, multinational army of hard-core jihadi shock troops. They only come around when there's serious resistance to Islamic Emirate forces, or they just want to send a message. Or if there's some really good booty to be had. They aren't nearly in the class of Saddam's old Republican Guard or the IRGC. They are primarily an instrument of terror, but they've apparently had enough training and have enough numbers and equipment to be a serious challenge to anybody they're likely to face in Somalia.

"Now, the Kenyans would have been able to take them down without even breathing hard a couple years ago, but, largely since Al Masri came on the scene, their stance in Somalia has been deeply eroded, largely because of the increasing AQEA activity in their own country. They already got pushed out of Kismayo, and the Ethiopians have been driven out of Baidoa. If the jihadis manage to push the Kenyans out of Baardheere, it'll be the end of resistance to Islamist rule in southern Somalia. They'll be able to turn to Galmudug, Puntland, and Somaliland next."

"None of which is our concern," Alek put in. "We're not here to liberate Somalia or ensure the stability of however many kleptocracies are crammed into this Godforsaken patch of dirt. We're here to get those hostages out."

"Just setting the stage, brother," Danny said. "If we're trying to operate in an area where Awale's set up shop, it's going to make things dicey. These guys are known for being sharia enforcers wherever they operate, and anything that looks out of place is likely to attract their attention. And once engaged, they tend to dog pile. We get in it with a squad of 'em, they'll probably have a battalion on us in less than an hour."

"Which is why we stay clandestine," Larry pointed out. "Unless I'm missing something, we're supposed to just be the recon element here." He looked around. "Did I hear that wrong?"

"No, you didn't," I replied. "But nothing else on this op has gone according to plan, and we haven't exactly stayed soft the whole time. Makes sense to know what we're up against if things go to hell again." I paused a moment, then fulfilled my chosen role of doomsayer. "Which they will."

"Now, Langley is telling me that Baird has some undocumented assets of his own," Danny continued with a frown. "I have no idea what they are, or what he's doing with them. Like I said, the guy is a little questionable. The seventh floor thinks he's dangerous, but he's got enough friends in Operations and provides enough actionable information that he hasn't been shut down or pulled out."

"You said you had some personal experience with him?" Hank asked.

"Briefly," was the reply. "We had some contact a few years ago, trying to hunt down some AQEA bad boys, but nothing extended." Danny shrugged. "He struck me as a little loose in his procedures, and his reputation is pretty shady, but that could be either earned or unearned. Could be he's just unorthodox, and has made enemies for purely political reasons."

He grinned suddenly. "Which is a possibility that actually makes me somewhat predisposed to like the guy a little, given how things are going."

Alek snorted. "If he's survived as long in this hellhole as you say he has, he'd have to be unorthodox."

"Alek," I said, "any word from Tom as to whether Caleb and his boys can get close enough to support us on this?"

He sobered. "Not at the moment. Kenya is pretty well locked down, with the increasing AQEA insurgency in the south. They aren't letting many foreigners in, except some aid workers, but definitely not heavily armed contractors with a helicopter, at least that aren't there to fight AQ. They're trying the Ethiopian route, but it's taking time."

"So we're on our own. Again." It wasn't a question.

"Yep."

***

We got a look at how bad it was going to get a couple hours later. We were about an hour from Baardheere, and could actually see it through the thick vegetation that grew along the banks of the Juba River, and around the farms that crammed into the Juba floodplain. We could also see the billows of black smoke rising from where the Lashkar al-Barbar had already struck.

"They moved faster than we expected," Jim said from behind the wheel. Both trucks had come to a stop under one of the biggest acacias I had seen yet.

"Danny's trying to make contact with Baird," Alek called over the radio. "No answer yet."

"Naturally," I replied. No way was this going to go smoothly. I watched the smoke boil skyward, and could even hear some of the shooting going on. Unfortunately, we didn't have any way at the time to know what was going on, who was shooting, or anything else about the situation. For all we knew, the Kenyans might have been on the run already. They were strung out pretty thin on this side of the border, since so many of the 2,000 troops who had been in country had been pulled back to deal with the rash of Al Qaeda in East Africa attacks across Kenya proper. Between the loss of Western support, the decapitation of the NFPS by Al Masri's lightning strikes, and considerable support for Shabaab from other Islamist countries, the operation that had been poised to end the Somali Civil War just a couple of years ago was on the verge of total failure.

"Vic Two, Vic One," Alek called. "We've got an RP, northeast of the city, on the bank of Juba. Also an update; the smoke is from a Lashkar al-Barbar raid, but the gomers have pulled back for the moment. Main body is still probably most of a day out. They're having fun with the farmers on the way." The disgust in Alek's voice came through loud and clear.

"Roger," I replied. "Recommend we go to ground until dark, then

179

move to the RP. I'd expect the Kenyans to be a little trigger-happy about unidentified technicals rolling around right after that."

"Affirm," Alek replied. "Take point, find us a lay-up point."

***

That didn't take long, as there was quite a bit more vegetation this close to the Juba than there had been up north, and it was thicker. Most of it consisted of thick, low trees that I couldn't identify, but looked like they were related to the acacias up north. There wasn't a lot of ground cover, just red clay with the bushes and trees growing out of it, but we found a thick enough grove to drive the trucks into after only a few minutes of looking.

We shut down the engines, and, after setting up security, which mainly consisted of three two-man teams in the weeds, we set to pulling the foliage back into place to hide where we'd brought the trucks in. Once that was done, it was a matter of watching and waiting to see if we had been spotted entering the grove. There wasn't any sign that we had, so we relaxed a little, and set in to wait for dark.

***

The bank of the Juba was more heavily vegetated than the Shabelle we had crossed a day ago, or at least it was where we were supposed to meet Baird. We approached slowly and cautiously, blacked out. We were barely rolling at a walking pace, and I probably could have gotten out of the Land Cruiser and walked alongside. Instead, I kept my window rolled down and my rifle muzzle resting on the edge, so I could get it out fast, and scanned the riverbank with the thermal imaging on my NVGs turned on.

The spot Baird had picked as a rendezvous was about two miles north of Baardheere, past where the Juba made a hard turn to the east. It was all farmland or open ground for about a mile in any direction.

We halted about one hundred meters from the river, and waited. I could see some movement down by the water, but shortly figured out that it was just more crocs. Other than that, and a few other animals out in the weeds nearby, I couldn't see any sign of life. Of course, there was plenty of brush to hide in.

Once the trucks were halted, Larry and I got out and headed east, while Hank and Rodrigo went west. We were spreading out to the flanks of the meeting place, getting into position to unleash hell if things went pear-shaped. We knew next to nothing about Baird aside from what Danny had told us about his rep, and that apparently he wasn't on the best of terms with Langley these days.

The brush was much greener and softer than the prickly stuff we'd had to thrash through up by Balli Gubat. It was also easily as thick, and grew higher, which made it more of an exercise in frustration to get through it. Branches and leaves snagged on kit, weapons, and arms, and had to be pulled away. It made noise, and it slowed us down, while the entire time I was more worried about stumbling into a croc that I didn't see because I was wrestling with an oversized bush.

I looked back toward Larry, who was having even more trouble than I was. I could barely hear his constant stream of swearing under his breath as he forced his way through the twining branches. I scanned around him as he came up next to me.

"I've still got visual on the trucks," he whispered as he came alongside my shoulder. "We're good."

"All right," I replied, just as quietly. I pointed ahead. "Looks like the veg extends toward the river right up there; we'll set in there." Larry just nodded and tapped my shoulder by way of acknowledgement. I turned back forward and forged toward our chosen position.

It turned out to be just about perfect, or so it looked in the dark. More than once I've gotten into a hide that looked like the ultimate evolution of concealment, until the sun came up. Fortunately, we didn't plan on being here when the sun came up. It was just short of midnight. I took a knee looking to the northwest, while Larry covered behind me, out toward the hinterland. I scanned toward the west, until I got eyes on either Hank's or Rodrigo's IR firefly. The fireflies were small, cheap IR beacons that plugged into a 9-volt battery. They worked almost as well as a full-sized military strobe, while being much smaller and lighter. Every one of us had one in his left shoulder pocket.

We stayed like that for the better part of a half-hour, while I had to switch knees a couple of times. I was pretty sure Larry had switched to sitting against the tree; a man that big cannot stay on one knee comfortably for any length of time. I was only able to because it was a damn sight better than trying it with seventy-five pounds of kit on. I was rolling with a chest rig, rifle, and bump helmet for my NODs, that was it.

My radio earpiece crackled to life. "Danny just got off the phone with Baird," Alek reported. "He's inbound now, five mikes." I just tapped my PTT twice to acknowledge.

It was quiet, or seemed so at first. After a while, the noise of night insects, frogs chirping, crocs grunting, the wind in the branches, and the slow gurgle of the river became almost a cacophony. At least, until the sound of engines and tires crunching on the ground came on the wind, and started drowning out the rest of the night noises.

The vehicle was running blacked out, and I could only see a silhouette and the faint gleam of NVG-amplified starlight off its windows and dusty paint. At first glance, I thought it was a minibus, but it was an old UAZ Bukhanka. It rolled out into the open ground below the trees, where the river looked to flood relatively frequently, and slowed, then stopped. The passenger door opened, and a man got out, with the telltale tube of a set of PVS-14s in front of his eye. He looked around, then, looking toward us, reached up to his NVGs and flashed the IR illuminator three times.

I replied with a double flash from my own, and he acknowledged with a single flash. I tapped the PTT on my vest. "This is Hillbilly. I have positive contact with the asset." Even before I got an acknowledgement, I stood up, tapping Larry on the shoulder to let him know I was moving. I heard him lever himself up off the ground behind me, as I moved forward toward our contact.

The guy was short, wiry, and cradling an AK in his hands. He had an old Halo mount that held the NVGs in front of his eye, and an AK chest rig over his short-sleeved shirt. I could make out that he was dark, with something of a beard beneath the NVGs, but that was about it. "Baird?" I asked.

"That's me," he replied, with a faint accent that didn't sound exactly East African. I couldn't put my finger on it, but I already knew the guy was an American, so I let it lie for the moment. He pointed to my shoulder. "You might not want to flash too much IR around," he said.

I raised an eyebrow he couldn't see. "Why not? Are you telling me the skinnies have night vision now?"

He stared at me for a moment. I couldn't make out all of his expression, but he seemed surprised and disgusted. "Really?" he asked, confirming the disgusted part. "They sent you in here that unprepared?" He shook his head. "Never mind. Bring your trucks up, and let's get moving. And really black out."

I felt almost a little embarrassed, which pissed me off. We'd come this far through this shithole country, and this guy was calling us out at first meeting. It also pissed me off that apparently we'd been left out of the loop somewhere, if he was on the level.

Another tap of the PTT. "Bring it on home. Our guide is here," I called. "And he's warned us to douse the IR lights."

"Roger," Alek replied. A moment later I could hear the trucks starting up, and then the HiLux nosed through the bushes, followed by the Land Cruiser. I saw the firefly to the west go dead, then the darkened forms of Hank and Rodrigo came walking up along the treeline, all but invisible except for the thermal imaging until they were right on top of us.

I turned to Baird. "You lead out, we'll follow in trace." He just nodded curtly, and Larry and I trotted over to the Land Cruiser and climbed back in.

"So," Jim said from the driver's seat, "you met our boy? What do you think?"

"I don't know," I replied, as I adjusted my rifle so I could get it out the window fast if I needed to. "He at least implied that the skinnies down here have night vision, which means either he's making shit up to make himself seem important and knowledgeable, or we've gotten shit intel again.

Both seem entirely possible at this point."

Jim just grunted. "The way the rest of this op has gone, I'm leaning toward option two," Imad said from the back seat. There didn't seem to be much to add after that.

To his credit, Baird led us away from the direction he'd come, angling out to the southeast, swinging wide into the hinterland before turning back west toward Baardheere. Most of the way we were actually on the rutted, packed tracks that somehow had survived the flooding of the Juba, but several times we were bouncing over open ground. Honestly, if I'd been blindfolded, I never would have been able to tell the difference.

Baardheere loomed against the river, a darkened hulk of buildings and trees. There were next to no lights visible; in a couple of places we could still see fires burning from the raid the day before. There didn't look like there was a single electric light burning anywhere outside of a building, not even at the checkpoints where Kenyan forces were set up. I could see one on the northeastern outskirts of the town, mainly identifiable by the BMP that was sitting near the sandbagged emplacement. There was a faint glow to the south, probably where the main Kenyan FOB was, but even that seemed to be minimally lit.

I watched the Kenyan outpost carefully as we rolled toward the north end of town. There was no activity, no sign that we'd been spotted, or if we had, that they had any interest in us. I found that disturbing, frankly. These were supposed to be the forces that were going to stop the Islamist takeover of Somalia; at least that was the line in the press, even after the disastrous reversals in Mogadishu, Kismayo, and Baidoa. But they were looking to be rather less than watchful, even after Awale's raid in the morning. Were they that beaten? Or was Baird just that good at making sure they looked the other way while he worked?

The UAZ led us to a small walled compound on the north side of the town; in fact it was the northernmost structure in the place, near as I could tell. There was what looked like a kind of superfluous extra wall sticking out at an angle from the south wall, and Baird led us into the funnel-shaped opening. The HiLux pulled aside, and I motioned for Jim to take us in after Baird; Alek obviously wanted the HiLux with the PKM furthest out.

The UAZ came to a stop, and Baird and his driver got out. The driver was huge, easily 6'4" and, unless I missed my guess, around two hundred fifty pounds. He was also carrying a Galil like it was a toy.

Jim shut off the engine, little more than a foot from the UAZ's rear bumper, and we started piling out. Baird started into the compound, but Alek called out quietly for us to wait a second.

"Bob, Nick, you've got vic watch," he said. "Keep an eye on things. We'll keep our radios on for the time being. This guy is apparently our contact--" he looked at Danny, who nodded. He'd apparently gotten the bona fides from Baird at some point since we'd linked up. "So, we should be on reasonably safe ground, but let's not take anything for granted." There were nods and murmurs of assent all around. Noticeably, none of us had either dropped kit or left our personal weapons in the trucks. Safehouse or not, we weren't going to be relaxing much here.

The big guy was waiting by the entrance. As Alek led the way in, he gestured for our gigantic host to go in first. I saw a flash of teeth in the dark as the guy grinned, and ducked through the low gate to lead the way into the compound.

It looked like just about any other Third World compound I've ever been in. The concrete wall was topped with what looked like a low fence, and there were three small buildings against the north wall, one in each corner, with another about centered. The main house was against the west wall, and while it was the same stucco with ill-fitting windows and metal roof of all the rest of the buildings I'd seen in East Africa, it looked solid. A generator was chugging away around the corner from the entrance, but if there were lights on inside, the windows had been blacked out.

As I glanced around, I saw that we weren't alone in the compound with Baird and the giant. There were at least half a dozen men in the courtyard, all armed. None of them were smoking, which I found interesting. Smoking at night kills your night vision, but that's a fact generally lost on Third World armies and militias. These guys were in kit, albeit light, armed, and held themselves like professionals. Just what kind of operation did the Agency have going here?

Baird was nowhere in sight when I came through the gate, but Big Guy was next to the door to the main house, and pushed it open as the team approached. Golden light spilled out, confirming that the windows had indeed been blacked out from inside. I was also able to get a good look at Big Guy for the first time. He was white, with thick red hair, dressed in shorts and a t-shirt, with a Rhodesian chest rig across his massive torso. I also got a good enough look at his rifle to see it was not the Galil I'd initially thought it was. It was close, as the South African R4 was closely based on the Galil, but it was different enough to be noticed in the light, at least if you have an eye for those sorts of things.

We filed into the house behind Big Guy, who walked across the room and leaned against the wall. Baird was standing next to a table that dominated the left side of the room. A small chest that at second glance was a storm case sat in the corner next to Big Guy, and several white plastic chairs were drawn up around the table. Another R4 was leaning against the wall. Other than that, and the rugs on the floor, the room was bare.

Baird looked us over, as we returned the favor. He was black, though not quite as dark as most of the Somalis I'd seen. His hair was short, and going gray, as was the short, neat chin beard. He was also obviously in good condition, in spite of living in this hellhole for who knows how many years.

He was also pissed. "Where do you people think you are?" he demanded. "For that matter, what year do you think it is? You think this is Iraq, in 2005, when the muj hid their faces, and never came out at night? You don't own the night here, you don't own the air, you don't own anything. Yet you carry on after dark as if you have no signature, blazing beacons on your shoulders, and have the nerve to say you want to meet covertly!"

I was about to respond, and not politely, but Alek wasn't having any of it, either. "Slow down, Baird, none of us have any idea what the fuck you're talking about. We didn't get briefed on Al-Shabaab having any sort of modern capabilities, aside from AKs and RPGs, and we only found out that they were this close to Baardheere within the last twenty-four hours, anyway. Since you're the man on the ground, you can calm the fuck down and fill us in, or you can shut the hell up and we can leave, to do what we can without your hysterics."

Baird looked shocked. "You mean..." He looked around at all of us, his gaze finally landing on Danny. He sat down heavily and shook his head in disbelief. "You really have no idea what's going on down here, do you?"

"Apparently not," Danny said tightly. "So how about enlightening us?"

Baird cursed under his breath. "I've been reporting to Langley about this situation for months, ever since Al-Khalidi showed up. Naturally they've been sitting on it. Didn't fit with what their whiz kids had dreamed up."

That got Danny's attention, fast. "Al-Khalidi? Which Al-Khalidi?"

Baird raised an eyebrow at him. "Mahmoud Al-Khalidi--'Al Masri,' he's calling himself here."

"Holy shit." Danny seemed genuinely rocked. I was missing something. "Are you sure about this?"

"Of course I'm sure!" Baird snapped. "Triple-sourced sure. I've even seen the man with my own eyes. It's him."

"Somebody mind filling in the rest of us knuckle-draggers as to just who Mahmoud Al-Khalidi is?" Jim asked, his voice just a little too loud. Jim never was a fan of people talking inside baseball in front of him.

Danny was still staring at Baird. "He's the number two man in the Egyptian Mukhabarat, and the brother of Said Al-Khalidi, who has been formally anointed to succeed Yusuf Al-Qaradawi as the spiritual leader of the Islamic Republic of Egypt. He is a very, very big fish. Now just what the fuck brings him to Somalia?"

"I think maybe we need to start this conversation over from the beginning," I put in. There was a general murmur of agreement.

Baird nodded, and waved to the plastic chairs around the room. "Please, sit down. This could take some time. You may as well bring your other two teammates in; this compound is secure." Alek just looked at him for a moment, before finally nodding fractionally and motioning to Tim, who stepped out to bring Nick and Bob in. Baird looked over to Big Guy. "I should probably introduce my associate, and number two man of this little operation here. Jason Van Voorhees has been with me since the beginning, when I was still an officer with our oh-so-well regarded colleagues in Langley." Van Voorhees grinned humorlessly.

"Wait a second," Larry said, "I was under the impression that you were a CIA officer?"

"I was," Baird replied. "I retired a few years ago, but maintained some of my contacts, and my activities here have provided my former bosses with enough information that they have decided to generally look the other way and leave me alone." He snorted. "As if they could touch me here, the way they've let their assets fall off in recent years. It's worse than the nineties."

Danny looked over at Van Voorhees. "So where'd he dig you up, Jason?"

"Special Task Force," the big man said, in a soft, Afrikaaner-accented voice. He didn't volunteer any further information, but if he was telling the truth, those three words pretty well established his bona fides, at least as a trigger puller. Special Task Force had been South Africa's premier hostage rescue and counter terrorism force for a long time. It had suffered a lot from the corruption under the ANC administration, but still was probably some of the best on the continent, that I knew of.

"All right," Danny said, pulling up a plastic chair and levering his geared-up bulk into it, as the rest of us followed suit. There was some commotion as Bob, Tim, and Nick came in and situated themselves around the room. Funny, none of us had our backs to either the door or Van Voorhees. "We already knew you had some kind of assets here, we just didn't know exactly what kind. Are you telling me you've got your own little company of shooters out here? What the hell for?"

"Same reason I came back over here after I retired," Baird replied. "To do something about the Islamists and the warlords." He scratched his beard, and stared at the floor. "Haven't managed to do all that much," he admitted, "mostly running some support missions for the AMISOM forces here, and gathering information.

"It was shaping up better when we first stood up. I had a good spread of former South African, British, and US military personnel, along with a handful of Kenyans and Somalis, mostly those who'd been somehow involved in the Jubaland Initiative." Jubaland was to be the semi-autonomous Somali-Kenyan state in southern Somalia, much like Puntland and Somaliland to the north. It was intended by the Kenyans to serve as a buffer between Kenya and the nonstop violence and extremism of Somalia itself. "At the time, things were looking a bit better down here. Then Al Masri showed up."

CHAPTER 22

"At first we didn't have any idea who he was. Hell, we didn't really care. He was small time, an up-and-coming Shabaab commander, but Shabaab was on the ropes. They were holding on to Kismayo, and that by their fingernails. They'd given up Mogadishu, and they'd lost Baidoa to the Ethiopians, bad. They'd been at each other's throats a year before and almost wiped themselves out. That's always been their biggest weakness; even when they had the NFPS outnumbered and outgunned, they couldn't make it stick because one leader or another was always taking time off from the fight to attack his fellows. They expended more ammunition on each other than they did the NFPS, the Ethiopians, or the Kenyans.

"The Kenyans, with a handful of NFPS troops, had had Kismayo surrounded for months. They were getting ready to push in; the only reason they hadn't yet was a combination of supply problems and harassing attacks on their bases, mostly mortars and rockets. Shabaab threw a lot of rockets at the Kenyans, but they got lucky twice, hitting a supply dump and burning the entire thing to the ground the first time, and actually hitting a CP the second time. Several higher Kenyan commanders were killed.

"But Al Masri didn't show up in Kismayo. No, he showed up in Baidoa.

"Somalia had never really seen the kind of bombings that have been used in Israel, Iraq, or Afghanistan. Even Shabaab kept their violence good and personal--shootings, kidnappings, beheadings...things of that nature. Bombings happened, but they just weren't an East African method.

"Until that winter. In the course of a week, fifteen bombs went off in Baidoa, mainly targeting Ethiopian patrols, but also the homes of two prominent Somalis who had welcomed the Ethiopian forces. Then the mayor disappeared, only to show up two days later hanging from a power pole with no head.

"The Ethiopian troops were getting hit hard; they lost almost a platoon in one day. Three separate patrols were ambushed and cut off. One was apparently hemmed in by the crowd in the market; I heard they used trucks to close off the exits, then detonated them. Another was hit in the street in the middle of the day, in what sounded like a classic L-shaped ambush.

"By this time, the Ethiopian troops were spooked, and they were starting to turn turtle, retreating into their handful of fortified FOBs within the city. It didn't get any better when 'Al Masri' came on the loudspeakers of almost every mosque in the city, praising Allah, and declaring the rebirth of the Islamic Emirate of Somalia. It was a long speech; I've heard recordings. He wove in threats against the Ethiopians and their allies, along with invitations to them to abandon their invasion, submit to Allah, and join the brothers. That alone was new.

"By this time, the Ethiopian command was barely keeping it together. They were being mortared or rocketed every night, and sniper fire was a constant. They tried pushing out a patrol one day. The point man got shot as soon as he stepped outside the wire, and the patrol mutinied, or so the story goes. They wouldn't go.

"A few days later, the Ethiopians pulled out of Baidoa, still taking losses the whole way. An IED hit the convoy leaving one of the FOBs, and killed about thirty troops who were riding in a troop truck. Al Masri and his troops weren't letting up, and they were sending a message, too, that they wouldn't be satisfied with just Baidoa.

"I was still here at the time. We were doing some basic support work, trying to lay the groundwork to keep the AMISOM and Kenyan forces from shooting us when we started going at it for real. The Kenyans weren't too keen on our being around, and AMISOM was even less so, but they appreciated the reporting we could do, and they had bigger fish to fry, so they tolerated us. I had developed enough contacts within the Kenyan command that I was hearing rumblings about what was going on in Baidoa. It sounded different enough from business-as-usual in this country that I decided we needed to check it out.

"I went alone, with Nigerian papers and a cover story that I was an arms dealer with ties to Boko Haram. I circled well around Baidoa, approaching from the Shabaab-dominated areas to the north, so it didn't look like I had somehow come from Kenyan-held territory as a 'brother-in-jihad.' I got searched thoroughly by a checkpoint as soon as I got within the city.

"I had to establish my credentials, and got taken for a meeting with one of the Shabaab captains. It was Muktar Abu Kadir; maybe you know the name. We'd been hunting him for some time while I was still with the Agency, though never all that hard; he was small fry at the time. He never rose to the level of the really bad guys; he was a tool, a particularly savvy and savage field commander, but he never led more than about a company.

"Two fighters loaded me into a truck and we wound our way into downtown Baidoa. It was still relatively crowded with people going about their business, but the atmospherics were all wrong. Everybody seemed furtive, on edge. When I saw the first few patrols, I understood why.

Shabaab had Taliban-style 'morality police' out, and they were accosting and beating anyone who didn't seem to be acting in an appropriately Islamic manner. Six of them were surrounding a man just outside the building where we stopped, and were kicking him and beating him with rifle butts. I never did find out why.

"I'm not sure what the building was. It was three stories, painted light blue. It might have been a hotel at one time, but everything had been torn out of it, and it was Abu Kadir's headquarters now. He was on the third floor, of course, and I was marched up to see him.

"As soon as I walked in the room, I could see how much things had changed, and quite possibly why. Abu Kadir wasn't alone. While he was obviously in charge, there were three Arabs, either Libyan or Egyptian, sitting in a half circle beside him. My first reaction was that they were advisors. They weren't armed the same as the Shabaab troops; one of them even had a SIG-Sauer carbine, and a modern assault vest, not the old AK chest rig or gunbelt that most of the Shabaab fighters were using.

"They didn't talk much, but let Abu Kadir do most of the jawing. He was shrewder than I'd expected, and I had to do some fancy talking to make my rather flimsy, thrown-together cover hold up. Funny what happens when you don't have all the resources of the US Intelligence community backing you up. He wanted to see samples of what I had to sell; fortunately, I had brought a handful of Chinese CF-05s. I didn't have any more to sell later, but he didn't know that. He was impressed, but most importantly, he turned to his Arab advisors and handed them the one he'd picked up out of the truck. They looked it over, and told him that they would be good purchases, but not all that useful in open environments, or against Kenyan or AMISOM body armor. They recommended more AKs, or QBZ-95s, if I could get Chinese rifles.

"I met with three more Shabaab commanders, and it was always the same. The commanders were Somali, but with Libyan, Sudanese, or Egyptian advisors, and they were all looking for weapons and gear, unless it was something they could get from Egypt or Sudan. One of them actually told me that, though I was pretty sure that was the case already by the time I talked to him.

"I was able to leave without too much trouble, although as I left I saw more than a dozen bodies hanging from electric wires in the center of town. I learned before I left that they had been executed for apostasy.

"It's just gotten worse since then. The supplies are coming in mainly from Egypt by sea through Kismayo now, after the Kenyan blockade was broken by submarine strikes and small-boat suicide bombers. They aren't sending the top-of-the-line stuff, most of which they got from us, but modernized small arms, anti-tank weapons, night vision, comms, it's all coming in. Shabaab and their cronies have never had it so good.

191

"On top of that, the weapons and training they've gotten from the Kalifah Alliance countries have allowed them to go so far as to capture Ethiopian and Kenyan armored vehicles and artillery. Not a lot of them, but enough to make a difference.

"They've pushed the Kenyans away from Kismayo, and the Ethiopians have been reeling so hard that Shabaab has a presence as deep into Ethiopia as Afder and Melka Chireti. Mogadishu fell pretty quickly when Al Masri and Lashkar al-Barbar showed up. Malouf's band of murderers had just appeared on the scene a few weeks before that, when they massacred a bunch of farmers they accused of being Ahlu Sunna Wal'jama members in Buur Hakaba.

"In short, gentlemen, you've taken a job to rescue hostages from the Kalifah Alliance, not just from a pack of rag-tag East African Islamists who've barely been managing to hang on against the militaries of no fewer than three nations, and the UN. They're almost as well trained and equipped as any of the top-tier Arab countries now, and those have been getting training and equipment from the Russians and Chinese lately. With Lemonier gone, there's now no drone coverage down here. And you were sent in without any of this information, with…eleven men."

CHAPTER 23

There was a long silence after that. I suspect all of us were thinking the same thing; was it even feasible to see this job through, or did we need to cut our losses and try to get out? That presented its own problems, especially as I was pretty sure our employers back in the States probably wouldn't be too keen on helping us extract when we'd just told them to find some other way to get the hostages back.

Not only that, but, despite the odds, I didn't much care for the idea of leaving those men and women to the mercy of those machete-wielding savages to save our own skins. Call me a romantic.

"Is that it?" Jim asked, the first to break the silence. There was a wave of dark chuckles as we got it. Baird looked nonplused, so Jim obliged him by explaining, "This entire job has been so clusterfucked already, that I don't see how this changes anything. It was damned near impossible before. Now it's really damned near impossible. Big difference."

"Joking aside, it's a valid point," Hank said thoughtfully, fingering his beard. "The overall mission hasn't changed, has it? We're still here for a deep-recon mission; locate the hostages, then call in the cavalry--Delta, DevGru, whoever's in the chute for it. We need to be a little more careful, certainly, but I don't see it as being impossible."

Danny was looking at the table, his fingers steepled in front of his face, a frown furrowing his brow. After a moment, he looked up. "If you gents will excuse me, I have a couple of calls to make." He stood up, pulled his sat phone out of his kit, and walked out into the courtyard.

"Hell," Tim pointed out, "we've already had plenty of reasons and opportunities to take our ball and go home, and we haven't yet. I think I can safely say that we're all psycho enough to see this through, no matter how many bad guys Murphy throws at us."

"True enough," I said. "We might have to alter the plan somewhat, but we were already in way over our heads anyway, so what's this much more?"

"I'd say it depends on one thing in particular," Alek said, watching Baird carefully. "That being; do the bad guys know we're here?"

"They might," Baird said. "They suspect something's up, at any rate. After the breakout in Djibouti City--I presume that was you?" At Alek's nod, he continued, "--I'm sure you were informed about the execution of the Qardho group. I've heard rumors that it was supposed to be the Berbera group, but someone got to them before they could be executed; supposedly the hit went down less than an hour before al-Khalidi showed up with his camera crew."

Nick chuckled. "Bet he was pissed."

"I imagine he was," Baird said coolly. "Which is probably why he took his time with the Qardho murders. I don't know how much of the video you've seen--" he glanced around at our shaking heads "--but it was bad. Very, very bad. I'm sure they've stepped up security on the remaining hostages in the meantime. And you can bet that any hint of Americans operating in Somalia is going to bring them screaming down as hard as they can. We'll have to make very thorough reconnaissance, and not make any moves until we're sure, and can get out fast."

"What's this 'we' business all of a sudden?" Imad asked. Imad had generally accepted Danny's involvement, but he was intensely clannish when it came to our operations, and even less trusting of outsiders than most of us, which was saying something.

"You didn't think I'd become involved, and then just sit on the sidelines while you went blundering about in my backyard, did you?" Baird replied levelly. "I've got a few assets here, in addition to my contacts, as you already know. I can't offer much materially, but sometimes just a few more guns at the right time and place can tip the balance. I also know this place far better than any of you. You won't have much of a chance without my help."

"We'll think about it," Alek said, before Imad could say anything more. "I appreciate the offer, but we haven't worked together, trained together, or even rehearsed together, and you'll understand if I'm a little reticent to throw new players in the mix this far into the game."

"I understand," Baird said, "but with the situation being what it is, don't take too long. I think you may find you need all the help you can get." He paused, eyeing us shrewdly. "Plus, I think you might change your minds when I tell you I can get us a couple of helicopters."

A couple of eyebrows went up. "You have our attention," Alek said.

Baird settled back in his chair. "They aren't much, I'll admit. One's an old Alouette III that has been kicking around Africa since the '80s. I think it might even have been used during the Rhodesian Bush War. The other's bigger, a Cougar that we were able to get through various means from Zimbabwe a couple years ago." There were a few grunts and grumbles at that; while many of us had had to trust our necks to old birds--I knew a Platoon Sergeant when I was with Recon who liked to point out every time we got on a CH-46 that the last of those birds had been built in 1967--but they'd all been maintained by Americans. We were in no way certain about forty-year-old helos that had been kicking around Africa for that whole time. No, we didn't have a very good opinion of the mechanical skill and conscientiousness of African ground crews. Still don't.

But Baird held up his hands. "I know what you're thinking, but they're in pretty good shape. Hans has had one of them since 2007, and went over the other one with a fine-toothed comb once we bought it from an NGO upcountry in Ethiopia a couple of years ago."

"Okay, who is Hans?" I asked flatly. I'll admit, something about Baird just kind of irritated me. I didn't really have a good reason at the time. Maybe I was just being belligerent. Stranger things have happened.

"Hans Van Der Boek is our resident gear-head and the man responsible for our little aerial contingent," Baird replied. "He was with the South African Defense Force, flew for the Recces. He got out shortly after Mandela's people took over, and he's been private sector ever since. His crew is about half-and-half, Afrikaaner and Russian. He's been keeping helos flying in African hellholes for almost forty years. I've trusted him with my life many times, both before and after I retired." He cocked an eyebrow at me. "Satisfied?"

"For the moment." I didn't really have a lot of reason not to be at this point, and, as Jim and Hank had pointed out, we had passed the BOHICA threshold a long time ago, so there really wasn't any reason to be an asshole about it. I guess I was just being tired and ornery.

"Where are the birds?" Imad asked, pointedly ignoring my crankiness.

"That's the problem," Baird admitted. "They're about fifty miles west of here, closer to the Kenyan border. We had them at the field south of town, but with Malouf's killers getting closer, we decided to move them. Of course, we didn't know you were coming at the time, or that we'd need them operationally."

"We might need to bring them in here," Alek said, as Danny came back into the room. "Let's go over the plan first and see which is more feasible, bringing the birds here or going to them." He glanced over at Danny, who said nothing, but shook his head. So there was nothing new from Langley. More than likely, whoever Danny had talked to was as surprised by the information as we had been.

"Part of the problem, as I see it, is getting an ID on this Abu Sadiq character," Baird went on. "I haven't heard of him, at least not by that name. But since most of these assholes use kunyahs, even here, that isn't necessarily a game breaker. I probably know who it is, by another name. I take it we don't have photos?"

"Not at the moment," Danny replied. "Just the name. The source said he is a major player with the Al Qaeda cadre attached to Al-Shabaab, and that he hangs out in Kismayo. He didn't know too much beyond that; he was mostly involved with the Djibouti side of the operation. It looks like they've compartmentalized this particular op pretty well."

Baird nodded, as he retrieved a case from the back corner and started pulling maps and photos out of it. "They've gotten good at that, especially as the AMISOM guys have learned more and more from US advisors. Let's face it; most of the active-stupid jihadists got nailed back when the US was in Iraq and Afghanistan. The ones who survived are now the major commanders, and they are the ones advising and supplying Shabaab now. Even the Iranian high command cut its teeth with Qods Force in Iraq." He laid out maps of southern Somalia and overhead imagery of Kismayo. "I don't have many contacts in Kismayo anymore," he said. "My best one was arrested for drinking alcohol, panicked, and was shot trying to escape." He sighed. "Can't get good snitches these days." His delivery was so deadpan, and we were so damned tired, that it took a minute to realize he was half-joking.

"That means we're going to have to develop our target package on the ground," Jim mused, rubbing his chin. We were all more than a little bristly by that time, even Jim, who generally tried to go clean shaven. The gray in his beard showed more than his temples. "Which means a lay-up point and preliminary recon first and foremost. What are the atmospherics there? Is some kind of partisan link-up even a possibility?"

Baird was frowning at the map, now joined by another man, a lanky, almost hairless individual in shorts, boots, and a t-shirt. He was darker even than Imad, and looked almost spidery as he spread his long-fingered hands on the tabletop. "I was there only a few weeks ago," he explained. He had a faint accent, all but undetectable. "Anyone who might have been willing to give the Islamists trouble has either been shot, hanged, stoned, or has fled. Everyone else seems to be keeping their heads down. Any known collaborators with Kenyan forces were beheaded in the first two weeks after Shabaab retook the city.

"Three months ago, I would have said that the best option for gathering intelligence is going to be posing as khat traders," he continued, "but Shabaab has taken one of their hardline swings against khat and other drugs lately. Three khat dealers got burned alive in their car just two days ago, near Baidoa. So that's out."

"What about the NGO approach?" Alek asked.

"You mean come in as some sort of rich, clueless, oh-so-concerned Westerners trying to ease the suffering of the people?" Baird asked sarcastically. He frowned. "Maybe, but it's a roll of the dice as to whether they accept the propaganda and the possibility of money or just take you hostage for more money. Or kill you on the spot. Especially with Egyptian support now, they don't have to kiss bleeding-heart ass so much anymore, and they're more likely to just show their contempt for infidels. Possibly violently."

"Then a couple of us show up as new recruits," Imad said. He looked over at the lanky guy. "I don't know about you, but I daresay I've gotten pretty good at the East African mujaheddin routine."

Lanky nodded. "Either that, or arms dealers. We do have the examples available to pull that off, but I think especially with the Egyptian involvement, your idea is probably more workable."

My turn to frown. "I'd say go with the gun-runner option." Imad and Lanky turned to look at me, so I explained. "Look, recruits aren't going to go straight to the Big Man, they're going to get shipped to a training camp, or handed either an AK or a suicide vest, and sent north. Arms dealers are more valuable, even with the Egyptians on the ground, and have a better chance of talking to somebody higher up, like Baird was doing in Baidoa." I scratched my chin. My beard was greasy, salty, and gritty, and it itched. "We've just got to think of what you can be trafficking that the Egyptians can't supply."

"Drones," Larry said suddenly. I cocked an eyebrow at him, and he plunged onward. "Think about it. These guys have been getting pounded by JSOC Reapers for years now. I'm pretty sure the Egyptians don't have much in the way of UAVs, and probably aren't giving them to Shabaab. If we can convince them that we can get them armed UAVs, and train them to use them, they'll probably jump at it. It's not like the muj have ever been picky about the source of the weapons they use--if they can use an infidel weapon to kill lots of infidels, they'll do it."

"You're assuming they didn't already get all or most of the drones out of Lemonier," Hank pointed out. "There were supposed to be a lot of UAV assets there."

"Then we offer subject-matter experts," Larry replied. "They can't have too many people who necessarily know how to use the drones to their full potential."

"Might be doable," Alek said. "We'd need a fair amount of information to make these guys sound convincing. And I don't think either of you have ever actually operated a Reaper or Predator, have you?" Both Imad and the guy I was already starting to think of as Lanky shook their heads in the negative.

"I think we need to set up a link back to the Colonel, and see if we can't get some useful information pushed about drone operations," Rodrigo suggested. "I can have the link up in about ten minutes."

Alek nodded, so Rodrigo jerked his head at Tim before leading the way out into the night. Our comm gear was still on the trucks. That brought another concern to mind, and I reminded myself to bring it up to Baird when we got to that point--did he have batteries for the comm gear? It was one thing that we hadn't been able to load up on nearly enough, and we were unlikely to find much in the way of lithium batteries for SATCOM radios and laptops in Somalia.

"So, who exactly are we sending in?" Hank asked.

"I will go," Lanky said. "I have been there before."

"I'll go, too," Imad said. He held out his hand to Lanky. "Imad," he said, by way of introduction.

Lanky clasped his hand firmly. "Harith," he replied. "Call me Spider."

Wonder where he got that nickname, I thought wryly.

***

With the general mission determined, namely to get Spider and Imad into Kismayo to find our mysterious target, we got down to the heavy duty planning. Maps and imagery were pored over, our assets were gone over with a fine-toothed comb, and various courses of action started to come together. Through it all, the imminent arrival of Lashkar al-Barbar hovered like a shadow. We hoped we'd get out before they attacked.

It was a vain hope.

CHAPTER 24

We had decided to catch a few hours' sleep in the early hours before dawn. We'd been up most of the night hammering out the plan. It was rough, but as good as could be expected with the tiny force we had. Baird had set security with the small number of his people who wouldn't be coming with us, and the rest of us had crashed. Alek and I briefly discussed the wisdom of this, but Alek finally made the call, based largely on Danny's say-so. Danny insisted that he had it from somebody he trusted in Special Activities that Baird was good, even though he was considered a bit of a dangerous nut by the seventh floor. So, we went ahead and trusted to his security, especially since all of us had been up for nearly thirty hours by then, anyway.

I awoke suddenly, with faint, pale light leaking through the cracks around the shoddily-fitted metal door. It took me a second to place what had disturbed me, but only a second. The thumping of rockets or mortars impacting to the south was pretty distinctive.

I rolled out, grabbing my kit and my rifle. Most everybody else was rousting out, too; if you've spent time in a war zone, you don't tend to sleep through that sort of thing. I was the first one with my kit on, so I slammed out the door and went for the first rooftop post I could find that was facing south.

"You got eyes-on that shelling?" I yelled up.

"Sure do," came the reply, in a faintly British accent. "It's still about a kilometer away, looks like they're shelling the southern edge of the town."

"Any sign of ground forces?"

"Not yet," he answered. "Tell Baird if we're clearing out of here we'd best get moving, though. LaB doesn't usually start shelling this heavily unless they're ready to push. If we wait too long, it could be a stone bitch to get out of here."

"Roger, I'll tell him," I shot back, and started in as Baird came out. "They've started shelling the south edge of the town," I told him.

"Damn," he said, as the *crump* sound grew more intense. "They're earlier than I expected." He started to move to yell at the guy on the roof, but I saved him the time.

"He says the shelling's still a klick away," I said. "We need to get moving before it gets this far north." My statement was punctuated by a long shot hitting less than two hundred yards away with a whistling *bang*.

"Right," he said. "My boys are already packed up, we don't settle in anywhere without being ready to punch out at short notice." I was already heading inside, while the rest of the team dragged out what gear they had brought in instead of leaving on the trucks. "I see you follow the same SOP."

"Most of us were Recon, at one time," I tossed over my shoulder. "It goes with the territory."

I dashed into the darkened room where my go-bag was sitting next to where I'd slept, grabbed it, and headed back out. By then, the shelling had intensified, and was now a rolling, thunderous roar to the south. These guys were serious.

As I chucked my go bag into the back of the Defender, I took the opportunity to watch Baird's guys work. I'll admit, I was impressed. They were smooth, practiced, and showed no sign of panic. Go bags and equipment cases came out of the main house and the sheds and were loaded on their trucks, along with several heavy guns, mostly PKMs and a couple of Pechenegs, and the cases of ammunition to go with them. We got some extra ammo and fuel, as well. Baird apparently wasn't poor, and he wasn't niggardly with his supplies, either.

Since we had been pretty much ready to grab-and-go, and Baird's people weren't too far behind, our little Mad Max convoy was ready to roll in about forty-five minutes. By this time, we were starting to hear sporadic small arms fire, and the shelling was getting a little ragged. As the last of Baird's guys came down off the roof, he reported that there were dust plumes closing on the Kenyan positions on the far side of the unnamed tributary wadi that ran roughly east-west through Baardheere to connect with the Juba. There wasn't much water in it at the moment, so it didn't afford the defenders much of an advantage. If the LaB were using four-wheel-drives, which they likely were, they'd plow through the wadi without even having to slow down much.

All of which added up to it being time for us to leave.

Baird's UAZ took the lead, with our HiLux and Land Cruiser pulling in behind him. Another UAZ and two older, open-top Land Rovers took up the rear, each retrofitted with mounts for one of the PKMs and the two Pecheneg machine guns. We turned out of the little staging area that the odd walls of the compound had set up, and immediately doglegged north. None of us wanted any part of the fight that was brewing up to the south.

But it quickly became apparent that we weren't going to get clear of Baardheere that easily. And it wasn't the jihadists we had to worry about. It was the Kenyans.

The Kenyan forces had a fair amount of their support base outside the city, ostensibly for the sake of keeping collateral damage down, but also because the city was the target, and the jihadis would have a bunch of Somalis to go through before they could get to the Kenyans' rear area. Cynical, yes. Hard not to be in Africa.

They also had security forces in and around their rear area, that got a little twitchy when they saw armed vehicles coming north during a LaB attack.

I figure we got spotted by guard posts on the corners of the big supply FOB that straddled the main dirt road heading northeast out of town. We hadn't gotten more than about a half mile away from the compound when the dust plumes of three AML armored cars came billowing toward us. Worse, an MD-50 helo lifted off from the FOB and started toward us, holding above the AMLs.

Just what we needed. People who were supposed to be our allies, but scared, suspicious, and trigger-happy, coming after us. Fuck this country.

"Contact, right," I yelled at Jim and Larry, who were crammed in the back of the Land Cruiser. We had a little more room than before, with Imad and Tim riding in the front UAZ, but it was still cramped. "They're friendlies for now, but I'm betting they're going to be a little paranoid, so it might not last."

We could outrun the AMLs, but not that helicopter. I keyed my radio. "Coconut, Hillbilly. You see our friends to the east?"

"Roger, Hillbilly, I've got 'em," Alek replied.

"Plan of action?" I asked.

"Try talking to them first," he replied. "We can outpace the armor, but I'd rather not have to shoot down a Kenyan bird if we can help it."

"Affirm." We certainly had the firepower to turn an MD-50 to scrap, but that would be pretty counter-productive in this situation. Not to mention we'd probably get a little shot up ourselves in the process. I twisted my head back to address Jim and Larry over the engine noise along with the banging and creaking of the suspension. "Gonna see if we can talk our way through this one, gents."

Jim just nodded. "Good call," was Larry's assessment.

I didn't hear it, but apparently Alek got through to Baird, and the lead UAZ slowed, coming to a stop in a slowly settling cloud of dust. As the HiLux moved slightly to the right before stopping, I motioned to Rodrigo to steer us to the left. We were forming a loose sort of modified herringbone as we came to a stop. That way we could still be in a defensive position without being too in-your-face about it. We didn't want to make the Kenyans' trigger fingers any itchier.

The AMLs rolled up to us and spread out on-line, while the MD-50 swooped overhead in a big circle, going into a tight orbit over us. I looked up through my open window, and saw the door-gunner watching us from behind an HK21. He didn't have it pointed at us, exactly, but he didn't have it pointed elsewhere, either.

"All dismounts out," Alek called. "Don't get in their faces, but let's not be timid, either."

I didn't need to pass that one on, as all of us except for Rodrigo were already kicking our doors open and pushing out onto the dusty ground. Rifles hung on slings, muzzles angled toward the dirt, gloved hands rested on firing controls.

There was a squad-sized group coming toward us from the lead armored car. They were dressed in either British camouflage or something similar, with light tactical vests, old Fritz-pattern Kevlar helmets, and G3s, except for one, who walked slightly ahead of the trigger-pullers. He carried no rifle, but had a shiny leather pistol belt and flap holster around his waist, and wore a green beret. Officer, no doubt. He marched up to Baird, who was standing a little forward of the group. He was flanked to the rear by Alek and Jason Van Voorhees.

I stayed back with the truck, and Jim and Larry hung back behind me, watching the Kenyans and our rear at the same time. These weren't technically hostiles, so we kept our stance easy, relaxed.

I kept toward the front of the truck where I could watch, but was plenty glad not to be in the thick of this conversation. I've never been much of a "hearts-and-minds" type of guy, and I find the sort of political posturing and give-and-take of these sorts of meetings and engagements more than a little tiresome. Jim and Larry were of generally the same sort of temperament. We didn't talk, concentrating on keeping an eye out for unpleasant surprises. At least, anything more unpleasant than the rising pall of smoke and dust behind us, continually roiling with the *whump* of explosives, as well as the sporadic, but increasing, rattle of small arms fire.

The conversation seemed to last forever. The Kenyan officer was arguing vociferously, and Baird and Danny were stonewalling him. Alek was standing in that way that told me he was starting to think about going ahead and shooting these clowns. I couldn't hear what was being said, but I could make some informed guesses.

We hadn't been authorized to pass by his command, meaning we hadn't bribed him, or hadn't bribed him enough. He had no assurance that we weren't terrorists, meaning we hadn't bribed him, or hadn't bribed him enough. He had orders to lock down everything coming or going around Baardheere, meaning we hadn't bribed him, or hadn't bribed him enough.

I kicked a rock as I let my gaze rove again, picking out pieces of cover where shooters might be huddled. It was automatic now, almost unthinking. My mind wandered, sort of, while my eyes scanned. Once something out of the ordinary popped up in my vision, my focus would

202

immediately snap to it, but for the time being, even with the noises of increasingly intense combat coming up from the south, fatigue led me to woolgather a bit.

Damn, but I hated this bullshit. Making nice with greedy assholes who pretended to give a fuck about their country while they really just did their damnedest to line their own pockets, using the chaos around them as an opportunity. Conversely, making nice with the bureaucratic assholes who obstructed operations that could help their country, just because the latest set of chickenshit boxes hadn't been checked. I hated all of them. I hated the games. Just let us pass and let us get back to killing assholes.

That's why I never even thought about being an officer when I was still in. Officers have to be politicians. Enlisted guys just have to make sure their shit's wired tight, and wreck house. "In case of war, break open glass." That's me.

Jim came up to my shoulder, both of us still watching, neither of us looking directly at the other. Jim and I have known each other a long time. He can be wise beyond his redneck exterior, or he can be the utter epitome of "cranky old bastard." Sometimes, he was both. He also wasn't terribly consistent about how he came around to either mood. What can I say, he's old. Says the guy who's in his thirties, but feels more like he's in his fifties...

The noise to the south was getting more intense. Sustained automatic fire was now audible, over the continuing rumble of shelling, and the occasional detonations of RPGs. It sounded like lead elements had made contact with whatever defensive positions the Kenyans had in place. From what I'd seen so far, I wouldn't give the Kenyan defenders a lot of time, but then, I hadn't been terribly impressed with *anybody's* fighting prowess out here.

Jim spat a brown gobbet of dip spit on the ground. That said something about his mood right there; he'd been hoarding his remaining Copenhagen for the last few days. "We need to get moving," he muttered. "Take a look toward the river."

I looked over to the west, where the Juba ran between Baardheere proper and B-ur-ae-ore. Sure enough, there were small motor boats coming upstream, positively overloaded with people. I had little doubt that they were LaB shooters. How the Kenyans had let the river go unblocked I didn't know, but it sure looked like they had. I reached for my radio, but it looked like Alek had seen it as well. He stepped forward and tapped Baird on the shoulder. There was a brief exchange of words, and Baird looked west, then, scowling, pointed out the incoming boats to the Kenyan officer.

The man looked startled, and immediately got on his radio, speaking rapidly and excitedly. His goons still weren't standing down, though they did keep glancing nervously toward the river, as well as the swelling cacophony of gunfire and explosions to the south. I really didn't like this. They were scared and probably a bit trigger-happy already, and with the real bad guys closing in on them, it was going to get worse. I traded a quick look with Jim, and he nodded fractionally. He felt it, too. We had to stay calm and collected, and not give these guys a reason to go over the edge and start shooting.

Alek was now standing back from the parley, his hands noticeably resting on the buttstock of his rifle, not the firing control. Baird had his hands spread in a pointedly non-threatening gesture, and Danny was leaning against the hood of the UAZ, his arms crossed, looking nonchalant. It was a marked contrast to the Kenyans.

It also seemed to be lost on them. The officer was looking more and more agitated, and wasn't calming down with Baird's reassurances. That was bleeding over to his subordinates. I didn't see anybody who looked like an NCO; that was a major problem with militaries that didn't have a solid NCO corps. There wasn't the practical voice of experience to calm down the connected amateur that was "leading" the unit.

That was when Spider stepped in. To this day, I don't know what he said, but the officer went very still all of a sudden, just staring at him. Then he waved to his subordinates, turned around, and left.

Just like that.

My estimate of Spider went up several notches.

The officer climbed back into his AML, and they did a reasonable formation turn away from us and back toward the FOB, as the MD-50 roared by overhead, its rotor wash beating at us, the door gunners still not *quite* aiming their HK machine guns at us. Alek turned back to the rest of us and made the raised-hand circle signal. *Mount up.* I nodded, and Jim and I climbed back into the Land Cruiser. Rodrigo put the vehicle in gear as I slammed the door, maneuvering my rifle so that I could point it out the open window if need be.

"We good, then?" he asked.

"I guess," I replied. "They're leaving and not forcing us to go with them. I'm going to take that as 'we're free to go.'"

Rodrigo pointed toward the river. "You guys see that over there?"

"Yeah, we did," Jim said. "So did the Kenyans, and I'm guessing they figured that those guys are more of a threat than we are, so they skedaddled to get some HESCOs between them and the Lashkar assholes."

"Maybe," I said. "They didn't look too interested in letting us go until that Spider dude said something to the officer. Then they took off like scared rabbits."

"What'd he say?" Rodrigo asked, as we started bumping across the ground again.

"How the hell should I know?" I replied. "I was back here. Even if I wasn't as deaf as I am, I wouldn't have been able to hear it."

"Who cares?" Jim pointed out. "We're on our way."

He had a point, but I couldn't help but wonder just what was going on with Baird's lanky associate. It usually takes more than a few words to get a uniformed bureaucrat to shut up and leave you alone, especially in these Third World shitholes. It implied a few things about Spider that made me curious. And yes, a little more suspicious.

***

We went bouncing and roaring north, rattling over farmland, following the narrow tracks between fields that often weren't much more than footpaths. It was a painful ride, and I wondered how much longer the suspension on the Land Cruiser was going to last, even as my knees ached from my rifle banging into them. We had to fare pretty far north to find a river crossing; we didn't want to try too close to the LaB boats. As it was, we were kicking up plenty of dust; they could probably see us heading north. The question, that none of us asked as the noise of our passage was generally too loud and none of us felt like yelling, was would they bother following, or write us off and go after the big prize of the city? I was reasonably certain that they would choose the latter, but it never hurt to be a little paranoid.

Baird's people already had a crossing picked out and scouted, and we splashed across the Juba where it doglegged to the east, then turned to the northwest and banged out into the badlands. Familiarity didn't make the roughness of the ride any less painful, I'm afraid.

I kept an eye on the battered, dusty rearview mirror, trying to pick out signs of pursuit through our own not-inconsiderable dust cloud. I couldn't see anything, but that didn't mean it wasn't there. I stayed tense until well after the low outline of Baardheere and the plumes of black smoke and dust rising into the midday sky above it faded into the horizon.

Then I tried to settle into the battered stuffing of the seat, keeping the increasingly hot metal of my rifle and the vehicle door off any exposed skin, and held on for the ride.

***

Naturally, we had to stop in the middle of nowhere.

The pitch of the Land Cruiser's engine changed, and Rodrigo started cursing, before he keyed his radio, and called Alek. "This piece of shit is overheating, we've got to stop."

"Roger," Alek called back. "All stations, we're halting for ten minutes. Circle up, Hillbilly's truck in the center."

The UAZ in the lead immediately slowed, and the HiLux pulled off to one side. With trucks alternating directions, we soon had a ring of vehicles in the desert, facing out, with the Land Cruiser in the middle. No sooner had we halted than the dismounts started getting out, rifles out and ready. Rodrigo piled out of the driver's seat, and popped the hood. I took the opportunity to get out, my M1A hanging from its sling, and walked over to Alek's HiLux.

As I did so, I looked around some more. There wasn't much to see. Miles and miles of rolling red dirt and low brush. There was little other sign of life aside from our little band of trucks.

At least, there was until I turned my eyes south, and saw the reddish plume against the horizon. It was still a long way off, but something out there was kicking up dust, and coming our direction.

I continued the last ten paces to Alek's vehicle, keeping my eyes locked on that plume. When I reached the HiLux, where Alek had just finished pissing against the front tire, he looked at me and immediately asked, "What is it?"

I just pointed. Alek followed my finger, and squinted. "Somebody's moving out there," he said.

"Yep," I replied. "Any guesses as to who?"

"A couple. And only one fits." He keyed his radio. "Stand to, we've got company." At this point, he didn't really have to say anything more.

I joined Jim and Larry moving to the south side of the perimeter. Since we had stopped in the bed of one of the many wadis that made up the tortured terrain of western Somalia, we had high ground to our south, at least for certain values of high ground. It didn't really afford us any elevation advantage on whoever was coming toward us, but it did offer some cover.

Several of Baird's guys were already down in the prone against the side of the wadi; little but their heads and weapons would be showing to the south. It was a pretty good position, and the three of us spread out and set in among them. I found myself between a massive black man, who greeted me with a glance and a "What's up, man?" in a distinct West Texas accent, and a skinny blonde white guy who didn't even look in my direction, but kept his focus solidly on the south.

I nodded to each of them, and concentrated on setting in, without tearing myself up too much on the rocks and stiff desert brush. We were actually on a slight rise, so we could see pretty well. I had been worried about getting up here and finding ourselves staring at just more brush, or even facing an uphill slope, with visibility that cut off barely a few tens of meters in front of us. It was a relief to see that we had a good field of view for several hundred meters.

The dust plumes were getting bigger now, and we were starting to see little glints of sunlight on metal or glass at their bases. They were definitely vehicles; the only question was, whose? I peered through my scope, but couldn't make out much detail. They were pickup trucks, and had either a bunch of cargo, or people, in their beds. That was all I could see.

They were moving fast enough to kick up dust, but out in the desert, that isn't necessarily that fast, and going too fast without a road is a ticket to a bad day. They wouldn't be in range for a while yet.

I called Alek. "Are we setting in and waiting for these guys, or heading out as soon as that truck is up?"

"I'd rather not have them tagging along all the way to Garbahaarrey," he replied. "We'll stay put and see what they do. If they're just nomads, once they're out of sight, we move. If they're coming after us, we educate them as to exactly why that is a very bad idea."

"Roger." I couldn't argue with his reasoning. In his place, I'd probably make the same call.

It was hot as hell, lying there in the dirt with my vest and my mags digging into my ribs, feeling where the bits of brush had made their way into my shirt and my trouser legs, hot, sharp rocks digging into various parts of my anatomy. None of us talked; there wasn't a lot to talk about, and all of us had developed the habit of quiet in tactical situations a long time ago. We just lay there, sweated, hurt, and watched.

As the oncoming trucks came closer, they started to resolve into what were unquestionably technicals. They were mostly HiLuxes, with a few older two-and-a-half ton trucks, with gunmen in the beds and hanging out passenger windows. At least two had heavy guns mounted; I saw what I was pretty sure were a couple of PKMs and a DShK. That pretty much sealed the deal--they were LaB, and they had to be looking for us.

So much for the city holding all their attention.

But did they know where we were? Had they spotted where we had stopped, or were they still searching? Could we lie low and hope they'd pass us by? Or should we ambush them, and hope we could take them all out with minimal losses?

After all, as much as these particular assholes might need killing, they weren't the particular assholes we were there to pick a fight with. The mission came first, and the mission was to get to the hostages and get them out. Fighting these punks if we didn't have to endangered that mission.

Not that I didn't want to waste the whole lot of them.

Scanning across the dust cloud, I noticed something. There was one HiLux well out in front of the two deuce-and-a-halfs, and two more well out to the flanks. Somebody had sure been teaching these guys tactics; they had point and flank security out. Used to be that such things were pretty much beyond these gomers, but it appeared that the Kalifah support had taught them a few things. Of course, the GWOT had taught the Kalifah Arabs a few things about tactics, too, often courtesy of American trainers.

There was a tall guy in the back of the point HiLux, with a radio. At first, even through the scope, I couldn't tell what he was doing, but soon enough I figured it out. He was looking at the ground ahead of the truck.

Motherfucker was tracking us.

I called Alek. "Coconut, Hillbilly. We've got technicals, and they're following our tire tracks. They're going to come right to us."

"They in range?" he asked.

"About two more minutes," I answered.

"Waste 'em."

"Roger that." I looked over at West Texas. "You guys ready?"

"We'll initiate on you," he replied, without looking up from his own Leupold scope, which looked downright weird sitting on an R4 in the middle of East Africa.

I set my eye back on my own scope, and settled the sights on tracker boy. It was still a decently long shot at six hundred, though easily within the capabilities of even a short-barrel M1A. It was a little far for the R4s, so I held off a little bit longer. I still wanted to hit them at least one hundred meters outside the range of the AKMs most of them appeared to be packing.

I waited, breathing slow and easy, watching the tracker bob in my sights. When he filled enough of a milradian, I started shooting.

Now, I was a sniper when I was a Marine. One shot, one kill was the mantra, but it rarely worked out that way in real life, especially if the target was moving as much and as randomly as a guy standing in the back of a moving vehicle. Often it boiled down to taking a shot, watching where it impacted, and adjusting to get the target with the next shot. You had to be quick on that follow-up shot, too, because very few people will just stand still and look around when a bullet just cracked past them.

I wasn't looking for a precision kill this time, though. While single disabling shots was still our standard, there were more people and a vehicle to put holes in, so general area was acceptable. I made sure to aim each shot, but I wasn't adjusting much.

The booming reports of the Praetorian .308s were quickly joined by the lighter cracks of Baird's guys R4s. Dust flew up from the muzzle blasts all along the line.

I saw tracker boy drop. Bullets smashed through the HiLux's windshield, and it suddenly veered to the left, as a red splash appeared on the spider-webbed glass behind one of the bullet holes. The death-spasm-induced turn was too tight, and the HiLux flipped over with a horrendous crash, sending bodies flying out of the bed.

The rest of the LaB vehicles tried to jam on the brakes, as one of our M60s opened up to my left, and hammered rounds across the cab of the right flank HiLux. That truck simply slowed to a stop, as its windshield shattered and its grill came apart. I saw one fighter try to leap clear of the bed and run away, and gunned him down with two shots that smashed him sideways to the dirt.

The rear vehicles were trying to pull backward, out of the kill zone. I loosed a couple of shots at one of the deuce-and-a-halfs, to little apparent effect. They were backpedaling fast, leaving the three trucks we had caught on the X to their fate.

The two HiLuxes that remained were trashed, their occupants obviously dead or soon to be that way. The lead deuce-and-a-half, however, while disabled, wasn't out of the fight. There was still a DShK mounted over the cab, and several of the fighters in the bed had survived, and were now on the ground and starting to shoot back.

Our M60 thumped again, raking the truck. Dust kicked up and the truck rocked as bullets slammed through its skin. Fluids were already visibly dripping from the shot-through engine, and its tires were shredded. I came up to a knee, saw movement near the rear of the truck, and slammed off two quick shots. I don't know if I hit anything.

Looking past the kill zone, even while AK rounds snapped past, I saw the rest of the enemy trucks had halted their headlong flight and were starting to turn. I looked down at the rest of the guys. "We've got to finish these motherfuckers off before their buddies can come back around and flank us," I yelled, trying to be heard over the gunfire. Nobody said anything in reply, but West Texas, Jim, and Larry all started getting up out of the prone.

I dashed forward, aiming for an angle that would put the wrecked HiLux between me and the shooters for as long as possible. Sporadic gunfire kicked up dust around me, and snapped painfully through the air overhead, as I sprinted across the uneven ground toward the overturned truck. I half-slid/half-dove into the meager cover provided by the smoking engine, and planted my hiking boot in a muddy puddle of fluids that was seeping into the ground. I steadied myself, swept up my rifle, and was about to pop up over the wreck when I heard something to my left.

I looked over to see a badly wounded gomer crawling toward an AK. I didn't hesitate, but shot him in the top of the head. Blood, brain, and bits of bone splashed away from the entrance wound. I didn't see the bullet come out. He dropped face down in the dust and didn't move.

I quickly looked over the rest of the bodies lying around the truck, even as Larry ran up to drop to the prone nearby. Before the booming reports of his FAL drowned him out, I heard him yell, "You gonna start shooting or what?"

"Once I'm not going to get shot in the back, sure," I yelled back. Satisfied that everyone who had been in that particular HiLux was dead, I popped over the side of the overturned pickup and searched for a target.

Jim and Baird's boys were keeping the bad guys at the deuce-and-a-half generally pinned, though as I watched, two of them tried to rush forward under cover of hastily and poorly aimed covering fire, only to be beaten back by a flurry of 5.56 fire. One cried out as a bullet smacked into his calf, blowing out a splash of meat and blood, and limped the rest of the way back to the cover of the big truck.

A third gomer stuck his head around the stricken truck's tailgate. By a terrible coincidence, he did so just as my scope settled on the very space where he stuck his head.

I was a little startled, enough so that I almost didn't get the shot off. The timing couldn't have been better; I just wasn't expecting old boy to try to hit my bullet with his head. But he did, my rifle boomed, his head jerked back, and he dropped like a marionette with its strings cut.

With the two others hidden behind the deuce-and-a-half, Larry and I were clear. I tapped Larry hard on the shoulder with my non-firing fist, and came up to a high crouch, then ran around the far side of the HiLux. If I could get in position while the pinned gomers concentrated on Jim and the others shooting at them, I should be able to get a decent shot.

My lungs were starting to ache. Regardless of what kind of conditioning you may be in, sprinting in body armor, however minimal, at midday in East Africa is murder. Sweat was dripping down my entire body mingling with the dust and grit and smearing my Oakley lenses. I was panting as I hit a knee, and brought my rifle up.

There were three left, huddled in the lee of the truck, as bullets pinged off the metal or smacked into the dusty ground near them. There were at least three more bodies on the ground, and I saw a foot hanging off the end of the truck bed. That was all I had time to see before my finger finished its squeeze, and the trigger broke on the first shot.

It was short, brutal, and to-the-point. They never even had a chance. I tracked across them, putting a single round into each torso, then back, finishing off the crumpled bodies. Only one had been still trying to move. The range was way too short to miss something vital.

"Cease fire," I rasped into my radio. "Truck's clear." The shooting tapered off, then stopped.

We weren't out of the woods yet, though. The other trucks were still out there, and as I straightened up out of my fighting crouch, I could see them coming on line out to our east. They wouldn't be so surprised the next time.

CHAPTER 25

Jim and I descended back into the wadi to find Alek. Larry stayed up on the lip with Baird's guys. We could see the remnant of the LaB force closing on us, but they were moving at the pace of a slow walk; they had been hurt bad, and were being cautious. They had to be well aware of what had befallen their comrades who had stumbled into our ambush, and had no desire to repeat the performance. Their problem was that slow and cautious only works in combat when the enemy doesn't know you're coming.

We found Alek already on the flank where the LaB fighters were coming. He was watching them with binoculars, over the hood of one of the UAZs.

"So, we fight this bunch, or run?" Jim asked without preamble.

"Fight," Alek said flatly. "If we run, they can still follow us. We've got a decent position here, especially in this direction." He pointed. "They don't see it yet, but that side wadi is going to funnel them in to a group about two trucks wide, and it's right at five hundred out. That's when we hit 'em. Even if we don't get all of them, the survivors aren't going to be very enthusiastic to keep coming after us. They're ready to break already." He half-grinned, half grimaced. "Garbage."

I nodded, squinting toward the line of technicals and fighters. The ones we'd already wasted had been little better equipped than most militias we'd seen out here; they were dressed in mostly long, baggy shorts or pants, t-shirts or wife beaters, and had minimal equipment aside from their rifles, most of which they'd probably been using before the new Chinese stuff started showing up. I suspected that was why they'd been sent after us, instead of getting to join in the storming of Baardheere. These were the dregs, the guys that Malouf wouldn't miss when they got shredded.

Of course, there were a lot more of them than there were of us. Even with Baird's guys, we still only came to about twenty-five strong. It looked like most of a company out there; we were outnumbered about three-to-one. We had the advantage of skill, but numbers can count for a lot, especially over mostly open ground.

For almost half an hour, the enemy fighters paced toward us in relative silence. There was only the whisper of the slight wind that did next to nothing to cool the sweat gathering under our gear and clothes, and the faint buzzing of the insects that gathered in the brush. They had stopped the vehicles almost fifteen hundred meters away; they were that unenthusiastic about coming to grips with us.

After what we'd done to the front three vehicles of their little strike force, who could blame them?

I had briefly argued for pulling out the .338s. The long guns could easily reach that far out, and shooting a few of them from five times the max effective range of their weapons might just break them without having to come to grips. Alek had declined, preferring both to save the sniper ammo, which we couldn't restock anytime soon, as Baird didn't have any, and to really waste as many of them as possible, to make sure the message got across loud and clear.

Do. Not. Fuck. With. Us.

I could see his point. In fact, in an observation that got me a grimace and a glare without much force behind it, I told him I was starting to rub off on him. I punched him in the shoulder and went to find a firing position before things cooked off.

I wound up finding a lump of slightly higher ground on the side of the wadi that I could sort of squeeze myself behind, and got down in the prone. Kneeling or standing shots at five hundred aren't easy, especially when the target is moving. I settled myself in behind the rifle, peered through the scope as I blinked the sweat out of my eyes, and settled on a skinny guy who was charging forward a little more enthusiastically than his fellows.

As Alek had said, we had established the wadi as a limiting feature that was about five hundred meters out. It was our trigger line, a concrete gauge of when to open fire, without need of any overt commands. They pass that line, they die. That simple.

They passed the line. We started shooting.

The initial fusillade roared out over the desert, smacking half a dozen Somali jihadists into bloody heaps in the dust in seconds. At least two rounds hit my guy; I'm pretty sure one of them was mine. There was a mad scramble for cover, and I'm pretty sure one of their trucks ran over at least two of their own men trying to get out of the kill zone.

Most of what the rest of the line was doing faded slightly into the background, as I picked off another gomer running for a hillock. I led him a little too much, and the round smacked into his outer ribs. He staggered, and kept running behind the hillock, where I lost track of him.

By now, they were starting to shoot back. Puffs of dust and faint flashes that were almost completely lost in the sun's glare started to flicker across the desert where they had gone to ground, and a breath later, a cacophony of harsh snapping noise started crackling overhead. One or two

212

rounds smacked into the dust way too closely in front of me, throwing grit my way. I flinched backward, ducking down as several more rounds passed close enough that I could feel the shockwaves.

They might still have crap equipment, but it looked like their advisors might have started actually teaching them some marksmanship. Either that, or they were getting lucky through sheer volume of fire.

I glanced back down the line. Their fire was getting close in a couple places, and was nowhere near others. It looked like their accuracy was still pretty hit-and-miss. Good. I rolled back up, leveled at one of the dust puffs, and started squeezing off shots. It only took two before the shooting from that position stopped; whether from his being hit or suppressed, I couldn't tell. I shifted right, and dropped a skinny who was running forward with a round through the upper chest.

Then they were pulling back. Some were careful, moving in short, bent-over sprints, trying to keep cover between themselves and us. Others just ran, and paid for it, as our .308s reached out across the distance to knock them on their faces in the dust.

Finally, they were far enough away that Alek had to yell at a couple of us to cease fire. I levered myself to a knee, watching them go, then stood up, my knees starting to protest, and started making my rounds to make sure everybody was all right, and see what our ammo situation was.

I kept an eye down the wadi as I went, watching what the gomers were doing. And damned if they weren't rallying. Our hoped-for rout had just turned into a tactical withdrawal.

That wasn't good.

I finished my rounds and came back to Alek, who was back to watching the gomers through his binoculars, his OBR hanging from its sling across his chest. "Everybody's up. Tim caught a ricochet in the meat of his shoulder, and one of Baird's guys got grazed, but nobody's hit bad. Ammo's at about eighty percent per remaining."

He nodded without taking his eyes out of the binos. "Good. We may need it. These guys may be the dregs, but somebody with them is a pro. Whoever he is, I'll bet he's got them back on us in another half hour."

"Attack, or move?" I asked.

He finally lowered the binoculars, and kept watching to the east, thinking. It was a tough call. Attacking might take the initiative away from them, but it was pretty damned risky, with the shoestring we were operating on. We stood a good chance of losing people, and, aside from the immediate desire to continue breathing, we really couldn't afford to lose anybody this side of Kismayo, at least. The mission still had to have priority.

Baird and Danny came over to the UAZ. Baird was impassive; Danny had that expression of weary unhappiness that he'd been wearing for some time now. He had the look of a man who was caught in an avalanche, knew it, and couldn't do a damned thing about it. I didn't know what he was getting from his bosses back in Langley, but given what we had on the ground here, it wasn't much.

"We need to go now, while they are disorganized," Baird said. "They might not follow."

Alek didn't look at him, but kept watching the activity around the old deuce-and-a-half trucks. "They will. Their commander has a vested interest in killing us now. We've made him look bad."

Baird frowned. "That is not how they usually work. We have hurt them badly, twice. They will not want to press further."

"Their commander isn't a skinny," Alek said, finally turning to face him. "Can't see much detail, but he's not black, and he's not acting like a warlord. He's acting like a trained infantry commander with a concrete mission." He locked eyes with Baird. "And I'm pretty sure that mission is to take down anyone trying to get out of Baardheere. That means us. And if he's not a skinny, that means he probably doesn't have a lot of concern for using up a few more of them to accomplish his mission."

"Particularly if he's an Arab," I pointed out. A lot of Arabs, especially in Africa, held black Africans in contempt at best. Sudan was the prime example of this attitude, as the predominantly Arab government slaughtered black Muslims in Darfur and black Christians in South Sudan.

Baird was nodding thoughtfully. "I suppose that makes sense, given what's been going on. The Kalifah advisors want strategic control of the Horn of Africa. They don't really give a damn about the people here. Of course they'd see Somali fighters as expendable."

Danny looked at me. "You think you can nail him from the roof of one of the trucks?"

Alek and Baird turned to look at me. I squinted to the east, trying to gauge the wind. "If he stays put for a couple more minutes, easy day," I replied. I turned and hollered down the line, "Hank, you want to spot for me?"

Hank nodded silently, and heaved himself to his feet. I went to the HiLux, where we had the long guns stashed, and drew out my Sako.

It took some doing to get both of us up on top of the UAZ. I'm kind of long and lanky, but Hank is short, built like a fireplug, and for some reason objects to using his three-inch long goatee as a handle to haul him up. Fortunately, since the Bukankha was kind of a van, there was enough space for the two of us and the rifle. The TRG is a long weapon, and takes up a bit of room. I unzipped its drag bag, and laid it out as a shooter mat, both for the padding to give the steel bipods something to grip, and to keep from burning myself on the steel roof of the vehicle.

Hank was prone beside me, almost on top of my left side, with a spotting scope laid over the top of an assault pack he'd grabbed at random out of one of the vehicles. He settled in as I popped the lens caps and settled in behind the rifle, getting my body lined up to absorb as much of the recoil as possible without throwing the muzzle off on the first shot. I was already concentrating on controlling my breathing, slow and shallow.

"Eleven fifty," Hank murmured. "Wind...five right."

I picked out the commander. Alek was right; the guy was unmistakably an advisor. He was dark, but not black. I couldn't make out a lot of facial features at eleven hundred fifty meters, but he appeared to be an Arab; either Egyptian or Sudanese. While most of his troops were dressed in various civilian clothes, equipped with bandoliers at most, and older Soviet or Chinese weapons, he was in desert camouflage, with a soft cap, chest rig, and a Beretta AR70 or similar knockoff.

"Shoulda blended in with your troops a little more, Achmed," I whispered. "Shooter ready."

"On you," Hank said.

I let out my breath, relaxed, and squeezed the trigger. It broke like glass, and the rifle slammed back into my shoulder with a thunderous boom. I worked the bolt before even getting back on glass to see the aftermath.

"Hit," Hank reported. "Upper left chest. He ain't getting up from that."

Despite Hank's optimism, I stayed on glass. I wanted to make sure, for one thing, that old boy hadn't been wearing body armor, in which case he might be able to get up. I'd had a buddy get hit with a 7.62 NATO AP round in the plate, and just feel a shove.

I also wanted to see if dropping the commander had the desired effect, or if I needed to start spending ammo on more of them.

The commander lay in the dust, his tan cammies quite visible against the red dirt. He wasn't moving, and no one was rushing to aid him, either. In fact, a few were staring in shock at the corpse of their erstwhile leader, while the rest were either running for cover or piling into the trucks.

"I think that did it, buddy," Hank said, still peering through the spotting scope.

I came off the scope, and started unloading the rifle to slip it back in the drag bag. "I think you may be right. Sure looks like that was the straw that broke the camel's back."

Hank chuckled as he stowed the spotting scope and went to drop off the side of the van. "Or the camel jockey's."

I just shook my head. "Even for you, that was bad. I mean, it was just sloppy."

He dropped to the ground, grinned, and shrugged. "It's been a long week. I'm a little off."

I handed down the drag bag, then followed it. Alek nodded to us once, and then headed for his truck. I took the drag bag back from Hank, carried it over to the HiLux, stowed it, and then headed for the Land Cruiser.

The LaB cordon wasn't going to give us any more trouble. We'd definitely do some antitracking on the way out, but they'd have to find another leader who could beat and cajole them back together and back after us, and that would take some time. We could make the best of that time, and hopefully be at the helos and moving before they could get anywhere near us.

We just had to move fast.

***

I can't say that moving fast across the Somali desert is that much fun.

If you're into Baja racing, it might be fun for about the first hour. After that, it just gets punishing. No matter how padded the seat, and these seats weren't all that well padded anymore, the bouncing starts to hammer your tailbone and send shocks up your spine that you're sure will cause some lasting pain later in life, should there be a later in life. Add in even our lightweight body armor, ammo, and weapons knocking around, and it gets worse.

It took five hours to cover the red, rocky badlands between Baardheere and Garbahaarrey. Nobody talked much, just keeping an eye out for further pursuit. The last we saw of the LaB force that had come after us, they were scrambling back south toward Baardheere in a cloud of red dust. But, while we were technically within the Ethiopian sphere of control, the truth was that anywhere outside of the little enclaves around the Ethiopian garrisons, Somalia proper was still as lawless and wild as ever. Bandits and militias were an ever-present threat.

As we moved away from the Juba, the main source of water, the country got increasingly barren. Though it had been carved by streams and flash floods in the past, for the most part it was now a wasteland of dry, dust-choked washes and eroded rock outcroppings. The tenacious green scrub remained, drawing what little water it could out of the ground. The terrain slowed us down; we had to stop twice to get the Bukankhas unstuck.

Finally, as the sun started to dip toward the horizon, Garbahaarrey started to come into view.

It wasn't much--just a group of brown stucco houses and a white mosque surrounded by the same scrubby trees and bushes. Our little convoy angled to the west of the town, where a long dirt airstrip had been carved out of the bush.

There wasn't any sort of airport facility; the strip was just there. There were a few prefabs at one end that looked out of place; I suspected they were where Baird's people kept the helos. An old twin-engine Antonov sat at the northeast end of the strip. It was dusty, but all the windows were intact, and it looked like it still had the engines and props in one piece. It would probably still fly.

We were alert, in spite of the spine-pounding trip and the heat. There had been raids in Garbahaarrey barely a month ago. Being in the passenger seat of the Land Cruiser, I had a good view of the town as we got closer. I was watching for anything--vehicles, patrols, sniper positions.

I didn't see a damned thing. The town was quiet, and movement was minimal. A couple donkeys cropped what little greenery they could find outside a house on the outskirts. A woman watched us from the window. A couple of kids squatting in the dust outside another house stopped playing to watch us, but otherwise showed no reaction.

As I had expected, the lead UAZ took us right to the prefab hangars on the west side of the strip. As it slowed and stopped, and the rest of our vehicles spread out into a loose perimeter around it, a short, skinny man burned so dark by the sun I might have thought him to be an Arab if not for the fact that his eyes were so light blue they were striking even from inside the vehicle, and his hair was a blond so bleached by the sun it was almost white, came out to meet us.

He was dressed in a white t-shirt, khaki shorts, and sandals. He also had a leather pistol belt slung around his hips, and an FN HiPower in his hand. Baird got out of the UAZ and walked toward him. The blond man, on seeing Baird, grinned widely and embraced the former CIA man, slapping him heartily on the back.

I got out, with a needless admonishment to Rodrigo to keep the engine running. Alek was already out of the HiLux, and Danny was coming over from his truck. We converged on Baird and the blond man, who was talking rapidly to Baird in slightly Afrikaans-accented English.

"...all ready to go," he was saying. "They're gassed up, and I went over them just this morning. As soon as you are ready to launch, we can lift."

Baird turned to us as we came up. "What do you think?" he asked. "Do we need to spare a few hours to rest, or do you want to launch now?"

"We'd best take a few hours," Danny said. "I know we're on the clock here, but fatigue is going to be our worst enemy the longer this goes on. Tired shooters make mistakes, and we can't afford mistakes at this point."

Alek was nodding, and looked at me. I had to agree. "I don't want to push this too far to the right, but we need to get some shut-eye. We're not going to do those guys any good if we miss something because we're ready to drop."

It was agreed. First, we set security, with about a quarter of our guys and Baird's watching the perimeter, while the rest loaded our gear on the birds. While that was going on, I checked with Baird that we had confirmation from his contacts down south. He assured me he did, that they'd meet us with vehicles, a place to go firm, and a meeting set up for

Imad and Spider. "I'm on top of it," he said.

"Not trying to question you too much," I said, "just haven't had a lot of good luck with other people's arrangements so far this trip." He nodded knowingly; we'd told him about the clusterfuck at Socotra and Hobyo.

"We'll be fine, at least up until we get into Kismayo," he said. "After that, of course, all bets are off."

I nodded, and went back to making sure my ruck was secured properly in the Alouette. I'd be one of the guns covering Imad and Spider on their insert.

After that, we found what space we could to stretch out in the shade of the prefab, and tried to get some sleep. For most of us, myself included, it wasn't that hard. We'd been in either condition orange or red for the better part of three weeks. That alone, never mind the mileage we'd covered, the heat, and the limited food and water, was exhausting.

It seemed like I'd barely closed my eyes when somebody was kicking my boot. I opened my eyes with a grunt, and sat up, rubbing the grit out of them. My tormenter had by this time moved on to somebody who wasn't moving.

It took a few minutes to get my head together, a sure sign that, in spite of the circumstances, I was getting tired enough that my edge was starting to slip. It bothered me, and I smacked myself in the back of the head a couple times to make sure I was awake and ready to work. After that, it was short work to throw on my vest and grab my rifle, then start helping to push the birds out onto the strip.

It was dark, in a way that you only see out in the wilderness or the Third World. I hadn't seen any power lines going into Garbaharrey, and there weren't any lights showing in the town now that the sun was down. The air had cooled, and a light breeze was blowing in from the east.

We got the helos out of the prefabs and on to the strip, spaced far enough apart to lift without interfering with each other. Then, with a last huddle to make sure everybody, including the pilots, was on the same page, we loaded up and got ready to lift.

The Alouette started up smoothly, the engine rapidly climbing in pitch to a howling whine, and the rotors started to turn, biting the air with a staccato roar. After a moment, the bird started to rock as it lifted clear of the ground, the terrain around us momentarily obscured by a massive cloud of dust. In a few more minutes we were high enough to clear the brownout, and turned south.

There was no moon. We roared over the barren East African desert in near total darkness, broken only by the stars overhead, which, given the lack of light pollution, were brighter and more numerous than I'd seen them in a long time. The pilot, whose name I hadn't caught, was flying dark and low, without running lights. Looking back, I could just barely see the

Cougar hulking behind us, also blacked out. After about an hour, we turned east, while the Cougar rumbled past us, heading south to the lay-up point.

Soon enough we could see the coastline ahead, and the Juba River as a dark ribbon passing through the desert, meandering toward the sea. Our designated insert point for Imad and Spider was at an intersection a few kilometers outside a nameless village near the mouth of the Juba. The pilot took us on a long, circular turn around the LZ, and from the open door next to Jim, who was manning one of the Pecheneg door guns, I scanned the LZ. There was nothing on the road but the single van that we'd been warned to look for, and as we passed overhead, a red light blinked twice. That was the signal. I let the pilot know we were clear and we started coming in to land.

The Alouette flared in another billowing cloud of dust, then Imad and Spider were on the ground and running toward the van, with little besides the small satchels they carried with them. They didn't have any kit but a pair of battered AKMs and a 9mm Makarov, a little bit of water, their bona-fides, and that was about it. I didn't envy them.

The pilot had feathered the rotors when he landed, so the dust was settling, and we were able to see our two guys meet up with their driver. Apparently everything was kosher, because I got the "all clear" signal from Imad, so I turned to the pilot, and gave him a thumbs-up. He returned it, and the dust and sand started to get kicked up again, as he gave us lift and started us back into the sky.

We turned northwest to swing wide around Kismayo, and headed for our lay-up point, where we would wait for word from Imad and Spider. Behind us, the van's headlights came on, and it started trundling down the dirt road, heading for one of Shabaab's largest strongholds in the country.

CHAPTER 26

There was no word for three days.

Our lay-up site was in the middle of nowhere, sixty-two kilometers from Kismayo. There was nothing but dust and low, dark green scrub as far as the eye could see. Baird's contacts had three HiLuxes and two Unimogs for us, with the requisite armament--two Pechenegs, a PKM, a DShK, and an HK21. We had fuel for the trucks and the helos, water, and chow, even if it was mostly rice and goat. We even had some extra ammo and explosives. I had no idea where they'd scrounged NATO ammo out here, but Baird said that anything was possible if you knew the right people and had money.

Baird's contacts were a pair of Darod Somalis who had been part of the Jubaland Initiative before they gave up in disgust as the independent Jubaland failed to materialize. Both were also American expats, one of whom had served in the Army for four years before getting out and immigrating to Kenya to be part of the Initiative. They generally kept to themselves, but I had talked to Aden, the former soldier, enough to know he had lived in Seattle for ten years, and had been stationed at Ft. Lewis. He liked America well enough, but still considered Somalia to be home.

Both of them had a taste for rap music that most of us did not share. They stayed under their cammie net, and we stayed under ours, while I tried to keep Disturbed, Metallica, and Lamb of God songs going through my head to counteract the hip-hop from their side.

It was getting on toward dark on the third day when the sat phone rang.

Alek grabbed it and answered. It was quiet enough I could hear the single word that was spoken before the connection was severed.

"Wildfire."

That was bad news. It meant Imad and Spider had been compromised, and whoever had made the call was heading for our preplanned emergency RV site, hopefully with both of them. Either way, it meant one thing for us. We immediately started grabbing our gear and getting ready to move. Bob ran off to warn the pilots to start getting the Alouette ready to lift.

I grabbed Alek. "I'll take Jim and Hank," I said. "We'll pick 'em up, hose down whoever might be after 'em, and get back here."

He nodded. "Go." I already had my kit on and my rifle in hand. I barked for Jim and Hank, and sprinted toward the helo.

Hans, the blond-haired South African, was already in the pilot's seat, and had the rotors turning. We scrambled aboard, Jim and Hank taking the door guns, and no sooner were we on than we were rocking into the darkening sky.

I don't think we were more than a hundred fifty feet up before Hans pitched the nose down and sent us racing over the desert. He'd made it clear that he wasn't all that invested in the overall mission, but he was invested in his part of it, namely, getting us where we needed to go quickly, and getting us out again. The guy was a daredevil who didn't give a shit about the danger. He just liked to fly.

We skimmed the ground, which was mostly flat as a plate anyway, heading northeast toward the grid that was our emergency RV. I hoped that Imad and Spider had been en route when they made the call; the quicker we could pick them up and get back, the better.

It only took a few minutes. There was already a car sitting there, with the recognition symbol in tape on the roof. Hans took us in a fast circle, checking for any other company, then set us down less than one hundred meters from the car. Hank stayed on the outer door gun, and Jim and I hopped out and moved warily toward the car.

Imad was the only one in it, sitting behind the wheel, an AK across his lap. He had what looked like a makeshift tourniquet set high on his left arm, and his left side was dark with blood. Even through night vision, he looked shocky.

"Imad, brother, you with us?" I asked. I didn't want to try to open the door and get shot because he was too far gone to recognize us.

"Get me out of here, Jeff." His voice was weak, but clear. I slung my rifle and moved to open the door. Jim stepped in to help as I stuck out my hand to help Imad out of the car.

He grabbed my wrist with his uninjured hand, and I levered him out of the car and slung his arm over my shoulders. "I can walk," he said.

"Where all are you hit?" I asked. I'd do a quick blood sweep when we got on the bird, but asking helped determine how all-there he was. Behind us, Jim was rigging a thermite grenade to the car. There wouldn't be anything left shortly after we disappeared.

"Just my arm," he said. "I think the humerus is broken."

"All right, hang in there; we'll get you out of here." We were only a handful of paces away from the helo. "Imad, where's Spider?"

"Taken." That single word made my blood run cold. I didn't know the guy, but he was technically one of ours, since we'd linked up with Baird. I didn't want to think about what was being done to him. "We're burned,

Jeff," he said. "We fucked up, and now we're burned."

"Let's get you back to the lay-up, and we'll figure it out from there," I told him. Jim jumped up into the bird, then turned back to help pull Imad in as I pushed. He was a skinny bastard anyway, and not wearing any kit, so it wasn't that hard. I grabbed a handhold and followed. As soon as I was in, I banged on the bulkhead next to the pilot's seat and yelled at Hans to take off.

We roared into the air and swung to the west, as the car burst into flames. Imad was slumped in a seat in back, where Jim had hastily secured him, and I started checking him for further wounds. He was right; it just looked like a nasty bullet wound to his left arm. The humerus was definitely broken. I couldn't tell how much blood he'd lost, but he was out of the fight.

Which meant we had to find a way to get him out of the country. Being this far out in the cold had a lot of problems, that being one of them.

He was still awake, in spite of everything, but was in too much pain to talk over the scream of the Alouette's engine. I yelled in his ear to relax, we'd debrief when we got to the lay-up. He finally nodded, and we settled in for the ride.

We had taken a fairly straight-line course to get to the RV. On the way back, Hans hooked us about twenty kilometers north, so as not to cover the same ground, and, if somebody was watching our approach and departure, obscure where we were based. It took an extra few minutes, but we landed back at the lay-up, and most of the team came running as the rotors spooled down.

Nick and Bob helped Imad down out of the bird, and over to our shelter in the lee of one of the Unimogs. I stuck an IV in him as soon as we got him down, and went to work on his mangled arm. I didn't know how long it had been since he'd been hit, but there was likely enough damage that he'd be lucky to get full use of the arm back. I had to throw a pressure bandage on the wound, while trying not to make the break worse, then splint it and tie it up so even if he moved around he wouldn't damage it further. That, the IV, and a shot of morphine for the pain were about all I could do. He'd require surgery when we could get him to some decent facilities.

Imad had passed out while I was working on him. We had no idea how long he'd been pushing to stay conscious with that much blood loss, not to mention the mind-numbing pain of a bullet-shattered humerus.

Alek was on the sat phone with Tom. It sounded like Caleb and his team had managed to get into Ethiopia, since Kenya wasn't letting many foreigners in at the moment. That put them a couple hours away by helo, the better part of a day by ground.

Finally, he hung up. "Caleb and his boys are in Dolo, with the 407, and the DC-3. We've got the 407 on the way to medevac Imad. They'll be wheels-up in thirty minutes. So we've got about two and a half hours to figure out what went wrong, and decide on our next move."

"Are we getting reinforcements from Caleb's team?" Nick asked.

"Negative, they're still in support. Mike's team is inbound overland, they'll rendezvous with us here, or if we need to move, at an RV we pick," Alek said. "They're bringing a few more toys, but mainly men, ammo, and food."

"Finally," Bob said.

"Are we hoping that nobody's going to notice the better part of a company minus out here in the middle of the desert?" Danny asked. "Even out here there are nomads, and they talk. Baird's guys and the helos make a big enough signature, do we really want to add another ten guys?"

"After that shitstorm in Djibouti City," Jim said, "yes. I personally want as much backup as possible. It's not like the bad guys are completely clueless that there's somebody out here killing their guys. We've left enough of a trail of corpses already."

"Not to mention," I added, "that Imad said they were burned. Which means the bad guys definitely know we're here, and we might be at the stage where we need to consider being able to fight our way out of the country. If that is the case, then we need as many guns as we can get. Face it, Danny, this stopped being nicely covert some time ago."

"We're not going overt here," Alek put in. "It's not like we're going to lose our minds. If need be, we'll spread out to reduce our signature. But we're at war with Shabaab and all their allies here, with a handful of men. I'm not going to turn down another team."

Danny finally nodded, but he looked even more unhappy than before. I kind of understood. He was the one that Langley was going to hold responsible for what happened out here, regardless of their own reluctance to support us with anything but money. Of course, all of our lives were on the line, and I thought he should probably focus a little harder on that, but given the fatigue levels we were all working under, I could sort of see where his mind was going.

There was some more discussion, mainly about options once Mike and his guys got there, but we were interrupted by Imad's quiet call. He was awake, and although the morphine was making him fuzzy, he could talk.

"Easy, brother," Alek told him, as we gathered around. "Take it slow. You took a hell of a hit."

Imad swallowed and focused on Alek. "We got burned. We fucked up, and we got burned. I don't know how…"

"Easy man," Alek said. "Start at the beginning."

He blinked a few times. The morphine was really doing a number on him. When he started talking again, his voice was quiet, but steadier. "We got into the town easily enough. They've got checkpoints…map?" Danny held out the overhead photo we had of Kismayo. It didn't have a lot of notations, but it showed where everything was, as long as it could be identified. Imad squinted at it, then pointed out several major intersections. "But the checkpoints aren't all that tight. They're only on the major roads; most of the minor back streets are clear. Half the time we went by them, the troops were high on khat, when they thought they could get away with it. At night, they sleep more than keep watch.

"The first day we just kind of set up shop in the suuqa, offering some arms with hints that we had bigger and better toys for somebody with the money and influence. Just before sundown, we were approached by a guy who said he represented the Kismayo Islamic Council. He had instructions from his boss to bring us to a meeting.

"We accepted. We didn't know whether the Kismayo Islamic Council was actually affiliated with AQ, Shabaab, or Al Masri, but it was a place to start. So we packed up what we had, and followed him to his car. He had point and chase vehicles, both packed to the gills with militia, so whoever this guy was, he had some pull around there.

"They took us to a two-story building on the west side of town." Again, he pointed out its rough location on the map. "About here." He squinted harder at the photo. "I think it was this house, here. It was in a part of the city that was well patrolled, lots of guards. Even more on the rooftop. They took us inside, and we met with a group of Somalis who wanted to know what we had to offer, that could kill their enemies without notice. They'd gotten the hint that we could offer drones, and they were almost drooling at the possibilities.

"But when we started talking, I started to get the feeling that something was off. There weren't any Arab advisors, for one thing. The guards' equipment was shit, and their discipline was worse. These guys were making all the usual noise about jihad, evildoers and all that, but they seemed...well, kind of desperate and half-assed, I guess you could say.

"That was when Spider leaned over to me and said that they weren't who we were looking for; these guys weren't Shabaab, they weren't AQ or Kalifah-affiliated, they were the holdouts from Hizbul-Islam, who'd been fighting over Kismayo with Shabaab since '09.

"That was a problem. We couldn't do business with Hizbul-Islam and then hope to get close to Al Masri's people. We had to disengage and get back out the next day to try to contact somebody Kalifah-affiliated, and this time we couldn't use the same place because we'd have to avoid the Hizbul-Islam crowd."

Imad had to stop and lay back for a moment. He was breathing hard, the pain and blood loss taking its toll. I checked his IV; it was still half full.

"Spider did most of the talking; he was more familiar with how things work here. He explained that we were just representing another dealer who works out of Bahrain, and that we didn't have anything here yet, but were just feeling out the market.

"They didn't like that. Two of them especially started getting agitated, and I was getting sure that we were going to get our heads cut off, but Spider reassured them, and said that he would pass the information along to his supplier, and that in a few weeks we would be able to provide them with a demonstration.

"They got even more vocal at the few weeks' timeframe. I heard one of them say out loud that Malouf would be back before then, and they would lose their chance. It sounded like they hoped to launch a coup and take over Kismayo while most of Lashkar al-Barbar was out overrunning Baardheere."

As Imad took another break, Danny mused, "That could actually be pretty useful. If the split between Hizbul-Islam and the AQ-affiliated groups is that wide, and we can spark it, it might be good cover for a recovery op."

"Might be," Alek replied. "Might also just get the hostages killed in the crossfire."

"They're scared shitless of Malouf and his boys," Imad interjected. "The only way they'd be willing to risk it is if Malouf and most of the Kalifah advised and led units are gone. And then, half of them are even more scared of what Al Masri will do once they act against his puppets."

"I take it you got out without an incident?" Jim asked.

"Eventually," Imad said. "Spider had to do some fast talking, and make a lot of false promises, but we got out, and headed for our hostel. We'd try again in the morning.

"The next day was a complete bust. We talked to a few people, and kept our eyes open, but didn't make any contact. We did see some things, though.

"There is a definite split in the city. About a third, to the west, is held by Hizbul-Islam, while Shabaab bully-boys control the rest. There aren't very many Shabaab troops there now, but Malouf's reputation is apparently scary enough that the Hizbul-Islam types don't try to push their luck very much, even when he's gone.

"But there is one area that the locals stay away from, and it looks like there are still a good number of guards. That's the old Kismayo University, up north. One of the men who did stop by our little setup to talk said that Shabaab drove out the professors a year ago and took it over. I asked a few questions, but he didn't know what goes on there. Just that there was a lot of activity a couple of weeks ago, and that the Shabaab soldiers kept it under heavy guard even when everything else was drawn down for the push on Baardheere."

The whole team kind of sat up and took notice at that. It sounded like a pretty big indicator to me. Maybe that was where they were keeping the rest of the hostages. Or maybe it was a Shabaab/AQ headquarters, where we could at least pin down where the rest of the hostages were. It was more than we'd had, anyway.

"I decided we needed to check it out," Imad continued. "Spider argued against it, said we needed to stick with the plan, but the plan wasn't getting us anywhere. It looked like all the honchos were out of town. The man I talked to even said Al Masri had left last week, going back to the Arab states. He didn't say which one. I asked if he'd heard of Abu Sadiq. He said he hadn't. We hadn't heard the name the whole two days we had been there. The man was a ghost; he didn't seem to exist.

"When we got back to the hostel, I said I was going to go recon the University that night. Spider argued that I shouldn't, but I pointed out how shitty the security was at night, and promised I'd be careful. He didn't like it, but he couldn't do much about it without raising a ruckus. So I went."

He started feeling around his pockets. "I made a sketch. It had all the guards and patrols I could see. I made a thorough recon, then headed back to the hostel at about 0300. But when I got back, Spider was gone.

"I hadn't gone in the front; that's probably the only reason I wasn't taken. There were half a dozen men with AKs out front, waiting for me. I heard them talking. They were laughing about the handful of Americans trying to rescue the hostages, when so many hadn't been able to stop 'the brothers' from taking them in the first place. That was when I ran, but I made some noise getting out, and they came after me. That's when I got shot. I was able to evade, steal a car, and get out of town. Good thing they didn't put enough checkpoints in to lock the city down." He winced and lay back again.

There was a long silence, as we all took it in. We were close; it sounded like the burst of activity at Kismayo University fit with the rough timing of the hostages being moved away from Djibouti. Whether they were all there or not, we couldn't know unless some other intel surfaced, but it looked to me like we needed to confirm that there were at least some there.

Apparently, my opinion was not shared all the way around. "If they know we're in the vicinity, and Spider's been taken, we need to abort," Baird said. "We're burned, and they will be ready for us if we attempt to move on them."

"What do you think, Danny?" Alek asked. "Is this enough to get higher to send in the cavalry, or do they need more? Do we need to go in there and try to confirm?"

Danny sighed, and pulled his sat phone out. "I'll ask." He got up and walked away from the trucks, searching for a good satellite signal, while Imad, exhausted and pain-wracked, lapsed back into his morphine-induced torpor.

***

It was a short conversation. "They won't risk it," Danny reported. "They won't so much as move any assets until we have solid confirmation on all targets." His shoulders were slumped in defeat. "And yes, that means we have to know exactly where all one hundred fifty remaining hostages are being held before they'll commit anything." He ran a hand over his beard. "Damn it to hell. I'm sorry, guys." He looked at Alek solemnly. "If you make the call to abort, I understand."

Alek didn't say anything for a long time. None of us did. Most of us just stared at the imagery of Kismayo and thought. There weren't many good options. Hell, there weren't *any* good options. Rock, meet Hard Place.

It was Larry who finally broke the silence. "By all rights, the smart thing to do would be abort," he said. "But I have one question before we make that decision." He looked around at the rest of us. "What other option do those hostages have at this point? If the powers-that-be aren't willing to do anything until they have one hundred percent confirmation, does that mean they get abandoned to be human shields or worse if we call it quits? Are we really the only chance they've got?"

Eyes turned to Danny, who held up his hands and shook his head. "I'm not really part of the team on this one, guys. I've told you what I've gotten from my superiors. I'll leave the decision to you."

"I think Larry hit the nail on the head, guys," Rodrigo said. "Washington has written these men and women off, unless we do something." He looked down at the dirt for a moment, then looked up at Alek. "I don't like that. I don't like that we already lost Colton on this clusterfuck, and the idea that he went down just for us to turn around and abandon the mission turns my fucking stomach."

"The odds suck," Tim said.

"The odds always suck," Hank replied. "Why do you think we used to say, 'alone and unafraid?'"

"If we're burned, we can't take our time," I pointed out. "If we're going to go ahead and push, we need to do it soon, or those poor bastards are going to go the same way the ones in Qardho did."

"I'm not going to make this call by myself," Alek said. "We're all here by our own choice. I personally don't think we should turn tail and leave those guys to rot, not while we still have ammo and freedom of movement. But I'll leave it up to the team. All in favor of continuing on mission?"

All but Tim raised our hands. He looked around, then said, "Aw, fuck. Fine. I think it's suicide, but I suppose there are worse ways to go." He raised his hand too.

"That makes it unanimous." We turned to Baird. "We've got another team inbound," Alek said. "I'll leave it up to you if you and your boys continue on. I know this seems a little psycho."

Baird said nothing for a while, then chuckled. "We've been hanging out here, hoping for something that might stand a chance of doing this much damage to the jihadis for over a year, Alek," he said. "Forget what I said before. We're in. Every man I have working with me knows what we've gotten ourselves into."

Alek nodded, and held out his hand. "Welcome to the psych ward."

"I've been here longer than you have, my friend," Baird replied as he shook Alek's meaty paw with a grin that seemed to glow in the darkness.

***

The Bell 407 swooped in to land in a swirl of dust, and we hurried to get Imad loaded up. As we passed him to Caleb's and Dave's willing hands, Caleb leaned out and yelled, "Mike's team left early, about eight hours ago. They should be in position to link up with you guys in about another five or six hours."

"Good news," Alek shouted back. "Saves us some time." He pointed to Imad. "Get him to a hospital as fast as you can. He's your priority now."

Caleb threw a mock salute, and waved to Sam. We jogged away as the rotors bit and flung sand and gravel at us hard enough to hurt, and the helo pulled for the sky.

We had less than a day to plan, link up with Mike's team, finish the plan, and get into position to infiltrate Kismayo with a reinforced platoon. Sleep and chow were going to be secondary considerations for a while.

Time to get to work.

CHAPTER 27

It was just about midnight as we crept into the outskirts of Kismayo.

The idea was to probe the outskirts for a dead zone, and start slipping through. We had to signal carefully, since, as Baird had pointed out, the bad guys weren't anything like as unsophisticated as we had come into the country expecting. Any transmissions had to be short and clipped, or we ran the risk of alerting them we were coming.

Of course, with total radio silence, we had another problem; namely, keeping the teams coordinated and getting everybody through the gap in a timely manner. This was why Jim, Bob, Tim, and I were creeping ahead, while the rest of our guys stayed hunkered down in the bush about seven hundred meters north. It meant that it would take longer to infiltrate, but staying clandestine was our only hope at the moment, so we did what we had to do. It had meant stepping off a little early, too, to make sure we had as much darkness as possible to work with.

The goal for tonight was to get eyes on any hostages that the bad guys were keeping in Kismayo, and, if we couldn't account for all of them, snatch somebody who knew where the rest were. Easy day.

Right.

Jim went to one knee at the corner of the first big compound we'd come to. In the dark, Kismayo looked like just about every other desert city we'd been in, whether in the Middle East, South Asia, North Africa, or East Africa. Mud or cinder block walls surrounded courtyards and squat, mud or cinder block houses. Dusty, deciduous trees and bushes grew where there was water to support them. Here the houses seemed to mostly have metal roofs, but other than that, most of these places weren't all that different.

The lights were on, but only in certain places. The neighborhood we were poking around the edges of was dark, which was a large part of the reason we were there. Whether they didn't have electricity because they were too poor, had pissed off the local ruling council, or just due to the overall incompetence of the Islamist-run power plant, we had no way of knowing. Frankly, my money was on option three. Just as long as the power stayed off, we'd be in business.

Tim moved from cover to join Jim at the base of the wall, facing off to the east, while Jim peered around the corner to the south. Apparently satisfied that the way forward to the next compound was clear, he turned and signaled to Bob and me to move up.

I came to my feet while squeezing Bob's shoulder. He reached up and returned the silent signal with his off hand, and rose smoothly to follow.

We didn't run, and we didn't move in an exaggerated "stealthy" crouch. For one thing, that just wears you down physically. Don't believe me? Try moving a hundred meters with gear and a rifle, in a half-crouch. You'll be smoked and in pain by fifty. Running makes noise, plus the human eye is drawn to movement. Walking slowly presents a lot less eye-catching movement than dashing from cover to cover.

This is not to say we strolled. It was a controlled, quiet glide to the next compound to the south, across the bare dirt track that passed for a street from Jim and Tim. Keeping to the shadows, out of the line of faint light coming from the lit portions of the city, I came to a stop, and after making sure there wasn't a can or bottle there, lowered myself to a knee. Once Bob had settled, watching our six-to-three o'clock, I stayed there motionless for a handful of heartbeats, watching and listening.

There was no movement. No sound, aside from the whisper of the wind, the buzz of insects, and some movement inside the compound we were huddled up against, that I identified as a donkey when it brayed loudly. Another moment of waiting to see if the owner was going to come out to investigate why his jackass was making noise in the middle of the night, and I relaxed fractionally, and signaled Jim and Tim forward.

We moved like that for another fifteen minutes or so, using a combination of the shadows of compound walls and bushes in between to mask our movement. The entire time, we were cataloguing what we saw, trying to imagine how the rest of the teams would have to move through. It was going to be dicey, and most likely, they would have to choose multiple infiltration routes through the neighborhood, to reduce their footprint. I hadn't seen any room for more than two or three shooters to hide at any one time.

The structures started getting closer and closer together, and our maneuvering room started getting cramped. We still hadn't seen a soul, which was good, but I didn't think it could last. Urban infiltration is not my favorite sport, but it certainly was a challenge.

Jim and Tim had just slipped across the northeast-to-southwest dirt road that was the major thoroughfare through the neighborhood. I was about to follow, when I got a sudden clenched fist signal from Tim. Freeze. I stayed on a knee, motionless.

It took only seconds to see what Tim had seen. A faint glow on the side of the wall that Jim and Tim were hiding beside began to intensify, until it was the unmistakable white glare of headlights. I shrank back from my corner, trying to stay in the shadows as much as possible, and brought my suppressed rifle into a half-ready position, just in case.

I didn't want to have to use it. Contrary to a lot of movies and video games, when you kill somebody on an infiltration, you can't just drag the body into the shadows and go on your merry way. A killing on an infiltration means the infiltration is over, and you just fucking failed. Sooner or later, somebody is going to wonder where that poor bastard you just slotted went. If he's a sentry, somebody is likely to wonder that sooner rather than later. Then they come looking for him, likely with the suspicion that he met with foul play. Whether you get spotted immediately or not, you just got compromised, and, as it says on the door of Scout/Sniper School, "Compromise is Failure." Out here, failure meant we'd be dead.

And that is leaving aside the noise of the shot, which would give us away in the first place.

The vehicle turned out to be an open-topped jeep knockoff, with four skinnies in it, all armed. The two in the back were standing up and looking around. Fortunately, they didn't seem to have NVGs, or we'd have been screwed, sitting not ten feet from the road. They did have a radio, and I was close enough I could hear chatter in Somali crackling on it even over the noise of the engine and creak of the suspension. They cruised on past, not slowing down or showing any sign they'd spotted us.

Well, shit. They were patrolling, and by the sound of that radio, they were patrolling aggressively. That was going to put a serious crimp in the night's activities. I waited until the taillights disappeared around the bend, then made another careful scan, focusing as hard as I could on the thermal outlines, making sure that there wasn't anybody else hanging out, or that the jeep hadn't dropped somebody off to watch their rear.

Nothing showed up. The thermal showed nothing aside from a couple of chickens pecking in the dust outside another wall, and a mangy dog rooting through the heaps of trash on the side of the road a few hundred yards away. It was ignoring us for the moment. I willed it to keep its attention on the garbage, and got up to cross the road.

We moved deeper in, until we found ourselves in a little, brush-choked, dusty cul-de-sac. It was sheltered by another compound from the road, and there was plenty of concealment in the brush and the shadows. It wasn't safe, by any means, but nothing in this city could be considered safe. It would do for a team minus to stage. I got on the radio, and sent Alek the description and directions before advising to send no more than six shooters, and keep them in pairs until they got in position.

It took a few moments to send this, as I was sending in bursts of no more than a few seconds at a time. When I finished with, "Over," I got back simply a double squelch-break. We were taking Baird's warnings seriously.

The four of us stayed put, spread around the open space where we

233

could see out onto the streets, with Jim and Tim covering the general area to the north, while Bob and I kept our eyes south, toward the target area. Staying on a knee for a long time gets tiresome and painful, but we didn't dare relax too much so we endured the discomfort while we waited for the rest.

It took about thirty minutes for the lead pair to link up with Jim and Tim, and make their way into the little staging area. Glancing back, I could see by movement and profile that Alek and Larry had led the way in. Figures, put the two biggest guys on the team on point. I'd give Alek shit about it later. For now, as the next two came in, Jim, Tim, Bob, and I moved out, going deeper into the house of our enemies.

A short distance from our little staging area, two compounds sat close enough together to form a narrow alleyway that we immediately made use of, slipping between the two walls in the shadows and out of sight. Then we hit a sticking point.

There was a solid wall of interlinked compounds facing us. We'd have to either go around, which at least to the southwest led straight to another major road, or try to go through. I dropped to a knee while still in the alley, and took my time, looking it over, acutely conscious that time was ticking by, and we were losing darkness with every passing moment.

Finally, since I couldn't see any other way, and there was no sign of human or canine movement nearby, I decided to chance going through. I signaled to Jim to stay put, and led Bob out toward the walls.

I crept to the base of the compound wall I'd picked as our tentative entry, and went to a knee, waving Bob in close. I grabbed him by the shoulder and, my lips less than an inch from his ear, barely whispered, "I'll be the base. You peek over the top, see if the compound is clear. If it is, we'll signal to Jim and Tim and go over. If not, we move." He nodded, and I braced my back against the wall, carefully slinging my rifle across my chest to keep it from banging against the cinder-block, and interlaced my fingers as a stirrup.

Bob slung his rifle tightly to his back, put his boot in my clasped hands and his gloved hands on my shoulders, then carefully lifted himself up to the top of the wall.

My arms and shoulders started to ache almost immediately. Holding a man in full gear above you with main strength is a bitch. I had to keep my head down, too, to avoid having my NVGs catch on his kit. So I stared at my knees and Bob's boots, trying not to shake with the effort of holding him up, all the while hoping that no Shabaab patrol happened by while we were doing this.

It seemed like forever, but was really only a few seconds before Bob stepped back down. "Clear," he whispered. "Not even any animals."

I nodded, and signaled "come ahead" to Jim and Tim, then bent down, reaching into my shoulder pocket. I pulled out a tiny triangle of glint tape, and stuck it to the base of the wall, then got back into position. It wouldn't be visible unless you were looking for it, but it would reflect enough ambient light to show up like a beacon on NVGs if you were. The last man over would retrieve it, leaving no sign of our passage except for footprints and scuff marks on the walls. "You first," I murmured. Bob nodded, and as quickly as he could while being as quiet as possible, stepped up and pulled himself up on top of the wall.

He stayed there, pressed as flat to the top of the cinderblocks as he could. Fortunately, the Somalis didn't line the tops of their compound walls with broken glass or nails like I'd seen done elsewhere. As soon as he was set, he reached a hand down to me. Once my own rifle was slung securely, I reached up and grasped his wrist, and he helped haul me up the wall. There was some noise, as my boots scuffled on the wall for purchase, then as I dragged my gear over the edge and lay out on the top, facing Bob. He nodded, and spider-dropped off, hanging down by one hand and one foot as far as he could before letting go, keeping the actual drop as short as possible. I followed, as Jim and Tim got to the base of the wall.

Coming to my feet, I scanned the courtyard, keeping close watch on the house that squatted at the center of the back wall. It was silent and dark. Thermal showed nothing moving, either. Watching my footing carefully, I moved toward the back wall.

Now that we were in the compound, I wasn't entirely sure about the wisdom of going through this way, but we were pretty well committed. We'd have to go over the back wall closer to the house than I'd like. On the other hand, a careful, guarded look at my watch showed it was almost 0200. Time was a-wasting.

Once Jim and Tim were in the courtyard, we repeated the same dance on the back wall. This time, we found ourselves in a compound that actually had an open gate in the general direction we wanted to go. Easing my way around the wall at the gate, I saw just brush-scattered ground between us and the target.

That wasn't all I saw, either. There were sentries on the roof of the University, and from their body language, they were alert. The place was also lit up like a Christmas tree. That might well explain the widespread blackouts in the city; all the juice was going to Shabaab's headquarters, or whatever the fuck they had this place staked out for.

I ducked back inside, as a Bongo truck practically overflowing with armed men bounced past, apparently circling the University. They weren't taking any chances with security on the place, that was for sure. And if all the higher-ups were gone, that probably meant the hostages were in there.

Probably wasn't going to be enough, though. I eased back until only the eye with the NVGs over it was exposed, and watched the target, thinking.

As I did, Jim and Tim joined us in the compound. Jim leaned forward and whispered, "Rest of the team is inbound. Next element is in the staging area." I nodded, and went back to watching the target.

There was a low wall running all the way around the campus, except for two large gaps, one of which was directly ahead of us. It looked like it opened on the soccer field, with one of the three large main buildings beyond it. Not many of the windows that I could see were lit, but the field lights were on, bathing the open ground in harsh white light. We weren't getting across there without being spotted.

As I looked at the main building, I began to wonder just how the hell we were going to find the hostages in that mess. Those buildings were huge, guarded, and well-lit. Finding anything in there was going to be dicey, not to mention getting back out. For all our determination out in the desert, this was looking more and more unlikely.

But, as I watched, I started to think I saw an opening. Not the obvious wide open gap in the wall, but a shadowed area further down the southwest wall. There was a shack up against the wall, and not a lot of illumination. In fact, the more I looked at it, the more I saw a gap in their lighting, and a path up to the wall of the main building that would be generally out of sight, unless they had somebody in the windows with night vision. Which they might, but we'd scan it thoroughly with thermals before we even tried going over the wall.

It was so thin a chance as to be damned near transparent, but it was the only chance we had to find these guys. I dropped back into the compound, as Danny and Rodrigo came over the wall behind us. Alek and Larry were already in, so I hunkered down with Jim and Alek to explain what I'd seen.

"I think we might be better off taking a house and setting up surveillance, to be honest with you," Jim said. "Sooner or later there's got to be some outward evidence of the hostages. I don't like this setup."

"I don't like it, either," I said. "We should just get eyes on over the wall first; see if we can locate anything from outside. Going in should be our absolute last resort."

"Agreed," Alek said. "But if they're deep inside, we won't see shit."

"Only so much we can do with this situation," I pointed out. "This is worse than we thought. I say we get close, see what we can see, see if we can grab anybody of medium importance who might know more, and get the fuck out."

Alek nodded. "Let's do it." He laid a hand on my shoulder. "You guys have been on point for the last couple hours. Let's push the next element." I nodded tiredly, until Danny and Rodrigo stepped up.

"Danny?" I whispered. "Aren't you supposed to kind of hang back and let us expendable contractors do the dirty work?"

"Like hell," he murmured, as he slipped out of the compound with Rodrigo, Nick and Hank standing by to follow them.

The new point element moved carefully through the spaced-out buildings and bushes, working their way toward the corner of the main wall. Once there, they sent a quick glint to signal that they found a decent staging point. I led out, as their thermal signatures disappeared around the corner of the wall.

The staging area turned out to be some thicker bushes surrounding what turned out to be an abandoned house. We went into the house, relying more on the brick to mask us than the brush. I found a window facing southeast, where I could watch the point element get into position.

I watched as they set in between the wall and a small shack, that, if I was reading the ground right, was just across the wall from the shack I'd seen inside. I took my eyes off them to scan the roof of the University building, and spotted one of the sentries, who seemed to be pointing toward the wall...

The night exploded.

CHAPTER 28

The shockwave of the explosion slapped me in the face, hot air rocking me back on my heels. The noise was deafening, even this far away, and I almost didn't hear the hiss of flares being popped off, or the sporadic pops of small arms fire, as the sentries started shooting into the kill zone.

Through my NVGs the area around the shack was a huge thermal bloom. Smoke and dust was still billowing out from the blast point, and glowing wreckage was strewn across the ground. It didn't seem possible that any of the point element had survived that. The bullet impacts that were smacking dust up from the ground just seemed to emphasize the hopelessness of it. Danny, Nick, Hank, and Rodrigo were dead.

Somewhere inside the campus, some fuckstick started up a PA, and started shouting "*ALLAHU AKHBAR!*" at the top of his lungs, over and over. It was so loud it was clearly audible over the steadily intensifying roar of gunfire as the Shabaab fighters hosed down the kill zone frantically with rifle and machinegun fire.

All around us, the city came awake. Engines roared, headlights flared to life, and more small arms fire popped off. My earpiece crackled to life with Mike's voice.

"Coconut, Speedy," he called. "All hell's breaking loose out here; we've got mounted patrols coming out of the woodwork. What's your status?"

"Same thing here, Speedy," Alek replied. "Hold what you've got, we had an IED go off, and we've got casualties. I'll fill you in when we've got a better handle. For now, go firm and get ready for us to come to you, fast and hard."

The rest of the team was already at the windows, guns up and ready, but as yet, no one had started shooting. The flares were starting to white out my NVGs, so I flipped them up and started using my scope. We weren't taking fire yet, and if the guys out front were gone, we wouldn't do them any good by bringing hell down around our own ears. Alek came up to me and took a knee, and was about to say something when I held up a hand to stop him.

I'd seen movement, out there in the kill zone. At least one of our was still alive. I pointed, and whispered to Alek, "We've got to get er there. Somebody's still breathing. We can't leave 'em here."

He looked at the long stretch of open ground we'd have to cover to get there, the fighters on top of the campus building that were still shooting, and the half dozen trucks that were rumbling in from at least three different directions. "Good thing we brought at least one sixty," was all he said. He turned, tapped Jim on the shoulder, and pointed toward the roof.

It was going to be a drop in the bucket, but if we were lucky, it would get their heads down long enough for us to get to our casualties. Jim and Larry would stay put, Alek, Bob, Tim, and I would head for the blast zone.

Heaven help us, we were about to run *into* a fucking kill zone. I swallowed the hollow feeling in my gut, and got ready to run.

We peeled out the back door of the abandoned house and headed for the wreckage of the shack at a sprint, as Jim and Larry opened fire on the campus, the *thud-thud-thud* of the M60 being punctuated by the hammering reports of Larry's FAL. We ran bent over, as friendly rounds snapped past overhead. My body immediately started to protest, and the dusty, smoke-laced air burned in my lungs, as my boots pounded the ground, and my gear bounced and rubbed against my torso with every jarring stride.

We were halfway there when two of the enemy technicals rolled into the open.

Their headlights glared across the open ground and silhouetted us against the wall. I don't think they knew quite what to do, at first. The sight of four large men running full tilt *toward* the gunfire must have thrown them, because they seemed to falter at first. Then somebody shouted something in Somali, and AK fire started to strobe out of the darkness behind the headlights, reaching out for us.

I didn't slow down as I returned fire. They were probably the least-aimed shots of my life, but they might have bought us a few precious seconds. One of the headlights shattered, and some of the gunfire slackened, as I heard frantic shouts in Somali. We were almost to the knee-high remains of the shack.

Then Tim dropped on his face. Bob skidded to a halt, turned, and ran back to him. Alek and I dropped to the prone and started shooting at the trucks, concentrating our fire a little better from a stationary position. My chest was heaving, making my aim waver, but they were close. I saw two skinnies drop as I unloaded an entire magazine at the truck, and the rest scurried back to try to shelter behind the bed. I was glad I'd loaded up for bear as I rolled to one side to get a mag out of my vest to reload.

Bob was yelling at us, as I rocked the fresh magazine in place and sent the bolt home. I fired four more rounds at the truck, which looked like an old 5-ton, before twisting my head around to see Bob dragging Tim's limp form into the semi-shelter of the wrecked shack walls. He was yelling and waving at us to come on. I scrambled up onto a knee, then scuttled over to Alek and hit him on the shoulder. I stayed there, alternating between the two trucks, which were becoming increasingly bullet-riddled, firing a pair at one, then at the other, until he could get to his feet. He was breathing harder than I was, but we couldn't afford to slow down. We sprinted for the shack, as Bob opened fire from its dubious cover.

I vaulted the shattered wall, and landed in a mess of rubble. I noticed at that point that Bob wasn't the only one in the shack shooting. Nick was alive, covered in blood, and sitting up against the back wall, popping desultory shots up at the campus building. He looked shaky; I guessed he had a severe concussion at the very least.

Hank lay in the rubble of the shack wall closest to the blast. His right arm was nothing but mangled meat just past the elbow. Because of the way the rubble had fallen, I didn't see until I tried to move him that both legs were just gone. Before even thinking to check him, I grabbed his tourniquets off his gear and threw them on the stumps of his legs, cranking them down so hard that if he'd been conscious, he'd have been screaming in pain. Only once they were in place did I check for his pulse.

Nothing. He'd bled out while we'd been regrouping and trying to get over to them. Hank was dead.

My adrenaline was cranked so high that I didn't feel anything. I just stared at the man who had been my friend for almost ten years, and was now nothing more than inanimate, bloody meat. It didn't seem real. Even the boom and crack of gunfire didn't quite bring it home that he wasn't ever going to sit up, or open his eyes again. I probably would have stayed there for a long time, but many years of training and instinct stirred me to action before my brain even caught up.

I went to check Tim, but Bob just reached out to grab my arm, and shook his head. It took only one good look to see why. The bullet had gone in just under his right eye.

I looked around for Rodrigo and Danny. At first I couldn't see any sign of them, like they'd just vanished. But then I started to see the pieces.

Danny's head was mostly intact, lying on its side in a patch of dirt that had been turned to mud with the blood that had flowed out of it. A little farther away was a Lowa hiking boot, with mangled flesh and a jagged bone sticking out of it. Over by the corner was part of a ribcage.

Four men dead. Just like that.

I hurriedly checked Nick for any serious bleeds, while Alek and Bob laid down their hate on the two trucks, as well as a third that came in from the west. He wasn't very coherent, but he was conscious and shooting back. He had a broken leg and a lot of frag in him, but no arteries had been hit, and he was breathing all right. We'd need to get him checked out, but for right now he was alive.

Now we just had to get out of this deathtrap.

The firing from the rooftop had slackened considerably. I couldn't tell just how effective Jim and Larry's fire had been, but the Shabaab fighters had fallen back off the roof, and weren't shooting at us from above anymore. But I could see movement down on the ground floor. It looked like they were massing to rush us. Meanwhile, the fighters out by the trucks were chewing up the shattered cinderblocks we were using for cover. Dust and fragments filled the air with a harsh crackling thunder.

Alek was yelling into the radio, but I couldn't hear him over the gunfire. I settled my rifle on the edge of the smashed wall and got ready to start denying the rush.

When it came, it wasn't particularly disciplined, but it was a little more than the usual mob that we had expected when we first got to this shithole country. They moved forward in bounding rushes, firing from the hip as they came. They still weren't hitting shit, and I dropped three in the first rush alone. Nick got another one, whether by aim or luck I still don't know.

Then I got a look at the guy in the back, directing the attack. And I recognized him. It threw me for a second, but when I got him in the scope, it was undeniable.

It was Spider.

In spite of the fatigue, the adrenaline, and the mind-numbing noise of the fight, I felt an upwelling of rage and hate like I don't think I've felt before or since. My usual combat calm cracked, just for a minute, and I dumped six rounds into Spider's chest as fast as I could squeeze the trigger with a snarl of sheer animal fury. He staggered backward in a welter of blood and shredded meat, thumped against the wall behind him, and fell on his face, leaving a dark splatter on the cement.

It was at that point that Jim and Larry came running up, using the lull in the firing from the roof to link up with us. Jim yelled, "Friendlies, coming in!" at the top of his lungs, and vaulted the low, broken wall, the M60 held chest high, then dropped down between me and Nick, laying the machine gun on top of the wall, and opening fire. Larry came in a little bit slower, blowing hard. Guys Larry's size aren't built for speed.

Alek turned from the far wall as Larry took up position and opened fire. "Baird's choppers are incoming!" he yelled. "They're apprised of the situation, and are coming to us, and coming in hot!"

That was the first good news of the night. "What about Mike's team?" I threw the question over my shoulder as I continued to engage enemy fighters in the University building. The first half dozen deaths had convinced them that trying to rush us was a losing proposition, and now they were trying to shoot at us through the shattered windows on the first floor.

Alek's answer was momentarily forestalled by Jim ripping a long burst at the Shabaab positions. As the pig fell momentarily silent, he called back, "They're falling back out of the city, and linking up with the rest of Baird's people at the vehicles. They'll meet us at the RV point in the desert."

I squeezed off a pair of shots and dropped an RPG gunner who had popped out of a doorway. He convulsively clenched the trigger as he spun and dropped. The rocket smacked off the doorway and spun off into the night, and the backblast pulped the man who had been next to him, whose body fell out into the door. Nick shot him again, apparently just to be sure. "How far out are the helos?" I asked. "We aren't going to be able to keep this up much longer." We were going through ammo like crazy, and once the bullets were all gone, that was all she wrote.

"Five mikes," was the reply. I just hoped they didn't rally and try a bigger push in the next five minutes. Not to mention, I hoped that they didn't have RPG gunners set and ready for helos. We were in the same country where two SOAR Blackhawks had been shot down with RPG-7s within 15 minutes of each other, after all, and that was over twenty years before.

"North!" Larry yelled, turning his FAL to hammer out a booming trio of shots. I turned to join him, and saw three big panel-sided trucks rolling into the open, their beds almost overflowing with fighters.

Even as I started shooting, Jim pivoted, took one step to take a knee right next to me, and dumped the rest of the belt into the back of the lead truck.

It was a long burst, at least twenty-five rounds, and it shredded the side panels along with anyone who didn't have the presence of mind to jump off the far side of the truck. The truck slewed to one side, giving us a view of the heaped bodies in the back, after Larry shot the driver. The occupants of the other two trucks immediately started bailing, and Larry and I started picking them off as best we could.

They started spreading out through the walled compounds on either side of the dirt road that had sort of faded into the wide open area in front of us. They had a long way to go to flank us, but either way, we were running out of time.

We actually saw the helos before we heard them. To be accurate, we saw the muzzle flashes and streams of tracers from their door-mounted guns. Hans and his fellow pilots had also considered the history of helicopters being shot down in Somalia, and weren't taking any chances. They were coming in low and fast, and their door gunners were shooting at anything that looked like it might be carrying an RPG.

The Alouette was in the lead, and came in on a low curve over the campus, as the port door gunner raked the main building with 7.62 fire. The other gunner was giving our attackers from the north the business, playing his stream of tracers across the three stopped trucks, which shuddered, and started to come apart under the hail of steel and lead. A tracer found the rear truck's gas tank, and it erupted in flames, further adding to the hellish scene.

Then the Cougar was swooping in to land, fire spitting from both side doors and the back ramp. It settled in a swirl of dust, and then two figures were running off the back ramp, firing at the enemy to the north as they ran. I recognized Baird and Jason Van Voorhees as they got closer. I grabbed Nick, making sure his rifle was pointed in a roughly safe direction, and got him up. I shoved him at Jason as they ran up. "Get him on the helo!" I yelled. "We'll get the bodies!" Jason just nodded, threw Nick's arm over his shoulder, and started toward the bird, supporting his weight easily.

Bob was already throwing Tim's body over his shoulders in a fireman's carry, but Hank was going to be more difficult. I ended up slinging my rifle across my back and picking him up by the armpits. He was lighter than he had been in life, with the amount of his body that was missing, but he was still heavy as hell. I had to back toward the chopper, while Alek, Jim, Baird, and Larry bounded back slowly, keeping themselves between Bob and me and the enemy.

I staggered up the ramp and found a spot forward where I could lay Hank down. I positioned him as best I could, across the fuselage from Tim, as the rest of the team pounded up into the bird and Baird ran forward to yell at the pilot to take off. The tail gunner was already going to town again, hammering away at the University buildings, as we rocked into the sky and pulled away from Kismayo.

I looked down at Hank. His eyes were still open, so I reached down and closed them before I got into one of the mesh seats and slumped against the fuselage. The pilot had pitched us over hard, and we were tearing away from Kismayo as fast as he could get the old helo to move. The guns fell silent as their targets receded behind us.

At that point, I confess I wasn't thinking about the hostages who'd been left behind. They were as far from my mind as anyone back in the States. All I could think about was the brothers we'd just lost, in less than an hour of hell.

As we flew north, the first, silent tears began to fall.

CHAPTER 29

Conversation on the bird was impossible. The howl of the engines drowned out any words that weren't hollered directly into someone's ear. But as the flight went on, I started to study Baird carefully.

I'd been too busy staying alive before to think through the implications of what had just happened. Baird and Jason had come with air support, and were getting us out, so I hadn't looked a gift horse in the mouth. But now, as the adrenaline drained out of my system, and we were no longer in danger of winding up as mutilated corpses in some celebratory jihadi video on the Internet, I had some time to think, and I didn't like where my thoughts were taking me.

I didn't think anyone else had seen Spider on the ground back there. Nick had been the only other shooter facing that direction, and he was still a little out of it. There hadn't been time to tell anyone else, in the mad scramble to get airborne. So I was left pretty much alone with my thoughts, and my suspicions.

The question was, did Baird know about it, or had Spider betrayed him as thoroughly as he'd betrayed us? Or was it all a setup? Was Baird really back in Somalia for the reasons he'd said, or was he there to keep the CIA from doing the Muslim Brotherhood's lackeys too much damage?

But if that was the case, why fly into that hornet's nest to lift us out? He could very well have abandoned us to be overwhelmed and slaughtered as soon as our ammo ran out.

It was a conundrum.

After a couple of minutes, I felt more than saw Alek's eyes on me, and I looked over to see him watching me, a faint frown on his face. His eyes flicked over to Baird, then back to me, with one eyebrow raised. I shook my head, and mouthed, "Once we're on the ground." He watched me for another moment with narrowed eyes, then nodded, and put his head back against the fuselage.

***

We touched down in the desert to pick up Mike's team before continuing on toward Ethiopia. The Cougar was getting fairly full, but with three of Mike's guys getting on the Alouette, we were still well within the limits of both birds, so we cruised north as the sky began to turn pale in the east.

***

The sun was all the way up and getting hot as we touched down in the desert just outside of Dolo. Caleb's team had a small temporary FOB set up, with several GP tents, fuel bladders for the helos and the DC-3 that had been parked nearby, and three smaller tents that looked innocuous from the outside, but were lined with sandbags on the inside. Each held a mounted M60E4 and over one thousand rounds of ammunition.

Our two choppers landed together, the rotor wash flapping the sides of the tents and hammering the FOB with grit. Caleb and his team minus were waiting for us, and started forward to retrieve Hank and Tim's bodies. I waved them off, as I bent down to pick Hank back up, and Bob maneuvered Tim back onto his shoulders. We'd carry them off ourselves.

As we got up, and I adjusted Hank's dead weight in my arms, I caught Alek's eye, and jerked my chin to one side fractionally, while glancing at Baird and shaking my head. He nodded without a word, and we walked down the ramp, off the helo.

Caleb and Dave had a couple of litters waiting, so we carried our dead to them, and laid them down gently. Dave took Nick in hand and helped him toward the smaller GP tent, where I guessed he had the aid station set up. Bob crossed Tim's hands over his chest. Hank didn't have enough left of his right to do that, so I just adjusted him as well as I could. Then I stood up and faced Baird.

Consciously or unconsciously, the remainder of our team had drifted into a group with Baird and Jason opposite. There was a growing tension in the air, and Caleb picked up on it first.

"Guys," he said, "What's going on?"

I brought my rifle off my back, and kept it slung in front of me, my hand on the pistol grip, the muzzle pointed at the dirt. "That's a good question, Caleb," I replied, not taking my eyes off of Baird. "Seems we got set up."

"What do you mean?" Alek asked. Baird was frowning in puzzlement and a little anger, his hands pointedly held out at his sides, empty.

"Ask him," I said, nodding toward Baird. "Care to explain why your boy Spider was commanding the fighters trying to get at us from the target building, Baird?" I asked.

He looked taken aback and a little insulted. "You must have been mistaken. I've worked with Spider for five years."

"Oh, I wasn't mistaken," I said. "I shot him from less than fifty yards, through an eight-power scope. It was him."

Baird was watching me with as much intensity as I was watching him, his eyes searching mine for any trace of a lie, or uncertainty. I knew he wouldn't find any. "Why were those Shabaab fighters waiting for Imad at the hostel that night?" I asked. "Why did he leave Spider's side, and was almost immediately burned?"

He was as pale as I've ever seen a black man turn. He wasn't looking at me anymore; his gaze was questing around, his thoughts churning, trying to find an explanation for what I'd seen, for what had happened. I could tell he wasn't having any luck.

"He sold out Imad, and was waiting for us," I ground out. "He was Shabaab, or Al Qaeda, or Brotherhood, or some fucking thing the whole fucking time, Baird. So here's the question: did you know, in which case you've been playing us from the get-go, and we should just shoot you dead right here and now, or does your security just suck?" I was beyond pissed. I wanted to kill him so bad I could taste it. I wanted to do it with my bare hands.

Only many years of discipline and restraint were keeping me rooted to where I was standing, and my rifle pointed at the ground.

Jason was looking at me with narrowed eyes, as if trying to gauge whether or not I was telling the truth just by staring. Then, he turned his attention to Baird, a cold, expectant look in his eyes.

Baird continued to look at us in disbelief. He couldn't accept it yet.

"I knew he'd spent time with the militias. That was what made him so valuable," he explained. "I'd recruited him while I was still working for the Agency. He helped me bird-dog two warlords who were doing business with Baseej gunrunners who were bringing in weapons from Sudan, about five years ago. He saved my life at least twice. His contacts with the militias were what got me into Baidoa on my little fishing expedition. He got me the initial introductions." He looked at me, then at Alek. "I can't imagine he'd turn."

"I've known Jeff a lot of years," Alek said. "I've never known him to be wrong when he's this certain before. So what's the deal? Is your team compromised? Danny warned us that Langley considered you less than reliable. Were they right?"

"I don't know who's been saying that bullshit, but it's a lie," he protested angrily. "If Langley had had a problem with the way I worked, they'd have recalled me. I retired, I wasn't forced out."

"I knew Danny for a lot longer than I've known you," Alek pointed out remorselessly. "Why should I trust you over him?"

"I have a feeling that there isn't a right answer to this, is there?" Baird said. "If I deny that Spider could have done what you're saying he did, I'm a Shabaab double agent. If I admit that he was Shabaab, that he sold out your man and staged an ambush for us in Kismayo, then my security is unreliable. And if that's the case, then by extension, so am I." He looked steadily at us. "For what it's worth, if it's true, and Spider was dirty, which I am not admitting he was, then I had no knowledge of it."

"That's small comfort to the guys we lost, now isn't it?" Jim said harshly.

Baird spread his hands helplessly. "I can't change that. I can't go back in time and undo last night."

"No, you can't," Alek said. "Neither can we. Unfortunately, all we can do is try to make sure there isn't a repeat performance." He pointed with his off hand, his meaty right still wrapped around the grip of his rifle. "So get on your birds and get out of here. We don't need your help anymore."

"Just like that?" Baird said. "I pull your asses out of the fire, and this is the thanks I get?"

"Just like that," Alek affirmed. "I just lost four good friends last night. I can't afford to take chances with the rest, and as far as I'm concerned, I've got enough evidence to call working further with you taking chances."

Baird stared at both of us in frustration, then, his fists clenched, spun on his heel and strode back to the Cougar. Jason looked at us coolly for a moment, then nodded fractionally, touching one hand to his hat brim in a mock salute. He turned and followed his boss without a word.

The lot of us stood there stonily watching as both helos spun up and lifted. The wind of the rotor wash blew grit and gravel over us and the bodies. Bob bent down to brush the worst of it off the fallen. It wasn't going to do them any good, but it was the gesture that counted.

Bob was taking it hard. He hadn't known either man as long as most of us had, but he'd been in the "peacetime" military. He'd never lost a buddy in combat before Colton, and now three more teammates and one who was close to being a teammate were gone in a night. He was trying to stay stoic like everybody else, but I could tell he was hurting.

All of us were. But we weren't out of the woods yet, so we pushed it into the dark places in the back of our minds and tried not to think about it. We'd all pay for it later, and I fully expected most of us would spend a couple of days blind drunk when we got out of Africa, but for now we couldn't afford to hurt. So we clammed up, went stone-faced, and drove on.

Once the birds were out of sight, Caleb came back over to us. "What the fuck was that all about?" he asked.

"Some son of a bitch we were supposed to trust turned out to be a bad guy," Jim said. "And as a result, we lost four guys."

Caleb looked down at the bodies. "Fuck." It wasn't eloquent, but it got the point across. He jerked a thumb at the big tent behind us. "The Colonel's on VTC inside, wants to talk to you guys." We all involuntarily glanced at the bodies. "Go on. We'll take care of Hank and Tim." He paused. "Was there any way to recover Rod?"

Alek just shook his head. "Wasn't enough left."

Caleb closed his eyes. "Fuck."

"Amen, brother," Larry said, as we filed past and into the tent. Mike and Eddie followed along, leaving the bulk of their team to help Caleb.

There wasn't any air conditioning, so it was, if anything, hotter inside than it had been outside, under the sun. An industrial fan was blowing in the corner, trying to stir enough of the air to keep the occupants breathing, but it didn't help all that much. A couple of folding tables were covered in satcom gear, and Tom Heinrich's face was already looking out of the screen of a laptop set on one of them.

"Gents," he said solemnly as we gathered around the table. "Caleb's filled me in on some of it. What the hell happened?"

Alek gave him the short version, up to our little confrontation with Baird outside. By the end, Tom had reached off screen, and come back with a cigarette, which he promptly lit up. "I don't have the words, gentlemen. I know how you're feeling right now." He took a long drag. "I thought you should know that Al Masri has put out a new message, proclaiming that the infidels tried to rescue several of the 'infidel criminals' that their 'brothers in Islam' were holding righteously in Kismayo, blah, blah, and failed. He's holding it up as a sign that Allah is with them, the time of the infidels' superiority is at an end, and calling for all Muslims to strike down infidels wherever they can. The usual jihadi boilerplate, there really isn't anything new."

"Did they kill any more of the hostages?" Mike asked.

The brief flash of anger across the Colonel's face answered that question even before he spoke. "Only fifteen this time, but yes. They hanged them in front of Kismayo University at sunup this morning. It hit the web just a few minutes ago. I'll spare you the video."

I almost told him to play it anyway, but we really didn't need to see it. We had enough of a reservoir of hate and discontent built up from last night to take us a long way.

"I've got some other bad news," Tom said carefully. "The CIA's been told to pull the contract. This shit-show in Kismayo got enough of the wrong people concerned that the whole mess is now supposedly getting handed over to 'negotiators'" He practically spat the word. "There were apparently some NGO handwringers in Kismayo, trying to do relief work. They're decrying the 'indiscriminate use of air support' on your extraction. The local UN toady is screaming about illegal mercenaries being the greatest threat to stability in the country, again. The usual suspects are bleating about unauthorized special operations, and some of the biggest leakers on Capitol Hill are screaming that they weren't informed in detail about what was going down. I don't think they know it was a PMC on the ground, but that doesn't matter. This operation is now officially high-visibility, and that makes it politically unacceptable. Some poor sod in the Clandestine Service is probably going to be hung out to dry for running a rogue operation. They might even put the blame on Danny's head. Lord knows he's not going to be able to defend himself now."

"Wait a minute," Bob protested. "They're up in arms about what we did, but not about the hundred fifty or so hostages that the bad guys are still holding?"

"Most of them probably don't even know about the hostages," Tom admitted. "Most of the media's been downplaying this ever since it happened. They couldn't hide that there was an attack, but the official word is that with the GWOT being over, Lemonier was all but closed down. The only people who seem to actually know how many were there are the military and to some extent the families of the people stationed there. And the military leadership isn't talking, because they've been ordered not to. It would reflect poorly on the present administration, and since it didn't happen on US soil, it can be generally swept under the rug." He stubbed out the cigarette and lit a fresh one. "Oh, there are some voices who are raising hell about it, but they're considered, 'unhelpful,' I think is the new wordage. Those men and women are in the wind, now, and there's not a damned thing we can do about it."

"Has the Agency been told about Danny?" Alek asked quietly.

"They have," Tom replied. "So has his wife. I added my condolences, and told her that you'd be by as soon as you could get back." Alek nodded his thanks. There was an awkward silence for a minute after that. None of the rest of us knew Danny very well, but he and Alek had been close at one time.

"So now what?" I asked into the quiet. "We just go home, bury our dead, and hand another success to these assholes? Fuck that."

"What else can we do, man?" Larry asked. "We're a little outgunned here, and now we don't even have what little support we had before. We're as much in the wind as the hostages."

"Actually…" the Colonel put in carefully, "There is something. It might not save the hostages, and might make us all even more a bunch of pariahs back home, but we can still put the hurt on these fucking savages."

We all looked at him for a moment. "You have our attention," I said.

He gathered his thoughts for a moment, those icy eyes looking somewhere above the screen. "I was struck early on with just how little information we were getting from the CIA about the situation. Obviously, they let their assets slip, and then they pointed you to one that turned out to be unreliable in the worst way. I didn't know about Baird at the time, but I figured it was time that we started developing our own intel base.

"It's still a project in its infancy," he went on. "But I have already managed a couple of rather significant recruitments, which have already started to bear fruit. Given the nature of the present contract, I of course concentrated on subject matter experts in the Middle East and East Africa. What I've managed to dig up in the short time we've had to work on this is…interesting. One of my new recruits has been able to access certain realms of SIGINT that were previously out of our reach, as well as putting a few pieces together that we didn't have before.

"The new Egyptian Mukhabarat is becoming the Muslim Brotherhood's equivalent of the Iranian Revolutionary Guard. They're very well-funded, they're hardline Islamists, and they're quite interested in exporting the Islamic revolution as far as it can go. Apparently, strategic control of the approaches to the Suez Canal was on their 'to do' list.

"Their problem seems to be that they're upset Hezbollah and the Qods Force has been upstaging them lately. While they got a good amount of traction in North Africa and the Arabian Peninsula, and have been making progress in East Africa, the Iranian proxies have them on their heels in Lebanon and Anbar. They mostly seem to consider AQ to be unreliable these days, so they wanted to strike a major blow against the US to advance their own credibility with the Muslim street. Even as neutered as our foreign policy is these days, to Muslims, the US is still the Great Satan, and it's still the primary symbolic target, even if the US government won't lift a finger against them for fear of being called Islamophobic.

"The Lemonier hit was their first big push. Apparently they're comparing it to Osama's gambit in Somalia in the '90s in some of their strategy calls. I don't know if you remember, but it was the Black Sea shootdowns and the subsequent withdrawal that convinced Bin Laden that the US was a paper tiger, and emboldened his operations leading up to 9/11. Al Masri, or Mahmoud Al-Khalidi, now that we've had that particular kunyah exposed, sold the operation as a litmus test. In effect, they took our people to see if the response would be as overwhelming as the attack on the Taliban in '01 or the invasion of Iraq in '03. Since it wasn't, he's ecstatic, and is pushing for the 'next step,' whatever that is."

He stubbed out his second cigarette and lit up a third. "This is where our opportunity comes in. Al-Khalidi's holding a meeting to discuss the next stage. We don't know what that is, but it apparently either involves AQAP, or he's suspicious enough of his own people that he doesn't want to meet where there are a lot of ears around, namely in Cairo. The meeting is apparently going in Yemen, in a small town outside of Aden, called, imaginatively, Little Aden. We don't have a solid place yet, but I've looked at the imagery of the town. It's not big. In fact, the Al-Hiswah power station is almost as big as the whole town. It should be possible to get in, kill or capture the attending jihadists, and get out."

There was a long moment of silence, each man in the tent thinking over what had happened, and what the Colonel was offering. If the Lemonier hostage-taking really was just the first move in a new wave of attacks, we couldn't really stand aside if we had a chance to take out the guy responsible.

Of course, we weren't technically soldiers anymore. We were contractors, guns-for-hire. If we wanted, we could walk away right now. There was no money in a raid in Yemen, and with the very real possibility that we wouldn't get paid for the hard work and loss of the last month, that was a real concern.

But, looking around at the rest, fresh from losing Tim, Rodrigo, and Hank to Al-Khalidi's pals, I could see that none of us cared. Even Bob, who in the past would have been the first to argue for the money side, didn't care. We had a shot at the guy responsible for the deaths of our friends, regardless of any wider geopolitical considerations, and we were going to take it.

You fuck with us, you pay the bill.

Alek turned back to the laptop. Tom was waiting impassively. "Give us all the targeting data you have," Alek said. "I also need as up-to-date maps and imagery as you can get me, up to one hundred klicks from the town. I'll check with Caleb and see if we've got the logistics to make the move to the Yemeni desert from here, or if we need more."

"You'll have everything I can dredge up," Tom said. "I might be able to get in touch with one of our previous clients with a ship in the area, in case we need a staging area for materiel."

The maps were already downloading. We started dropping our kit and getting to work.

CHAPTER 30

We had to do a little reorganizing. Alek's team was desperately under strength, and while Caleb was also at half numbers, because half of his were still on the *Lynch*, we still needed them to hang back and run support. Without support, we probably would not make it out of Yemen.

None of them were happy about it. They'd been stuck on the sidelines for this entire job, and we weren't a very large company, so they'd known the guys we'd lost almost as well as we had. They were itching for some payback, but necessity can be a bitch.

So, we sat down with Mike and he gave us Bo, Charlie, and Lee. Bo was a former Ranger, while Charlie and Lee had been Recon. They were all solid professionals, even if Charlie had a tendency to get a bit of an inter-service chip on his shoulder sometimes. The fact that none of us were still in the military, and that many of us had cross-pollinated between the Marine Corps and Army SOF seemed to be a little lost on him sometimes. Lee was the consummate gray man; he rarely said anything at all, and was in fact something of an enigma to his own team. Bo was a solid, soft-spoken, two-hundred-fifty-pound black guy who'd escaped Detroit by joining the Army.

That left us with eight, and Mike with seven. We had two maneuver elements and a support element in the rear. It would be enough for a quick in-and-out, but if we got pinned down like we had in Kismayo, we'd be in trouble. Yemen had a standing military, and though the Egyptian and Sudanese advisors had improved Shabaab's training, the Yemenis would be a step above that. They were also better equipped, and since the takeover in the wake of the Yemeni Revolution a few years back it was a good bet they were going to be sympathetic to the bad guys.

They also had air defenses, which was going to make getting in under the radar difficult. You could fly into Somalia with impunity, as long as you stayed above RPG range when you went over any cities. Yemen had radar, SAMs, and MiGs. Add in the fact that the target was pretty close to one of the country's largest and oldest cities, and the likelihood of significant defenses became even higher.

The more we looked at it, the more it looked like coming in from the sea was going to be our best option. It still wasn't a good option, given our assets, but a maritime raid stood a better chance of success than trying to fly in to the desert undetected, move overland, make the hit, disengage, and move overland again to the bird, then fly out without getting shot down.

As we were trying to figure out this particular problem, the Colonel called with another interesting proposition.

"What do you guys think about going back to Socotra?" he asked.

There was a chorus of, "Fuck that."

"The last time we went there it was a fucking disaster," Alek said. "There's no way we're doing business with those assholes again."

"Not talking about doing business with pirates," Tom replied. "Quite the opposite in fact. If you get lucky, you might even have a chance to put a bullet in one or two of the sons-of-bitches who double-crossed you last time.

"The Somali pirates have been using Socotra as a refueling point for hijacked shipping for several years now. At any one time, there are usually two or three commercial freighters at anchor there. My sources say that there are five right now. There is one, however, that is of interest to us."

He brought several photographs up on screen. They gave several angles on an older container ship, painted blue and green. Its white superstructure bore the name *Frontier Rose*. One of the pictures was an overhead shot of the ship at anchor near a long concrete pier jutting off a sandy beach.

"The *Frontier Rose* was hijacked three months ago. The company that owns it was already in bad shape financially when the ship left port; this run was their last hope of avoiding bankruptcy. Obviously they are in worse straights now. They can't afford to ransom the hostages, and the captain has already been killed. The pirates are getting more and more irate, but the company simply doesn't have the money to pay them, and their insurance ran out just before the run started.

"We have recent video confirmation that the pirates are keeping the crew on the ship, thanks to their latest message to the company demanding payment. They're in bad shape, but they are alive.

"Here's the deal; I've been in contact with the company, and they are desperate. They made me an offer. If we can get their people away from the pirates alive, we can have the ship."

Several sets of eyebrows went up at that. Eddie blurted, "Is that legal?"

Larry turned to him. "If this works, we're going to use that ship as a launch platform for an armed invasion of a sovereign country, for the purpose of assassinating several people, at least one of whom is an actual official of *another* sovereign country. And you're worried about whether or not it's legal for us to get paid for a rescue with a container ship?"

Eddie thought about it for a second. "You know, you're right.

254

Forget I said anything."

"My first thought would be to say that this idea is kind of jeopardizing the raid," Jim said. "Another raid to set up for the first one just multiplies the chances of a critical failure. We'd have to run it perfectly. We can't afford any more losses at this point. And every time we make contact with armed opposition, which this will be, we chance taking losses."

"Noted," Alek said finally. "Face it, boys, we are so far across the Rubicon we can't even see the motherfucker anymore. Either we do this, or we pack it in. And I'm not ready to do that yet. Yeah, it's gonna suck, and the prospect for even worse suckage before we get to go home is pretty fucking high. Oh fucking well." He looked around at the whole group. "Clear enough?"

Nobody objected. He was right. We were all too proud to go home now. The mission was there, and we planned on finishing it, or dying in a pile of empty brass. Binary solution set. Win or lose, live or die.

"I've got our standby bird on the way to Socotra right now with boats and amphib gear," Tom said, when he was sure the byplay was over. "It should meet you there. Logan will make sure nobody fucks with it." Logan Try was an old hand who was, if anything, meaner than most of the guys on the teams. He tended to be a bit too much of a lone wolf, which was why he wasn't on a team. He could be trusted to make anyone's life who tried to steal our shit short and painful, though.

"How much is this costing us, Tom?" Alek asked quietly.

"A lot," Tom admitted. "But we're good. You worry about operations, Alek, and let me worry about the financial side. I won't let us go under, I promise. Besides, you pull this off, I'm already figuring out how to leverage it into other opportunities."

"All right, Tom, I'll leave it to you. Unless there's more info you can give us, we've got a lot of work to do if we're going to get to Socotra in time," Alek said.

"I'm sending all updates I've got as an attachment," Tom said. "I'll let you guys get to it." The video window winked out.

"Well, let's get this shit packed," I said. "We've got a date on Socotra."

***

It took most of six hours to get everything broken down and packed on the DC-3, while still maintaining security. It was getting dark as we finally took off, leaving the 407 behind to follow us by a longer route. The helo didn't have the range the DC-3 did, and would have to stop to refuel en route. Most of Caleb's team was riding with the helo to make sure no one decided to hijack it, since they'd be stopping in Somaliland and Puntland on the way to Socotra.

I sat in the uncomfortable web seat against the fuselage and closed

255

my eyes. It was going to be just over a four hour flight to Socotra, and we'd likely hit the ground running once we got there. We could all use the sleep. I drifted off quickly enough, in spite of the drone of the engines and the ghosts waiting behind my eyelids.

***

We landed in the middle of the night, apparently to the ground controller's great displeasure. Mike had woken us all up about fifteen minutes out, so we'd gotten to watch as the strip lights didn't come on until we were on final approach. Logan must have had to go wake the guy up. It was one in the morning, after all.

Paul brought the DC-3 down with a brief chirp of rubber on cement, and hardly a bump, even in the dark. The bird was his baby, and he took great pride in how well he knew her every quirk. If the landing had been even remotely rough, he would have been pissed at himself for days, never mind that it was on an unfamiliar strip in the middle of the night. Like Sam, Paul was a perfectionist.

We got up and stretched as he taxied the plane over toward the tiny terminal. I'd gotten a look at it out the side window as we landed, and it really wasn't much. There was a separate tower, and the terminal itself was a two-story block of a building that squatted next to a large cement pad where airliners could offload their cargo of mostly French tourists. We'd have to go through the terminal, as we were masquerading as similar tourists, in order not to alert the pirates that somebody very scary had just landed. I didn't know for sure what cover Logan had used for all of our amphib gear, but the bulky kitbags full of armor, ammunition, and weapons might get interesting.

It turned out to be a little less interesting than I had expected. As we taxied, we slowed to a stop still a fair distance from the terminal, as an ancient diesel truck pulled up to the side door of the aircraft. Logan got out and climbed up into the bed, and then called over to toss him our gear. He'd hold on to it until we cleared Yemeni customs, then we'd link up with him down by the shore, where he'd been getting the boats set up. It seemed workable, so fifteen heavy kitbags got heaved out into the bed of the truck, then Logan climbed back down into the cab and pulled away, still without lights. We continued to taxi toward the terminal.

When Paul finally brought the plane to a stop, the door opened again, and we climbed down, notably unarmed, and clad in the closest we'd been able to scrape together to summer tourist clothes, which wasn't much. We were still wearing mostly khaki tactical pants, hiking boots, and short-sleeved shirts, plus there was no disguising the fact that fifteen fairly large, fit men, most with beards, had just landed on the island. There was a noticeable lack of women or older men, and we all had to work to tone down the "fuck off" meat-eater vibe that we tended to wear like a second skin.

The inside of the terminal was a single big, open room, filled with black plastic chairs, and punctuated by several square support columns. A long reception desk sat along the back wall, along with a customs checkpoint, and that was where we headed, with our 3-day go-bags slung over our shoulders, hoping they wouldn't appear overly tactical to the customs goons. Our excuse was that we were there to do some serious hiking in the inland mountains. It might be believable.

There were half a dozen airport police scattered around the terminal, most looking like they'd just been rousted out from a nap. They didn't look too concerned about us, in fact they looked mostly concerned about getting done and going back to sleep. Perfect.

Alek led the way, presenting his passport and his bag for inspection. The blue-uniformed policeman shuffled through the bag disinterestedly, found the bribe that had been placed carefully just for him to find, and waved him through. The rest of us followed, the same ritual being repeated without fanfare or fuss. I don't think they even noticed that half of our packs were made by Kelty, or if they did, they didn't know what it meant.

We met Logan with the same truck in the mostly empty parking lot behind the terminal, and climbed into the back. He ground the rickety thing into gear, and we started rattling down the main road out of the airport.

It was surprising how normal everything appeared. There weren't any armed patrols, in fact there was no sign of the pirates we'd run into up in Hadibu. The gas station just outside the airport had its lights on, and was apparently open for business. There wasn't really any traffic, which wasn't all that surprising given the hour, but it felt strangely calm, as though none of the hell that was going on around the Gulf of Aden had any effect here. It was an illusion, one that we would shatter soon, but it was eerie, all the same.

We trundled down the road, which was in really good shape, better than some of the roads back in the States, as a matter of fact. There weren't a lot of lights lit on Socotra at night, and the clouds had started to roll in off the Arabian Sea, so there wasn't much starlight, either. The hills loomed on our right, their dark bulk more felt than seen, outside of the cone of light from our headlights. Nobody talked much.

After a while, Logan pulled the truck off the road, and we bounced along a rough dirt track in the dark, until the ground ahead suddenly disappeared from the headlights. Then he stopped the truck, killed the lights, and shut off the engine. When he got out of the cab, he simply said, "We're here," and started walking away.

We jumped out, hauling out our kitbags with us, and started after him. It quickly became apparent that the ground had disappeared because we were parked on the edge of a steep bank that sloped sharply down toward the shore. It was going to be rough climbing with our kit, but Logan already had a path picked out, and was marking it with small chemlights as he descended.

It wasn't fun, but it wasn't as bad as it initially looked.

At the bottom, the waves lapped against the shore and the three Zodiac rubber boats that were mostly set up just above the waterline. The engines weren't hooked up yet, but they were on the beach, along with five storm cases full of gear.

"Holy shit, Logan, you didn't haul all this crap down here by yourself did you?" Larry asked.

"Yeah, I did," was the gruff reply. "So what?"

"Just...damn." There had to be the better part of a ton of gear down there on the beach, and Logan had humped it solo down that embankment. The guy gets a little...single-minded, sometimes.

Glancing at my watch, instinctively shielding the Indiglo with my hand, I saw that it was about 0230. We had about three hours or so before first light. That was going to make it unlikely that we'd manage to take the ship tonight. We still had too much setup to do. We got to it.

None of the boats was fully assembled; we had to finish inflating them and install the deck plates. The outboard motors had to be unpacked, fitted to the boats, and secured, then fueled, primed, and tested. All of our kit had to be brought out and checked. By the time everything was ready, it was almost dawn.

"Were you able to get eyes on the target?" Mike asked Logan, as we all sat down either on the storm cases, the boat gunwales, or rocks.

"No," was the answer. It wasn't surprising, considering that the weird bastard had spent however many hours hauling three boats and all their assorted gear down a rocky slope, instead of leaving it in the truck and waiting for us to get there to help out.

"We're going to have to do some kind of reconnaissance," I said. "The Colonel's information is as up-to-date as he can make it, but it's still old. We need eyes on before we try to board."

"Well, anybody bring shorts?" Eddie asked with a laugh. "We can be tourists running around in a boat, skin diving."

Without a word, Logan got up and hiked back up the bank toward the truck. We all kind of looked at each other, not sure what to make of this. When he came back down, he had a small overnight bag over his shoulder, which he tossed on the ground in the middle of the loose circle we had going.

"The Colonel thought they might be useful," was all he said. Bob went over and opened up the bag. Inside were several sets of tropical shirts, shorts, and sandals; just the sort of thing tourists would be wearing in a place like Socotra.

"Leave it to the old man to think of shit we didn't even think to ask about," Bo said. To Bo, Tom was always "the old man," since the two of them had served together in the Army, many years past.

"I'll go," I said. "I'll take Jim and Lee." I tossed each of them a pair of shorts and sandals that might fit, and pulled out a loose white short-sleeved shirt and pair of board shorts that looked like I could get into. Without much fanfare, we started peeling out of our khakis and t-shirts for the tourist gear. "I'll need binoculars and at least one camera, plus a cascade bag for weapons. Pistols only; if we need rifles, we're fucked anyway, and the mission is blown." I stopped talking to pull my t-shirt over my head. I got a good whiff of myself as I did, and damn near gagged. I couldn't remember the last time any of us had had a shower. At least playing tourist out on the ocean for most of the day would give us a chance to rinse off, even if it was with salt water.

"It's still about eleven klicks to the target area," Alek said. "That's within range of the icoms. I don't want you taking tactical radios if we can avoid it. Keep comms up the whole time; if we've got to come after you, I want to know immediately."

"Not my first rodeo, Alek," I reminded him. "We'll be up."

He clapped a huge hand on my shoulder. "Not trying to armchair quarterback, here, brother. Just can't afford for this to go sideways."

I returned his shoulder-thump. "We'll get it done, brother." I rolled my trousers and shirt up and lay them on top of my hiking boots, next to my kitbag. I pulled my .45 out, checked the mag, and slipped it and two spares into a small waterproof bag, which was then clipped securely into the inside of the boat, next to Jim's Kimber and Lee's SIG. Lee already had the radio and the binos, and Jim was putting a digital camera in a waterproof case that would still let us use it.

On a thought, I grabbed my fins and a pair of Chuck Taylors out of the amphib gear, and clipped them in the boat, along with a mask and snorkel. They might come in handy. Jim saw me do it, and as soon as he was finished with the camera and had it installed in another waterproof bag, he did the same. As I clipped mine in, I saw that Lee had beaten me to the idea.

With our gear checked and loaded, we heaved the boat down the beach and into the water.

CHAPTER 31

It was almost possible to momentarily forget just how serious a situation we were in, as we started leisurely motoring our way along the Socotra coastline. As the sun climbed in the sky and cleared the broken clouds that had gathered over the island's central peaks, we seemed to be a world away from the fire and bloodshed that had consumed our lives for weeks now.

The water was crystal clear, and we could look down and see schools of fish darting past. A pod of dolphins skimmed alongside the boat for a couple of kilometers, leaping clear out of the water on more than one occasion. We could almost relax and enjoy ourselves a little, especially since that was what we were supposed to be appearing to do anyway.

I've never made a good tourist, and from the looks of things, neither have Jim and Lee. It was all we could do to lounge in the boat rather than lay down on the gunwales and open the throttle, heading for the target. But there were eyes on shore, and out on the water, that would notice if we acted too much like American gunfighters, and not enough like tourists in awe of the natural beauty of Socotra.

It *was* a striking place, now that I took a moment to really look at it. The last time we'd been there, I had been watching the pirates, not the scenery.

The island reared up out of the Arabian Sea in a jumble of jagged towers, their slopes covered with more verdant greenery than any of us expected this close to either the Arabian Peninsula or the Horn of Africa. It wasn't Hawaii, don't get me wrong, but it definitely got more rain than Somalia did.

The water was warm, and we each took a turn or two going over the side to swim a bit, stretching tired muscles while rinsing the grime from our skin and looking like dumbassed tourists frolicking in the ocean only a little way from where pirates were openly operating. We never got too far from the boat, and kept away from anybody who might be a spotter. We didn't want to get taken ourselves. It was unlikely; they used Socotra as a port, and most tourists went unmolested, most of them blissfully unaware of the nature of the murderers they got their pictures taken with.

After about an hour, we were roughly halfway to the port, and we could see three large merchant vessels sitting at anchor. We were getting close to where we could start actually reconnoitering the target vessel. We'd have to do it carefully, looking like slack-jawed gawkers taking pictures of everything, so there'd be quite a bit of junk around the important pictures. Jim had taken the role of our resident shutter-bug, and had already set the pattern of taking enough photographs that if we had been actual tourists, our families would be looking for a shotgun to end it all about a quarter of the way through the slide show.

We drifted closer, and I picked out the *Frontier Rose*. She was sitting slightly farther out to sea than the other two, and while there was some activity around the two closer in, she seemed abandoned at first, almost dead in the water. There was no movement at all, except for the lap of the waves against her hull.

I brought the binoculars up, and peered at her, watching the superstructure and the bow more closely, trying to find lookouts or other signs of armed occupation. "Looks dead," I said.

"I hope not," Lee replied. "That would mean the crew is somewhere else, and I doubt we'll be able to find them before tonight."

Jim grumbled something under his breath. "What's up?" I asked him.

"This whole damned clusterfuck started out trying to find hostages," he said irritably. "And now here we are trying to find a *different* set of hostages."

"Just the way the game plays out, brother," I said, getting back on the binoculars.

"Wait a second," Lee said. "Jeff, take a look over there." He was pointing to our starboard, toward the far side of the pier. "Is that what I think it is?"

I turned the binoculars to where he was pointing. There was a dhow floating just on the other side of the farthest ship, drifting slowly down the coastline toward us. There were definitely armed men aboard it; I could see one with a badly-wrapped turban in the bow, with a Krinkov slung across his chest. There was a machinegun mounted on the forecastle behind him, too, though I couldn't get a very good look at it.

"Yeah, it looks like they've got a patrol boat covering the port," I said. "At least one heavy gun on it, and probably RPGs, too." I lowered the binoculars. "Fucking hell. That's going to make things more complicated."

"Let's just hang out for a while and see what they do," Jim suggested. "At least we can try to figure out a pattern for their movements, so we might be able to avoid them at night. I doubt those Muslim Brotherhood assholes have been supplying the *pirates* with night vision, too."

"Let's hope not," I said, as I raised the binos again. "This would work better if we had a couple of days to watch, but we're getting a little down to the wire, if we're going to make that meeting."

"We can always hope they go home for the night," Jim said.

"Yeah," I said, watching the guy with the Krinkov. The longer I watched, the more I was convinced that he really wasn't paying attention to his surroundings at all. He was leaning against the bow, letting the gun hang, and appeared to be smoking something. "You can hope in one hand, and shit in the other, and see which one fills up first." Jim chuckled.

We floated, making an effort to look like we really were snorkeling like good little tourists, while drifting closer to the seaward side of the *Frontier Rose*. We finally saw some movement on her deck. A single man in local clothing was walking along her side, from the bow toward the superstructure. At first look, he appeared to be unarmed, but Lee took the binoculars, and announced that he had a pistol in his waistband, sticking out of his shirt, in the usual "blow your own balls off" gangster carry.

So, there were armed pirates on the ship. We still didn't have any confirmation that the crew was still aboard, aside from the last video message from the pirates, which was over five days old. They could very well have moved them, or even moved them from shore out to the ship to tape the message, then taken them back to shore. It didn't sound likely, and pirates had shown a tendency to keep their hostages on the ships they hijacked, with a few exceptions, but it was a possibility.

The sun was starting its long slide toward the Somali coast, and we still didn't have any confirmation that the crew was aboard. If we didn't get the crew, we were fucked. I was increasingly convinced we could take the ship relatively easily; the pirates we could see were slacking off, bored, and paying little attention to their surroundings. There hadn't been any attempt to take any of the ships they had, they probably hadn't seen a US Navy ship in months, and they certainly weren't worried about their captives trying anything.

But without the crew, taking the ship would be pointless. None of us knew how to run a container ship, plus the use of the ship was conditional on our rescuing the crew. We *had* to find them.

Just as I was starting to get to the point of thinking of doing something crazy and/or stupid to get in and see if I could get eyes on the crew, the pirates did us a favor.

It was probably about five in the afternoon when a small fishing boat with a single occupant pushed off from the shore and slowly motored out to the nearest inshore cargo ship, a bulk carrier called the *Hyram Horizon*. It disappeared behind the ship, but we could hear some yelled conversation, then the boat came chugging out from the shadow of the *Hyram* and headed for the *Frontier Rose*.

263

This time, the boat pulled up to the ship's flank where we could see. The guy in the boat yelled up to the deck, and after a minute, was answered by one of the pirates. This guy was carrying an AK and a radio, and spoke into the radio for a moment after the guy in the boat yelled up to him. Jim was taking pictures as fast as he could.

A few minutes later, a hatch in the superstructure opened and two men came out, with a third carrying an SKS behind them. When one of them didn't move fast enough, he got a hard shove from the guy with the SKS.

The two men were herded to the bow, where they took a coiled rope and let it down for the guy in the boat to tie on several bundles, which they then pulled up and started carrying toward the stern. The guy with the boat backed away from the side of the ship and headed for the third vessel.

"Tell me you got all that," I said to Jim.

"I got all of it," he replied. "I think that pretty well establishes that the crew is on board."

"I think you're right," I replied, checking the time and the angle of the sun. "And I think that's our cue to head back. Tourists probably wouldn't be out here snorkeling until the sun went down."

"Probably wouldn't be out here stag, either," Lee muttered. He had a point, but we didn't have a lot of choice there, and we hadn't been accosted, so I figured that anybody watching us had bought it.

We took a long, curving turn, and headed back west toward our launch site. I found myself hoping we'd get back in time to get some rest before we headed out again. It was going to be a long night.

***

Our three Zodiacs purred toward the *Frontier Rose* from the seaward side.

It was one in the morning. We had launched two and a half hours earlier, heading north, straight out to sea. The former Marines on the team were at a little bit of an advantage; Recon did this kind of shit a lot. And if you think navigating on open water in a Zodiac at night is easy, well, just try it.

Our kit really hadn't changed much. We had our fins with us, and small air bottles with demand valves in case we went in the drink and needed air before we could strip our kit and get to the surface. Flotation collars went over the vests. Other than that, we were kitted out pretty much the same we had been on land, with rifles, vests, FAST helmets, and NVGs. Larry and Rick each had a compact, lightweight Wilcox cutting torch on their gear, with the copper cutting rods strung through the MOLLE weave on their backs.

As we neared the *Frontier Rose*, the throttles were cut back until the outboards were barely idling, and we didn't so much motor toward the ship as we drifted. Everyone but the coxswains lay low to the gunwales, trying to present as low a profile against the water as possible, rifle muzzles covering the ship's deck.

The ship was mostly dark, with light shining through a handful of portholes, and only the most basic running lights. I suspected they'd shut down the power plant, so any lights were probably running on batteries. So much the better for our approach, but it could make things more complicated when it came time to try to steam out of here.

The first two boats sidled slowly and quietly up to the side of the ship, while the third hung back, the shooters on the gunwales keeping their eyes and their rifles on the deck, watching for pirates who might either sound the alarm or otherwise interrupt our boarding.

I was on the lead boat with Larry, Lee, Jim, and Alek. Lee was driving; he was one of the better coxswains we had. He brought the boat alongside the *Frontier Rose* with a touch that was so light we didn't even really feel it.

Jim and I steadied the collapsible caving ladder we'd stored in the bottom of the boat, raising it to the edge of the ship's hull. The hook at the top had been taped, as had the nubs to rest it against the hull itself, to keep the noise down.

It wasn't a long climb. Jim went first, while Mike took the lead on the second ladder. They each paused just short of the top, drawing their pistols and then easing over, facing in opposite directions. There was a brief pause, then they each clambered the rest of the way up and disappeared over the edge.

A handful of seconds later, a hand came over the edge and flashed a small green LED twice. That was the go signal. The rest of us headed up the ladders.

I was the second man up. The caving ladder felt flimsy as hell, even though I knew it could even take Larry's weight, with gear. It took only seconds to get up and over the rail, dropping carefully to a knee, clear of the ladder. I reached back and unslung my rifle, joining Jim facing back toward the superstructure.

The ship was silent, except for the sounds of our guys scaling the caving ladders. The coxswains were the last up, bringing mooring lines with them to lash the boats to the rail. We figured we'd need all the shooters we could get. Lee and Chad would stay at the boarding point, making sure no pirates came around behind us and cut the boats free while we were clearing the ship. Everybody else was on pirate-hunting duty.

A hand squeezed my shoulder. We were up. I came quietly to my feet, Jim mirroring my movement beside me, and we started to glide sternward, careful not to let our boots slap on the metal deck.

The *Frontier Rose* wasn't very large as container ships go. She could only carry about four container boxes across, and only had them stacked two high above the main deck. A quick glance down showed that there wasn't much room between the containers and the outer hull. It also looked like the superstructure was only about three decks high. That would narrow down the crew's location rather significantly.

It would also make it harder to clear out the pirates without any of the crew getting hurt or killed.

We climbed the short ladder to the rear deck without seeing any sign of either lookouts or hostages. There was a single hatch on the side of the superstructure, without any portholes. I moved immediately to the far side, facing where the door would open, while Jim took the other, the rest of the team stacking behind him.

Jim tested the latching wheel. It moved easily, so he carefully turned it. I waited, my rifle pointed at the seam where the hatch would open, praying it didn't squeak.

It didn't. Even after three months of doubtless complete neglect, the hatch swung open quietly on well-greased hinges. I stepped over the lip and into the superstructure.

The interior lighting was on, so apparently they were keeping at least one generator running, they just had most of the external lights shut off for some reason. I moved quickly but quietly into the narrow corridor, with Jim flowing in behind me.

There was only a blank bulkhead forward, with three hatches astern. One was open, leading to the ladderwell up to the bridge. I held on that one, while the rest of the stack pushed past me. Alek and Larry were barely able to squeeze through, essentially sliding along the forward bulkhead. I really hoped there weren't any bad guys on the other side.

Jim and Alek went in the center hatch, and then Charlie and Larry kept going, moving to the far one. I glanced at them, and got a signal saying that it was the ladderwell down, probably to the crew quarters and machinery spaces.

Alek came out of the center hatch first, and came over to stack on me. I immediately started up the ladder, my rifle raised and pointed at the open hatch at the top.

The hatch opened onto the bridge. It was a narrow space, made smaller by the steel island of controls set in the center. Plate glass ports opened on all four sides, providing a decent view in all directions. Nothing really could be seen outside at the moment, as the bridge lights were on.

Those lights starkly illuminated the two pirates who were leaning against the control panel bullshitting. They turned at the sudden movement as I came in the door, checked the corner, and then stepped out of the way as Alek came in after me.

For a second, they obviously didn't know what the hell they were looking at. They weren't expecting any of their friends, and the fact that they'd just been boarded by large, heavily armed men in full combat gear took a few moments to register. By then it was too late, anyway. Both of their weapons were on the deck, leaning against the forward bulkhead. By the time they could get to them, they'd be dead, and they knew it. Their eyes widened as it dawned on them what was happening. The one closest to me pissed himself.

They didn't offer any resistance as I moved up and took them to the deck. The fact that Alek had moved up on the other side of the control panel, his OBR covering them the entire time, might have had something to do with it. They were too used to waving a gun at unarmed merchant crews. Facing armed men ready and willing to kill them was a little too much. The guy who pissed himself even started whimpering as I slammed his face into the deck and put my knee in his back while I flex-cuffed his buddy.

The radio crackled with Mike's voice. "This is Speedy. Forecastle's clear."

"Roger," Alek replied. "Bridge is clear, two tangos down. Moving to lower decks."

Jim and Bo simply turned around, Bo taking point down the ladderwell, and Alek followed. I took the few seconds to gag the two pirates, one of which was now actually crying, using curtains torn down from the aft ports, then went down after Alek.

We flowed through the crew cabins relatively quickly. None of them were very large, so we could only get maybe two men in at a time. The pattern quickly established itself--two men stack on one hatch, go through, the next guys go to the next hatch. The first two had been taken, and Alek and I were on the way to the third, when another hatch forward opened, and a skinny Somali with a shitty turban and an SKS stepped out. I was pretty sure that it was the same guy I'd seen on the deck during our recce. The turban looked the same.

Alek pounded forward and shoulder-checked him into the edge of the hatch, and he yelled out in pain and surprise, the SKS clattering to the deck. Something cracked audibly, and his shout quickly turned into a long wail of pain. Alek wasn't in a sympathetic mood, and he simply slammed the guy face down on the deck and zip-tied him.

Bo was coming out of the second cabin as I finished. There was a pale, sickly-looking man with dark eyes and sunken cheeks behind him. "The first mate tells me there were only three aboard," Bo said. "We should finish clearing, but it looks like we're in business."

"There haven't been more than three of them for the last month," the man said. His voice was dry and quiet. "With only eight of us to guard, they must not have felt like sparing more than that."

"We'll make sure, anyway," I said, moving past Alek and heading for the next hatch, with Larry in tow. The hatch wasn't dogged, and swung easily. I threw it open, and Larry went through.

***

It didn't take much more than another five minutes to determine that the first mate was correct. There had only been three pirates aboard, all of whom were now flex-cuffed and being held below decks in the bow. We still had to figure out what to do with them, but getting the ship away from Socotra came first.

Alek, Mike, Eddie, and I were in the bow, discussing our next move, as the engines rumbled to life and the anchor came up. Chad, Jon, and Lee were on watch, in case the pirates decided to object to our absconding with the ship they'd hijacked.

The Zodiacs were now lashed to the bow and stern, wherever we could fit them after hoisting them up out of the water. The more we looked at it, the more we saw that we wouldn't be able to launch our Bell 407 off the *Frontier Rose*, at least not without some considerable modifications. We didn't trust the containers to hold up the weight of a loaded helicopter.

That was going to put a serious crimp in our options on the raid. Not only would we not have an aerial medevac, we wouldn't have any fire support either. What we took ashore on the boats would be it.

We were in the middle of hashing out some of our possible contingency plans to counter this problem, when the first mate, who it turned out was named Sean Summers, came up to us with a frown on his face. We all stopped talking and turned to look at him. He hesitated for a moment, looking from one to another of us uncertainly, then apparently figured out we were going to wait for him to say something.

"I just had probably the strangest conversation with my employer I've ever had," he said. "Actually, I suppose I should technically say my ex-employer, as apparently the company has gone under while we've been in captivity. But apparently you already knew this." There were a couple of nods. "So the *Frontier Rose* belongs to your company now?" Another nod. He shook his head, rubbing a hand over his scruffy beard. "That's a new one on me," he confessed. "If you are indeed the new owners, I have some questions."

Again, none of us said anything, but Alek made a go ahead gesture, so he took a deep breath and dove in.

"I don't know what a security company needs with a container ship, but I suspect I probably shouldn't ask. So, what is the plan for us? Do we stay on, or are you going to ship us home and bring in a replacement crew?"

"Well, Sean," Alek replied. "That's kind of up to you. You and your boys have been held on this ship against your will for three months. What would you like to do?"

Alek was playing an angle that could threaten to derail the entire operation; if the crew of the *Frontier Rose* backed out and demanded to go

268

home, Tom probably couldn't get a replacement crew out here fast enough for us to be in position by the time the meeting started. We'd miss our window.

However, I immediately saw why he was taking the approach he was. These guys had been held by pirates and forced to watch their captain be murdered for the sake of a ransom that wasn't going to come. They probably weren't on the most solid psychological ground at the moment in the first place, and if we tried to play hard-ass, we could very well find ourselves in the position of acting exactly like the scum we'd just taken the ship back from. These guys weren't terrorists or pirates. They were just ordinary guys trying to make a living. We couldn't force them to work for us at the point of a gun and be able to look ourselves in the mirror ever again.

The question gave Mr. Summers pause. I don't think he'd been expecting it. He'd confessed earlier that he had thought we were Navy SEALs when we'd broken into the superstructure and taken down the pirates. He was a bit confused, and probably a little disappointed, to find out the truth, regardless of the fact that every single one of us had at least eight years in some sort of SOF-related field before we'd gone private sector. A lot of people still weren't comfortable with the idea of PMCs, even when they'd just had their asses pulled out of the fire by one.

"I think we'd all like to go home," he replied finally. "But at the same time, most of us have been doing runs on the *Rose* for six years. We're not ready to just abandon her out here, even if we don't have a controlling interest in her anymore. And, we still have the cargo to either deliver or return to the client. I'd rather deliver it. Call it professional pride. So I guess the question is, what do you have in mind for her?"

"We do intend to see that you guys get home," Alek said carefully. "We do, however, need you to do us a favor, and make a little detour along the way."

"I was afraid of that," Summers said. "What kind of detour are we talking about?"

"Not one that is going to put you in any more risk than you already are," Alek assured him. "Just up by the Yemeni coast for a day, and then back out to sea."

"I'm not sure that qualifies as 'no more risk than we are in right now,'" Summers replied. "That's still well within the pirates' operating radius, and it's the opposite direction to our destination."

"Where is your destination, anyway?" Eddie asked.

"Mumbai," Summers answered. "Which is kind of a long way from Yemen."

"As for the detour," Alek explained, "you're already three months behind schedule. A couple more days won't change much. And you aren't going to have to worry about the pirates. You have my word on that."

269

"Are you guaranteeing our security, then?" Summers asked. "Because it sounds like you have some other errand in Yemen that I probably shouldn't ask about."

"You're right, you shouldn't," Alek agreed. "But yes, we are guaranteeing your security. There will be no fewer than five of my shooters on board at any one time, from now until you hit port, and we decide what to do after that. Any pirate so much as looks cross-eyed at this ship, and they'll regret it."

Summers pursed his lips, looking down at the deck, as he thought it over. Finally, he looked up and said, "I'll have to talk it over with the rest of the boys. That all right?"

Alek nodded sagely. "That's fine. Make sure you're all on the same page."

Summers nodded vaguely, his mind obviously elsewhere, and just kind of walked away, heading aft toward the crew spaces.

"Bit of a gamble, isn't it?" Eddie asked.

"Only way to go," Alek replied. "Because I'm no fucking pirate, and neither are you."

"Which way do you think he'll jump?" Mike asked quietly, watching Summers as he walked toward the superstructure.

"I don't know," Alek admitted. "He could sink this whole op, but I had to give him the option. The alternative was to hold him and his crew at gunpoint, and I'm not comfortable with that."

"I don't think any of us are," I said. "Like Eddie said, though, it's a hell of a gamble. We've come this far, just to put the entire operation in the hands of somebody who has no idea what the fuck is going on."

"He has some idea," Mike said. "If he's been held by pirates for three months, he's got to have some idea."

"Some people are just oblivious to anything that happens outside their little bubble, Mike," I replied. "Even after getting slapped in the nuts with reality."

"None of which matters now," Alek said. "The decision's been made, and we're just going to have to hope that Summers makes the call our way. Otherwise, we've just got another maritime security op to run. In the meantime, let's assume that the crew is going to turn our way, and get back to planning this abortion."

***

It didn't actually take that long for Summers to get back to us with the crew's answer. They weren't thrilled by the idea of going deeper into pirate waters, but as long as we had shooters aboard the entire time, they would follow the course we set. I think they also figured that since our company was going to be their new employer, at least if they wanted to stay aboard the *Frontier Rose*, they shouldn't try to refuse.

So, we turned toward Puntland, where we'd pick up Caleb and his boys. Then on to Yemen.

CHAPTER 32

We were floating about a mile off the coast of Puntland. Dawn was spreading across the sky, but the *Frontier Rose* was all but alone on the waters of the Gulf. The barren hulk of the Puntland shore was little more than a dark shadow limned with the faint white foam of the surf. Somewhere on that shore, Caleb's short team was waiting with their gear for our boats to come in and get them. The timing and the light were far from ideal, but we didn't have a lot of choice, if we were going to get to Yemen in time.

But before we launched, we had one more task to finish. We still had the three pirates we'd captured during the boarding down in the bow. We couldn't take them with us, we sure as hell weren't going to turn them over to their buddies on Socotra, and none of us, except maybe Charlie or Bob, was exactly comfortable with just shooting them in the back of the head. Everyone I'd killed, and I'd killed a few people over the years, had been a clear threat. Not kneeling, bound and gagged, waiting for the bullet. I'm a warrior, not a butcher.

So, Alek had come up with a solution that might seem a little dubious in some circles, those inhabited by people who weren't out in the middle of nowhere, operating on not a shoestring but a thread, surrounded by people we could only assume were enemies.

They were lined up against the rail with their flex-cuffs cut off, but still covered by blank-faced men with rifles. One wrong move, and they would be dead, and they knew it. They looked at Alek, who just pointed over the side. "Jump," he said.

I'm sure they understood, but they acted like they didn't. Their fear was palpable. It should have been. There were plenty of sharks in the Gulf of Aden.

"I said jump, motherfuckers," Alek said. "Hope you assholes know how to swim, 'cause it's a bit of a distance to shore."

They still huddled against the rail. They were going to make us do this the hard way. "Fuck this," Charlie snarled suddenly, and stepped forward. He wrenched one of the pirates around by his shoulder. He then grabbed the pirate by the back of his neck and the waistband of his shorts, and heaved him overboard. "Get the fuck off!"

The pirate yelled as he went over, his arms and legs flailing. He hit the water with a splash and came up spluttering. His buddies were yelling too, and tried to back away from Charlie, but he wasn't having any of it, and they quickly followed their fellow pirate into the ocean. They tried paddling toward the ship, calling out for help, but were met with rifle muzzles, and soon started moving away. They kept looking back toward the ship as though they thought we'd relent and let them back on board. No such luck. You make your living by theft, extortion, and murder, you get no sympathy from me. They could swim, or drown. It was on them now. As the *Frontier Rose* powered away, it began to dawn on them.

Once we were well away from the floating pirates, Mike, Eddie, Chris, and Marcus launched two of the Zodiacs off the stern, and headed in toward the shore. The rest of us got back to preparing for the mission ahead.

***

Only a few hours later, Tom was back on the satellite link with more intel.

"We've got a location for the meeting, and something of a timetable," he said. "You're gonna love this. The location is the old parliamentary building for the Federation of South Arabia. It's close to shore, but it's big." He clicked an overhead photo up on the screen. He wasn't kidding. The building was only a little over a kilometer from the shore, but it was a massive, two story rectangle with a central courtyard. It would be hell to try to clear that with fifteen shooters, especially considering the fact we were expecting heavy resistance. The bad guys were sure to bring a lot of security.

"The good news is, according to the message traffic we've been intercepting, they're not expecting much trouble. Somebody going by Al Dhi'b has talked some shit about what you guys were able to pull off in Djibouti and near Baardheere, but Al-Khalidi has thrown Kismayo back in his face, and is telling him there's nothing to worry about. It does sound like most of them figure they're on friendly ground, that there's no way anybody is coming for them. They're not even worried about Reapers anymore, since Lemonier is out of the picture.

"Short version, while there will be extensive ground security, you shouldn't expect much in the way of hardened defenses, and I'd be very surprised if they have IEDs out. They think they're safe. If there's anybody they're really worried about at the moment, it's each other.

"We don't have a lot of specifics, but it sounds like there are leaders of several different groups attending, at least two of which have been at each other's throats within the last year. I can't give you names, or even kunyahs; the concerns have all be voiced by security people talking in codes, but there is a chance that there might be some bad blood floating around that you might be able to take advantage of.

"As for the timing, you've got exactly forty hours from right now before the meeting starts. It sounds like there are already security personnel for at least one of the attendees on site, but you might be able to infiltrate overnight and lay low until the meeting."

I looked at the imagery and frowned. "I'm not seeing much in the way of good hide sites in that," I said. "Definitely not for any length of time with hostile security forces actively patrolling."

"Can you feed us any sort of detailed intel on strength and armament of the security?" Alek asked.

"Sorry," Tom admitted. "Most of what we're getting is SIGINT that my hacker gnomes are picking up, and then it's only bits and pieces. I'm afraid the picture's still a little incomplete. I'm dumping everything we've got to you, so you can see the raw information, such as it is."

"All right," Alek said. "We'll look it over. Thanks, Tom."

"I'll be sending regular updates as I get them," the Colonel said, and signed off.

***

In the end, it was going to come down to adaptability. We couldn't get a lot of on-the-ground information until we were actually on the ground. We'd have to roll with the punches once we were ashore.

There wasn't a lot of room on the ship for rehearsals. It was a small ship to begin with, and its full hold left pretty much the crew quarters, narrow passages along the rails, and the bow. With the bow now once again occupied with the Zodiacs, since Caleb and his boys came aboard, that left the main deck and the crew quarters. We did a lot of tabletop talk-throughs.

We had a lot to take into consideration. There was a lot of open ground to cover on the movement from the beach. There was also a major, four-lane highway, followed by a wall, followed by more open ground before we even got to the target building. The only way to approach that was under cover of darkness; and if the bad guys had thermals, that might not even be enough. In the old days, we could count on the muj not even having so much as 1st Gen night vision, but especially with the increased backing they'd been getting from the Chinese, those days were over. We had to consider all kinds of nasty possibilities now.

We did, however, have two more of the small Aeroseekers that Logan had brought. They wouldn't necessarily level the playing field, but they'd give us a bit of a better picture, once we were on the ground.

So, we planned, wargamed, planned some more, prepped our kit, and waited for darkness.

***

There was a Yemeni patrol boat watching us.

It had been lurking around the entrance to the wide bay that led into the port of Aden, and for some reason decided to come out and take a look at the *Frontier Rose*. We tried to keep a low profile, and generally stay out of sight. I was a little concerned about the Zodiacs, but we'd thrown tarps over all three of them, so they weren't obvious at least. Caleb and his boys were visible, with weapons, but armed maritime security contractors weren't a strange sight in the Gulf of Aden anymore. Now, if they'd seen twenty of us on a ship the size of the *Rose*, that might have raised some eyebrows. As it was, they just seemed to be doing some sort of show of force, to demonstrate who owned these waters.

It was also getting uncomfortably close to launch time, and these clowns were still off the ship's starboard bow, posturing.

We couldn't do anything to chase them off, either. Doing so would mean instant compromise. We'd have to scrub the entire mission and run. Al-Khalidi would have his meeting, and kill more people. Colton, Tim, Rodrigo, and Danny would have died for nothing.

So, we watched and waited, staying below decks as they finally pulled alongside and their commander gestured and yelled that he was coming aboard. Alek went up to meet him, leaving his rifle below, and carrying what we hoped would be enough cash to cover the bribe the Yemeni captain was going to be demanding.

As we waited, listening to the clang of the gangplank running between the patrol boat and the rail, the sat phone started to buzz. Larry scooped it up and tossed it to me. I unfolded the antenna and brought it to my ear. "Talk to me, Tom."

"We just picked up a fragment of a transmission confirming that Al-Khalidi is on site," the Colonel told me. "They're still waiting on one from Dubai; it sounds like the Emir might have some idea of who made his nephew disappear. It wouldn't surprise me if Al-Khalidi is using Ali's unknown fate to manipulate the Emir. It's another big cash cow for his operations if he gets the Emir of Dubai on board."

"As if he didn't already have enough backers," I growled. "At any rate, we're stuck at the moment. We've got a Yemeni patrol boat looking for its protection money."

"Dammit," Tom said. "You should have enough cash to get rid of them without too much trouble, but if they see the hardware you gents have, the op could be blown."

"Teach your granddad to suck eggs, Tom," I said. "We're staying out of sight, and the boats are covered. We know the risks."

There was a pause, and I could almost see the flash in those icy blue eyes of his. The Colonel didn't care to be snapped at, even by the guy on the ground, but he was also wise enough to know when to back off. He'd railed against TOC commandos when he'd been in uniform; he couldn't very well start being one now. "All right," he said finally. There was a stiff, clipped tone to his voice. He was pissed, but not letting it out. "I'll let you guys handle it. You're the guys on the ground. Just don't get too eager. I don't want to be informing any more families that more of you guys aren't coming back."

I almost snarled at him that it was his intel that had us sitting here, but held my tongue. If he hadn't suggested it, one of us probably would have. There was no going back now. There was too much blood.

"Sorry, Tom," I said finally. "We're getting a little strung out here, is all."

"I understand," he replied. "I would be, too. Didn't mean to be REMF here. Just wish I was out there with you guys."

If he had been anybody else, I would have said, "No you don't," but I knew Tom. I knew he was sincere about wanting to be out in the field. These kinds of operations may not have been his forte, but he still would rather have been in the field, leading troops and busting heads, than stuck back at The Ranch, shuffling data.

Overhead, we could hear the clatter of boots as the Yemeni captain came aboard. We couldn't hear voices, but we could imagine what was going on well enough.

Officially, the Yemeni government, what there was of it, opposed the piracy on the Gulf of Aden, and operated aggressively against the Somali pirates. Unofficially, the government was so weak and fragmented that there were factions within both the government and the military that were actively aiding the pirates. That lent some uncertainty to what exactly the Yemeni patrol really wanted.

Whatever was happening up there, we had to stay quiet and out of sight. We had bigger fish to fry on shore.

"I'll keep you guys informed," Tom said. "Out here."

Larry, Jim, and I were trying to keep ourselves occupied by looking over the imagery again, along with the crappy little mockup we'd built out of scraps we'd found in the crew spaces, trying to skull out how to do the takedown. About all we were coming up with was get in fast, hit hard, kill as many as we could on the ground, and get the hell out. The lack of air support was going to be a major stumbling block. We couldn't swoop in like Delta or DevGru, land on the roof, clear the building, and then get back on the Little Birds and fly away. We had a klick to hump in, and another klick to hump out. And the hump out was probably going to be under fire.

Finally, there was another clatter of footsteps overhead, followed by the scrape of the gangplank being pulled away. A few minutes later, Alek came back down to join us in the narrow passageway we'd commandeered as our quasi team room.

"That was surprisingly straightforward," he said. "All they wanted was their bribe, especially with Caleb sitting on the forecastle watching them through his sights. Anything new from the Colonel?"

"Yeah," I told him. "Our primary target is on-site, but they're still waiting on somebody from Dubai. Apparently, Al-Khalidi's using our hit in Balbala to get more backing from the Emir. What it looks like, anyway."

Alek checked his watch. It was only an hour to sunset. "Is he sticking overnight?"

"Sounds like it, but we'll have to see."

Alek looked around the shooters scattered along the length of the passageway. "Well, it's decision time, gents. We get one shot at this guy. If we commit, and miss him, there's no next time."

There was silence for a moment, then a round of nods. "Let's do it," Eddie said. No one disagreed. We got our kit on and got ready to launch.

CHAPTER 33

Boats One and Two floated seven hundred meters offshore, waiting. The motors were turned off, and the only sound was the slap of the mild waves against the black rubber gunwales. We could just see Boat Three two hundred meters closer in, dropping off the scouts.

Jim was huddled under a glorified poncho back across from the coxswain seat, stooped over the small PDA that he was using to control the Aeroseeker that was even now quietly orbiting the target site. We hadn't been able to launch the UAVs from the ship; they didn't have the range, at least they didn't if we wanted to keep our RF signature low. But here, at less than a mile, it was easy.

I felt a tap on my leg, and looked back to see Jim holding out the PDA, wrapped in the blackout cloth. We could have turned the PDA's brightness down to where it could be read with NVGs, but the PVS-14 sucks for fine detail, so we just covered up as we used it. I took the PDA, threw the damp blackout sheet over my head, and brought up the display.

Jim had the mini-UAV set to orbit automatically, keeping about three hundred meters away from the target compound. The little drone had some serious cameras on it, so I was able to zoom in on thermal and take a good look.

There was a *lot* of security around the building itself. I counted at least twenty very expensive cars and doubtless up-armored SUVs parked in the open field in front of the building. There were ten guards on the rooftop, and what looked like a reinforced squad out on the grounds. I counted four at the main gate, along with what looked like a sandbagged machinegun, maybe a Kord. It was going to be a hell of a nut to crack, just getting in, never mind finding Al-Khalidi in there. Especially when I considered that it was one in the morning, and there was probably at least one more shift worth of soldiers inside, sleeping.

But they had made one mistake. For all the strength of their security, they didn't have anybody on the outer wall. Their shooters weren't moving much past the parking lot. The outer wall was clear.

I pulled my head out of the blackout cloth, wrapped up the PDA, and passed it to Larry. At almost the same time, Chad's voice hissed in my earpiece, "Scouts inserted."

"Ten minutes," Alek whispered. "Then we head in."

Ten minutes seemed to drag like ten hours. Ashore, we could see the lights of Little Aden, including the red warning lights on top of the three tall smokestacks over the Al Hiswah power plant. There didn't seem to be any traffic on the shoreline road at this time of night, fortunately. We couldn't see Marcus and Chris, who were probably halfway to shore by now.

Finally, Lee cranked the outboard to life, and we started to move, sliding slowly and quietly across the water toward the Yemeni beach. All three boats were aiming for a very narrow spot; there were several little fishing shacks down on the shoreline itself that we wanted to avoid. Back from the beach, and east, there were several bungalows. Though all were dark at the time, we didn't want to chance getting too close and waking somebody up. They'd wake up soon enough.

The boats puttered up to the sandy strip of shore. Larry and I leaned out over the bow, trying to see the bottom, and both put our fists up at almost the same time. Lee cut the throttle, and we bailed out into knee-deep water, trying not to splash too much. The two of us held the boat steady while Jim and Alek got out, then Lee reversed the engine and backed off the beach. To our right and left, the other two boats were doing the same thing. They'd hold position about four hundred meters offshore until we needed to extract.

We waded to shore, spread out in a loose wedge. The muted surf drowned out any splashing we made. The sand of the beach was soft, and our steps made no sound as we moved up toward the dusty scrub. Two at a time, we split off into our raid elements and moved to our positions.

Larry and I had paired up for this one. We moved carefully up to the edge of the highway that ran along the shore, and took a knee in the bushes, side by side, our boots touching so we could communicate, even facing opposite directions, without having to move very far or whisper very loud. We waited and watched in silence, looking and listening for a car. There was nothing, and we would be able to see headlights a good long distance away. Long enough to count, anyway.

I hefted my rifle in my shooting hand, and thumped Larry on the shoulder with my off hand as I came to my feet, then sprinted across the highway. It felt like the longest sprint I'd ever run, even though it was barely fifty meters from the south side of the road to the low wall that surrounded the target site. It wasn't so much the actual distance, of course, but the exposure. Even in the dark, I felt like a bug on a plate.

Larry came huffing after me, and thudded into the side of the wall. Unfortunately for him, he didn't have a lot of time to take a breather. He braced his back against the wall, and cupped his hands. I put my boot in his hands, and hoisted myself to the top of the wall. A quick look showed nothing nearby. I hoped like hell I wasn't about to silhouette myself on the wall just as a hajji guard happened to be looking this way with NVGs.

I slung my rifle to my back and planted my gloved hands on top of the wall, pushing up as I swung one leg up. With some effort, and Larry's help, I was soon lying prone on top of the wall. I reached one hand down to Larry, who grabbed it. I dropped down the inside as Larry climbed the outside, acting as something of a counterweight. With some scuffling and one clink of a rifle against concrete that made my heart just about stop, we both got over. Crouched in the shadowed corner of the wall, I scanned the huge courtyard, watching for any sign we'd been spotted or heard. Nothing.

Keeping next to the wall, we got down on our bellies and started to crawl, slowly and carefully. It was a lot like a stalk at sniper school, except there were real lives at stake.

The ground was all hard dirt and rocks, and my hands and knees were aching in short order. But finally we were settled in the prone a bare few meters from the guard post at the main gate.

There was indeed a Kord heavy machine gun mounted behind the sandbags. Only one hajji was manning it, while the other three lounged and shot the shit. They were wearing older but still serviceable body armor, and some kind of tactical vests. Their weapons were new, HK G36Cs. No beat up old AKs for these boys.

"Hillbilly in position," I whispered into my headset. Two clicks answered.

All around the compound, our two-man teams were getting into position to wreak the most havoc. When all the pieces were in place, the show would begin.

Finally, Alek's voice came over the radio. "Start the music," was all he said. It was all he needed to say.

There was a flash and a bone-shaking *thud* from the west wall. Dust and debris rose high into the air, and started to rain down on the courtyard. Marcus and Chris had brought one hell of a charge with them. But that was just the diversion.

Even as yelling in several Arabic dialects started to sound across the courtyard in the aftermath of the deafening explosion, Larry and I got up, lined up the guards at the gate, and shot each of them twice. They never even knew what was happening. The guy on the Kord didn't even get to turn around before his head exploded all over the heavy gun's receiver.

The rapid thumping of two of our M60E4s started up soon after the blast, raking the roof of the target building. Larry rolled the dead guard off the Kord, before quickly stripping it and taking the firing pin. I watched the number two building, where Tom's source had said the majority of the guard garrison was going to be housed.

Sure enough, moments after the attack had started, hastily kitted out soldiers and fighters started to rush out the front door. It was a turkey shoot.

They were lined up neatly in the narrow doorway. There was enough light from the building that I didn't need my NVGs. I laid the scope on the first one and opened fire.

The M1A thumped heavily, the suppressor muffling but not completely eliminating the harsh crack of each shot. The Troy stock helped even out the recoil, and the barrel stayed where I put it, as I dumped the entire mag in less than ten seconds. As I stripped out the empty and rocked in a new mag, the enemy fighters who'd survived the initial fusillade were scrambling back into the building, trying to find another way out.

"We've got to move," Larry said next to me. He was right. If we stayed put, they'd maneuver on us and we'd be done. I scrambled to my feet, and we started running toward the target building. Behind us, I heard several muted *thump*s, and then the entrance to building two dissolved in multiple explosions. Mike was having fun with the MGL rotary grenade launcher he'd gotten his hands on, thanks to Logan.

Larry and I met Alek, Jim, Bob, and Bo at the entrance to the target building. The doors had been glass; they had shattered, and the shards were scattered across the steps. Jim pulled the igniter on the fucking *huge* concussion charge he'd brought ashore, and chucked it up the steps and into the foyer.

Being closer, that blast felt and sounded ten times bigger than the charge Chris and Marcus had set. Dust and smoke billowed out of the smashed doors and debris whickered through the air. As soon as the patter of second-hand shrapnel stopped, we charged in.

The dust and smoke was still pretty thick, but the thermal attachments on our 14s cut through it well enough. There were about half a dozen guys on the floor in the foyer, and I was pretty sure they were dead, from overpressure if nothing else. We shot each one as we went through, just to be sure.

We were across the foyer before anybody on the balcony above was able to unfuck themselves enough to do anything. Alek went straight to the first set of doors and kicked them open. Larry and I flowed through, while Jim and Alek covered our six.

It was the old parliamentary chamber. The lights in the foyer had shattered from the blast, but they were still on in here. It was fairly small for such things, amounting to little more than a large meeting room, with raised seating. I guess there hadn't been very many parliamentarians in the Federation of South Arabia.

Whatever the British, who had built it for the FSA, had had in mind, I was pretty sure they hadn't been thinking of what we saw. Jihadi flags were on all four walls, along with inscriptions in Arabic, and pictures of Said Al-Khalidi, five times life size. He looked to me like a pussy; he was fat, and had a weak chin.

Other than the seats, the podium, and the posters and flags on the walls, the chamber was empty. There was also only one way in or out.

"On the door!" Alek snapped. He and Jim immediately turned and faced out the opening. A moment later shots snapped in through the open door, smacking plaster off the far wall. Larry and I scrambled to get out of the line of fire, and wound up on opposite sides of the door.

Just at that moment, Mike's voice came over the radio. "Coconut, Speedy. We are receiving heavy fire from the vicinity of building two. It looks like you have more bad guys headed your way from there."

"Roger," Alek replied, as he ducked back from the doorway, as more rounds splintered the wood doorjamb. "They're already here."

I peeked out into the doorway over Jim's shoulder. There was the better part of a dozen men in the foyer, dressed in black. They wore tactical vests and body armor, and were packing more G36s. The well-to-do jihadis seemed to be going increasingly to HK for their armament.

I ducked back as a round snapped by my face so close I could feel the shockwave. I leaned in to Jim's ear. "High-low," I said. "I'll go high." He nodded, and I kneed him in the ass, then popped out behind my rifle, as he dropped to a knee and leaned out, leveling his Mk 17.

I couldn't have leaned into a more perfect position if I'd tried. A bearded, black-clad man's face blossomed in my sights just as my rifle steadied, and I shot him. Red splashed out the back of his skull, as I tracked toward the next man, a little weasely-looking fucker who was crouched behind the granite monument or whatever it was in the center, and put two rounds into him as he tried to scramble back into cover. Below, Jim was putting out rapid double-taps at anything that moved.

I ducked back behind the crumbling cover of the wall, and fished in my vest for a grenade. We couldn't afford to get pinned down here. Letting my rifle hang on its sling, I pulled the pin, yelled, "Frag out!" and tossed it out into the foyer. A moment later, Larry did the same thing from behind Alek, as Alek and Jim were still shooting. They ducked back just as the one-two blasts rocked the building, blowing more dust and smoke around the foyer.

Alek led the charge out, flowing through the door behind his rifle. We couldn't see much at first, but we were at an advantage over the black-clad fighters who'd been out there when those grenades went off. There were a half-dozen near the door who had avoided most of the shrapnel and some of the overpressure, but we came out of the smoke and killed them, the sound of our four rifles sounding like the air was being ripped apart. Only one got a shot off, and that missed, snapping by a few feet from my head. I shot him just above his plate, the rounds ripping through his lower throat. He dropped to the concrete, choking on his own blood. A single brain shot as he thrashed on the ground stilled him.

The shooting had paused momentarily, so we took the few moments to reload. "We've still got to clear this building," Alek said. "I'm starting to think that our target might not be here, but we've got to make sure. Clear left." We mostly responded with nods, and I led out, heading for the western hallway.

The hallway was lined with offices and small conference rooms. We went methodically from one to another, kicking in the door and clearing each room. We didn't find anything; they were empty all the way down the hallway. It was starting to look like there wasn't anybody in the target building at all, aside from the guards we'd already killed. The sound of gunfire outside had intensified, and we stayed away from the windows after a stray round shattered one in the second room we cleared.

We came out of the last room on the end just as more bad guys came in the front door. We met them with a withering barrage of fire that dropped the first three in a welter of blood and steel. The rest moved to the walls, dropping to knees or the prone. We didn't give them any breathing room, but glided forward, firing on the move. Larry was in the rear, and chucked a grenade ahead after cooking it off. We stopped and dropped to a knee, continuing to lay down fire, as they tried to scramble clear of the deadly little ball. Most of them didn't make it. Smoke, dust, and shrapnel stormed down the hallway. One of the jihadis came stumbling out of the smoke, bleeding from his nose, ears, and a dozen shrapnel wounds. Jim finished him with a single shot to the forehead.

I checked my ammo situation as I reloaded. We were burning through magazines at a ridiculous rate. I still had four, but I'd come ashore with eight. Half my ammo gone, and we still hadn't gotten eyes on the target.

Just then, the radio crackled. "Coconut, Speedy. The target is building two. I say again, the target is building two. There's no activity in the target building; it's all coming from building two. Will attempt to provide covering fire for you to move on it. Element two has the rear isolated."

That wasn't all. Before Alek could acknowledge, Lee came on the radio. "Coconut, this is Mr. Big. Be advised, Yemeni security forces have been alerted to the fighting, and are inbound. You haven't got much time left."

"Roger all," Alek snapped. "All right, we're going to move to the east side of the building, find an exit, and move to building two. We've got to be fast and aggressive, but I don't need to tell you guys that, do I?"

"Fuckin' A you don't," Jim growled. "I'm up, let's move."

It was a careful balance between speed and security. We moved as fast as we could down the hallway, carefully clearing each door as we passed it, our muzzles never coming down from the low ready. We reached a door at the end of the hallway and kicked it open, moving in to clear the room beyond without even slowing down. From there, Jim, Larry, and I moved to the windows, while Alek covered the door.

Quick strikes of rifle muzzles shattered the glass, and we swept the ground beyond for hostiles. In the process, we got a good look at the fight that had shaped up outside.

We had split up into elements of two to better cover multiple lanes, and shut off the target building. We had four guys to the west, covering down the north and west sides of the target building. They didn't have much to the west to occupy them, but they were taking desultory shots at anybody on the north side of building two who tried to poke their head out. Four of us were in the target building. And four more, with Mike leading them, were south, covering the main gate and the south and east sides of building two.

Mike and his boys had the heaviest part of the fight at the moment. There was fire coming from both floors and the main entrance, as blasted to hell as it was, of building two, and more fighters were trying to get out the back and sides to try to get at them. Some were just doing the time-honored hajji form of combat shooting, sticking their rifles out the windows and spraying south without aiming. An M60E4 and Mike's MGL were making an unholy mess of the front of the building, along with anybody who tried to get out, but they only had so much ammo, and it looked like there were a lot of bad guys in there. Several fires were already burning on both floors, I had no doubt due to Mike's grenades. The fires and muzzle flashes lent a flickering, hellish illumination to the scene.

Four men wearing camouflage jackets and cheap chest rigs bailed out of the lower windows. They were armed with a couple AK variants, an SKS, and a G3, and they crouched low as they tried to maneuver toward Mike's team. Larry, Jim, and I didn't even have to say a word. We swung our rifles out the windows and opened fire. The jihadi shooters dropped like sacks of meat. They never even knew what had happened. Our suppressors apparently masked our own muzzle flashes enough that nobody in building two knew, either. We didn't take any fire.

Alek started shooting from the doorway, a series of rapid, muted *cracks* announcing his shots. "Got shooters in the hallway!" he yelled. Where the fuck were they all coming from?

"Speedy, this is Hillbilly," I called, as Jim turned and sprinted to the opposite side of the door from Alek, leaning out to finish off the last three SIG 550-toting terrorists. "Four friendlies coming out of building one, east side. Shift fire."

"Roger, go ahead," Mike replied.

I turned back to the door and yelled, "Alek, Jim, we're going, move!" Then Larry and I hoisted ourselves into the windows and jumped out.

I landed badly, falling on my side but managing to keep my suppressor out of the dirt. I was able to roll out of the way before getting crushed by Alek's huge self unassing from the window. As I got up on a knee under the trees that lined the side of the building, half a dozen more bad guys came out a side door, where they were masked from the western element. The lull in firing had opened up an opportunity.

Larry had already seen them, and his FAL started barking almost as soon as they cleared the doorway. The lead shooter flopped to the ground, and the rest scrambled for nonexistent cover as Jim, Alek and I joined in. They were shooting back, but although they were showing better firearms training than I'd seen hajjis use before, they still sucked in the dark. Rounds were snapping high overhead and smacking into concrete and tree limbs, shredded vegetation falling down around us as we moved forward in a sort of half-crouch, firing as we moved.

The flickering light, along with the smoke and dust in the air, was making it hard to see, even with NVGs, but the thermals helped. I was able to pick up outlines in the green haze, something they couldn't. We swept from one side to the other, each putting two rounds into any thermal signature he could pick up. A moment later, the gunfire coming our way died down, the only sound from the destroyed team the pained gurgles of a man not yet quite dead.

We picked up the pace without a word, heading for the opening the enemy shooters had come out of. I called Mike again. "Speedy, Hillbilly. We are making entry northwest side of building two."

"Roger," was the reply. The shooting suddenly redoubled again.

We paused to stack on the door, as Alek prepped a frag and tossed it in. We followed the earthshaking *thud* of the explosion, moving fast into the smoke and debris. There were more corpses in the hallway; it looked like another team had been on its way out when the grenade had gone in. We had well and truly kicked the hornet's nest. It was starting to look like there was at least a reinforced company of troops of one kind or another here.

There was an open door ahead, leading to a stairway. Alek led the way to it, while Larry popped the corner of the intersecting hallway, holding it as the rest of us headed up the stairs. Jim thumped him as he went past, and Larry fell in with the rest of us going up.

The top floor was kind of strange, with a hallway running around the outside of the building, and what looked like it might be a conference room in the center. There were several shooters, of the camouflage jacket and AK chest rig variety down at the south end, taking shots at Mike's element. They never even knew what hit them. Staccato pairs of suppressed shots dropped them into heaps of meat and rags leaking blood on the tile floor.

There was another stairwell at the far side, and shouts in Arabic were starting to come up from the one we'd just ascended. Larry was posted on the landing, his FAL aimed down the stairs, waiting for the first hajji to show his face. Alek took the corner, facing down the long hallway to the south, watching the far stairs. Jim and I moved to the nearest door.

It was wood, or at least wood veneer, and it looked like it was pretty good quality. Most of this place had been pretty fancy at one time, before decades of neglect had been topped off by us blowing the shit out of it. There was a lot of yelling on the other side, most of it that I could make out was in Arabic. Somebody didn't sound happy. I reached for the doorknob and turned it. It was unlocked.

The door splintered inches from my hand, as someone on the other side fired a long burst from what sounded like an AK-74 through it. So much for that option. I moved to donkey-kick it open, while Jim pulled out his last frag.

There was more defiant yelling from inside, and another burst tore up the door some more. Jim had the pin out, and his hand clamped around the grenade's safety lever, and nodded to me. I wound up and slammed my foot straight back into the door.

The door latch ripped right through the splintered doorjamb, and the door slammed open. Jim lobbed the grenade inside, throwing it high to bounce it off the ceiling, hoping to lessen the chance that somebody could scoop it up and throw it back out.

He must have cooked it off while I was winding up. It detonated a bare second later, and I felt the concussion in my chest, even through the wall. I pivoted and went in, Jim on my heels, with Alek and Larry falling in on the door behind us.

The room had been a conference room, and a very nicely appointed one. Rich wood paneling was now gouged by shrapnel, and what I could only assume was a very expensive deep red carpet was smoldering where the grenade had gone off. Several burning papers were still fluttering in the smoky air.

The first half of the room was a charnel house. Whoever had been shooting at the door was down, missing both his arms and one leg, along with a good chunk of his head. His AK was a smashed ruin, bathed in blood at the foot of the now thoroughly smashed end of the conference table. Two more lay crumpled off to the side, similarly mangled. We cleared the corners and moved forward, stepping over the mutilated bodies.

There were four men at the far end of the conference table. They had been knocked senseless by the overpressure, and were bleeding from several shrapnel wounds. We closed on them quickly, rifles leveled.

One was dressed in traditional flowing white Bedouin robes, with a black keffiyeh on his head. The other three were all dressed in expensive suits, marred now by dust, blood, and shrapnel holes.

The first one to start to pick himself up was a short, spare-framed man, in a black silk suit, with short, oiled hair and a short, neat beard. He came to his hands and knees, and looked up at us, his eyes bleary. He obviously wasn't seeing straight.

I recognized him, though. After Baird had provided the ID, we'd gotten photos. The man on the floor was responsible for hundreds of dead Americans, and who knew how many dead Africans and Arabs. He had plans to be the next Osama Bin Laden. He was Mahmoud al-Khalidi. Al Masri. I leveled my rifle at his forehead.

As his eyes started to clear, he looked around at us, then at his associates on the floor, who were also starting to shake off the effects of the grenade blast. Recognition lit in his dark eyes, followed immediately by a flash of hatred so intense that if looks could kill, his would have incinerated the side of the building. He stared up at me for a moment, then simply said, "*Allahu akhbar*," and reached into his suit.

His pistol had just cleared his lapel when I shot him.

The round hit him just to the left of the bridge of his nose, and blew the back of his skull out, splashing the white thobe of the Bedouin-dressed man with blood and brains. In the next second, the other three were shot dead, before they could do the same.

We didn't stop to reflect on what had just happened. That could come later, provided there was a later. As we moved to the next door, leading out into the hallway, the radio came to life again.

"Coconut, Speedy," Mike called. "We've got Yemeni security forces at the gate. They've got armor, and we can hear at least one helo incoming. We have to go, now."

CHAPTER 34

"Roger," Alek responded. "All callsigns, primary target is down, I say again, primary target is down. We are moving to extract. Fall back by pairs to the west wall." He turned from the door we were stacking on. "Back the way we came!" he said, heading for our breach point. "We'll use the building to shield us from the armor."

We pounded across the room to the shattered door, and stacked on it quickly. A bare second's pause to ensure everyone was ready, and we flowed out and into the hallway. Jim almost collided with the hajji who had led the way up the stairs.

The man wasn't ready for us to come boiling out of the conference room, and staggered back, staring in shock. Jim muzzle-thumped him in the throat, squeezing the trigger even as his suppressor crushed the guy's larynx, blowing fragments of his spine out the back of his neck.

He dropped like a rock, clearing the guy behind him, who was bringing up his SIG 550 as I shot him in the head. It was a fast shot, and just blew out the side of his skull. He spasmed in pain, his finger tightening on the trigger, and shot Jim in the leg as he fell.

Jim grunted and staggered, as the 5.56 round blew a chunk of meat and blood out the back of his calf. Alek and I raked the rest of the fire team coming up the stairs, pumping shots as fast as we could, just making sure that there was a body in the sights each time we squeezed the trigger. Several of our shots hit body armor, but enough were placed well enough to kill or wound, driving the team back down the stairs, stumbling over the bodies of their dead, or their thrashing, screaming comrades.

Larry got to Jim before his leg collapsed under him, whipping out the tourniquet that Jim had strapped to his vest and hastily wrapping it high around Jim's wounded leg. Jim leaned on him, his rifle pointed, if somewhat shakily, at the corner where anyone coming from the other stairway would have to expose themselves.

"Can you move?" Alek asked, facing toward the opposite corner, while I covered the stairs.

"Damn straight, I can," Jim growled. "I might be a little slower, but it's either that or stay here and die."

"Fucking right," Alek said. "Jeff, you take point. Larry, you stay with Jim, I'll take rear. Let's get down the stairs and out of this building before the Yemeni Army decides to come in."

I didn't wait for much of an acknowledgement. Larry reached out and thumped me in the back of the shoulder with a meaty fist, as I pulled my last frag out of my vest and prepped it. "Frag out," I called over my shoulder, and chucked it down the stairs, hard.

There was a burst of panicked shouting in Arabic from below, cut off as the grenade exploded. I followed the jarring explosion down the stairs, intent on not giving the bad guys time to recover.

There were still five of them alive at the base of the stairs, though two of them were rolling on the floor screaming, clutching at mangled or flat-out blown-off limbs. I worried about the ones that were still standing, halfway down the hall, trying to shake off the concussion and bring their AKs to bear. I shot two of them, and a shot from above me took out the third. I glanced over my shoulder. Larry had both hands on his FAL, and Jim was holding on to the drag handle on the back of his vest to hold himself up as he hobbled after him. Good thing Larry's a big guy.

I drove on, pushing through the short hallway to the side door. "Speedy, Hillbilly, four coming out," I called. "Kemosabe is hit, but mobile."

"Roger, we've got you covered," Mike replied. "We are at the south wall, taking heavy fire from the gate. Rock is down. We're going to have to blow the wall and go out this way. We'll rendezvous at the BLS."

"I copy, Speedy," Alek replied. "Shiny, we're coming to you, north side of building one."

"Roger, come ahead," Bob answered. "Make it fast, we can see the helo. Looks like a Kamov." That was some good news, anyway. The Ka-29 couldn't carry more than about six people; they weren't going to be dropping troops on us with it, at least. On the other hand, it could be fitted with a minigun or cannon, which would be a bad day. Better to just get the hell away from it.

"Let's go," Jim yelled. "I'll hobble as fast as I can. Let's blow this Popsicle stand."

I dug in and sprinted to the northeast corner of the big building, pivoting and dropping to a kneeling stance as soon as I got to it. The Yemenis weren't advancing into the compound very quickly, thanks to Mike's fire, but that wouldn't last long, especially if Charlie was out of the picture. Larry and Jim ran/limped past me, heading toward the far end of the building, then Alek ran past all of us to take point. I held on the corner for a few more moments, and then started after them.

We ran through Bob's position, past Chris and Marcus, and headed toward the breach in the wall, as they got up and came after us. Some fire was starting to snap past us from the gate, but it was unaimed and didn't come close.

Coming around the corner of the three-story building that butted up against the west wall, I saw that Chris and Marcus hadn't fucked around. There was a thirty-foot hole blasted in the wall, and it looked like part of the corner of the building had taken some damage from flying debris. There were fragments of concrete and brick strewn around for a hundred feet. The crater was still smoking.

Alek rounded the crumbled edge of the wall, as Larry popped the opposite direction. There was a crackle of gunfire, and Larry yelled, "We've got company!"

Alek grabbed Jim and kept going down the length of the wall, heading for the road. I dropped to a knee beside Larry and took up firing on the hazy shapes of armed men coming toward us from the north. Bob skidded to a halt next to me, but I yelled at him, "We've got this! Go! We'll catch up!" He looked at me for a second. I could see him out of the corner of my eye, even as I took a shot at another armed silhouette and missed. Then he was gone, sprinting toward the road.

There was more gunfire from behind me, back in the compound. I risked a glance back to see what looked like Mike's team trying to bound along the inside of the wall, laying down fire with the remaining rounds for the M60. One of them was lugging a body in a fireman's carry. It looked like Bo, which meant the body was probably Charlie.

"We've got to hold," I hollered at Larry, over the noise that seemed to be tearing apart the night itself. "Mike's coming."

"He'd better hurry the hell up," Larry yelled back over his shoulder.

I scrambled back to the hole in the wall, dropping to the prone in the crater, to try to help cover Mike's team's fallback. There were Yemeni troops starting to fan out into the compound, following an AML-90 armored car. They were shooting, but not heavily. They seemed more interested in keeping the AML between them and Johnny's M60. Most of their shooting was definitely of the "spray and pray" variety, which helped. It didn't look like they could see very well, either; no night vision.

We didn't have anything that could even scratch that armored car, at least not without getting way too damned close to it. The fact that Mike wasn't using his MGL told me he was already out of grenades for it.

I lined up the first Yemeni soldier who got a little too aggressive, and squeezed the trigger. He dropped, and his buddies scrambled to cram behind the AML. I kept up single shots whenever I saw a target, as Mike, Bo, and Johnny came closer. Mike was on point, and Johnny was taking up the rear, firing short bursts from the M60, and immediately moving. The AML was returning fire, but it was slow and inaccurate; I could only guess that they didn't really have night sights on the vehicle, either, which was good news, such as it was.

Mike led the way into the breach, pounding past me and up to Larry's side. Larry was putting out a constant barrage of fire to the north; it sounded like the bad guys in that direction weren't getting the message. A moment later, Bo staggered through, carrying Charlie's body over his shoulders. I pointed him toward Alek, Jim, and the rest, down by the road, and he kept going. Johnny dropped down next to me with the 60. He was wrestling with a 150-round "nutsack," one of the soft-sided ammo carriers we'd gotten for the machine guns. "Last belt," he gasped.

I drilled four more shots toward the AML and the advancing Yemeni infantry. I couldn't tell if I'd hit anything or not. The soldiers didn't seem to be getting any more eager to charge forward, and their sporadic fire was still high and wild. It was the AML I was worried about. That 90mm gun could make it a very bad night.

However, even as the air above us started to be ripped by bursts of 7.62 fire, the main gun stayed silent. I guess they had orders not to blow up too much of the city, at least apart from the damage we'd already done, but at the time, we couldn't take the chance. "Larry, everybody's through, let's go!" I bellowed. My throat hurt from the yelling, the smoke, and the dust, but I hardly noticed it. I would later.

"Peel off!" Mike shouted, and slapped Larry on the shoulder. Larry got up immediately and trotted toward the road, while Mike kept shooting at whoever was trying to get at us from the north. He yelled over his shoulder, "Jeff, get ready to shift your fire north!"

I came up to a knee, as Mike turned and pounded past, and turned up the alley. The bad guys weren't trying to advance up the alley, as it turned out, but they were peeking around the corner and trying to get shots off. I discouraged that by sending 7.62 rounds skipping off walls and blowing concrete in their faces whenever they tried it.

I gave Mike ten seconds, then turned, thumping a fist into Johnny's leg as I went, and he took my place, as I sprinted, my knees protesting and my lungs burning, south toward the road. Ahead of me, Larry and Mike had already stopped halfway, and were waiting for us to clear them before they opened fire. My hearing was so shot by that time I couldn't hear Johnny running behind me, but Larry started shooting, so he must have turned and started back.

I pounded to the end of the wall, to find Alek kneeling behind it, and the road filled with thick white smoke. He waved me toward the road and the brush beyond. "Armor at the intersection!" he yelled at me. "Keep moving!"

I did, running across the road in the haze of HC smoke, and skidding to a stop next to Chris, who was on a knee behind a low tree, watching back toward where we had come. I bumped him and took his place as he fell back toward the shore.

Shortly, Mike, Larry, and Johnny came sprinting out of the haze, followed by the errant cracks of wild, unaimed gunfire, with Alek taking up the rear. I waved them past me, toward the shore. I'd take the rear.

Just as Alek ran past, the helo arrived, and things got more complicated.

It roared over, low, the downblast from its coaxial rotor shredding and tattering the smoke that was hiding us from the limited eyes of the ground forces. It didn't fire, but looking up I saw that there was indeed a weapon slung underneath the bulbous cockpit. I hoped it wasn't as big as I was afraid it was, but even if it was a light machine gun, it spelled bad news.

"Cover!" Alek bellowed at the top of his lungs. Except there wasn't any. We might be able to dodge the helo in the bushes, but we were exposed on the long flat run to the beach.

"Fire on it!" I yelled, as I tracked the helo with my own rifle and started suiting actions to words. "Get some lead on that motherfucker!" I remembered learning about VC and NVA counter-aircraft techniques, some of which were still taught in the Basic Reconnaissance Course. It was a long shot, but there was a chance to bring down a helo with massed small arms fire.

In a staggered line leading toward the beach, the teams started opening fire, even as we fell back toward the water. I was banking on the Kamov being thin-skinned enough that we could either hit something vital in the engine, or kill or maim the pilot. It swung out over the water, and started in on its first firing pass. Most of our smoke was gone, torn away by the helo's low passage. I tried to ignore the blossoming muzzle flash in its nose as it bore down on us. Gouts of sand and gravel were blasted into the air along the beach as the pilot walked his fire toward us.

I was aiming for the windscreen, dumping the magazine as fast as I could squeeze the trigger and get the muzzle back on target. Nearby, Johnny was dumping the last of his M60 ammo into the oncoming helicopter.

The Ka-29 suddenly banked sharply, or was it veering out of control? It almost half turned over, seemed to right itself drunkenly, then nosed down and started to drop. Somebody must have hit the pilot. Unfortunately, it was dropping straight toward us.

Johnny and I had nowhere to run but back toward the road to try to evade the plummeting twelve tons of metal, fuel, and spinning rotor blades. As we scrambled out of the way, more shots crackled overhead. I glanced toward the road, and saw two AML-90s rolling toward us, firing their coax machineguns, followed by what looked like close to a company of Yemeni infantry.

The helo hit with an earth-shaking impact, the fuselage crumpling and the rotors spinning into whirling shrapnel as they bit into the earth. Dust and sand blew outward with a hammering shockwave that knocked both of us off our feet. Sparks and flame started to pour out of the engine cowling as the engine seized and caught fire, then the fuel tanks exploded.

A massive orange fireball lit up the night, and the heat hit us like a wall. I scrambled up on my feet, grabbing Johnny by his kit as I went, and shoved him toward the west, away from the Yemeni troops. A glance showed they'd been rocked by the crash, and it would take them a few precious moments to get their shit together after that. I was determined to take advantage of the shock.

Half running, half stumbling, we scrambled around the wreckage, trying to put it between us and the advancing Yemenis. Flames billowed through the night, and the heat scorched both of us as we pounded past the fiery crash. My lungs burned as I breathed in the foul smoke, but we couldn't slow down.

As we got some distance from the conflagration and ran toward the beach, the warm night air seemed positively cool, after the inferno heat of the burning helicopter. Rounds were still cracking overhead, but they were pretty far off. Ahead, I could see the rest of the team running for the beach, every few yards stopping, dropping to the sand, and sending a few more rounds back at our pursuers to discourage them.

Then we were at the beach, spread out in a skirmish line, already half in the water, shooting back toward the city. I heard the second M60E4 go silent, and Eddie yell, "I'm out!" He was followed shortly by both Bob and Chris. Just as Chris sounded off, there was a flash up by the road, and a 90mm shell howled just overhead to splash into the shallow surf and detonate. Apparently, now that they were aiming out over the bay, the AML gunners felt they could use their main guns.

We scattered, trying to provide as little a target as possible. A second gun boomed, and sand geysered into the air only meters in front of us. They'd have the range in a second, and then we were dead. I glanced back at the water. Where the fuck were the boats?

"Into the bay!" Mike yelled. "Swim, we'll RV with the boats away from the shore!" He started shoving the guys closest to him into the water. He was right. Swimming out to meet the boats was our best hope of getting off the beach alive. Almost as one, we surged out into the surf until we were up to our knees, then dove in and started to stroke for open water.

The guns continued to fire, and shells howled and splashed far too close for comfort, but we swam on, gathering together into what would have been a suicidally close group on land, but was necessary to make sure we had everybody. Bo was still towing Charlie's body, and Alek had his hand clamped around Jim's pull handle, helping him swim with only one fully working leg.

We hadn't made it very far out before Bob lifted his head, listening.

A moment later, I picked up the sound of outboards, then spotted the faint white trails of the boats' wakes. All three were headed toward us, their throttles wide open. A flash of a red lens let them home in on us. Lee was in the lead and chopped the throttle just in time to keep from running Chris and Marcus over. They each grabbed side handles and hauled themselves aboard, reaching back for the next guys.

It took mere moments to load up, and then we were pulling for open water, followed by desultory fire from the shore. Patrol boats, probably including the one we'd bribed earlier, were converging on the beach, drawn easily by the towering pyre of the downed helo. Lee led the way, circling far enough out to the west to evade them before turning south into the Gulf of Aden.

There was silence in the boats as we bounced across the waves, heading back toward the *Frontier Rose*. We'd accomplished the mission. Al Masri was dead, and most of us were out, alive. But we'd lost Charlie, and the empty spaces where Colton, Hank, Tim, and Rodrigo had been haunted us. We were exhausted, and probably a little shell-shocked. It had been one hell of a few weeks.

EPILOGUE

There was a knock on the door, and everybody in the hostel room we had to ourselves turned, hands close to concealed weapons that would have the Mumbai police down around our heads in an instant if they were seen. But it was just Bob, his arms full of the food we'd sent him out to get. He was drenched from the monsoon rains, and it looked like some of the water had gotten to the food, but it was still light years away from the fare we'd had in Somalia, so nobody complained. Johnny let him in, then closed and locked the door.

It had been a long trip from the Gulf of Aden to Mumbai. We'd had to bury Charlie at sea; there was no way to preserve his body, and even if there had been, Indian customs officials would have flipped out if we'd pulled into port with a dead body on board, that had obviously been shot. We kept Jim's leg bandaged, and avoided the hospital, so there were no real questions asked, after the initial explanation of an accident. All the weapons except our pistols had been carefully hidden in the *Frontier Rose*'s keel; we'd retrieve them once we left Mumbai.

Now we were gathered in our simple, unadorned hostel room, waiting to talk to Tom. Right on time, the icon lit up, and Alek opened the videoconference.

"You guys alone? No curious ears around?" he asked first.

"It's just us, Tom," Alek said.

"All right, then." Tom looked out at us with his usual icy impassivity. "The dust is starting to settle a little bit, and I'm starting to hear things, both official and unofficial. You guys did a hell of a job in Little Aden, let me tell you.

"Not only did you kill Mahmoud Al-Khalidi, you shwacked most of his personal security unit. I have it on good authority that the other three big shots you killed were very important people from Saudi Arabia, Dubai, and the UAE. Together, those three were worth probably about ten million gold eagles. One of them, Ahmed Faisal Farouq, was a Saudi who also had access to the Brigade of Salah ad Din. They're the unit that was formed from the hard-core jihadis who dragged the royal family out into the streets and beheaded them a couple years ago. That's leading some to think that Al-

Khalidi was trying to put together a wider alliance of Brotherhood-linked killers. For what, we have no idea.

"Nobody knows for sure who pulled off the hit; you guys did a good job of getting in and out clean. The Egyptians, Saudis, and Dubai are now mightily pissed at the Yemenis, and how that's going to work out, we don't know. There have already been a few incidents that point to some serious bad blood over this. You might have just put a wedge into the Brotherhood's cohesiveness for a while.

"Back home, well." He sneered. "Most people don't know that anything that's gone on in the last month even happened. The government's keeping quiet about it, and most people are worried a lot more about where their next paycheck is coming, or when the currency's going to take another nosedive, to really give a fuck about what's going on halfway around the world. Some of the sharper blogs are talking about it, but most people aren't paying much attention. Too far away.

"The Agency suspects something, I think, but from what I'm hearing, they can't prove it. Some, particularly in Special Activities, don't really care, from what I'm hearing."

He leaned forward. "But we need to be careful. There are some very powerful people who have quietly taken notice, and not all of them are happy about a private organization pulling off a raid like this. Don't forget, the UN managed to get Executive Outcomes shut down for very similar stuff. There are some people on both sides paying attention now, and some of them will probably stop at nothing to shut us down. Not only are we 'mercenaries,' but the Brotherhood has a lot of clout in Washington now. You guys hit them at home, and they're not happy. They find out it was Praetorian, and we could be in for some trouble.

"On top of that, we're already persona-non-grata over the earlier job in Somalia. We won't be getting work from the Agency again, that's for sure. It's going to take some serious legal-fu to make sure they don't try to charge us with anything, but I've got that covered."

He looked down, then looked back up at us. "Any thoughts?"

Alek looked around at the lot of us. "What about the hostages?"

Tom sighed. "As near as we can tell, there are about eighty left alive. It sounds like they've been consolidated in the Egyptian Mukhabarat's new prison complex south of Cairo."

"Any chance of getting to them?" Jim asked.

Tom shook his head. "No way. They are in the heart of the Brotherhood's power, and a couple hundred miles inside Egypt. You guys could pull off a coastal raid on Yemen, but this is a whole other order of magnitude. Maybe someday, but not now."

"Someday?" Alek asked. "That sounds like you've got ideas, Tom."

The Colonel nodded. "I do, as a matter of fact." He steepled his fingers in front of him. "This operation went way beyond what we originally set this company up to do. Back here, I've already had to expand our intelligence and support arm far faster than we had planned. This has actually had a side benefit that I hadn't foreseen.

"Turning our little intel shop into a mini-intelligence agency cost money, a lot of it. To defray the costs, I've already set up our own little private intelligence service, rather like Stratfor or the Cavell Group. It's already bringing in some not-insignificant revenue. It's also highlighting some opportunities that we didn't know were there. Opportunities to hurt the Brotherhood and its ilk.

"Now, I know we all went into this to make money. I know I did. But we're all still warriors at heart, and I know all of you well enough to know you're not happy with the way the world's going. I think I can find a way for us to hit back at the bad guys, and still make money. What do you think?"

There was a long silence. It was Jim who finally broke it. "I think all of us went into this business more for the chance, however slim it looked a few years ago, to get back into combat." He looked around at the rest of us. "Most of us got out because we thought the Army, or Marine Corps, was getting too political, turning into a bunch of pussies more concerned with cultural sensitivity than fighting. We all fought these assholes before, and got choke-chained when we needed to cut loose. We've all felt the frustration."

He looked down at the floor for a second, gathering his thoughts. "I guess what I'm saying is, as long as we can still pay the bills, I'm happy to kill bad guys, wherever, whenever. And I don't think I'm alone."

I shook my head. "You're not. The assholes are just getting stronger and stronger. Our people just keep knuckling under, and scolding anybody who doesn't. I say fuck all of them. If we see an opportunity to fuck these assholes up, let's go for it."

Everybody in the room was nodding by then. Alek looked at the screen. "That answer your question, Tom?"

He smiled, a tigerish expression without warmth. "It does indeed. Welcome to the time-honored profession of privateer, gentlemen. Get back here as soon as you can.

"We've got a lot of work to do."

DON'T MISS OUT!

SIGN UP FOR THE NEWSLETTER!

When you sign up, you'll get an email whenever a new action story comes out. We won't spam you; emails only go out with a new release.

Sign up here!

Made in United States
Orlando, FL
08 November 2023

38716991R00189